CONVERGENCE
JOURNEY TO NYORFIAS, BOOK 1

TERRY ROY

A Zapstone Production

ISBN-13: 978-1-937899-80-6

ISBN-10: 1-937899-80-2

Fourth Trade Paperback Edition

Library of Congress Catalog Number (LCCN):
2010922017

Wasn't getting stuck with a dimwitted alien mindforce enough of a disaster for one day...?

The discharges from enemy weapons distorted Corporal Kraym's voice over her pcom. "We're cut off all around," he reported a little breathlessly. "We've no place to go but straight ahead. Com's out—blocked. Just have local to each other."

Rett checked that information for herself, quickly cueing up her pcom. She looked in the direction of the bridge—straight ahead. There was plenty of activity there now.

Stunned was just as bad as dead. Worse in most cases.

"We can't just sit here and wait to get zapped. We may not have a way out, but we're not using stun force!"

"Right," agreed Kraym. "Let's see how many of them we can take out permanently before we're down."

"Com connect all Fang team!" The voice command opened channels from the communications patch in Rett's headband to all her platoon. "Fang leader to Fang team, take them out any way you can!"

Someone set them up. They knew exactly where they would be; that they would be tired. They had expected them, and well enough in advance to set up traps that couldn't be detected until it was too late.

But who?

~I can tell you that. Mott and Shamos.~

She didn't notice that thought came from the alien presence in her mind, only that it came. And it shocked her. Mott and Shamos?

Unthinkable.

But it made terrible, logical sense...

More Books by Terry Roy

~ ~ ~

Science Fiction/Action
Convergence – Journey to Nyorfias, Book 1
Gravity – Journey to Nyorfias, Book 2
Stratagem – Journey to Nyorfias, Book 3
Carakenne – Journey to Nyorfias, Book 4
Kyarta Girl – Journey to Nyorfias, Book 5

~ ~ ~

Sff-Romance
Discovery – A Far Out Romance

~ ~ ~

Romance
Fear of Flying (Romantic Suspense)

~ ~ ~

Humor
as Terran Moffat
First Bass and Other Stories

Visit
https://teryvisions.wordpress.com/
for the latest news, updates, sneak previews, and more!

Contact the author!
terzap@gmail.com
Please write with any comments, concerns, or questions

For my sisters of birth and of soul,
we'll be forever together.

AUTHOR'S NOTE

THIS IS THE FIRST BOOK in the Journey to Nyorfias series, the first three installments make one epic story that is simply too long to put into one printed book. (Even cutting some parts out!) The saga is composed in a series of connected episodes rather than conventional chapters. This story can stand alone, but please note: it does not end with the end of Book One. I suppose I could have ended it on a cliffhanger, or in the middle of something, but then I would get notes from readers claiming I was just trying to "lure them in" to get more books. Honestly, I'm not. It simply made more sense to split it out into manageable chunks. Had I split each story section out, I would also be getting hate mail about how I would be ripping people off charging them for each story section, some of which are short novel-length in themselves. Thus: three parts. Three decent sized volumes.

Also part of the complete series, and containing important insights to the continuing saga, are the shorter novels *Carakenne* (the events take place during JTN2 *Gravity*) and *Kyarta Girl*, which should be read immediately after JTN3 *Stratagem*.

I highly recommend reading them in this order: *Convergence, Gravity, Carakenne, Stratagem,* and *Kyarta Girl*.

I hope you enjoy the adventure!

Convergence

Journey to Nyorfias, Book 1

Terry Roy

1.0.0 PROLOGUE CONVERGENCE

"**I** AM GOING TO FAIL. I am going to lose this match even before the second level begins."

It wasn't the personal failure to advance to full Guardian of Balance that worried Pheasyce. Nor was it stress about the ultimate price for defeat in the Game: the inescapable fate of having her life essense dissolved into the matrix of the Universe. This fear that clawed into her soul was for her protectorate. Losing meant that an entire solar system would be crushed—every living thing, every rock, every molecule within it would be lost, in death or to the Dark.

She needed help and turned her thoughts and life essence toward one of those distant solar systems that others of her Order protected.

All thoughts of failure were firmly dismissed as Pheasyce appeared in the presence of the two Guardians assigned to the world they called, simply, Earth.

"I bring you greet—"

"What brings you to us a second time?" demanded Naguta.

Tuneme was more hospitable. "Be welcomed, Pheasyce. How are you managing in your trials to hold the Balance for Nyorfias?"

Pheasyce bowed. "The situation is not good. I have to ask for your help yet again."

"You strain the limitations of the rules with this radical stratagem of yours," the first Guardian said with a stern shimmer.

"But I am not going beyond them," Pheasyce pointed out. "And since my opponent cannot detect the source, it causes no harm to those under your protection—"

"That point can be debated," Naguta said, hard, metallic glints threading through its form. "There have been consequences. You cannot ask another?"

"The others who agreed are not in a position to provide help at this time."

Tuneme sighed and dimmed. "This is not good news, Pheasyce. Balance seems to be losing ground in too many places. Every time a world falls completely to either the Dark or the Light, we all draw closer to losing our free will. But this is the last time we can risk those we must also protect. The battle for Balance in this solar system is against *both* extremes. We are losing Players to Light and to Dark. We don't need to lose any to our own Order."

"Please." Pheasyce wasn't above pleading. "It is nearly the end of the first level. I need to prepare my new key Player before the second level of the match begins and the Dark has the upper hand. Perhaps, this time, it will be—"

"We can plan strategy and create situations that suggest better choices for our Players, but we cannot speculate," Naguta said. "None of us have the power to foretell the future. And none of us has the right to take away a Player's freedom of choice. What will be, will be. We will give you the help you seek—this one last time. Show us your new key Player so we can make the proper decision."

Pheasyce opened a path for the others to make their assessment.

* * * * *

Holding her breath, she remained as still as the tree in which she perched. In her color and light-reflecting uniform, the featherweight hood covering her head, she was secure in her invisibility to the naked eye. She had to hope someone wasn't about to swing a targeter her way, though. In spite of the cool, damp day, her body temperature wasn't as low as she would have liked. Even the quickest of scans in her general direction would be sure to pop an alert. Sure, it was nice to think that most enemy troopers never thought to look up, but the last time she had counted on that she ended up paying hard credit for her oversight.

Firmly dismissing the memory, she kept the count, as usual hyper-aware of the passage of time on a mission. Deities, could they be any slower?

A tingly prickle made her shiver. It wasn't anything she expected to feel, nor had ever experienced. Had it come from the inside, out? It was so unusual it attracted her attention, but before she could even take a breath the sensation was gone...as if it had never happened. She was sure whatever it was hadn't been dangerous, but damn, now she had to pee. And that was the last thing she needed to be thinking about. That—and the last time she'd slept.

Snarling to herself, she forced her mind and body back on the business at hand. It was time to go. Her empathic second-in-command's familiar mental poke let her know the platoon was ready, too.

Rett slanted her gaze as her targets approached. It was a small advance foot patrol for a company of enemy armored. The path they followed led to what should be the only possible crossing of a narrow ravine, unless the armored vehicles were capable of flight. The sturdy bridge had been a short distance beyond her tree. It hadn't taken very long for a handful of her clever engineering types to, ah, relocate it. Rett had felt a little twinge of sympathy for the infantry personnel who were going to have to retrieve it from the bottom of the chasm, some two hundred lengths down, but it had to be done. Letting even a small company of armored through to bolster the defense of the Wide River Gap bridge wasn't an option.

Three of them. The shorter one, obviously the patrol leader, was wary and alert. But still, she noted, not looking in the right directions. Too widely spaced to hit them all in one jump. As she watched, and as they drew nearer to the ravine, the gaps between the individuals started closing. Good.

She dropped out of the tree, hitting the patrol leader like a silent bomb. The second trooper's astonished, open-mouthed expression disappeared as her right foot slammed into his face. He went over the embankment, and she launched herself at the third, who hadn't even had time to react.

* * * * *

THE TWO GUARDIANS DREW BACK, their energies shifting in brightness and pattern as they conferred.

"Very well," Naguta said at last. "We have made our selection. You may assess."

Pheasyce followed the opening made for her observation.

The first impression wasn't encouraging. There was a pile of clothing in a heap in one corner, jacket and boots tossed near the door. Wood crates stood on end, with haphazard arrangements of books and small items. A pile of wire-bound books, some with lines, some without, sprawled on the floor. Loose pages, pencils, and pens peeked from beneath and between at random.

In the midst of this, a chunky, humanoid woman half-sat, half-sprawled, on some bedding laid on the floor, scowling at a computing unit resting on her knees.

"This?" The hope that had started to fill Pheasyce receded as the very strong emanations of frustration, uncertainty, and defeat from the human registered. Those were certainly not the qualities she so desperately needed for her key Player.

* * * * *

PAM SHIVERED AND TUCKED HER legs into the pocket of the blue sleeping bag that was both her bed and blanket. She glanced over her shoulder at the window. She wasn't cold, hadn't felt a draft, but she had felt, just for an instant, as if she'd see a face in the window. Which wouldn't make much sense, since she was on the second floor of the house.

And Pam didn't do ghosts. She rolled her eyes. Aliens, ninjas, giant crawling things, yeah, but ghosts, no.

She made a final face at her computer, one so exaggerated and twisted it tickled her nose and made her laugh. "Well, it was a long day. I'll be able to figure out how to get my character out of trouble tomorrow. Or at least feel like sketching something, that usually breaks a writer's block. But not tonight." She closed the lid of the laptop and set it aside, then poked up her glasses to rub at her still-itchy nose. "Tomorrow."

* * * * *

"THERE MUST BE SOME MISTAKE? Another, perhaps, not yet entered the room?" Trying to quell a flutter of dismay, Pheasyce turned to the shining entities standing outside of mortal time with her. She couldn't remember having a solid form: she only knew that at one time, she had been a creature of physical needs. The sensation that assaulted her now was perhaps the closest reminder of what gravity felt like. She pulled her thoughts together. "Are you sure—"

"You forget your place, neophyte! How dare you question a full Guardian willing to provide you the help you so desperately need."

Help, or hindrance? Pheasyce couldn't help wondering even as she shrank away from Naguta's blistering reprimand. The source spirit was certainly in Balance, as far as individual leanings to Light and Dark went. But—

She couldn't help turn back to Nyorfias, to the individual around whom the next plays of the Game would depend. Although she and other Guardians stood outside of time, they could not control it. Already her hesitation had resulted in time lost: her key Player had returned from her mission, and the full effects of her condition were distressingly apparent.

* * * * *

RETT SLID A FINGER BENEATH her headband to scratch an itch and returned to her scribing. She held on to a vague hope that if she rushed to finish this report, maybe she could keep up an illusion of busyness without actually doing anything. That way she could snatch five minutes to close her eyes before she was supposed to show up at the Division command post.

She covered everything that mattered. At least she hoped so. Taking a deep breath, Rett told the Omni to check for obvious errors. Her spelling left a lot to be desired, even on a good day. She had to blink several times to ease the burning dryness in her eyes in order to read the results. Done. Letting her breath out in a long exhale, she signed off with her personal code and sent the file off to the division commander's daily report queue.

Eight minutes to her meeting. Hopefully it wouldn't last more than ten. She had a three-day break to get to and she planned to sleep for at least half that time. The rest of her platoon—she hoped—had already started in on the sleeping part.

She was so tired. It had to be what had thrown off her focus and concentration before, something she never lost on a mission. Damn it. She was glad they were standing down. She didn't think she could move even if the command post were attacked.

14

At least this new location was more secure than the previous. It had to be. The 52nd needed to have a secure, solid location from which to launch the upcoming all-out push that would crack their enemy's single most important grip on Nyorfias. Hopefully.

She was thankful that Colonel Mott had, at least, taken her advice about the new location. The way he and his adjutant had been running things the past few months was starting to tell on the entire infantry division and any satellite unit assigned to support it, such as her Special Forces platoon. At least she had the comfort of knowing that, while she and F-troop were here to support and clear resistance for the 52nd, she didn't—technically—have to answer to Colonel Mott or any other infantry officer. Unfortunately, he didn't quite see it that way, but Rett's Special Forces CO had advised her to humor Mott. At least for now, while tensions were so high and the upcoming offensive so critical.

Damn it, she was tired of all this. It was more than physical exhaustion. She was tired of war. Fighting. Death. There was no way she'd quit, even if she hadn't sworn an oath, but she wished it would just...stop.

She would give everything she had for thirty minutes of solid nothing.

* * * * *

PHEAYSCE WAS AWARE THAT THE two Earth Guardians had followed, that they had seen. She dared to hope that they would see their choice wasn't appropriate; that her Player needed someone stronger.

"There is no mistake, you can decide yes or no." The metallic qualities in the sterner Guardian's energy ambiance were bright and hard enough to be solid matter.

Tuneme moved a little closer to Pheasyce. "You must understand we did not make this decision lightly and are in accord that this being is the best choice. It is hard for other Guardians to deeply read Players from worlds to which they are not responsible." The Guardian paused. "In truth, it has never been done before you dared to try. So look beyond the surface, and if you cannot, trust us. We do not want to see you fail."

Pheasyce, chastened, bowed. "I—"

"If you change your mind, we might not be able to help you in the future."

There was no better reminder of her lowly status as a neophyte Guardian in training than the constant interruptions by one senior and more experienced.

"And you must remember the parameters and limitations we have set. Your stratagem is already far too risky for one of our Order who is still only in the testing phases."

"It is. But I have to do this. I cannot change key Players once they have been chosen. And I am running out of them." Pheasyce looked back toward the solar system she loved. As mortal beings measured space and time, it was unimaginably distant. Yet, for a Guardian—or for one aspiring to be a Guardian—it was as close as a thought. She focused on the one that had, unwittingly, become her current key Player.

The soldier leaned forward over the small computing unit in her hands, features weary but intent, scowling over something on the display. Once, this tall, dark woman had been full of dreams and energy, with an imagination as lively and strong as her physical body. Now she was burdened by duty, aged with responsibility. Her spirit so worn that she no longer dared to dream, either while sleeping or awake.

But she hadn't lost hope, nor her determination to succeed. Both qualities, however, teetered on a dangerous edge. This was the reason Pheasyce had hoped to find a strong and influential spirit that would steady and infuse her key Player with fresh spiritual energy.

"You must decide, neophyte. Already our attention has been diverted for too long. We fight to balance both Light and Dark here."

"I—" Pheasyce took a moment to compose her thoughts, taking the time for another measuring look at the offered source-spirit. There was something different about her now. Maybe, just maybe, this would work.

Of course, it could also go horribly wrong.

She had to take the chance. They had gone so far out of their way for her, she couldn't keep them waiting. Nor could she afford to wait any longer.

"Thank you," Pheasyce said then to the two Guardians. "I will do my best with this."

1.1.0 EGO-MERGE

THE EARTH FELT COOL AND slightly damp. The clean odor of outdoors: sharp, green-blue-brown smells, made her smile and take a deep breath. She adjusted her tense position into one more relaxed. The breeze, faint but steady, tinged with the electric, ozone scent of nearby snowcapped mountains, was so clean it all but sparkled right through her closed eyelids.

This was great. So her imagination hadn't deserted her after all. She'd dreamed herself out of New Jersey and into the Rockies.

"Sergeant!" A boot nudged her hip. "Hey! Sergeant. Wake up!" snapped an unfamiliar male voice.

She didn't exactly remember moving. But as realization dawned, Pam found herself staring into an unfamiliar face. There was a gun of some kind practically jammed into the stranger's nose, and a long knife a molecule away from opening his throat. To her shock she realized that she was the one holding the weapons.

What the hell was that? What did she just do? She stepped back, arms dropping to her sides. Taking a huge breath to replace the one lost in her gasp, she let it out again with a curse. "Shit! Holy shit!"

"Wake up, Sergeant," the man said again in a voice that was hoarse and shook. He cleared his throat. "What in two worlds was that all about?" Still keeping a wary eye on her, the stranger felt his throat.

That was what Pam wanted to know, too. So her day hadn't been the greatest. Work had been hell, and the evening stop at the barn she rented to care for her horses hadn't been the relaxing, winding-down routine it usually was. So she'd come home in a black mood, to the bleak little room she rented in a house exactly halfway between her farm and her day job. She tried to imagine herself into a better place and wanted to work on the story she was writing, but all her creative Muses had deserted her. She hadn't wanted to sketch; none of her books had any appeal. Not even *Trixie Belden and The Gatehouse Mystery*, which usually cured her writer's block.

So, she had finally, simply, decided to call it a night. She'd put on some music and started daydreaming herself to sleep, finally feeling happy.

Now this.

"Am I dreaming?" Taking a step back, Pam noted the wild expression in the stranger's pale green eyes calmed somewhat with more space between them. But it obviously wasn't quite enough for him. He sidestepped so that his back was in open space.

"Maybe you were. I'll give you that. But you need to wake up now." He had spiky, shaggy eyebrows the color of wheat straw. Pam took special notice of them since they came together in a single irritated line over his nose.

"I'm awake."

"Then why are you still looking at me like I've two heads? Did you forget about the meeting, Killer?"

"Whoa. Hold it a minute. Killer? I've never killed anyone in my..."

Her voice faltered. She remembered the position she'd just had this man in. Then she glanced at the weapons she carried, the ones just seconds ago that had felt so familiar, and now just felt hard, cold, and *used*.

"...in my life," she finished lamely. "Of course the evidence is not in my favor," she added in a mumble, her focus going from the handgun in her right hand to the left holding the knife. Streaks of blued steel showed beneath a worn covering of camo paint. This blade, easily fourteen inches in length, was not the utilitarian tool one carried on the average camping trip. As for the hand holding the weapon... it wasn't her hand. This hand was strong and square with long, sinewy fingers. An uneven coating of dirt covered skin the color of golden brown whole-wheat toast. There were some other, questionable stains mixed in with the dirt. She wasn't sure she wanted to analyze them at the moment.

Swallowing, she checked the right hand again, which matched the one with the knife.

These hands were far from the stubby-fingered, freckled appendages Pam was familiar with after more than thirty years. "Holy shit." Glancing downward, she saw close-fitting material covering a long-limbed, hard, toughly muscled body. The colors in the material altered with every movement and breath she took. Some sort of camouflage, obviously, but not like any she had ever seen before. The shifting color and patterns mimicked every play of color, light, and shadow around her. Moreover, looking straight down, Pam noticed two things right away. The ground was much farther away than normal. Second, she saw a lot more than the usual glimpse of her toes. Without leaning.

She gulped.

"Sergeant," snapped the man she had attacked.

Attacked, hell, she had nearly killed him. Thoughtfully this time, Pam regarded the stranger. The clothing he wore didn't match hers. It was all muted greens, blues, and browns, a different but still more familiar camouflage pattern that didn't change and move. But it was a uniform. He stood well clear of her reach with his arms crossed over his chest, head to one side, and an expression of perplexed worry. He certainly didn't present the appearance of a forest ranger, game warden, or police officer. That left military.

This had to be a dream. She was convinced of it. She figured it had to have a connection to that paintball place in the Poconos that the guys at work had been talking about earlier. She didn't even look like herself. What a super body! It sure would be nice to keep it when she woke up.

"Sergeant!"

It took her a moment to understand the man was talking to her. "Uhm—" She scrambled through everything she remembered growing up as an Air Force brat, all those war movies she watched with her dad, the conversations she'd had with current and ex-military people; the research she had done to satisfy her interests and curiosity for a million different reasons. "Yes...?" There was no rank insignia on his uniform...at least none that she recognized. Just a few designs and enigmatic shapes in understated colors. "...sir?" she added anyway, to be safe. "Sorry about that, sir. I'm...ah...not quite myself."

He let out a breath. "Well, that's the *first* thing you've said that makes any sense. Forget it. I was warned what might happen if I touched any of you while sleeping without identifying myself first. I suppose I can't blame you, either, with the way you people having been running your butts off lately."

"Sir—"

20

"Forget it. Did you send the report already?" He bent to pick up a device on the ground near the tree trunk. "Let's go, Sergeant, you're supposed to be in Colonel Mott's office right now. As a matter of fact, you were supposed to be there ten minutes ago."

"Oh, yeah, right. I-I forgot," stammered Pam. What the hell was he talking about? Sergeant? Sergeant who? Colonel Mott? For that matter, who was this guy?

Noting her pistol didn't appear to be a type that fired bullets—either the regular or paint variety—she carefully replaced it, not wanting a demonstration of what it did shoot. She found an open holster in one of the two sturdy belts around her waist. A sheath for the knife. Also handily detachable ammo clip magazines, which puzzled her since her movie watching and research let her recognize them as such, but the gun she'd almost shoved into this man's left nostril didn't use them.

The second belt contained a plethora of little compartments and pockets. A shoulder harness carried more mysterious items. It clipped to the other belts front and back, presumably to help anchor them and support some of the weight.

Yep, a dream. Damn, she thought then. From the way she jumped on this guy just minutes ago, someone would think she really know how to use this stuff.

Pam had some small experience with firearms. She deer hunted every once in a while to satisfy the man from whom she rented the farm. She also kept a .22 caliber rifle in the barn for emergencies and impromptu target shooting with her friend Jen. But what she knew had no relationship with the ammunition she found herself carrying.

Whatever kind of gun these clips were for, it certainly wasn't one that shot paint pellets.

Replacing the knife in the empty sheath turned out to be a problem until she discovered at least a third of the blade length retracted into the hilt. A light touch from the thumb took care of that matter. She also found the same light touch caused the blade to instantly extend. Feeling a chill, she gingerly replaced the weapon in the sheath.

This knife certainly wasn't for chopping vegetables.

She shifted her stance and a solid weight tugged at a wide sling over one shoulder. Ah-ha. As the shape of the object suggested its purpose, she realized she'd discovered what the bullets were meant for. Adjusting the strap, Pam refused the temptation to examine this accessory more closely at that particular moment. Instead, she noted the man she'd assaulted had fully recovered from his near-death experience. He waited, watching her, his face patient but shadowed with perplexity.

21

Trying to put it all together and deciding there was only one conclusion, Pam let out a soft whistle. She was fully equipped and ready to kill people, and not to engage in a friendly paintball war game.

"Are you okay, Sergeant? Ready?"

"What? Oh, yeah, sure. We're going somewhere." Since this was a dream, she might as well just play along and see what happened.

"You're sure acting strange, Killer. Are you sure you didn't catch stuns this last assignment?"

"There you go again. What's with Killer? Is that some kind of codename or something?"

Pam saw some of the tension return to the man's expression. Then he rubbed his forehead and grimaced. "I'm sorry, I know you hate that name. I have to listen to it all day from them, and it sort of slipped out." He offered the tiniest of grins. "Will you let me live?"

She appreciated the fact he was trying to keep his sense of humor, and hers—if she was supposed to have one in this dream—but she had to set one fact straight. "Look, I've never killed anyone in my life—people, anyway—" she amended hastily, "and I'm—"

"Stop." The officer's voice took on the tone one reserved for the very young, very old, or those suffering from severe head injuries. "Look, just get a grip, okay? At least enough of one to get through this and then you get to your break." He scratched his chin with his left middle finger and stared at the device in his hand. "I'm not sure you're really awake."

"*I'm* sure," muttered Pam, barely under her breath. "I'm sure I am not awake at all. I'm positive this is all a dream and I am going to wake up, run to take care of the horses, and go to work." In a normal voice she asked, "I do feel pretty weird. Maybe I did hit my head. What's your name again?"

"Sergeant—"

"Humor me, sir?"

"You're lucky I like you, you know that?"

"I do, sir. Very lucky." Pam did feel an odd sort of gratitude toward the stranger, but she had to wonder just how well this man knew the person he thought she was. Or appeared to be. Or was supposed to be.

He let out something that sounded like a laugh. "Captain D'lano, F-troop's infantry liaison officer. You know, go-between supreme? Or as your seconds like to say," the captain lowered his voice, "the only person who stands between you and you yanking out what hair remains on Colonel Mott's head. Colonel Mott and his second-in-command, Major Shamos, are waiting—for you—for debriefing and discussion of F-troop's next assignment. I tried to talk him out of it, but he's in a bad temper."

"F-troop?" queried Pam then as the man's words sank in. F-troop? She couldn't recall anything about military units that involved a des-ignation as "troop" unless it was cavalry. But if there were any horses around here, she would have been sure to know that already.

Okay, maybe this wasn't some military thing, rather a really odd-ball detachment of Canadian Mounties or New Jersey State Troopers. Cops dressed in military style uniforms sometimes, right? No, he said "infantry liaison", she reminded herself. She was in the Army. Shit. Maybe he meant an armored unit. And a liaison? Did that have anything to do with the fact their uniforms were different? Maybe—

She looked at D'lano expectantly, hoping he'd explain further.

The man just shook his head. "Let's go, we've wasted enough time. Here's your Omni. And try to stay mellow. The Colonel's in one of his moods. Something's eating at him and the Major, so do some deep breathing and get your head together! After we're finished, I'll go with you and we'll track down your medtech."

Pam took the device, wishing she knew what the hell it was. She hunted without success for a brand name or familiar fruit-shaped logo of some kind. Despite the obvious dents and scratches on the camouflaged casing, it looked much more sophisticated than the average PDA on the market in the real world. "This gizmo's certainly been tossed around some," she muttered as she followed D'lano. "Hey, what language is this in anyway? Any cool apps on this?"

He either didn't hear or pretended not to. She caught up to walk alongside and when she glanced over, she saw his brows had once more formed a thick hedgerow across his forehead. He mumbled to himself and stared at a similar device in his hands.

Pam shrugged. She did feel strange. Even for a dream. Wearing such formfitting clothes, as comfortable as they felt, was strange. Moving in a taller, long-legged, and more muscular body than she ever imagined having was strange. Despite the body's super-fit shape, it was muscle-sore; aching to the bone in more than a few places. At least she recognized the feeling of outright fatigue, from toenails to hair.

This body felt exactly like Pam's after she'd been on her feet dealing with holiday shoppers for ten to fourteen hours a day since the week before Christmas.

Thank God, an element of reality.

Pam shook her head, hoping to dispel some of the congested, achy, turbulence inside. Her action produced a brief second of dizziness. Great. This really neat dream was about to interrupted by the sinus headache from hell. She willed herself not to think about it.

Focusing her attention on the surroundings helped. It could have been a set from a modern war movie. A headquarters or something: it had the busy, businesslike look she knew from visits to military bases. Any structures looked temporary. The few vehicles that went past rated second glances. Fascinated, she watched them skim over the ground in near silence. Whatever sort of engines powered them emitted only a soft whine-hum-swish. A silent hovercraft? Hardly any engine or fan noise, just the same sound a passing breeze would make.

"People'd think you never saw a rover before. Come on," she heard the captain say. After feeling a brief, gentle tug on her arm, Pam realized she'd stopped in her tracks. "We're already late. Come on, Sergeant."

"Uh, thought I saw someone I knew," Pam said lamely, but the officer had already resumed stride.

People in uniform, all armed, moved around intent on their own affairs. She'd catch a glance or two from them once in a while. Those would add a peculiar sort of diagonal nod, a wave, maybe a quick grin. Most of them wore uniforms like the captain's, with the addition of what was, unmistakably, light armor. Why didn't she have anything bulletproof on? Compared to them, she was practically naked. Who was she in this dream?

The wooded area containing the site held a population of plants and trees, again vaguely familiar in appearance, yet different. Startling shades of greens, browns, and rust, a snatch of gold. Bright, true blue so intense it didn't look real. A smattering or sheen of violet color here and there. The glimpses of sky visible through the overhead tangle of foliage revealed a gorgeous, jewel-like shade of deep, pure azure with exactly enough red added to put it in the violet range.

Wow. It was looking through a sapphire-amethyst gem of some kind. What a gorgeous color! A sharp twinge made her press a hand to her temple. Felt like a horse had just started kicking in there. Ow! She wondered if there was anything for a headache in one of the belt pockets. Then again, if this wasn't her real body, maybe it wasn't really this body's head that was hurting, either.

The instant her uncertainty surfaced, the pressure increased. The kicking sensations turned to thoughts. Like this body, these thoughts didn't belong to Pam. And they were as hard and sharp as the knife she'd held a few minutes ago.

Damn it, get a hold on yourself! You're losing it! Your name is Rett. Rank, Sergeant, platoon leader, F-troop! ID number 90674SF, otherwise known as Sergeant Killer! Which you hate! Damn it, wake UP!

Pam's stride faltered. This was getting ridiculous. Of course it was her mind. It was her dream, after all! And, she reminded herself, she only heard other voices in her head when she was trying to think up dialogue for her stories.

Dreaming? Of course I'm not dreaming! This is real! Why do I keep having these thoughts?

Pam sucked in a deep breath and firmly packed the distracting feelings and thoughts in a mental box. This was a dream. She added some imaginary duct tape and dusted off her imaginary hands for a finishing touch. This was a very unusual, interesting dream. That's all. Period.

"Sergeant."

Pam focused her vision on D'lano, who now had a firm grip on her arm and a concerned expression on his face.

"Head hurts." Pam grabbed the first excuse she could find. "Can't remember hitting it."

"Too many stuns will do that," agreed D'lano. "And you're definitely showing the right symptoms. Well, this meeting won't take too long."

She was glad to note he didn't look mad. Just resigned and, dare she hope, sympathetic? Maybe she should ask him about getting something in case her sinus headache started coming back.

The two officers inside the command post broke off their conversation as she entered with D'lano.

"Killer," greeted a heavyset man seated at a desk. He frowned. "You're late."

"Sorry." So she sounded sarcastic, but that's what she felt. Now she did hate that name. Especially the way he said it.

The man glanced up, eyes narrowed.

"Sorry, *sir*," amended Pam, realizing that unlike Captain D'lano, she wasn't about to get any sympathy or understanding from this guy.

"The report should be in your daily file, Colonel Mott," D'lano said. Pam was grateful for the cue and by process of elimination figured the second officer must be Major Shamos.

Mott turned to the console on his desk and grunted. "That can wait. I have a few more jobs for your unit, Sergeant. Important jobs. First, you have to get us some of those updated ML-12 SMG rifles the enemy's been using lately. We have to figure out exactly how those different low power settings can affect our defenses. MainTech also wants to test them against the targeting jammers we're trying to develop. After that, I'll need a thoroughly detailed survey of the Wide River Gap Bridge and the surrounding area..."

The imaginary box Pam had thought firmly sealed started rumbling. A sensation of anger, denial, and protest started seeping though it. Pam pressed two fingers against her head as the box jumped and made it ache even more.

"SMG rifles?" she said aloud. "Power settings...good grief. You mean like *lasers* and things?" She thought about the odd handgun on her hip. No way! "For Pete's sake, next I'll be seeing guys in long robes with light sabers and asking Scotty to beam me up! Sir," she added.

Incredulous looks exchanged between the two officers, then they fixed their astonished gazes upon her. "What's that supposed to mean?" Colonel Mott's heavy face darkened with anger. He made a motion to smooth out what little hair remained on his head.

"Colonel, Sergeant Rett seems to be suffering a..." Captain D'lano cast a concerned and warning glance at Pam. His look said plainly that she should just shut up and not push her luck. "...ah...she uhh... dozed off. A few hard stuns the last time out. I had to wake her just moments before we came in. I'm sure it's temporary."

"I don't recall seeing anything about any personnel catching stun, much less mention of any significant injuries, in the report. And the platoon medical report mentions only a badly bruised finger and several abrasions, none of which were disabling or required further treatment or consideration."

"Special Forces, sir, you know how they get about what they consider trivial."

"I did notice, however, that F-troop failed to replace the bridge they dismantled."

Captain D'lano didn't hesitate. "And the infantry detachment that took over that position is reassembling the bridge—as they were told to, sir, in *their* mission briefing. You *know* how hard F-troop's been working, sir. None of them have slept for days. And they're supposed to be on a three-day stand down. Sending them out right now isn't a good idea—"

"It'd better be temporary," said Colonel Mott, waving his hand impatiently, "because I'd certainly hate to file a complaint against one of Major Yidnar's finest. I might not be your direct commanding officer, but don't forget, Sergeant, that you are here on assignment, to assist me and the 52nd, and I don't appreciate insubordinate behavior." He ended his statement in a tone blending sarcasm and serious threat.

Realizing she was getting herself into big trouble, Pam pulled herself together and adjusted her outward expression. Something was definitely wrong. Should she apologize? No, that might have worked with the captain, but right now she'd just better stay quiet and at least try to act as if she knew what they were talking about. The captain had tried to cover for her—she'd ride on that for now. She couldn't help wondering if she—her dream self, rather—was supposed to be doing something else right now. After all, she'd dreamed herself into the middle of other odd situations and scenarios in dreams before. But this one...this one didn't feel like any of those other times. If *feel* was the right word.

"Do you understand me, Sergeant?" inquired the Colonel acidly. "We have important targets to acquire. The entire operation to retake the bridge and the city of Circle depends on everything we can do right now. The stand-down will have to wait."

She could do this. It was very simple to be in the military. He might not be her commanding officer, but when someone outranked you and looked that grumpy, there were only two choices for an answer. One—Yes, sir. Two—No, sir. That was it. She only had to pick one.

"Yes, sir!"

"Good. Major?"

Pam shrugged off a sudden, sick thought that she'd given the wrong answer. Oh, well. Too late to take it back now. She directed her attention on the second officer.

Major Shamos was a lean, dark faced man who had been staring at her this entire time as if she was some sort of bizarre new bug that needed to be popped into a jar of formaldehyde for later classification.

Piss off, she thought, inwardly delivering him a heartfelt third-finger salute. On the outside, she gave the sour looking officer the saccharine polite attention she reserved for customers with the same attitude. He responded with an "hmfph" and started to turn aside. Right before he looked away, she nailed home a split-second eye contact that told him exactly what she thought of his staring.

His sudden, hard, coughing fit turned his ears maroon. Inside Pam's head, the muffled—yet undaunted—turbulence from the other presence stilled for one breath, two breaths. A sensation of complete, shocked astonishment replaced it.

All right, so maybe she overdid that a little. She'd never managed that reaction from anyone before. Maybe it went over stronger because this was a dream. She winced as the pummeling in her head started up again.

Major Shamos cleared his throat and then gestured to a large video screen in the wall that displayed a detailed topographic map. He touched a spot on the screen and the video flickered and focused into a specific sector with unfamiliar code letters, numbers, and names. At least Pam thought what she looked at were numbers and letters since, as with the small computer she was still holding, she couldn't read or identify the language.

She was speaking, hearing and understanding it, so why couldn't she read it? She'd have to try to figure that out later. For now, she forcefully returned her full attention to the video display on the wall. One area of the map highlighted with another light touch, and Shamos nodded toward it.

"There's always Coalition patrols up here, in the Gateway Overlook, you know. Scouts say they're all armed with the updated weapon." He fingered the highlighted area on the wall display and it enlarged and detailed.

"Wow." She couldn't help the soft exclamation as she gazed over the rugged beauty of the terrain. Not to mention the quality of the resolution on the big screen.

"You'll have to be careful here." The officer indicated a particular spot on what looked like a huge ruined building. "Always seems to be lookouts stationed on the overlook, but at best, patrols will be light and, of course," he finished on a slightly sarcastic note, "you should be able to snag at least ten of them yourself."

Pam closed her mouth and raised an eyebrow. Oh, right. Whatever. So not only was she some sort of soldier in this dream, she was a soldier that these two officers had some issues with. They didn't like her. Or, they didn't like whoever she was supposed to be. And it wasn't just because she was late, or sarcastic, or taller than anyone else in the room, either.

Interesting.

"Yes, sir!" she said aloud.

Shamos continued talking about things. Pam remained clueless. Colonel Mott would interject a comment occasionally. She tried to appear as if she was paying attention. Something about a bridge, was that the Gateway Overpass? Going to check it out. No, the bridge was called the Wide River Gap Bridge. And it led to a circle. What sort of circle? A traffic circle? Crop circles in a cornfield?

Gee, imagine. She crossed the Delaware Water Gap Bridge just last week at Christmas and just days ago almost got into an accident at a traffic circle. Factors from her everyday life, like the guys talking about paintball war games, reassured her even more that this was a dream.

More than a bit troubled, Pam realized she couldn't remember any other dream where she was so worried about details. Great graphics on that computer, though. She quickly coughed to stifle a giggle that threatened to break loose, despite the seriousness the situation demanded. This dream was just too weird.

Major Shamos shot her a glance. "Hmm?"

"Dry throat, sir," Pam answered truthfully. "Oh, and Major, do you use one of those new Macs? Just how fast are the processors on that thing? And the resolution on a screen that huge is better than I ever thought. What sort of—"

"That will be all, Sergeant," interrupted Mott. "Move out as soon as possible." Colonel Mott dismissed her with a wave of his hand.

"Come on," muttered Captain D'lano. "Let's get out of here."

"Captain, if you'll stay, please."

"You're on your own, Sergeant." D'lano's voice was low, soft, and worried. "You can call this off. I think you should." With that, Captain D'lano turned to join the other two officers by the big computer screen. "Colonel, I really don't think this survey is a good—"

Pam ducked out while D'lano was still speaking. Her body shivered as if flooded with adrenaline, like almost getting into an accident and missing by the tiniest fraction. Unfortunately, once outside, she hadn't the slightest idea of what to do next. Her creepy crawly feeling was elevating in intensity, giving her chills.

The mental box she had filled and taped was threatening to burst open. It shook and shuddered with even more force than before. All she needed was for a slime-covered alien to come bursting out of her brain…

Turning a corner, an automatic reaction of her dream body's hard muscles brought all forward motion to an abrupt halt. Talk about close! Had she not been looking down and glimpsed two pairs of boots, she would have sworn no one was there. The color and light- reflecting material of the uniforms extending above the footgear nearly faded the bodies wearing them into the very air.

Uniforms—like hers. Except when she looked down, she didn't have the illusion of air. Hm.

"What's the rush, Sarge!" A deep male voice came from one of the uniforms. "No hurry now, is there?" He chuckled.

Taking a step back, she studied the pair standing before her. Or tried to. She discovered quickly that angling her gaze just a little ended the illusion of invisibility and the disquieting impression there was nothing but air between boots and heads. Both new arrivals wore black headbands edged with a thin blue band and emblazoned with a subdued gray lightning bolt and star emblem. Both headbands also displayed barely visible symbols: two interlocked gray rings followed by a half diamond, another ring below that. One quick motion, as if to smooth her hair, told Pam she also wore a headband and the hair on this dream body's head felt thick, surprisingly silky, and rather short.

Rank insignia, guessed Pam, returning her attention to the rings. The insignia design repeated on the left shoulders and right forearms of the uniforms, so subtle against the unusual color-reflecting material she had to look twice to make sure they weren't a trick of the light. Her attention traveled from the uniforms and rank patches to the people themselves. Like her, they were dirty and stained, from hair to heels, the harness and belts loaded with gear well-worn and scratched. She wondered if their eyes were burning like hers, and if hers were as bloodshot and shadowed as theirs. But despite their obvious exhaustion, they both regarded her with attentive concern.

Other than uniforms, accessories, and tiredness, however, the two newcomers were nothing at all alike. One was a young man with brown hair, mustache, and the thick-muscled, rugged look of a defensive linebacker from a professional football team. His companion, a beautiful young woman with pale hair and huge gray eyes, had the hard, slim body of an aerobics instructor or gymnast. As the silence grew between them, the newcomers began to look worried.

The man pushed up his glasses with a hand the size of a dinner plate. It was bruised and swollen between wrist and pinky finger, as if the edge had been mashed in something.

Ah, one of the not-casualties from the…last mission, the details of which remained unknown to her. Well, she knew only that it had involved another bridge. Or the same one they were supposed to go to now.

The golden-haired woman bit her lower lip and wrinkled one side of her nose, eyes narrowing slightly. "Troop's all settled, Sarge," said the woman at last. "Captain D'lano pcom'ed a few minutes ago and…uh, asked us to pick you up. Anything wrong?"

Pam scratched her shoulder as an excuse for checking the rank circles on her own uniform. There were six: four interlocked, followed by a full diamond, two more opposite. She remained unenlightened.

But she figured since they had less circles, rings, whatever they were, these two looking at her so expectantly must hold some rank less than the one she had. Her glance downward only confirmed the body she occupied had the look of one seriously auditioning for a spot on *American Gladiators*.

The huge young man cleared his throat. "Come on. Let's go get some sleep. Or is there something you need to tell us from the meeting?"

Oh, shit, Pam thought in growing bewilderment. *Oh. The SMG rifle mission…better get on that.* "Ah, yes. There is," said Pam in a very businesslike tone, noticing for the first time the voice she used had a strange sort of accent she couldn't identify. For that matter, all the people she'd met so far had odd accents.

Did that have anything to do with being unable to read the language displayed on the computers, or just the fact that she was in a dream and some things, as in most dreams, were just plain wonky?

"What's up, then?" persisted the young man.

She scrambled for words. "Ah, we have to get Colonel, ahh, whatshisname? Right, Mott. Colonel Mott some of the new SMG rifles."

"Right now?" asked the woman in surprise. "Did you tell him to shove his—"

The man's bruised hand covered his companion's mouth swiftly. He moved the hand to her upper arm, reached for Pam with the other, and pointed with his chin to a spot away from the command post. She went along without protest.

The young woman shrugged off her companion's grip, gray eyes stormy. "Damn it, Sarge, this has to stop. I know we're concentrating on this upcoming push for Circle, but this is ridiculous. I thought we were standing down for three days. None of us are in any sort of condition to go out."

"That's right, Sarge. We've already had a delay on this once. This break was supposed to start an hour ago! We're not exactly at peak form. You can't even remember Colonel Mott's name, and Ariam almost went off right outside his office! Is getting a few SMGs such an emergency that it can't wait a day or so?" asked the man.

She had that awful, sick, sinking feeling that she had royally screwed something up. Something important. She didn't know what to say. It didn't help that whatever she had thought safely put away had almost burst free, already struggling for control. And this presence wanted out, kicking like an angry Clydesdale.

"Ow!" Pam's hands went to her head.

"Yeah, something is definitely wrong." The woman exchanged a perplexed glance with the man. Then she reached toward Pam with both hands, her irritation transformed into puzzled concern.

Pam had no control over her feet—they took an involuntary step away. Whatever was inside her didn't want the young woman to touch her.

"You don't seem to be yourself, Rett," the one called Ariam said gently. "If you're not going to let me try to see what's happening with you, we're going to take you to Med."

Pam's thoughts on this wavered between complete opposition and total agreement.

No, said the other presence in her mind, once again manifesting as a clear, strong thought. *Whatever is happening to me has to stop NOW!* The imaginary box vaporized.

Pam winced again with the pain of it, unable to respond.

"I'll give Med a wakeup," said the man immediately. "Com connect—"

* * * * *

WITH THE THREAT OF MED added to the complete worry coming from her seconds, Rett threw everything she had against the alien presence. *Damn it, let GO of me!* She let out a sharp breath through her teeth. Yes, they were hers again, thank all deities!

"No, Kraym." Rett forced a laugh. "No, sorry. I was preoccupied. And have just a bit of a headache. I dozed off earlier and totally lost track of myself. We don't need Med. You should know by now that if he's not already vectoring in on me, nothing's wrong."

Her seconds looked unconvinced. "All right, then maybe now you can explain what you mean about getting Mott some of the new

SMGs." Ariam crossed her arms. "And then we'll all go in there and tell him exactly why we can't go. We're probably the only ones in F-troop still conscious at the moment."

No doubt Ariam and Kraym wished she were unconscious as well, thought Rett. She even wished she had that excuse. Unconscious or not, she'd heard every word spoken by Mott and Shamos inside the CP. And remembered the comments and answers that had come from her lips, if not from her.

She gave her juniors a quick report and ended it with: "If everyone is already settled down, we'll leave them be. At least they'll get a little break before the…" she winced, "…next assignment."

Ariam and Kraym exchanged glances. "The survey?" said Ariam. "Right after this?"

"I screwed up," Rett admitted. "I should have stood firm about the break. I didn't. Not only that, I acted like a complete idiot in there. Tiffed off Mott."

"Mott's always losing his temper lately," snorted Ariam, "even when people are polite. He needs a break."

"I know what I'd like to break him with," added Kraym darkly.

Rett agreed with both her seconds, but still she said, "We're all under stress. Be nice."

But being nice was getting harder every day. Two years ago, when Rett and F-troop had been first assigned to assist the 52nd, things were fine. Colonel Mott and his adjutant Major Shamos were always a bit taciturn, but no one had any complaints. The 52nd was hardworking, organized, maybe a bit down on their luck, but then again they'd been assigned to a tough area of the Branch Range, the Zen's Glacier River district. Mott seemed pleased enough to have F-troop as an asset back then, although after the first few days they didn't see much of him or his adjutant in person. Captain D'lano had always represented the majority of the contact the 52nd's command staff made with F-troop.

They'd pushed hard through the mountain district to establish this point convenient to the valley of the Wide River Gap. But since then, just about two months ago, the 52nd's luck seemed to take a turn for the worse. Rett was strongly of the opinion it had to do with the way Mott had started assigning missions: giving hard hit-and-runs and deep penetration raids to the infantry units instead of to F-troop. When she brought up the point, she didn't get anything but the last month of non-stop assignments. MainCommand was pushing them hard; after all, the Gap and the city of Circle were probably now the two most important strategic targets on the planet. She understood all that well enough, but casualties were too high, tensions even higher, morale was down, and the 52nd's commanders seemed to be caving in to pressure.

Mott had promised them a break, but now he was taking that back. She understood the need to press on, but they couldn't press on and expect success with exhausted troops. It was asking for trouble.

Aloud, Rett said: "This is just a snatch and run. I'll go myself. It's important to get these new weapons before we hit the bridge or Circle. When I get back, I'll see what I can do to hold off the survey. Once I get moving—"

"No." Ariam and Kraym said it in the same breath, the same tone.

"We're going with you," continued Ariam. "And when we get back, we're all going to see Colonel Mott. This way when your brain starts coming out of your butt again, one of us can kick it back into your head where it belongs."

Rett nodded. Now was not the best time to point out Ariam's less than acceptable word choices and tone of voice in a public area. Especially not after her own behavior in the past twenty minutes.

"I'll go and give Trebor the update." Ariam turned and strode off, displeasure evident in every step.

At least, thought Rett with a silent sigh, the adrenaline the three of them had just generated should last long enough to get Mott his rifles. Good gods and deities, what was that all about? What happened? She ran a hand over her face, through her hair, and let out another slow breath. Favoring her other co-second with a reassuring grin, she then attempted to focus her mind on the task at hand.

She should leave Ariam behind and take one of the others instead. Ariam and Kraym were teamed as co-seconds, but Ariam was senior and next in command. But Rett needed the younger woman's empathic abilities. Tired or not, she was indispensable. Rett needed Kraym, too. The three of them together were capable of sliding in and out of those ruins as one person, which was exactly what had to happen.

At least Rett felt certain that Trebor, as third-up, ensured the platoon of capable leadership. She hadn't spent much time preparing him or Gerrale, next after Trebor in the chain of command, for sudden elevation to commander and second. Yet she was confident enough in her people to know they'd be all right, no matter what. Everyone in F-troop told her constantly she worried too much about things like that. She couldn't deny it.

No trouble, Rett told herself firmly. She'd better worry about herself for a while. What she did affected her entire platoon; could affect the entire 52nd. Maybe she should allow Kraym to get Med. At least, if Med said she was medically unfit, Mott wouldn't file a complaint about insubordinate behavior.

The term grated on her already taut nerves. Sure, some infantry officers regarded her as arrogant. The formality that anyone wearing a Special Forces headband was required to display toward officers from other branches made some uncomfortable. The formal behavior could easily be translated into arrogance. And sometimes Rett's executions of orders bordered on the fringes of standard operational procedure, but were still well within Special Forces, if not regular infantry, methods. That caused some consternation among the infantry units her platoon worked with, although they couldn't fault her or F-troop for non-completion of an assignment. Ever.

But insubordinate?

Not in a million years! No matter how much she personally disliked the commanders of the unit she and F-troop had been assigned to assist, and would disagree with their plans and methods from time to time, she never in her military life had been insubordinate. Nor had she ever failed to show the proper respect. Until just before. She'd lost complete control over what her body was doing, yet had remained very aware of what was happening. That only made it worse.

Rett barely stifled a shiver of pure horror. Next to being immobilized and in tight spaces, not having complete control of her body or mind was her greatest fear, and triggered recollections of past events she thought firmly buried.

She mentally thanked Captain D'lano for trying to cover for her during that madness. He was a good friend to them all and went out of his way to make sure they had what they needed on and off the job. As Kraym liked to say, D'lano was as handy as two extra Omnis and a good set of VARs. Rett couldn't have asked for a better go-between.

He really came through for them again today. He tried. She knew he did. D'lano was a good man, and she was going to have to track him down later and apologize for that weird behavior before. She winced. She couldn't believe she'd jumped him like that. If anyone should bring her up on charges for something—it should be him. She was lucky he understood.

A light but definite poke in her arm brought her attention to Corporal Kraym. "What's up?"

"Humor me, Sarge, and tell me what galactic sector you're still in." The corporal snorted. "You're still far from a geosynchronous orbit. I was asking you if you needed anything from Supply for two minutes now. Is he someone from HQ?" His voice took a teasing, yet hopeful, sort of inflection.

Rett stifled another sigh. Her refusal to allow herself a personal life for the past few years had given her co-seconds a crusade to see if they could change her mind. To make it worse, lately the entire platoon seemed to be in on it, too. Normally it was a source of amusement to all of them, but right now Rett wasn't amused. Not after what had happened.

It wasn't important, she reminded herself. What was important was that Kraym was giving her another chance to show she hadn't completely blown her headband, just like Ariam was. She couldn't let them down.

She let go of the momentary rush of irritation and came right back in the same teasing manner. Taking a fast glance around the compound, she gave him a playful shove. "You wish."

"You'd tell me though, right?" He straightened, two long steps bringing him back to his former position.

"Now who's delusional? Forget it. And wherever I was, I'm all here now, Kraym," Rett said briskly. She checked her ammo supply, frowned at the way her knife sat in its sheath and fixed it. She felt for the familiar presence of her TT-1 automatic rifle on its shoulder sling, took it down, and checked it. Aware, the entire time, of Kraym's close, critical gaze. She wasn't too worried about it now. "And I'm set for this little playtime for Colonel Mott."

"You're sick, Sarge, definitely sick." Kraym's eyes glinted with mixed amusement and worry. "You'd better eat something before we go. This might be only a snatch and run, but you're going to need all the energy you can get. If we see anything else out of sorts, Ariam or I will turn us back before we get there."

"Agreed. Same goes for you and Ariam. And if I see either of you are going out on me, we'll turn back right away. Let Mott do his worst. His personal opinion of me isn't important." She gave a reassuring pat to the heavy forearm nearest her, adding one of her best smiles for good measure. "I'm all right now. You know how it gets when you doze off like that! Especially having a mind set on some time off."

"Don't try the sweet and innocent act on me, Sergeant," warned Kraym, but his expression relaxed into his normal good-natured mien. "I know better."

"Fell asleep thinking about that hangover you gave me last time we had time off," added Rett. She ducked her face from Kraym's sharp eyes before her shock surfaced. She turned her evasion into a pretense of adjusting her weapons and utility belts. Where in two worlds had that come from? Why would she say that when it was probably the farthest thing from her mind?

To her relief Kraym laughed. "No wonder. Deities, I can't remember ever getting that zoned, that fast. Every time I think about it I get a headache, but it was worth the credit."

"Your ale-swilling status will stand unchallenged in F-troop, Corporal. I'd stand a better chance running enemy fire with a broken leg than drinking you under the table." The deliberately sour note she put in her voice brought another laugh from her co-second.

"Especially when only three ales get you zoned."

"Yeah, well." Rett glanced at her chrono. "Let's get going. A patrol rover should be getting ready to go and if we can get a ride partway, we'll be back faster. The sooner we get Mott's little toys and get back here, the sooner I can remind him about that break."

"Maybe he'll be in a better mood, too," said Kraym. "I don't get what's up his butt. Shamos's either."

Corporal Ariam joined them in time to hear Kraym's last remark. "Well, they're right here in the hottest seat on Nyorfias right now, with the 52nd set to head up that big push for Circle. And our backups are nowhere in sight yet. Wouldn't that get you a little tense?" She handed Rett a fruit bar and a water bottle.

"I can appreciate stress," Rett said, noting Ariam's critical inspection of her from top to bottom. "I've worked with infantry commanders under stress during that big push we made with the 88th for East Ocean. We're not anywhere near that stress level yet here."

"Before my time," the younger woman reminded, "but I know what you mean."

"East Ocean was tough, but this push is going to tell if we shove the Coalition right off this planet," said Kraym. "I suppose that can be enough to put anyone on edge—being so close."

"Let's just get this over with. And, Sarge, I didn't hand you that stuff for decoration." Corporal Ariam gave Rett a meaningful glare.

"Thanks. I was just about ready for one of these." Rett shoved the water bottle temporarily in her shoulder harness and removed the wrapper from the energy bar, tucking the film into the recycle pouch on her utility belt. She firmly blocked up her thoughts and feelings, took a big bite, and grinned at her co-seconds. Deities knew why she held back on telling them everything. She'd never held back before. In this case, her deepest instincts warned against it until she knew more.

As Rett's direct second-in-command, Ariam had every right and duty to investigate any question of physical or mental fitness from her platoon leader and make a judgment call, just as Kraym did. For Ariam, it applied even to the point of using her talent, forcefully if necessary. If she decided to push, Rett knew she'd never be able to block it. She was too tired.

So, on a surface level, Rett concentrated on what she was chewing and her impatience to be off and get this assignment finished. "Trebor's awake?" Inside, she found time to feel a lingering amazement that both of them hadn't felt the intensity of her interior discordance right away, stunned her senseless, and turned her over to Med.

"Yes, he and Gerrale both are alert. I'm ready."

Maybe she was just overreacting to all this. She was overtired and a little disoriented from falling asleep. She'd take that, for now. At least until she found out exactly what had happened and how to keep it from happening again.

Somewhere inside Sergeant Rett, Pam drew her addled self together. Okay. She'd let this person Rett, or whatever her name was, be herself. All she was doing was screwing things up. She hoped she'd remember everything when she woke up. It might be great material for another story!

Rett shook her head, feeling another intrusion of disjointed thought. She had to stay focused. Well, a few hours, a few ML-12s, and she'd suck it in and try to charm Colonel Mott into reconsidering the survey. Sure she was tired, but not enough to be that brainless or forgetful.

Yet she had been. She couldn't change what happened.

Rett shivered and then dismissed her troubled musings. "There's our ride." Putting fingers to her lips, she let out a sharp, short whistle.

The gunner on the patrol rover swatted the driver in the arm with one hand and waved for them to come ahead with the other.

"Let's go." Rett suited action to words, hopeful that this foray would keep her from dwelling on her problem any longer. But all too soon her mind was back on her odd behavior, gnawing away at it the same way a river martun gnawed old bones. She was okay now. But what if it happened again? They'd have to make sure to be double alert going into the ruins of the landmark. What if it took her over, like back at the CP?

With a mental growl and a physical lengthening of her stride, she ordered herself to keep her mind on her mission and closed the remaining distance between herself and the small scout rover waiting for them.

"Hey, Sergeant Rett. Thought you guys were standing down."

"Yeah, so did we." Rett shrugged.

"Where's the rest of the troop, Sarge? I was going to call back the others." The driver spat the spicebush stem he'd been chewing over the side.

"No need. It's just us. Headed toward Gateway."

"Your lucky day, then," said the driver. "We lost the toss for that sector."

"Mmn. Funny thing, this. You always lose the toss for whatever sector I just happen to mention." Rett hadn't failed to notice that the instant she mentioned the location, the patrol rover's scanner operator had gone on com and redirected the patrol originally headed to that sector to another.

The four soldiers aboard the scout fixed Rett and her seconds with innocent grins so faked she had to laugh. The 52nd was a decent outfit. All they needed—*all* of them needed—was for Mott and Shamos to get over whatever was bugging them.

"Come on," urged the driver. "We'll see how close we can get you."

"Thanks." Rett and her seconds squeezed aboard, more off the vehicle than on it. As the rover lifted and started out, she was confident that whatever happened had passed. Everything would be fine.

1.1.1 UNDISCLOSED LOCATION
SOUTH CENTRAL BRANCH PROVINCE, NYORFIAS
0535.06.08 (LOCAL RECKONING)

RETT AND HER SECONDS HAD parted with the patrol a mile or so back, continuing on foot toward the overlook. A safe distance away, she halted them to scope out the target.

"It's sad," Kraym said as he handed over her VARs. "I remember coming through here as a kid, and all the fun we had at the center."

"My family traveled out this way once, too," Ariam said. "My dad figured since we came all the way to Circle, we might as well check out the sights…the first landing place, the temporary settlement, what was left of the ship. The museum was fun."

Rett shook her head. "The center can get rebuilt. Those rock formations can't. At least they're still intact. Stay sharp, you two." Tucking her VARs into her belt, she shouldered her weapon and started up the nearest tree for an unobstructed view.

Located well into the foothills of the Branch Range, the Gateway Overlook marked the end of the rolling plains so characteristic of the continental interior and the beginning of the northern high country. She would never forget cresting the last hill in the road and getting the first view of the unusual formations of rocky upthrusts that formed the "Gateway".

The view from her position was fine, too. She settled comfortably into the tree and retrieved her VARs for the scan. It was sad to see the center and park in ruins, though, especially after four hundred years of being a popular spot in this area. The building that once sprawled over the top of the hill had served as park headquarters, interactive learning center, and natural history museum. She remembered that the many viewing decks in and around the structure allowed unobstructed views for miles in any direction, from the southern expanse toward the Wide River Gap and lush green meadows of the Centerland plains, to the Gateway rock formations and first of the true mountains of the Branch Range to the west.

Only small sections of the building complex were in any sort of usable condition. She switched her VARs into combat mode, carefully combing the area, which was overgrown and all but hidden from eye view. With the VARs, however, it almost didn't matter what was in the way.

Although an odd sensation remained inside her, her tiredness had vanished. There was nothing like a good shot of fear to chase the sleepies. She bid her lingering nervousness good riddance. She didn't need the distraction of thinking about whatever it was that had possessed her. Or the potential results had it lasted any longer.

"Anything?" Kraym's deep voice was soft over the com.

Rett lowered the VARs. "Nothing easy. We're going to have to go around. Never can find an enemy patrol when you want one."

She slithered down the tree. Kraym, as usual, took charge of the VARs. She could have easily handled transferring the readings to their Omnis herself, but Kraym, ever since coming to her unit, had made it his habit.

"So much for simple, I guess," he said with a shrug.

"It's not that far. Let's find Ariam."

More vitality surged through her as she started off with Kraym. She smiled as his familiar energy, steady, warm brown and deep gold, made its familiar imprint on her mental vision. "Glad you're good to go, big guy."

"You can scope me now? I was concerned about that."

"Me, too."

After collecting Ariam, Rett led the way around to the south facing sections of the ruin. This time she didn't need the VARs. She was already sure an enemy patrol was up there. She pushed her awareness forward, alert for the telltale glow of energy sources.

She kept close to the wall, making as much contact with it as possible. She didn't have to check to know her seconds followed suit. The properties of their uniforms made them all but invisible to the unaided eye. In addition, staying close to the cool stone, moving slowly, and keeping their body temperatures down would momentarily confuse the body heat sensing abilities of the enemy's infrared targeting scopes.

The walls of native stone, strongly built yet covered with the rampant, creeping growth common to wild areas of this part of the continent, also merited close attention. Rett's ability to sense and interpret energy auras wasn't as reliable through dense stonework, and there were plenty of places available for the enemy to be hiding.

Surprising a Yixolryn Coalition trooper with a powered-up SMG was one thing. Having a Coalition trooper jump out and surprise you became a different story altogether, and a great way to get killed, since there was no way to avoid an already aimed and fired shot from an energy weapon. There was one way she knew of to avoid catching SMG: just make damn sure to be moving before the shot came.

She stopped short.

Behind her, the two corporals stopped, too.

It was time for Ariam to work. Rett couldn't push her energy sense through walls, but Ariam didn't have that problem. She signaled and the younger woman crept into the lead position, hand spread on the wall, head down slightly.

Rett could barely make out voices. When Ariam glanced back, Rett mouthed: *Four?*

Ariam opened five fingers.

Rett motioned with a slight movement of her head and they went on, slowly, in the direction of the voices. As they drew closer and the voices more distinct, she verified her earlier assessment of four different people from the variations in tone.

But Ariam indicated there were five. Where was the fifth? The voices were slurred, loud. Zoned? High? Both, probably. No officers around, she guessed. That was good, they'd never cut loose like that if there were. The fifth was probably on the lookout for them.

Her speculation was confirmed upon hearing a shattering noise and a round of tipsy laughter.

Pam had been sitting back, content to let her dream unfold naturally. This Rett character knew what she was doing, all right. But when she heard that shattering sound, it was a blast of the old familiar. Pam knew that sound very well, especially after working six years in a liquor store. She knew the sound of people who had too much to drink as well. So her working daily life was manifesting in this dream. She didn't know whether to be relieved or disappointed in that fact.

Rett started to shake her head as another weird thought surfaced. Anger surfaced with it—she thought that business was over with. Gritting her teeth, she concentrated even more on her situation at hand. She had no time for anything else. A head motion might be mistaken for communication at this point; a loss of focus could be a disaster. She halted in front of an old, thick-beamed door, firmly closed on one of the few completely standing sections of the ruin. From other briefings and her personal study of strategic structures, she recalled that this room had an excellent view of the entire valley.

Rett sent a wry glance to the two corporals. The squad of Coalition troopers hadn't been paying attention. Good thing.

After half a minute, she glanced to Kraym so he would understand he was to remain by the door while she and Ariam scouted ahead.

Kraym indicated agreement, also communicating his relief that she was completely back to normal. She gave him a half grin and bumped him slightly in passing.

Rett moved ahead with Ariam to make sure they wouldn't get any unexpected surprises in the next handful of minutes. Satisfied, she headed back to the door where Kraym waited.

Open it.

It's locked, Kraym indicated in return.

Rett answered with a nod and a toothy grin that brought an answering expression from Kraym. *Make like a missile, big guy.* She could have done it herself, but Kraym really enjoyed stuff like this. Besides, with her energy sense and Ariam's awareness helping to locate targets, it was better she and the younger woman were on their feet and ready to nail anything that might target Kraym before he recovered.

He hit the door. The wood didn't give, but the rusted metal hinges and latch cracked. With a loud, ripping, dust-raising crash, the heavy old door and one commando corporal slammed inward with all the force of a missile strike. Rett and Ariam were right behind him.

Four startled, openmouthed faces turned to stare down the barrels of Free Army weapons.

"Party's over," announced Ariam in a tone both sweet and hard. "Let's see hands, now!"

Four of the humanoid troopers complied. Rett finally spotted the fifth, one of the more alien races of the enemy Coalition. She slapped her short knife free of its holder on her shoulder harness and sent it flying as the alien made a mad dash for the passage leading outside to the overlook. The creature went down without an outcry.

"Get those weapons," Rett said.

Corporal Kraym relieved the remaining troopers of their sidearms, which he handed off to Ariam. Rett went to check the trooper in the passageway, sparing the yellowish-gray, scaly-hided creature a brief glance as she checked it for lifesigns. A Voi. Odd that one of its kind allowed the humanoids in its patrol to get that wasted. Usually those of its race were as hardline as the Yixolryns themselves. She retrieved her knife before checking the Voi trooper's utility belt for anything that might have information they could use.

These particular aliens were always kissing Yixolryn ass. But they also had a reputation for being mercenary and for always trying to make humanoids look bad, no matter whose side they fought on. Rett guessed that had been the creature's intention with the patrol. So she and her seconds had somewhat ruined its plans, but this particular little group of humanoids were still going to look really bad to their commanders.

She straightened and left the dead trooper behind. Kraym had arrayed himself with three of the bulky ML-12s and their powerunits and was just about to acquire a fourth.

"Let me have those last two, and give one of yours to Ariam. We have to move fast and I don't want any of us overloaded. We're leaving now. What's coming next is either their relief or their officers. Let's not be here to find out."

"We stay much longer, we're going to go off on these intoxicant fumes," agreed Ariam, blowing out a breath and allowing a grimace to appear on her face. "The alcohol is bad enough, but whatever they were smoking on top of that sure wasn't pipe herb. Don't stay in here too long." She adjusted her burden of extra weaponry and left with Kraym as Rett gestured them out, covering the patrol.

Rett grimly ignored the fume-induced headache she felt coming on as she stared down the troopers. Three males, one female. They still looked surprised and a little dazed, but were rapidly sobering. None of them dared move, hardly even to breathe. With or without the manipulations of their dead alien comrade, they would be in huge trouble for slacking off on lookout. She almost felt sorry for them.

At least she'd be merciful. Coalition cruelty applied as much to their own troops as much as it did to Nyorfian prisoners. But there wasn't time to do anything but leave them here to take their chances.

"One sound, one move, one step out of this room while we're still in range and I just may forget you're drunk and unarmed," growled Rett. "Understood?"

Three heads nodded in unison. The man on the end simply passed out.

With that, she joined her seconds, trying to snort the lingering fumes from her nose. "Let's move." No time to waste being stealthy or invisible now. At full speed Rett and her seconds tore down the steep bank and ran for the cover of the woods.

"Look sharp and scatter! We're spotted!" warned Rett, only a gasp before lightning streaked past them, searing the vegetation into steam and ashes.

Kraym and Ariam dove into the doubtful shelter of the trees. Rett, behind them, ducked instinctively to one side before a SMG beam sizzled past the spot where her head had been.

Yipes! That was close!

The strong intrusion of a thought that had no reason to surface and the overwhelming sensation of complete shock that came with it broke Rett's concentration. She jumped for the sheltering quartzite rocks inside the tree line. As she cleared the open space, there was a searing, burning, white-hot flash of pain through her leg. In the first two heartbeats of pained surprise, followed by instant redirection to maintain combat silence, she lost her balance. Without Corporal Ariam's quick assist, Rett's stumble would have rammed her face, nose first, into a tree.

Until just now, Pam's dream had the unreal quality of living in an action-adventure movie. Then the unnerving, very real sensation of a hot, lethal stream of energy screaming by at close range like a thunderbolt had shaken her from a passive state in to once more feeling as if she were a full part of the body she inhabited. She could swear the short hair above the black headband smoked from the nearness of the last shot. But that had been nothing compared to feeling the heat go through her—the dream person's—leg. Shit! It hurt!

Furious, Rett clamped her teeth and lips tight and wrenched her thoughts into order.

"You okay?" Ariam asked in a low tone.

She glanced down just long enough to make sure her uniform hadn't caught fire. "Yeah, come on. We have what we came for." She struggled to control her voice, to keep it low and calm. She didn't like the possibilities her situation was creating. Not one bit. She had to get herself and her seconds back safely—then decide how she was going to deal with it. "Let's go."

They ran on, then jumped into a deep, dry streambed and listened for sounds of pursuit.

"Surprised you hung on to the SMGs, Sarge," Kraym said.

"Me too." She took a few seconds for a closer look at one of them. "Clumsy things with these bigger power units. Heavier than the usual weapon. I'm surprised the troopers could maneuver!"

"They don't really have to maneuver with the targeters and range they have," reminded Ariam. "That shot you nearly caught came from the observation deck above that room we were in."

"I did catch it." Rett's level of tiff rose. "I don't always go around bashing my brains out on trees, you know. Thanks for catching me, Corporal."

"I swear you cleared it."

"Didn't." Rett shifted a bit so Ariam could have a look. She dragged her attention there reluctantly. Looking at it would just make it worse, but she had to know if it was going to cause problems. Baring her teeth, more in distaste than discomfort, Rett poked at the scorched, burned section of material covering her lower right leg, near the thick part of the calf muscle. A slight haze of smoke still rose from the wound, along with a peculiar burned meat smell. Aloud, she said, "Not too bad." Inside, her anger rose again. Exactly what she didn't need—another hole in her.

OW! For a dream, this hurts like hell! How can she be ignoring it so much?

Rett swallowed down an angry shout of frustration and tried to clamp down on the reason she should be having such odd, short-circuited thoughts. She wondered if she finally cracked; caved in to sheer fatigue.

Ariam gave her an intense glance and Rett answered with a head-shake. She reached into a belt pouch for a bandage, a cooling one for the burn.

"Want me to put that on?"

"No." Rett spoke more sharply than she intended, but she wasn't ready for a prolonged—and possibly probing—contact from her empathic co-second.

"We should go, Sarge," Kraym said after a minute. "Can you walk on that?"

"Let's go," she replied, scrambling from the cover of the ditch. "Have to cross the road while no one's coming down it."

She diverted her pain into movement and thought. Since she couldn't ignore or dismiss her symptoms any more, she had to formulate solutions. If going crazy or exhaustion offered no answer to her current state of mental confusion, there remained only one plausible explanation. Rett found it tough to even say the name of that phenomenon in her thoughts.

Ego-merge.

* * * * *

After covering five miles of the twenty between HQ and the overlook on foot, no one was happier than Rett to run into another scout unit. No amount of troubling thoughts, training, or pain tolerance made fast travel any easier on her wounded leg. And after they got back, it was habit more than anything that made Rett try not to limp as she and her seconds went to report in with their captured weapons.

"Wonder why Captain D'lano's not here?"

"It would be nice if he were getting some downtime, too. Like we should be. Let's just get these right to Colonel Mott and get it over with." Once they were all safely on some downtime, she could deal with her other issues. Other than hesitating to let a medical floater go by with a wounded soldier and two medical personnel in attendance, she didn't waver one step off her determined trajectory to the CP.

"Excellent work, Sergeant. That was fast. Any trouble?" Colonel Mott looked more pleased with her than he appeared earlier, much to Rett's relief. It didn't change the fact he personally didn't like her: that much was evident every time she caught a mental glimpse of his personal energy signature.

50   "Nothing extraordinary, sir. Now, Colonel, about that break…"

"Good, now about the Gap bridge—"

Rett blinked and peered at Mott to see if he meant it. She couldn't believe her own voice when she heard it say: "The bridge, sir? Right *now?*" She had absolutely no intention of saying that, not in those words and certainly not that tone of complaint! She stuck her tongue to the roof of her mouth and kept her lips together.

"You were given the briefing a few hours ago, Sergeant." Mott's pleased look abruptly faded. "These recons were given priority status from MainCommand."

This couldn't be happening. Rett instantly moderated her expression and tone of voice. "I understand that, Colonel Mott, sir. Is it possible this survey can wait a day, or a few more hours, at least? Colonel, my unit's dead tired, if I take them out now, even on survey, we're asking for trouble. If we can delay even a single day, it would make a difference, sir." She struggled to keep her voice even and polite. "You know we're already supposed to be on a three-day break. You cut those orders yourself. Is there something specific I should know, sir, that you need F-troop to survey and not your own observers?"

"I went over this with D'lano. He didn't see you first?"

"No, sir. We came right in."

A frown flitted over his face. "That's right, Shamos wanted him for something." Mott sat back and crossed his arms. "All right. Your unit is better able to get details and acquire important target areas. You know at this point in time, both the bridge and the city of Circle are the most important strategic targets on the planet." His gaze went to the map display on the wall.

"Yes, sir." Rett's unit out-qualified any of the 52nd's for performance of pre-combat surveillance and that was a small part of their job. "However, in F-troop's present condition—"

Colonel Mott glanced back to her sharply. "If I had someone else to send who would get the details your unit would, I'd send them. But I don't. MainCommand is expecting details. *Before* new day. So go and get some details, Sergeant."

She had priorities, too. First to the citizens of Nyorfias; then to the people in her troop. Taking her overtired platoon out, even for something as non-confrontational as a survey, only decreased their effectiveness on the first part, and increased the risk factor on the second, should things get hot. She had a right to find an alternative solution. If that didn't work and he made the survey an explicit order, she had a right to log protest, even if that didn't stop the mission.

"Sir—"

"You might not be a direct part of my command, Sergeant, but that was a direct order, which, in regard to the reason F troop was assigned to the 52nd in the first place, I'm allowed to give when I see the need."

Meeting the cold, hard stare he was giving her with one of her own, she said, "Yes, sir." She made sure her face and voice remained calm and impersonal. "Recorder on, clearance 90674SF, log and distribute! Sergeant Rett taking survey on the Wide River Gap bridge under protest. It is my personal opinion F-troop's personnel are under stress and in no condition for field mission." She added regulation sections, dates, and order numbers. The voice-address capabilities of any Omni in range and the CP's main computer systematically made notations of her words. "End record. Thank you, Colonel Mott, sir."

"Pull out within the hour, Sergeant *Killer*." Colonel Mott added emphasis to the name she hated.

Rett didn't care, this time. No matter how tiffed he was at what she had done, he couldn't fault her. Not this time. She'd kept cool, did everything by the rules.

"And the transport you've cleared us to use, sir?" Rett wasn't about to have anyone walk the sixty miles from where they stood now to the Gap. And diverting any more scout patrols was out of the question, especially since the entire platoon was involved. "Since this is a priority mission, sir. And since our liaison is busy elsewhere."

The top of Mott's balding head and ears darkened rapidly in anger. His energy registered a smoldering red-orange, a level that already increased the combat-ready tension in Rett's body. What did she do to get him so mad? Maybe he'd just had all he could handle. It had been a long war, and from what she knew, he'd been in it from the start. Three years longer than she had. Nor could she claim a decade or so before that with the system militia, or whatever experiences he might have had elsewhere before that.

She watched without moving as Mott snatched up the notepad for the vehicle pool so quickly a mug and two other notepads crashed to the floor. "Prep TC413 for F-troop immediately," he snarled into his comunit. "No, they don't need a driver. Dismissed, Sergeant!"

"Yes, sir, Colonel." Rett managed to keep her sigh inward and didn't roll her eyes until she was safely on her way outside. So much for turning on the charm. Not that she was much good at that, either. Charming wasn't a quality noted anywhere on her service record.

"At least you managed us a transport," mumbled Ariam, on her left. "Better than nothing, I guess."

"And the rest of the platoon had a few hours to sleep, at least. I'll go and get them ready." Kraym departed without further comment.

"Ariam." Rett stopped, chewing momentarily on the inside of her lower lip. "What did you get from that meeting? From Mott?"

The younger woman scratched her head. "I'm not sure. I didn't look all that closely. Stress. Irritation. Feeling overwhelmed. And I don't know what you did to tiff him that badly. He did say he didn't have anyone else to send that would get the same detail we can—he meant that. Also that MainCommand wanted it done. Maybe he screwed something up by not having this survey done already and is expecting us to pull his butt out of the fire."

Rett turned toward Ariam to comment, but before she could speak, a familiar, sour voice broke in.

"Hold it, Sergeant! Right there. Yes, you."

"Shit. Med." Rett turned and groaned when she saw the platoon medtech on an intercept course with her position. "Not now. It's minor, there's no time. We've 'important targets to acquire.'"

"So I heard. But there'll be plenty of time," Med said pointedly, "if I decide you stay behind." He indicated a convenient spot on the ground. "Sit. There. Now."

"If Colonel Mott wasn't on the edge of having a major fit with the lot of us," Ariam said as she took Rett's weapons, "I'd just ask you to decide we all had to stay behind, Med. A couple hours ago, I definitely would have. But we're not attacking anything, we're observing. And the Sarge has even managed us a troop rover."

"That's why I didn't pull Medical over Mott," agreed Med. "Those few hours the rest of us had were enough for this observation."

"Then everyone managed some sleep?" Rett felt hopeful.

"Some more, some less, but some. And it seems your little foray energized you a bit. But I'm not happy. You logged protest on this, did you?" asked the medtech.

"No choice but to, Med."

"Good. If anything blows up, I'll back you. I'm still waiting for you to sit down, you know. Minor or not, that burn needs attention."

Rett made a face. Unlike Ariam, Med didn't need to boost his peculiar sensitivity to pain in others with a physical touch. Most of the time, he knew if any of them were hurt or not feeling well. He didn't wait for people to come to him, either. No matter when, where, or what someone was doing, no matter the amount of training to block and reroute pain or discomfort Special Forces had given them, Med knew it. And if it was possible for Med to get to someone, he did.

"Sarge?" the medtech reminded impatiently. "Ground? Sit on it?"

She sighed, knowing she really was lucky to have two psi-talented individuals in F-troop. It just seemed so inconvenient. Especially now she was doing her best to hide something. She reminded herself to keep whatever concerned her tucked tightly beneath on what they were already focused the most. She was sore—that should keep Med occupied. And she was cranky—that should take care of Ariam. And the both of them knew she was better able to ignore being sore and cranky when she was busy and moving.

"Need help, Sarge?"

Rett glared at Ariam as she offered assistance. "I think I can plant my ass on the ground without help, Corporal," she snapped.

The corporal's return grin was a textbook example of impudence, and it lifted some of the stress from the younger woman's face.

The medtech knelt alongside to examine the SMG burn in Rett's leg, carefully removing the bandage she had slapped over it before. She felt tempted to ask him, casually, of course, what he thought about her spacing out, then thought better of it and remained silent. She wanted to be sure herself. Ariam and Kraym were still suspicious and would be keeping a close enough eye on her. She didn't need Med to add to something she kept hoping was an issue simple enough for a few hours of sleep to fix. If Med suspected anything wrong, he'd tell her straight off if he thought she or anyone else was unfit to go on this survey.

"Oh, this is lovely. Just what you needed, another hole," he commented in his usual grumpy manner, but his hands were deft and gentle.

Rett already knew that. Oh, it would get smaller over time, but it would never go away completely. She allowed her disgruntled feelings on it to surface, hoping to further disarm the two empaths in such proximity to her.

"Not much we can do but keep it clean." Med proceeded to do just that, adding some cooling unguent, finishing with a bandage to keep the dirt out. He continued with the usual running commentary, a sour grumble, making acerbic comments about wasting time with skin grafts and cosmetic surgery and how much little damned good that did anyway seeing she wasn't making time lately to take personal leave to have anything fixed. "…and what's the use, 'cause if you did you'd just go out later and blow any repair work all to shit anyway."

He went on with the woes of being a Special Forces medtech to a platoon full of self-destructive people. "And why did I have to choose this option when I could've had a far safer position elsewhere with another branch of the military?"

Rett tilted her head back to exchange glances with Ariam, who shook her head and rolled her eyes. Every single time Rett or anyone else got hurt, it was the same speech. It came in handy for diverting one's attention from the wound and what Med was doing. As long as Med was tiffing off, everything was fine. He only displayed solicitous kindness when things were serious.

"You'll see daylight through this one for a few years, at least," finished Med.

"Figured that out already. Thanks, Med."

He finished with his bandage and made sure it wouldn't slip. "When we get back I'll want another look at this. You were lucky it just went through a muscle, not tendon, bones, or ligaments. You don't catch many like this, Sarge." He looked at her closely. "Seem alert enough. Distracted, were you? You'll be paying attention now, I think."

"Yeah, Med," Rett agreed. "Don't worry, it won't happen again."

He began to replace his equipment in his pack. "In that case I'll leave well enough alone. I'll expect you to sleep part of the way on the rover. And, I hope you were planning to head over to the mess area just now," he added meaningfully as he stood up.

"Actually," Rett said, "I was going to..." She hissed as Corporal Ariam's boot connected with her burned leg.

"We were just going there." The corporal's slender, hard fingers dug into Rett's arm, as much in warning as in support. "And it's Thirdday... our favorite cook's on duty today. Did he make something good? Some of those stuffed rolls we all like so much?"

Rett kept her mouth shut and feelings neutral as she allowed Ariam to assist her upright.

"I was hoping that was what I caught a whiff of when we came in," Ariam went on with barely a breath after Med's confirming nod. "In any case, going out or staying in, we were going to run over and grab a bite and some extra to take on the way."

55

Rett nodded in agreement, since increased warning came through Ariam's tightening grip as clearly as spoken words.

"Good," replied the medtech. "I'd sure hate to leave anyone behind, especially our fearless leader, just because they were fainting from hunger."

"Good gods and deities, all right already!" Rett shrugged from Ariam's grip and rubbed her arm, wondering if her second's fingers had left bruises. "If you want me fully operational, I'll need that arm."

Corporal Ariam's glance was dark. "I wasn't about to let you come up with another one of your excuses. I know what happens when you're stressed and keeping it all locked up inside. So does Med. And unfortunately, so does Major Yidnar, and he's the last person I want to send any negative command fitness reports to. You need to eat. And you need to keep it down."

56

"I suppose I should be happy someone cares about me," groused Rett, wishing she could com her Special Forces battalion commander directly about this situation. Unfortunately, she couldn't. F-troop, as one of the 2023rd's splinter assault groups on assignment, still had to report to the 52nd Division. She'd jump up the chain of command only for a last resort, and only for something dire. A patrol survey didn't fit into that profile.

"We all do, Sarge. Particularly me! I'm not that anxious to make platoon leader!" This very familiar maxim was accompanied by a familiar smile, although it showed a little more strain than usual. "We need to talk, and we can do that as we eat. Besides, Gerrale and Trebor will pick up everything we need, they always do."

Rett decided anything other than agreement would only add to her co-second's tension. Especially after everything else that happened already today. Besides, Ariam was right. Rett could already feel the familiar churning deep in her guts.

This is all very interesting. I never had a dream where I felt so tired and sore—or hungry and nauseous at the same time. This one is certainly different! It seems so real, but I know it's not.

Rett stopped in her tracks as random thoughts surfaced again, stronger than ever. "Damn it, this has gone on long enough!" She wasn't dreaming. She definitely knew everything was real. Maybe she was the one finally cracking under the pressure, not Mott.

"Uh, Sarge?"

Rett heard, but didn't answer.

Her pulse pounded in her ears. She had thought the word before, but she hadn't wanted to even consider it. But there wasn't any other explanation. Unless…unless she had somehow been implanted with something. She started to shake her head in denial, stopping herself by raking her right hand through her short hair and wishing it was long enough to really grab. The thought she'd been compromised somehow by a Coalition device undetected by the rigorous routine scanning they endured was almost more unbearable than the idea of an ego-merge.

It was time to face this down.

She changed her course of thinking abruptly, directing her focus inward, toward the alien, insane leakage of thought invading her mind. *Hey, YOU!* thought Rett sharply. *Do you know where you are?*

No matter what, Pam had never expected the woman's mind she inhabited to confront her directly. Feeling entirely visible, she shrank back. All of a sudden everything felt different. The sensations, smells, sounds coming from outside more than unfamiliar: they were strange, alien. A group of soldiers hurrying past them, having a heated discussion as they went, spoke a language Pam's mind simply couldn't decipher. ~No. This is a dream. I guess I'm…nowhere, really.~

Anger replaced the deep, sick dread that had been churning up Rett's already empty belly. Her head on confrontation had demonstrated a definite separation of the alien presence in her mind. No longer did the strange thoughts manifest as an interior echo of her voice: they had a distinctive tone and, now she was focused on it, a unique energy. *Ah. There you are. Now I know I'm not crazy!* She let out a harsh breath through her teeth.

"There's something wrong in you, Sarge. I felt it before, I feel it now. I feel it now stronger than ever." There was no bantering, light attitude about Ariam now. "There's something—"

Rett made a swift, small gesture that stopped the younger woman's words, glanced around, and pulled her second-in-command into the space between two of the temporary structures of the division headquarters.

"Ariam—you're right." Rett spoke in a low tone meant only for her second to hear. "I didn't tell you earlier because I needed to figure things out for myself."

Ariam's gray eyes were dark with concern in her tense, pale face.

Rett licked her dry lips. "I'm certain I've had an ego-merge."

The corporal glanced around swiftly to make sure they were alone. "Certain? What makes you so sure, Rett? What if it's something else? A device? Like with—" Ariam swallowed. "Like when you were in C-troop, and—"

Rett didn't let her finish. "Oh, I thought about that, too. But our scans are thorough now. Plus, we have Med—who'd know for sure if something were stuck inside my head. And so would I, at least I would as soon as it activated. This *thing* has energy, but it isn't the sort of aura a device would emit."

"Well, that's a relief. Sort of. Ego-merge. Good deities." Ariam scrubbed a hand through her hair, loosening strands from the tight weave that kept it close to her head. "Shit. I suppose we should be grateful that at least, historically, an ego-merge isn't malicious. But there hasn't been record of one for over two hundred years! I thought that phenomenon was something from the past."

"All deities help me, Ariam, I'm sure," moaned Rett softly. "Why? Why did they pick me? Why now?" She glared up to the sky and the blackness of space that lay beyond, addressing the mysterious supernormal beings every Nyorfian knew existed and influenced their lives. "Why me?" She wanted to shout, but kept her voice in the same tone she used to speak to Ariam. "I don't have *time* for this! The last problem I need right now is having to cope with some dimwitted alien mindforce thinking it's dreaming!" There was no way she could combat an ego-merge. She would just have to put up with it.

"That's why you didn't want me to touch you earlier today?"

"I think so. That wasn't me right then…the alien had me blocked somehow. I managed to make it move away. I was trying so hard to get back in control, and thought if you touched my body and I wasn't all there—"

"Shit. And I didn't have a hand on you long enough to tell for sure when you stumbled before." More long golden strands came loose from Ariam's braid. "Well, right now, if it's from something alive and not something constructed, I'll definitely be able to tell if it's benign or malicious."

"I don't think it's malicious, just…" A suitable definition failed to come. Rett rubbed at her forehead wearily. "Just messing me up."

"Want me to check?"

"*Now* I do. Absolutely. Are you up for it?"

"After what you just told me?"

"Make it fast." Rett dropped all her mental barriers so the younger woman would be able to feel the second mindforce occupying her. "Just don't squeeze my face like you were squeezing my arm." She closed her eyes as Ariam's left hand, fingers spread, lifted to cover her face, making a light contact.

"Hush."

There was a familiar sensation of beautiful greens and cool silver blue as her co-second's energy aura slipped beneath Rett's outer defenses. It didn't take long. Ariam's cautious probe had made the alien shiver a bit, a reaction that made a few chillbumps tickle the nape of Rett's neck. But that was all. She opened her eyes as Ariam stepped back. The younger woman's expression was guarded.

"There *is* someone else. Confused, not believing this is real."

Rett didn't have to be told that, but having it verified went a long way to making part of her—a small part—feel better. But the verification of her condition also brought up the real seriousness of the matter. Again, she made sure her face was devoid of emotion. An ego-merge wasn't remotely comparable to a simple case of fatigue. What happened to her was now up to her second, whose responsibility it was at any time to make judgment calls on Rett's fitness to lead.

"It explains why you acted so strange earlier," the corporal muttered. "The merge must've happened when you dozed off and the alien mindforce was wide awake and dominating before you knew what was going on. I don't know whether I should be relieved or more concerned." Ariam looked up, meeting Rett's eyes. "That's why you caught that energy beam, too. The alien distracted you! What if it happens again?"

Rett said nothing. She stood still and silent. As still and silent as the presence in her mind had become after the initial shock and turbulence of discovery.

"You're not waiting for *me* to decide what happens now, are you?"

That's your job as ranking second-in-command, Corporal, thought Rett, remaining silent. The pleading, agonized expression in the younger woman's eyes wasn't something she could help right now, no matter how much she wanted to.

"If anyone finds out you'll get pulled off Active and sent to Research so fast..." Ariam took a deep breath, her tone firming. "That stupid rule should be dropped for this war, damn it. Nyorfias needs you here. We need you here, Rett. Here and now. But if something happens..."

She remained unmoved, her expression set. Waiting.

Ariam turned aside and pressed the heel of her right hand against her forehead. "Med didn't feel anything wrong. He passed you for this survey. I only really felt something strange when the alien was still dominant." The corporal turned back to face Rett squarely. "Once you shook off the alien mindforce's control, you were fine. Do you think now that you know what this is, that you've made contact, you can handle it?"

A huge knot of tension relaxed in Rett's chest and guts. "Yes."

"I agree. At this point in time, it's for everyone's best interest you stay on as platoon leader for F-troop. I'm not going to say anything. It's between us."

Rett closed her eyes for a few seconds. "Even if nothing happens, Ariam, we can both get in serious trouble if anyone finds out. Are you sure?"

Failure to make Rett's unusual predicament known to scientific authorities was stepping outside the law. As a rare phenomenon that might lead to clues to the Nyorfians' planet of origin; insights to alien cultures; and the effects of the merge on the subjects themselves, ego-merging was still regarded as a topic worthy of study.

The law demanded cooperation. The uniform they both wore demanded compliance with the law, military or civil.

Rett felt that alien presence perk up with interest at the track of her thoughts and ignored it for the moment. There were priorities to consider in this situation, too. Wasn't helping to eradicate the threat of the invasion forces of the Yixolryn Coalition more important than satisfying the curiosity of scientific research? Was it worth the risk of being brought up on charges for withholding information if anyone should find out? If something slipped out?

Was it?

Is it?

Yes. It is.

"We both know what's more important," said the corporal earnestly. "I'm willing to stand by my decision. And so are you."

"I am."

"We can't forget we're already committed, Rett," reminded Ariam, reaching out this time with her palm open and upturned. "We took an oath when we passed Special Forces training, all of us. *'Nothing is allowed to deter, divert, or stop us from the ultimate goal of protecting our worlds and people and preventing an enemy takeover.'* Nothing! Not even an ego-merge."

Rett covered Ariam's upturned palm with her own. "The minute you even suspect this thing in my head is making me do something I shouldn't—you take me down. Whatever it takes."

There was a slight wince, a tightening of her jaw, but Ariam's direct eye contact didn't waver. "I will."

Grasping the younger woman's hand firmly, Rett sealed more than just an agreement of silence.

"When this war is over, Ariam. When this war is over, then I'll take care of it."

"That sounds like a good plan. Right now, tell him or her or whatever it is to shut up and leave you alone!"

"Never fear," answered Rett grimly, "I'll take care of that. Now that I'm sure what's going on, I'll be ready for this...this..."

"Dimwitted alien mindforce," Ariam said. "Take care of it quick. We have to get going."

Listen you in there, Rett directed to the alien presence that cohabited her mind and body, *you are NOT dreaming! So shut up! You could've had me locked up, making people think I've flipped. And you damned near almost killed me! We've apparently have been chosen for an ego-merge.*

The alien's interest perked. Rett saw it as a brightening gradient of the energy source she'd identified earlier, one that was basically warm brown, violet, a bit of blue-green. ~Ego-merge! What's that?~

Some superparanormal beings in this neck of the galactic quadrant take someone's mind and spirit and merge it inside someone else's mind and body. No one knows why. I don't have time to explain anything else to you, so listen close, because this is the bottom line: where ever it is you come from, your body is dreaming without you. What makes you you is here, in me.

There just happens to be a very real, very serious, farthest from a dream war going on right now, and I'm directly responsible for the lives and performances of forty people, so don't mess me up or I'll—

~You'll what?~ A sensation of disbelieving laughter came from the alien. ~Get rid of me? How?~

Rett gritted her teeth. *I can make your life pretty miserable, especially if you feel everything I do. I'm trained to handle pain—are you? From the reactions you've been having, I don't think you are. Maybe I'll just stop diverting what I really feel. Like this!*

Pam recoiled from the force of that thought and the full, undampened extent of Rett's mental and physical pain, exhaustion, and frustration right then.

~Whoa! Ouch! Call 911! Okay. I'll stay out of it, no funny stuff, I promise.~ Pam made an effort to squash down her firm belief that she, no matter what, was positive she was dreaming. But she would humor this dream character, Sergeant Rett, or Killer, or whatever her name was, and cooperate, for now. She had thousands of questions all of a sudden, but…better to wait a while. Maybe they would get answered in time.

Felt nice, huh? Hey, and this is a good day! Rett snarled in her thoughts. *So look, alien, don't push me!*

~Aliens? Aliens merged us?~

I didn't say they were aliens. I said superparanormal beings. No one knows exactly what they are, just that they exist. You're *the alien.*

~Aliens merging people? That figures. And you guys really don't know where you came from? Wh——~

Rett wanted to scream. Somehow this foreign entity in her head was capable of reaching right beneath her surface thoughts to skim even more detail. No wonder she was thinking more than usual about the history of the Gap before, and—

I can't have this. You can't be doing this to me. KNOCK IT OFF! Again Rett whipped that thought with everything else she felt at the unwelcome presence in her mind.

~Good grief, all right.~

Pam shrank back. She was just giving herself, and this dream character, a headache. Again, she was suddenly deprived of understanding most of what was being absorbed through Rett's physical senses, as if a thick sheet of glass came between everything but her sight and access to the immediate concepts uppermost in the sergeant's mind.

She tried to absorb the sudden turn of perception. She understood Rett had dismissed her for the moment and was more concerned with this mission, but that was all it was—concepts, ideas, intentions. Not thoughts that manifested in words like there had been before. The words she was hearing through Rett's ears as the sergeant spoke with her second-in-command were foreign, flavored with an exotic cadence.

Cautiously, she edged forward again. As if emerging from fog into sunlight, things started making sense again. Okay. So she had to find a balance between cutting herself off almost completely and merely staying out of the way. But she needed to know more. Sitting back watching without getting any answers to her questions wasn't her idea of fun. Be patient, she counseled herself. Come on, how hard could it be to sit back and take it all in for a while? People did that all the time when they watched television. She didn't want to mess things up. She'd wait.

For now.

1.1.2 WIDE RIVER GAP
SOUTH CENTRAL BRANCH PROVINCE, NYORFIAS
0535.06.08 (LOCAL RECKONING)

RETT SMELLED THE RIVER THEY approached long before she caught sight of it. It wasn't just any river, after all. This river slashed a twelve thousand mile split in Main, from the northern ice to the southernmost point, following the course of the natural continental split. To the north, it was narrow and turbulent with rapids until it plunged from the high country into the more gentle, rolling, open spaces of Centerland. There, as the waterway dropped from its treacherous paths through the Branch Range, it widened and deepened. As the river flowed southward, in places it became a five to fifty mile wide expanse, like a seven thousand mile long lake. It was from those areas that Wide River had earned its name.

From Centerland Province, right below the last series of broad, shallow rapids above the Wide River Gap Bridge, the river was navigable straight through to the shores of the Great Southern Ocean. Before the war, shipping was a brisk business. The swift current made southward freighting an economical, ecologically friendly, resource saving enterprise. Northbound goods were carried by railtube or air freighter. As far as crossing the mighty expanse with heavy freight, well, that was different. Only in two places on the entire continent did the river both narrow and flow through terrain hospitable to the construction of bridges. And it was to the northernmost of those bridges Rett and her unit were headed now.

The Wide River Gap Bridge broke the main highway from the logging town of Branch, some hundred and twenty miles to the northwest, to the major spaceport and business center of Circle. Right now, the enemy invaders of the Yixolryn Coalition held this bridge, and the city of Circle, which lay twenty-five miles beyond. The Nyorfian Free Army had to take this territory back. With the northern spaceport cut from Yixolryn Coalition use, a tremendous dent would be made in the flow of enemy equipment and supplies pouring in from Epnoce, the captive sister planet to Nyorfias.

While they were still out of sight range, Rett brought her unit to a halt with a hand signal for those who could see her and a soft whistle for those who couldn't. Had her next cue been spoken she would have said, as usual, "All right people, let's drop what you don't want to keep inside until deities know when."

She found a likely spot to make her own contribution to the planet that nurtured them. Survey or not, they were moving out of a safe zone. Best not to have to worry about the need to relieve oneself if things got hot.

Once the Free Army finally made their move on this bridge, things were going to heat up. If they took it, they'd take Circle and the space-port. And then, they could finish the enemy on Nyorfias, kick their asses off Epnoce, and be done with it. It sounded so simple. Of course it wouldn't be.

Her sore leg twinged. Good thing they had the rover. They left it well hidden a mile or so farther behind them. If things were quiet enough, she might even send someone after it to bring it closer. Better yet, if things were quiet enough, they'd avoid going back to HQ at all for three days, pull back into the forest, and sleep. She rolled her eyes at such an improbable thought.

They moved on when the last whistle alerted them everyone was ready. After another short hike, she deployed her unit into positions from which to observe the bridge and surrounding terrain. Realizing she had been dwelling more than usual on the geophysical character-istics of the land she operated from, Rett frowned. *Hey. You. You have to stop that!*

The alien pulled back, and Rett turned her attention to the bridge. As usual, Corporal Kraym had the VARs ready and in her hand as she reached for them. She set the recording uplink with a soft vocal command: anything they observed would be sent directly to the main tactical station at 52nd Headquarters. The device hummed quietly as the focus and readouts changed with her scan of the valley. In the upper left hand field of the floating data display, the heat sensor spot-ters flashed an all clear green.

She bit the inside of her lower lip as she touched the zoom for a closer look. The heat sensors remained green. The metal detectors

65

registered normal for the bridge structure, buildings and few transport vehicles. She swept the area again, minutely, trying to focus her physical and mental senses through the visual enhancement in a futile effort to comprehend what she was seeing.

"Is this the right bridge?" Without stopping her scan, she hunkered down.

"There's only one for a thousand miles, Sarge."

"Well maybe they gave us the wrong intelligence. There's no one down there. Check with your VARs. Maybe something is wrong with mine."

"There's nothing wrong with yours. I take good care of them." He sounded a little insulted, but nevertheless reached for his unit. The husky corporal adjusted his corrective lenses before taking a look.

"There's supposed to be most of a…" Kraym started, then grunted, became silent for several seconds, and started muttering to himself. "Three big troop rovers, two small ones. Antiaircraft and heavy weapons batteries in place, but not powered up, no gunners. Gates are open, guardhouses empty."

Rett chewed on a stem as Kraym scanned up and down the riverbanks in both directions as far as the VARs allowed.

"Not a soul in sight or heat range…this is really irregular!"

"Why at least a third of a division would pack up and leave the second hottest target in this section is a bit irregular, yes," agreed Rett dryly, then spoke to her pcom. "Com connect Fang Two!"

"Fang Two, Fang Leader, are you seeing what I am?"

"Come up here," requested Rett. She opened the frequency to everyone in the platoon. "Fang Leader to Fang Team. Keep channels clean unless you've a situation."

"You feel something's up?" Kraym lowered his VARs.

"That's the problem," Rett said, again perusing the terrain with her device and getting an unchanged view. "I'm not feeling anything but puzzled at the moment."

Ariam joined them a few minutes later. "Trebor, Worren, and Nitraym are scanning and getting the same readings," she reported. "So the VARs are working. As far as what I can sense it's no good, Sarge," the corporal said in apology. "I've bottomed. My physical energy is okay, but—I can barely read you and Kraym. Can you see us?"

"Barely." Pulling enough focus to use her ability for her scan had started a dull headache. She concentrated again, but even being so close to her seconds brought nothing but teasing mental glimpses of their personal energy signatures: impressions so faint they couldn't even be called shadows. "Beyond barely. I think what I do see from both of you and the platoon is probably because I know what's usually there," admitted Rett. As tired as any of them were beneath their activity-induced liveliness, the energy auras she saw, or thought she saw, should have been dull and gray anyway.

"No one's seeing, sensing or feeling anything extra. But we all know something's really odd down there," said Kraym.

Rett slapped a hand to her Omni in the same moment it signaled. She read the short coded message on the display. "HQ wants us to get a bit closer for some new readings. Says they're sending an air recon patrol. Well, why in two worlds didn't they do that it the first place? It would've saved us a trip. Shit!" Rett shook her head and growled. "We do another scan and go home. We've three days off coming." Rising from her crouch with a grimace, she added: "Even if we're spending them on suspension, medical or otherwise." She could use a day off her feet, that was for sure.

"How much closer?"

"Down the ridge to the edge of the tree line," Rett said. "There's no cover after that." Only long grass, a tree here and there, and clumps of short bushy plants broke the mile and a half of open expanse between the forest's edge and the riverbank. "Stay well away from the road. We'll make it fast."

Rett and her platoon crept closer into the valley quietly, moving through the thinning woods like so many shadows. Vegetation offered no cover from energy weapons, but staying low and slow attracted a lot less attention. The heat and metal detectors remained clear. Nothing. Wind. Trees. The sound of the water in the distance.

Twenty lengths from the verge, a rush of adrenaline shot through her body. "Pull back, get out, now!" She heard Corporal Ariam shout her own warning so closely the younger woman's voice could have been an echo.

The ground erupted and the lightning strikes of enemy weapons blazed around them. The whine, sizzle and thunder-crack of the SMGs soon competed with the sharper, staccato chatter and reports of projectile weapons, shattering the sleepy quiet of the river gap. Rett cursed silently to herself and returned fire at targets she sensed more than saw. The enemy had been underground. All over the place! No wonder they detected nothing! It must have taken the enemy days...tendays...to set up such emplacements.

This was a trap, a setup, but who? Why?

~I have thoughts on that——~

Damn it! Not now!

There was no way to keep avoiding the enemy fire. Her people were dropping all around her. Rett winced as she watched another go down, feeling the shot as if it hit her own body. Stuns, she noted. The lack of smoke from both victims and surrounding vegetation absorbing near misses identified the lower power shot. Of course, she found time to think rather bitterly, in terrain like this, the Coalition had learned to be practical. They didn't want to burn down Nyorfian forests any more than the Nyorfians wanted them to.

The discharges from enemy weapons distorted Corporal Kraym's voice over her pcom. "We're cut off all around," he reported a little breathlessly. "We've no place to go but straight ahead. Com's out—blocked. Just have local to each other."

Rett checked that information for herself, quickly cueing up her pcom. She looked in the direction of the bridge—straight ahead. There was plenty of activity there now.

Stunned was just as bad as dead. Worse in most cases.

"We can't just sit here and wait to get zapped. We may not have a way out, but we're not using stun force!"

"Right," agreed Kraym. "Let's see how many of them we can take out permanently before we're down."

"Com connect all Fang team!" The voice command opened channels from the communications patch in Rett's headband to all her platoon. "Fang leader to Fang team, take them out any way you can!"

Someone set them up. They knew exactly where they would be; that they would be tired. They had expected them, and well enough in advance to set up traps that couldn't be detected until it was too late.

Who?

~I can tell you that. Mott and Shamos.~

She didn't notice that thought came from the alien presence in her mind, only that it came. And it shocked her. Mott and Shamos? Unthinkable.

But it made terrible, logical sense…

* * * * *

CONSCIOUSNESS RETURNED ALONG WITH MILD nausea, the hangover feeling resulting from SMG stun. It didn't seem as bad as usual. Still, holding back a groan took an effort as Rett blinked and tried to focus her vision. The first thing she saw was the business end of a SMG rifle, so close to the bridge of her nose it made her eyes cross. Even a low power stun from such proximity was fatal, so movement wasn't a wise option.

"Aw, shit," muttered Rett.

"Get up," a voice invited. "Nice and easy."

She did so, moving carefully. The effects were shaking off quickly, but she still needed a minute or two to clear her head. If she tried anything now she'd fall over.

"Hands where we can see them!" the trooper snapped.

Rett obediently placed both hands, palms out, in front of her forehead. Only when she stood fully upright did she glance around for a quick inventory of her troop. Looked as if everyone was operational. Reassured somewhat, she focused her attention at the enemy troopers surrounding them.

First the damned ego-merge! Now this! Rett wrestled back any outward display of her anger. *And you just keep quiet!* she commanded the alien presence in her mind.

Pam was keeping quiet. She felt a bit offended. This ambush wasn't her fault. Other than those few thoughts before, about Rett's commanding officers, she was doing nothing to break Rett's concentration.

You're doing it now, Rett thought back. *Every time you make me stop and think about something, need to know what it is, what is for, or want to take an extra look at something, you do it! Stop it!*

Rett looked toward Ariam, who caught her glance and raised her eyebrows questioningly. Ariam's subtle actions then asked what all of F-troop was thinking. *Should we fight?*

The situation didn't look good. Apparently the Coalition wanted them all alive, and that was never good.

Rett blinked twice, as if still trying to focus her vision, then glanced to the right, as if to look at the troopers covering her from that side. Her movements appeared very innocent to the enemy, but her motions were part of a silent language of body signals her platoon would interpret as clearly as spoken words. *Two seconds. Give them all you have!*

Rett didn't have to visually confirm her entire platoon moved at the same time. The trooper directly in front of her didn't even have time to cry out as Rett's muddy boot slammed into his face. She spun and rammed her elbow into another trooper's larynx. The man gasped for air, choked up blood and fell to the ground, his face contorted in a futile effort to suck oxygen through his crushed windpipe. Rett jumped over him, letting another catch a kick that sent him flying. She took two more down before she heard shouted commands to use the lowest stun settings only. She automatically seized and stored the fact there were now more than two stun levels. No wonder she hadn't felt as hung over as other times.

Maybe they'll fix that annoying whine next, she thought as the electronic hum of weapons charging for another blast reached her ears. Rett managed to dispatch three more troopers and twist aside from the full impact of someone's stun charge at close range, but the next one caught her.

Unconsciousness didn't last long this time, but long enough for them to get a start on securing her. The position of her arms and the cold bite of metal on her wrists told her that much. Fighting back the grogginess, she lifted her head enough to unsquish her nose from the smashed grass and damp earth, trying to catch her breath. It helped, but not much. Maybe that foot-sized area of heavy pressure grinding her spine, shoving her flat against the damp ground, had something to do with her current inability to inflate her lungs. A hand grabbed her right leg, clamping down hard over Med's bandage.

This extra twinge of pain cleared her head instantly and sparked a reaction of pure survival instinct. Rett moved, rolling free of the trooper's boot, both legs flying in vicious arcs. Each boot made solid impact. One trooper fell back and remained still. The other soon followed as Rett twisted again, her right heel smashing into the trooper's unarmored hip. Rett heard the hipbone crack. The female trooper went down with a scream, still clutching her smashed face with both hands.

"Keep it up, Killer, and we start using your people for some full power target practice," warned a voice before she could retaliate further. The command of Standard was correct. But the accent and garbled manner in which the words were formed tagged the speaker as one of the Yixolryn Coalition aliens in charge of the invasion.

The platoon was alive. She had to wait for another chance. She had to get them out of this.

Rett indicated surrender and didn't move as a new set of doubly wary troopers approached to snap metallic bands around each of her ankles. These bands weren't connected with a magnetic field like the ones on her wrists. Not yet, anyway. No doubt they would be. Sooner or later.

Then she was hauled upright to face the enemy officer in charge.

"Troop Commander Iheolon and our Leader are waiting, with great anticipation, Sergeant Killer."

"I hope they're not tiffed if we're running a bit late."

The alien laughed unpleasantly. "I'm sure they'll let our tardiness go, in this case."

"Too bad. Well, personally, I hate wasting time, and I've things to do. Are we going to stand here all day?"

From wherever it was she now lurked, Pam began to truly admire her host. Rett had a lot of guts, for sure. And she was doing an excellent job of outwardly hiding her intense fears for the fate of her unit.

71

Anxiety about what might happen to her personally was either not an issue or so deeply buried Pam couldn't detect any hints. No, the platoon leader's primary concern was F-troop. Anything else was trivial.

Pam pulled back a little more and imagined herself behind a barrier that would allow her to see and hear what was going on enough to understand, but keep her personal thoughts and feelings contained.

Rett felt the entity inside her head all but disappear, hoped it would stay that way, and then dismissed any further thought of it. After the enemy officer turned aside, she looked around and realized they had taken her platoon away already. They certainly weren't wasting much time! Then again, she reflected with an ironic, inward laugh, it wasn't every day they managed to catch her and her entire platoon. It was usually just her.

One of these days she'd let someone else run all the decoys and diversions.

She didn't feel tiffed any more, just tired. It was hard to keep her head up and look unconcerned as her rapidly fading burst of energy depleted.

"Go. Move." The words were flapped more than spoken.

She spared this trooper a curious glance, having never seen its species before. Good deities, it was huge. She caught a glimpse of its rank sigils before one of its three tentacled arms curled toward her and wrapped around her body as easily as she would grasp someone's hand. The powerful limb contracted and her feet left the ground.

She rapidly prepared herself for anything, but all the creature did was whisk her around and set her down facing the direction of a small troop rover.

"That way," said the flapping voice as the grip of the tentacle released.

She barely managed to stay on her feet as a powerful shove sent her forward. Was it trying to shove her all the way to Circle or what? Straightening, she complied without comment or resistance. She noticed the tentacled officer didn't join the ones that followed her. Maybe it was part of the permanent bridge defense rather than the ambush team.

"Good thing Captain Thip thought up those underground hides," she heard one of her guards say.

So that was who thought of it. She couldn't recall ever coming across a description of the race before and made a mental notation to check into it at her first opportunity. Smart. Strong. What would it be like to have to fight someone like that in hand-to-hand, or rather, hands-to-tentacles combat? She was glad she didn't have to find out at the moment. She no longer had the energy to do much more than breathe and walk until they wanted her to stop.

Two small rovers met them near the bridge. After activating the magnetic fields on her ankle bands without warning, her guards tossed her into the rear area of the nearest one before Rett had time to worry about losing her balance. Her body slid across the floor like a dry leaf on ice.

At least I didn't have to land on my face in the mud first, and then land on my... The impact of her head against the wall that separated the rear area from the cockpit interrupted that thought. *Ow!*

Trying to blink away the bright colored dots in front of her eyes, she managed to attain a sitting position on the floor, scrunching herself into a corner as the transport filled with troopers. One of them, humanoid this time, grabbed her collar and hauled her up to sit on the bench right before an equipment case slid across the floor, smashing to a halt in the corner where she had just been.

"Thanks," she mumbled aloud. That would have really hurt.

Aside from a momentary stiffening as he settled in beside her, the trooper didn't comment. She shrugged and wondered just how many guards they intended to fit into the small transport, which would just about hold two handfuls of soldiers and assorted gear. She watched as it filled, half uncaring, half astonished. Ten...twelve...deities! Fifteen? Just for her? She supposed she should take it as a compliment, but she was too tired.

She spent a useless few seconds attempting to take up less space. No matter how she tried to squeeze over, the trooper immediately alongside—the same one who rescued her from the equipment case—squished hard against her. She wasn't exactly slender, and his already bulky shoulders were made broader by his armor.

Rett sighed. It was too soon to worry about anything. With the load the rover had to carry, it would take it a good thirty minutes to reach Circle. She reminded herself the best way to stay out of trouble—and gather the energy she'd need for whatever was coming next—was to go to sleep.

* * * * *

HE FROZE FOR A MOMENT as the prisoner's tense, hard body went limp. It was hard not to notice the change: she was wedged between him and the front bulkhead so tightly it would take an explosion to dislodge her. Not wanting to attract extra attention in his direction, he held his position. Then a soft "thump" against the armor plating on his upper arm nearly made him jump.

Was that her head? He felt the added weight through the armor he wore. It couldn't possibly be comfortable, there were multiple plates for flexibility and all of them had hard edges. She must be unconscious. He finally dared to turn his head enough for a look. He had to bite the inside of his cheek in order to check his rush of relief.

Not unconscious—she was sound asleep. Just like that.

He made swift note of others in the rover. No one so much as threw more than a glance toward the Nyorfian squashed between him and the front wall, apparently satisfied with the view of her mud- splotched legs and restrained ankles. The hot topic of conversation all around him covered what just happened, how easy it had been; some grudging agreement that the Nyorfians' efforts during and after the battle had been admirable—and for a few, had caused real worry. Most voiced was the anticipation for their reward for pulling it off.

His attention returned to the prisoner. Her head was tilted up and toward him, offering a good view. He could see where the hard edges of his shoulder plates already creased the skin of her cheek and temples. Sleep softened the hard lines and angles of her strong features; erased the tough, professional mien more familiar to most of them.

He was surprised to see how long her eyelashes were. The dark, thick sweep almost brushed her high cheekbones. His fingers itched to wipe a smeary blob of partially dried mud from one of them. There was a dirt and grass stain on her forehead with a crushed leaf still firmly stuck against her skin. He fought back another incredible urge to brush away a crusty spot of dirt from right beneath her lower lip, as full and soft looking as a child's.

Did it feel as soft as it looked? All he had to do to find out was duck his head and lean just a little bit more to the right. He bit the inside of his cheek harder and swallowed.

Last time he'd seen her in person, two years ago, her face had been partially covered with a blindfold. The rest of that long, strong body had been entirely visible, but so tortured and battered it had been impossible to even guess what it looked like whole and healthy. He thought she was dead. So had everyone else.

And here she was. Completely, utterly exhausted. Bruised, muddy, and in dire need of a bath, maybe more than one. But alive. Alive, for now.

The salty, metallic taste of blood from the inside of his cheek reminded him where he was.

Jaq Pym stifled his thoughts, hoped no one saw the heat he felt bloom in the visible portion of his face.

What was he thinking? She'd never seen him. She had no idea he had tried to help her then. It was just as well—he didn't know if he could help her this time. He might be able to help the others. He had to wait and see—and hope.

He was glad when the rover bounced and the Nyorfian's face tipped downward, hiding her vulnerable look. He relaxed his position and the soldier next to him looked over.

"Careful, Pym. She's sneaky. She'll go all limp and next thing you know she'll explode."

"She's sleeping," replied Jaq.

"Sleeping?"

"Yes, sir," replied Jaq to the leader of the guard detail, who sat closer to the rear of the rover.

The detail leader made the trooper next to him change places, the next one slide down. The switch involved a lot of grunting and complaining in the tight space, but at last a spot opened across from Jaq and the detail leader squished himself into it. Then he reached out and twisted his hand into the material around the neck of the prisoner's uniform.

Jaq winced as his superior's practiced yank popped the Nyorfian's wedged figure from the corner and let her drop facedown to the floor among fifteen pairs of boots.

Killer just groaned softly, muttered something about it not being time to get up yet, turned her head to one side, and remained motionless.

The detail leader passed a small medical scanner over her, nodding as the reading confirmed his observations. "Pym's right, she's dead asleep," he announced. "We can relax." Resting his muddy boots on the Nyorfian's body, he leaned back, grinning. "She'll be safe for a while. Or should I say: we'll be safe for a while?"

1.1.3 YIXOLRYN COALITION HQ, CIRCLE
CENTERLAND PROVINCE, NYORFIAS
0535.06.08 (LOCAL RECKONING)

Dark. Cold. Indoors.

As Rett awakened, the automatic awareness of her immediate environment moved on to the next factors screaming for her attention. Like the pounding protests of her aching body, an acute sense of nausea and a fierce headache. *Stun hangovers...ignore.*

A discreet flexing of muscles and limbs crossed off the possibility of disabling injuries, but made her aware her magnetic restraints had not been removed. There was also the added restriction of a restraining band snug around her midsection and arms, pinning them close to her body at elbow level.

Good deities, how long was I lying like this? Her hands and arms were numb from her own weight pressing them into the cold floor. Her shoulders and lower back ached. Extending every trained and natural sense she possessed, Rett knew she lay in a small, empty area. Alone. At least for the moment.

Dampening her dry lips, she took a deep, shaky breath and attempted to find out just how far she was able to move. She had to get some of the pressure off her arms and back, even if only for a few minutes.

~Feels like they have you glued to the floor. It's metal, I think,~ said the alien voice in her head as soon as Rett discovered the facts for herself. ~Some hangover!~

Rett grinned into the darkness, relaxed, and let her head drop back. "Hah," she said, more a grunt than a laugh. Odd, she felt reassured, not so alone. "So you're still in there...in me?" she asked aloud, but softly. She definitely needed distraction now. Maybe finding out more about this alien would help. She might've been annoyed to be the unwilling recipient of an ego-merge, but she was curious. Since she wasn't doing anything else at the moment, it seemed like a good time to indulge in asking some questions.

She continued in her thoughts. *What's your name, anyway? You do have one, I hope. When people remember, mine's Rett.*

Her ego-merge visitor gave a little mental chuckle. ~I know. Mine's Pam. Also known as the "dimwitted alien mindforce".~

This is so strange, responded Rett after a minute. The tartness of the enigma's reply hinted at a cutting sense of humor and perhaps a wee bit of hurt. Rett decided not to comment on her uncomplimentary remarks and make up for them some other way.

~You don't have to make up for those remarks. I think your remarks and your reactions were, and are, justified. And so are mine. After all, I don't think something like this has happened to either one of us before. How are we supposed to know how to react to each other, or how and why to control what we think, much less know there are rules?~

Rett swallowed. Would she ever have a private thought again? It seemed so unfair. *So all along—you've known everything I've thought about?*

~Well, either what you are thinking is right here in the open or you're SHOUTING at me,~ protested Pam. ~I can't help know some of them. And no, I didn't do anything while you were unconscious—I guess I was unconscious, too.~

This is really weird. Like talking to myself, but not! What kind of being are you? I mean normally…in your own form? You're not some really freaked out looking alien, like the Serzzn from the Benwyr sector, are you? All jiggly and full of acid? Or that three-armed officer back at the bridge? What planet are you from? Are you male? Female? Both? Neither? I think you might be female, but your thoughts earlier were so hard to distinguish from mine, I can't be sure of anything.

~I suppose I look just as normal as most of you people seem to me,~ replied Pam. ~Human, female. I'm from a place we call Earth.~

I guess I should be grateful for that much. I'd sure hate for you to get a sudden craving for live food! Earth. Never heard of it, thought Rett. *Not as a name for a planet, anyway. I don't think it's anywhere nearby. But this system is somewhat far from the center of things. Listen, what you thought about Colonel Mott—*

Her thought checked abruptly as light exploded into her wide-open eyes. Rett swore, blinded for several moments, angry at herself for not being prepared as the outer door opened with a whoosh and fresh influx of air.

~Well, you thought before you couldn't sense energy though walls. Although I'm still trying to figure out how you can do that in the first place, visualize energy—that's so weird. Not to mention you're so tired I can't figure out how you can see normally, much less any other way.~

This isn't a good time. Back off for now, thought Rett as a heavy boot prodded her in the ribs.

"Have a nice nap?"

"Yeah," snarled Rett. "Watch your damned foot."

"Watch your mouth, smartass, or my foot'll be in it," the trooper returned coolly.

The troopers dragged her out of the smaller space before pulling her upright. It was hard, impossible, to find any sort of balance with the electromagnetic restraints activated. And now she was standing, she realized the devices felt different than the others: heavier, thicker. She risked a careful glance toward the bands on her ankles. The trooper in charge of the guard detail displayed his pleasure at her obvious discomfort.

"Latest models. They have some other special features I'd like an excuse to try out. Like them, Killer?"

"Oh, yeah. Very nice." Her attention sharpened. She tried to identify what was visible of the trooper's face beneath his helmet visor. Another Voi: leathery, yellow-gray skin, sharp narrow jaw, a mouth almost lipless. The description fit many Coalition troopers, including the one on her left. So did his aura, although she didn't waste too much of her precious regained energy trying to read that.

But his voice. She never, ever forgot a voice, and his had triggered an identification. She stifled her reflexive physical reaction: one to attack, knowing it was foolish at this point. Her chance would come. The surge of lethal force she contained for the moment, the same way she would bank live embers beneath a coating of ash.

"We like them, too. You killed eight of our buddies earlier with those feet."

"You guys should've learned by now to stay out of range," she said, then added in a disappointed tone: "Only eight? I was sure there were more."

"What a smartass, hey, guys? We can't have her talking to the Leader like that. He likes a little respect."

"We don't have time," said one of the two holding her, a female whom Rett instantly named Right, since she was on that side. Right's tone was regretful. "The Leader's getting impatient as it is. You know how bad he can get when he has to wait."

"Commander Iheolon will keep the conversation going, I'm sure," said the one in charge. "All those decisions they have to make."

"That's odd," commented Rett. "I didn't know your Leader had the mental capability to make decisions."

Her comment ended on a grunt as the trooper who had been baiting her aimed a vicious kick into her stomach. The troopers holding her, Right and Left, hung on, so Rett received the full force of the blow. She had to muster every ounce of training and self-control she had just to straighten up. When her vision finally focused, she fixed a cool stare on the alien.

"Well, thanks. At least that took care of my appetite. I don't think I'll be hungry for a few days."

"Can't deny you got nerve, Killer," the trooper admitted. "Let's go. Commander Iheolon and the Leader are waiting. I hope they let us have a couple of her people," he said to Right and Left with a leer.

"What, Trooper?" Rett asked coolly. "Don't want another round with me and some scared teenagers? You and your other friends seemed to enjoy that last time we met."

Mistaking her shudder of barely leashed rage as a prelude to a struggle, the troopers took a firmer grip. She let the troopers on either side of her take even more of her weight, no longer trying to find balance on her own.

Pam—whatever you did before to disappear, do it again. I don't need any complications.

The trooper swung back to face her, taking a step closer, catching her jaw and throat in a bony grip. There wasn't much flesh on the alien's three skeletal fingers. His breath smelled like a small dead animal. That too, Rett remembered, and added a gag reflex to the queue of mental and physical impulses she wanted to keep in check at the moment.

"As a matter of fact, I had that very situation in mind. Those kids we managed to get to before the rest of your unit crashed Commander Avok's party didn't last too long, but you…" He shrugged. "The Leader has other plans for you, Killer. And now that we have your people, I hope to discover they have your stamina."

He shoved her farther into the grips of the troopers holding her, made some adjustments to the restraining devices and stepped away in preparation to leave.

"I've plans, too," she said grimly as she felt the magnetic force change. It still bound her ankles closely together, but no longer dragged her boots toward the metal flooring.

"Oh, that's right. I remember. You said you'd get Avok, me, and the others for what we did to those kids. One at a time." He looked her up and down with interest. "Did you mean here and now?"

"No time like the present," she said pleasantly, her glance casual as it measured the distance between her and the detail leader.

All three troopers laughed. "She can't do anything now," said Right.

Rett stopped trying to keep herself balanced. As she became dead weight, Right and Left took even better holds. This was exactly what she wanted. Using Right and Left for leverage, she slammed both her bound feet forward, focusing every ounce of her strength and weight behind them.

The impact landed directly in the trooper's armor-covered groin. The flexible armor plates, meant primarily to deflect energy beams, crumpled like paper. The crack of his pelvic bone was audible. With a strange, squeaky scream, he doubled and fell to the floor.

The other two guards dropped Rett like a hot grenade. Right kicked her forcefully in the stomach, while Left went to the downed leader.

"She killed him! He's dead!" Left gasped. He slapped his comunit.

She noted clinically that yes, the reports that one good hard jolt in the right spot would take one of them out. The main nerve center in that race was low, in the pelvic area. And maybe she had used a little more force than she actually needed. The Voi were slight of build and very lightly boned, relying on their cunning and quick reflexes more than brawn. Well, that was one alien whose quick reflexes had failed.

And that's done. He had it coming, thought Rett grimly even as Right slammed another boot into her ribs with lung deflating force. Her breath left her in a wheezing grunt, but she wouldn't give them the satisfaction of a sound of pain.

"Hold it, trooper!" commanded a new voice.

Rett swallowed some of the blood in her mouth and then pressed her forehead against the metal floor, which actually felt blessedly cool instead of cold now.

No matter what followed, she would hold onto knowing that at least one particular perverted enemy trooper would no longer be able to terrorize Nyorfian civilians. Maybe she'd be able to tell the survivors of that particular event she'd kept her promise: to ensure the one who killed their friends so horribly wouldn't be able to hurt anyone ever again.

She forced that memory back where it belonged, down deep, with all the others.

Hands turned her over. A humanoid Yixolryn Coalition officer bent over her. "Damn you, Killer," he snarled. "You just don't know when to quit, do you?"

"I guess not," she replied.

He pushed her onto her chest again. Rett's bound ankles were forced up behind her, crossed over somehow with her arms, and ended up somewhere near the band constricting her chest. The added pressure from her own legs against the tightened band cut into her bruised ribs. Rett didn't have to make any attempt to test the limits of her movement or the strength of the magnetic force keeping her in a shape vaguely resembling the popular Nyorfian vegetable known as knotroot. After a control loop was made snug around her throat, someone pushed her on her side.

"Commander Iheolon wants to know what's keeping us, sir," said Left's voice uncomfortably. "He sounds furious."

"He's not the one I'm worried about," said the officer. "I don't answer to him. This idiot," he said, nudging the dead trooper with his foot, "was lucky she killed him. The Leader wouldn't have been so merciful knowing you three were wasting time playing around instead of bringing her upstairs *without delay.* Don't forget," added the officer in silken tones, "who Commander Iheolon's superior is, Trooper."

Rett's bruised guts froze. Iheolon! That was quite a few times his name had come up. First at the bridge. And just before. Damn! Why hadn't she instantly linked the trooper she'd just killed and the memory of his ex-superior officer to the name of their unit's senior commander?

Then again, this has been a most unusual day. But damn it, why was Iheolon still here, on Nyorfias? On their trip out from 52nd HQ, she'd had time to skim over the latest reports, cramming information with her meal under the stern gray eyes of her co-second-in-command. Intelligence said Iheolon had been scheduled to ship out to Epnoce with his division.

~Who's Iheolon?~ Pam asked.

The chairperson of my admiration society, thought Rett sourly. He's one enemy officer I've managed to make look stupid too many times. His personal goal in life has become my termination. The longer and slower, the better. He's a sick, perverted, dangerous half-Yixolryn. He hates his humanoid half, so he takes it out on anything humanoid. His officers and personal guards are every bit as sick as he is. He has the potential to become the most dangerous Coalition officer in this sector.

He's snagged me more than once. Never managed to keep me permanently, but kept himself and his troopers entertained. Just paid back one of those polluted bastards, too. Damn it, Pam, as soon as they took me back at that bridge I should have known...

Rett didn't dwell on any details of those situations and Pam felt the effort of her host's mental shift as Rett continued.

There's this huge price on my head, you see. He's promised to split that and bonus credits among his division. He's been so intense about it that the enemy Leader supposedly pulled him from this sector and shipped him out to Epnoce where he could concentrate on fighting us instead of just getting me.

~So,~ surmised Pam, ~without you to distract him, he'll be more effective.~

Exactly.

83

~Why do they want you so badly?~

I'm too good at my job, I guess, Rett informed Pam, feeling awkward. Sometimes Rett thought she would much prefer to crawl under a rock than face the formidable reputation she had earned during her years of service. *It's not as if I'm doing something no one else is doing. There are thousands of other Nyorfians risking everything.*

~Sometimes that's just the way things go. Especially during a crisis. I think people need to single someone out, either for praise or blame.~

You sound like Major Yidnar. He's my real commanding officer—my unit's only on loan to Mott—I mean to the 52nd. Anyway, you wanted to know about Iheolon. He really started getting obsessed about getting me while I still was platoon second for C-troop, but for the past couple years F-troop and I have been running into him and his junior officers constantly anywhere between here and the East coast.

Pam felt another mental shift. Whatever memories Rett had of those past occasions, she didn't want to remember them any more than she had already. Those brief flashes Pam had received of a few of the incidents only hinted at the full scope of the content.

Fine, Pam thought in the deep private section she had imagined. Something that made this woman react like that, she wouldn't push. This dream was intense enough. Pam didn't need to turn it into a nightmare.

~You're just a big pain in his ass, is that it?~ Pam asked.

Rett almost chuckled aloud. *I think I'm beginning to like you after all, Pam.*

A mental snort came from Rett's visitor. ~In such a short time, I've come a long way from just a "dimwitted alien mindforce", huh?~

Rett had no direct reply for this, realizing this once-unwelcome presence now cohabiting her mind and body did a lot to improve her failing spirits. She needed the distraction. She had to get her attention away from her physical condition, and this enigma named Pam certainly was a diversion.

Try not to be too much of a diversion, Rett thought in warning. At the same time she was amazed so much information was able to pass between them in such a short space of time. She resolved to think about that more later. If there was a later.

"Tell him we're on the way," snapped the officer to Left.

Left's voice shook. "Y-y-yes, sir."

"Are we going to carry her up there?" muttered one of the guards.

The officer tightened the choking loop on Rett's sweat-dampened throat, enough to cause an instant grayness and make getting breath a major chore. Then he took the long end, and did something with it behind her. "There. Lucky he wants you alive, Killer, or I wouldn't care if you strangled or got your neck broken along the way." He tossed the end of the lead to one of the guards. "Drag the bitch up there," he said.

Rett lost consciousness somewhere along the way. She was revived outside of what she assumed was the enemy Leader's office. Once some of the shock had ebbed, she realized her body had been released from the knot it had been forced into earlier. She wasn't so sure about her gratitude a second later when she was abruptly yanked to her feet. *Don't pass out, don't throw up. Just breathe.*

"You have enough leeway just to stand on your own," the humanoid officer told her, "so don't try anything, or you'll be flat on your ass."

No kidding. She was sure every hair on her body was still standing straight up. And if she wasn't mistaken, that familiar smell was scorched uniform and skin. If that jolt they gave her to revive her seconds ago was a mild example of what her new restraints could do, being on her ass was the least of her worries. Rett forced a swallow down her sore throat, pushing the dizzy and sick sensations with it.

"Take her in," he told the guards. "Keep hold of that choke and use that to keep her in line. Don't touch her otherwise, unless you're told. Just remember what happened to Negaller!" With that, they took her through the doorway.

Rett was unable to do anything about the sweat streaking down her face, but she composed herself the best she could. *Stay deep, like you've been,* she warned Pam. *Don't make me concentrate on stuff you might be curious about like you've been doing on and off. Especially not here, not now.*

~I don't know if what I've been doing is going to hold up if they decide to shock you much more, but I'll try my best.~

If you want to keep on seeing what happens next, countered Rett, *you'll do more than try.* She stood tall, made sure her attitude displayed only as cool and emotionless, and took another deep breath. She had the feeling she was going to need it.

"What a shame to destroy such a strong will."

Rett didn't move as the leader of the invading Yixolryn Coalition military forces scrutinized her from top to bottom. She made a brief, but very deliberate, eye contact with him, and then another with the hulking half-Yixolryn officer who leaned against the wall nearby. Iheolon. Then she pointedly fixed her gaze to a spot on the wall behind the Leader's head, dismissing them both as insignificant.

The leap from gloating condescension to anger in the Leader's energy output was gratifying. To her surprise it tempered quickly and the sound that passed for a Yixolryn laugh soon followed.

"I admire your control, but I'm in control now. If only you Nyorfians weren't so resistant and impossible to…work with. What an officer you would make for us."

Keeping her snarl inside, Rett thought there were two Nyorfians who hadn't been all that impossible to sway. If anything, she had to get a warning out about them. There was always a way.

"But unfortunately the best the Coalition could hope to get out of this system's remaining civilian population are laborers."

Right. She supposed it was easy enough for them to threaten the safety of parents and children to ensure compliance. They had proven that much already on Epnoce and a few other inhabited, occupied locations on Nyorfias. But as compliant as Nyorfians in occupied areas acted, they managed to make a million little things go wrong for the invaders.

"And of course your Nyorfian military personnel, in particular those with special training, are so admirably suited for other purposes. Some already have proven most amusing playthings for my loyal troops. And, of course, very useful for scientific experimentation. But those like you who've caused more trouble than they are worth and continually inspire resistance must be destroyed. Publicly."

NO. Don't. Rett had to struggle not to change her face as stronger reactions from Pam's came in response to the enemy leader's words and brief associations Rett made to them. *I've embarrassed some of his top officers—including that one over there—in front of their entire invasion force. Let it go at that for now. Back off!*

"Do you realize the amount of trouble you've caused me? Not to mention the credit involved! I'll have no more problems from you, Killer. You will be destroyed."

All right, now she could comment. "I've heard that before."

"This is the last time you'll be hearing it, then," the enemy Leader replied harshly. "At this time tomorrow you'll be nothing but a memory. It was well worth the trouble, Killer. Yes, well worth it."

Pam did her best to keep into the private corner she had created. The serious intensity of Rett's concentration right now was something she didn't want to break. She wasn't sure how an imaginary wall was doing anything, but like before, it seemed to be working. But it wasn't easy to quench her natural curiosity.

"Just think," the Leader was saying with pleasure. "Not only do I have you, but your entire gallant platoon!" He leaned back in his chair with a self-satisfied expression, as if he'd single-handedly captured them all himself. The smirk on his flabby, gray-hued face was repulsive in its intensity. "You won't die quickly, Killer. A fingertip at a time, how does that sound? I think we won't be disappointed. My sharpshooters are as precise as surgeons. We'll see if you can maintain that silence you're so famous for as pieces of you get seared off bit by bit. I'll make sure everyone in this system will see the vids."

"I have to admit it sounds original," Rett said calmly, adding the precise amount of "so what?" needed to raise the officer's energies back into the danger range. "Now," she continued, "take Commander Iheolon, for example. He always tries to kill me in the exact same ways all the time, even after the one episode where he actually thought I was dead and dumped my dead body out to cause public dismay. So he made a mistake. You'd think he would try something different after that, but no. He didn't, and it became boring. That's why, when I let myself get caught after that, I never stayed around very long."

She flicked an indifferent smile in Iheolon's direction, then continued to address the Leader. "Have to admit it doesn't look as if I'm going anywhere this time, though."

"I should say not," the Leader answered.

Rett sighed, allowing her posture to slump just a bit. "In that case, I'd like to ask a few questions."

The loop around her throat tightened in response to her daring. Her restricted circulation roared a protest in her ears; then the pressure released at a gesture from the leader.

"No, I want to hear this," he said, still gesturing to the guards.

Trying not to gasp as the pressure slackened, Rett fiercely concentrated on remaining upright and motionless.

"Questions, Sergeant?" repeated the Leader, with a sickly smile. "Such as...?"

"How'd you set up that ambush?"

The Leader looked so full of himself, so pleased with his own cleverness, that Pam's mental gag reflex edged into Rett's tight control. Added to her own personal reaction, the results would have been as unpleasant as the Leader's vanity had both of them not struggled to contain the threat into one short, harsh cough.

"I said to slack off," snarled the Leader, blaming Left, who managed Rett's control loop, for the interruption. "Just drop it until we're finished."

After giving the guard a glare, he refocused his beady eyes on Rett. "You might say I have a lifetime business arrangement with the commanding officers of the 52nd."

"Yixolryn agents?" This time the roaring in her ears had nothing to do with being strangled.

"We've had agents in your system for a long, *long* time, Killer. We spent almost a century planning this invasion and takeover. Of course, there were some things we didn't plan for—the ability of your people to hold out for this long is one. But a century was enough time for us to get some people in place long enough for them to become naturalized citizens, for them to work their way into the confidence of the community, to become part of your military, even your government."

It wouldn't have mattered if her choke loop had gone snug again: she had forgotten to breathe. Only a sharp reminder from Pam started her up again, helped her lock down her face before the shock inside showed itself.

Of course agents and spies had been—and still were being—discovered. There had been soldiers and citizens that had also been brainwashed or implanted with some sort of device. Brainwashing hadn't proved successful, although it was still attempted, especially on the young. And devices—ever since the first few were discovered, doctors, scientists, and Adepts had quickly learned how to deal with them. Any Nyorfian who had contact with the enemy was routinely scanned.

But to think people who had been on Nyorfias as long as Mott and Shamos, who had managed the 52nd through eight years of successful campaigns against the enemy…

"As commander and adjutant for the 52nd, Mott and Shamos are responsible for killing a lot of your troops," said Rett.

The Leader made a dismissive motion. "All part of the plan. Small sacrifices for the greater result. We gained far more than we lost. And it really helped keep those two above suspicion, did it not? They wanted out after so long, preparing for this since they were striplings, and then spending over thirty years living in the back end of nowhere, pretending to be good Nyorfians."

The Leader made a face as if he'd eaten something rotten. "I can't blame them for reaching the end of their tolerance, they are to be commended for their endurance. Now that we have you, cleaning up the 52nd will be child's play, and the Nyorfian hope of retaking this city and the spaceport will be gone."

Rett's entire body was clenched. She barely managed to keep her inner turbulence from showing on her face, although she felt her eyes tighten. *They could do it, too. As far as I know, the planning for the Circle push relies on the 52nd—and us—for the primary thrust. We can't afford to lose an entire division. No wonder…*

Pam dared to offer her comment. ~I don't know why you didn't suspect them.~

I'd never a reason to suspect them. The way you saw them behave wasn't at all usual or what I've come to expect as normal from them.

~They really didn't like you. Hated you, actually.~

I don't expect everyone to like me, Pam, and don't make judgments off that. This isn't your planet. I don't know you or how you do things there, but it's pretty obvious there's a lot of difference. I mentioned F-troop isn't part of the 52ⁿᵈ, *much less the same branch of the military—we're just loaded to them as support. And Nyorfians, native or naturalized, just don't do things like that. At least not of their free will.* Again Rett had to quickly suppress a memory, forcing her mind into the present.

"I didn't know any of your more humanoid...allies...were so dedicated," she said to the Leader.

"They're only a quarter-humanoid. The better portion, of course, is Yixolryn, and they are loyal. They are part of a very committed, very loyal family with a high standing in the Coalition. Of course this factor is neatly hidden from your medical scans...right down to the molecular level, they appear humanoid. The one you know as Shamos is quite a clever scientist. Excellent with computers, as well."

That helps to know, thought Rett, *because I should have been able to tell they weren't human if they were simply Yixolryns in disguise. Yixolryns have a slightly different energy from humanoids. But good deities, that's scary—how many others might there be like that? Undetectable?* "Dedicated or not," she said aloud, "I know enough to know there had to be something in it for them."

The Leader tapped his flat-tipped fingers against the desk. "Of course. I agreed if they delivered you and your platoon they would get a bonus of ten million credits each and transport to the Coalition controlled planet of their choice. Or a neutral world elsewhere."

This is all going to need some checking out when we get out of here.

~I'm glad you're optimistic about that. The way the Leader's spilling his guts, he's pretty confident you're not going to be around to tell anyone else.~

"That's a lot of credit," admitted Rett. *If we make it out of this, they're dead. I've not killed anyone in outright revenge until that bastard Negaller. And I've another on my list, Commander Avok, if I ever run into her again. I'll make another exception for Mott and Shamos!*

"Worth it, I think, don't you?" The Leader was watching her closely.

"You should have checked with me first. I would have turned myself in, free, for one uninterrupted night of sleep," Rett said dryly.

"You are amusing," replied the Leader, sitting back in his chair and crossing his arms over his belly. "Because you amuse me, you can ask more questions."

"I'd like to see my people. To say goodbye. What'll happen to them?"

The Leader nearly giggled. "I've promised them to Commander Iheolon. After your execution, their fates are his to decide. He and his troopers will enjoy that. I'm sure they will not be affected by boredom."

Rett bit the inside of her lower lip without changing her outer expression too much. That shot hurt.

"As for your seeing them, I think that could be arranged. Yes, you may spend, let's see…fifteen minutes of your last hours in their company, if only to prove to each other the absolute hopelessness of escape."

At that, the hulking, brutish-looking humanoid lounging against a wall near the enemy Leader straightened. "My Leader, do you think that's wise?"

Pam hoped her observations stayed behind the imaginary barrier she'd erected. There was definitely the trace of alien about Iheolon, although he looked more humanoid than the Leader, whose jutting bone structure, tiny eyes, ridges and folds of skin made her think of a hairless gorilla crossed with a pug. She didn't try to make out details, knowing if she did it would distract Rett, but it was hard to observe that much without wanting to know more. She'd have to be patient. If this was truly a dream, she hoped this dream character would live long enough for her to find out more. If it wasn't a dream…well, she didn't really want to think about that. But she still wanted Rett to live, as slim as the possibility of it seemed at the moment.

"What could possibly happen? Killer is under a failsafe restraint, as long as it is used *properly*." As the Coalition leader sent another withering glare around Rett to Left, she felt the trooper shrink. "This building is strong and well guarded. There are two full divisions in this city in addition to your own, all with complete support units. What could possibly go wrong?"

Where have we heard something like this recently? What could go wrong? Everything! Rett thought to Pam. *He doesn't know me or my people as well as Iheolon does. He just told me all I need to tell them if any of us manages to get out of here! Three divisions in Circle! With armored and air support.*

Pam felt pleased to be addressed again and edged forward a bit more. She *didn't* know Rett's people or Commander Iheolon, so she wasn't certain how to answer. From what she saw back at that bridge, even though they were taken completely by surprise, Rett's platoon certainly was tough. If they had half the guts this woman displayed—and from Pam's position, Rett's guts were the real thing—they'd have no problems at all.

She chose not to respond to her host at the moment, since the Nyorfian's focus was back on the conversation between the officers. Pam followed suit.

"I don't like the idea," growled Iheolon, fixing an acidic glare on Rett, one hand moving to the weapon on his belt. "We should just kill her right here and now."

"Did I ask you?" The Leader's already high-pitched voice rose a full octave. His flabby, ugly face turned uglier. Apparently not even Iheolon had ever dared questioned his decisions before.

"I meant no disrespect, my Leader," Iheolon said swiftly. "I was only considering the past records. Including the disturbance on the prison level below."

"Yes, Commander Iheolon. Those past records are all yours and were handled by your command, including the disturbance below!"

Rett half stifled a derisive snort and glanced briefly at Iheolon, who stood rigid with anger. Behind her, Left shivered.

"Iheolon, you might be right about killing her right now," allowed the Leader. "But not after all the trouble I've taken to make this a public and highly visible execution. It will be uplinked into every public information and communication network in this system. Think of what it will do to Nyorfian morale. Think of what it would do for the morale of our own troops. Every officer here in Circle, and that troublesome platoon of hers, will have close and personal vantage points."

"There should be at least two guards for each of them, my Leader."

"It's been taken care of. Go," the Leader said to the guards. "Take her away. Give her fifteen minutes with the others—"

Iheolon dared to voice a protest again. "My Leader, she's managed to get some critical information during this meeting. If she—"

The Leader came to his feet and smacked his flabby hands against the surface of the desk. Rett was the only thing in the room that didn't jump or shrink back as the Leader rounded in on Iheolon in a fury. "I did not ask for your input again, Commander! So what if she heard? What good would it do them?"

~Is he for real?~ Pam wanted to know.

Most Yixolryns are full of themselves. But I don't care about the Leader. It's Iheolon that worries me.

As much as she enjoyed seeing Iheolon get reamed by the highest authority the Coalition had in the Nyorfian system, her insides knotted in fear for her platoon. Whether she died or not, he was going to take every bit of his anger and frustration out on her people for this incident, plus every single other trespass, real or imagined, she had made against him.

"Now take her out of here. Let her have fifteen minutes with her unit. Then take her back to the cell she was in—and make sure she remains undisturbed—by *anyone*—until I call for her again. I'm feeling generous." Then the Leader sat back down. He gave Rett another long look, thoughtful and penetrating, and she desperately hoped he wasn't suddenly going to change his mind about her seeing the platoon. "You're not at all what I expected," he said finally, and waved a hand toward the guard detail.

Despite her decision to remain in the background and her promise not to cause trouble, Pam absolutely could not resist a parting shot. So, unexpectedly, Rett found herself saying: "Who did you expect? The Terminator?"

SHUT UP, PAM! Rett barely kept the shout internal. She fought to retain her uncertain balance trying to redirect and conceal her shocked reaction to the words and tone of voice that had escaped her lips. After she'd tried so hard to turn that interview around so she got essential information—*SHUT UP!*

~Sorry. I just couldn't help myself.~

Try harder next time, damn it! Rett's return thought snapped. *You're lucky he didn't change his mind about me seeing the platoon!* This she added as the Leader simply laughed at what she hoped he thought was nonsense, shook his head, and gestured for the guards to take her away. *Just shut up! No one in two worlds knows what you're talking about, including me.*

The detail hustled her from the office.

* * * * *

THE ONLY REAL ELEMENT RETT ever clearly recalled about the trek to F-troop's confinement area was her struggle to stay breathing and conscious. Her guards were paranoid enough to perform a repeat of the process in which they transported her to the Coalition Leader's august presence—with one nearly fatal exception: they neglected to add a check that prevented the choke loop from tightening past a certain point. Lucky for her this trip involved less dragging. A few lifts, one set of stairs, and a few short stretches of corridor, that was all.

A haul upright, a push, and a falling sensation brought her to full awareness, her body tensing to absorb the shock of contact with whatever awaited her landing.

And that happened to be someone slender, warm, and humanoid. She knew instantly it was Ariam. Rett's taut body went limp for a few heartbeats in total gratitude. *Ariam's still alive. Thank all deities.* And if she was still alive, then the others...

"Ariam," choked Rett, but all that she heard herself say was "Argh".

"Oh, Rett," whispered Ariam, more of a high-pitched exhalation of breath than word. "Sarge," she said a bit louder, not trying to hide the tremor of anxiety in her voice.

The touch of Ariam's hands was cool against Rett's burning throat and neck. Soon the choking pressure was gone.

"Kraym, help me, she's all tangled up." The younger woman's voice resonated with anger and frustration.

Other hands touched her then, huge hands, lifting her from Ariam's slim form. "Hi, Sarge. Nice of you to drop in," said Kraym in a tone dry enough to blister the lush countryside of Centerland into desert. "I see our friends have come up with a new way to tie a humanoid into a security knot." If his voice had been dry before, it was dusty now, even gritting like sand.

Rett would have told them not to bother, but she was still too out of breath to speak, and her position wasn't helping. Thankfully it didn't take long for Kraym to figure that out.

"I'm sorry, Sarge. I can't get these off. But this should make it easier to breathe." His huge hands soon matched words to action and Rett finally got a full breath. Almost.

"H'tenneck," Rett heard Ariam say. "Come here please. And Med, we need you too."

"No time." Rett cracked an eye open to see the younger woman's anxious face close to hers. "M'okay, Ari." She cleared her throat a few times. If she lived through this, it would hurt for days. "Ev'erun else?"

"No one's seriously hurt, Sarge," Kraym told her. "We're just tiffed enough to spit. You look…" Suitable adjectives failed him.

"Bad," Ariam said and kept her voice at a normal level.

Rett shrugged as much as her restraints allowed, then saw Ariam flick a signal to the other platoon members. Various conversations started up around them.

"There's no cameras or listening devices we detected, but we're not taking chances," Ariam told Rett.

Rett grunted. She mustered up a sort of grin as a slender dark man with blue-black curly hair joined them. Corporal Nitraym's junior, Senior Specialist H'tenneck, had a knack for bending Coalition devices to his will andwas an accomplished tinkerer. He was barely eighteen, but looked much older. He was from Epnoce, which had been first to fall to Coalition troops twelve years before.

If H'tenneck can't get these off, no one can, Rett thought to Pam. *But he has to leave them on. I just can't get breath enough to tell him.*

A huge pressure released from her chest after a few seconds: he'd managed to loosen the band around her arms and body. Rett's lungs sucked in what felt like the first deep breath in days. Her sore ribs protested, but her need for oxygen was stronger. After almost another minute Rett heard H'tenneck say, "I'm sorry, Sarge, but no way we can get these off. They're not the same as ours. From these burns, looks like you might have found that out already."

Rett decided not to nod, her neck hurt too much. "S'okay. They'll be back for me." She strained to get a look at those around her. "Ev'erun has?" Her voice squeaked, even in a whisper. Shit. If everyone was shackled like she was, there was just no way she could even hope to get them out.

"Right now they're active only on our ankles," said Kraym.

"But—"

"But remember what H'tenneck made from the units we took off our prisoners a few tendays ago," reminded Ariam in a low soft voice.

Hope rose strong. "Worked?"

H'tenneck grinned. "Worked. It's under control, Sarge. They come in, we're secure. They go..." he shrugged.

"Tell me how."

As he did, Rett could only commend the quick thinking that allowed the young squad junior to get his own altered devices in place before a Coalition trooper applied regular ones and removed his weapons and utility belts.

"When they reached me," concluded H'tenneck, "they assumed someone else secured me first and moved on."

Rett made a mental notation to get that on his record and have his action recognized whether it worked or not. The effort counted.

She glanced at Ariam, who nodded assent, as usual in line with Rett's thoughts.

"Good job," whispered Rett. She gave him a big warm smile right from her heart, and H'tenneck responded with a mixed expression: half bashful reserve, half proud gratification. His return smile was wide, but it soon faded as he looked back at her restraining units.

"These," he touched her devices. "Haven't seen this type before."

"What's different? They look heavier." Another soft sound of anger from Ariam coincided with a light touch at Rett's wrists. "Burned!"

"Shocking, I know." This time, Rett didn't mind Pam practically putting words in her mouth.

"That might not be all," said H'tenneck. "So I'll not tamper with them. I think we prefer you keep your hands and feet attached as long as possible. You said they're coming back?"

"Better they stay." Rett gave him a look she hoped was reassuring. "S'okay. Least can breathe now."

Med patted H'tenneck on the shoulder and inserted himself between Ariam and Kraym. Nudging Ariam aside, he made Kraym arrange Rett's twisted body a little differently. Her circulation was starting to come back and her hands and arms, numbed for so long, were beginning to tingle painfully. *Bad timing,* Rett thought to her body. *Sure. Wait until Med's right on top of me and go ahead and rip.*

As Med eyed her from boots to head his eyes blazed as hot as plasma discharge from an SMG. "You look like shit that was stepped in, Sergeant," he said sourly.

Rett raised both eyebrows. "'N I love you too, Med," she rasped, feeling something like a laugh from the alien presence that had once more withdrawn. *Stay that way.*

His anger was directed at her, but wasn't for her. Reaching for her neck, he probed with gentle fingers. "Dragged you here by the control loop, did they?" He made a rude sound through his teeth. "You're going to be lucky not to have permanent damage."

97

"S' not imp—" Rett would have pointed out whether or not she had permanent damage at this point wasn't an issue since most likely after tomorrow she wouldn't give a damn. Med cut her short.

"Sarge," he said wearily, "please shut up. I don't want to hear it." His skilled hands and fingers found and exerted pressure over several spots on her head, face and shoulders.

On second thought, Rett managed to think through a gasp of intense relief, having Med around at this particular moment in time could not have been planned better. The sudden and drastic reduction of pain brought a second heartfelt smile from her.

Med's lips twisted in a sort of return smile, but he'd never allow any of them to call it that. Sitting back on his heels, he studied her now in a frustrated silence.

She cleared her throat. "Kraym. Time I was in here?"

"Bit over five minutes, Sarge."

Seemed longer. Then again everything seemed longer when she couldn't breathe. "I don't have much time left, so let me talk now that I can." Her voice was still hoarse, but clear, and she made sure her words didn't go beyond those immediately around her. "Priority is coming up with a way to get you guys out of this mess. With some information

I obtained." Rett wriggled a little in Kraym's supportive arms, trying to ease a kink in her back that turned instantly into an entire series of major cramps from shoulders to hamstrings.

Med was on the job before she broke into a sweat. Grateful for the relief now, Rett wished she could store it up somehow for later. If they left her twisted up like this, which was more than likely, it was going to be a long, *long* night.

"So, what's the story?" Kraym asked finally, freeing a hand to push up at his glasses.

"The usual." She drew a ragged sigh and made the rest of her body ignore the spasming muscles Med was working on. "I get terminated tomorrow." For a second, she felt a rush of amusement, then it faded as she remembered what she needed to do before the guards returned. "Listen, there's three divisions here, one of them Iheolon's. No one's known for certain just how many troops were in this city, and MainCommand will need to know for that attack they plan. I doubt they'll ship Iheolon's out of here any time soon.

"And by now we're all aware of just how the updated ML-12 low power settings affect humanoid targets: shorter time of unconsciousness, no burn. Less hangover, unless you're hit repeatedly. It'll save the effort of those on the wrong end of weapons testing at MainCommand maybe, so be sure to remember that in the debriefing.

"What's really news is Mott and Shamos are apparently long term Coalition agents who felt the need to retire. Not only that…they're three-quarter Yixolryn—or were born that way. They've been altered somehow so it doesn't show up on medical scans. Planted here for thirty years, at least. I'm sure that's what the Leader said. But the timeframe is right for the ages they appear and the rank they've had to have previous militia experience to obtain. So I suppose recently Mott and Shamos decided they absolutely can't take it anymore, so…they made a deal to get out."

Rett wrinkled her nose. "So, for ten million credits each, transport out of here, they've been running us and the 52nd into the ground." Her voice disappeared before she was finished, but at least she had time to get it all out. *Deities, my throat hurts. But I can't think about that now.*

A stunned, angry silence greeted that revelation. Even the platoon members keeping a conversation, one of which had turned into a mock argument, quieted for a moment. They resumed after Rett glanced their way, encouraging them to keep at it.

"What?"

Rett angled her gaze toward Ariam, wincing as even that small of a movement jolted pain through her body. "Don't make me say all that again." She could hardly hear herself; saw Kraym's quick jerk and a blink as he made the transition from merely watching her face to reading her lips. He had to repeat for his co-second what Rett had tried to say, since Ariam had been staring off to the side.

Ariam cleared her throat. She looked stricken. "No, don't repeat it. I mean about Mott and Shamos. I never felt it. I only ever felt they didn't like us—you—much. Personally. Not professionally. I should—"

"Corporal," Rett said, this time managing at least a sharp whisper, "they know you're an empath. Of course they ran some interference when you or any other Talented people were around. You know people can be trained to block. Now, about tomorrow."

"We're not leaving without you. Not again!" Ariam said, her gray eyes flashing. "I think you've pulled decoy duty too many times!"

"Ariam." Rett hoped her patience and what she had of her voice was going to last. "*Look* at me. We don't have much choice. Don't argue with me now, they only gave me fifteen minutes and they'll be back shortly. I can't run or fight very well chained up like this. But I can cause enough of a distraction to keep them occupied for a while. If things look good, and that interrupt control of H'tenneck's still works, you guys do your thing and get out any way you can. At least get out enough to get the information to the civilian resistance. Do you know where we are?"

Kraym and Ariam shook their heads. "We couldn't see out the rovers and they brought them right into whatever building this is," Kraym said. "Didn't give our location much thought until now," he admitted. "Maybe Mikel knows." Kraym motioned for the platoon member he named to join them.

The man immediately stood up and joined them, hunkering on his heels like Med.

"You're from Circle," Rett said. "You were a maint-tech on a lot of the main buildings. Do you know where we are?"

Mikel nodded. "That I do. Lower area of DIPA main offices. I just figured that from the ID numbers on the support struts. I know this structure well enough."

"Good. Tell the others what they need to know after they take me out of here. Don't think I'll need your briefing, if I'm *that* lucky I'll be leaving with you guys. But don't count on it—and don't disappoint me."

"Disappoint you?" Mikel looked suitably affronted. "Never, Sarge."

Rett hardened her expression as she saw Corporal Ariam getting ready to protest, another "But" on the tip of her tongue. "With or without me, Corporal. It's one, or forty. I'd rather it be one. Besides, the Leader mentioned what would happen to the rest of you after I was dead." Rett felt sick at the thought of it. Mott and Shamos knew Ariam was an empath. Did they mention that to the Leader yet? "It's better to die fighting it out than to wait and see what Commander Iheolon and his troopers want to do. I've been there, remember?"

"But—"

"That is an order, Corporal," Rett said. Her voice, even to herself, sounded all the more threatening between lack of volume and hoarseness. "Your first responsibility now is to this unit. Tomorrow I make whatever sort of diversion I can. You're in charge from there, Corporal Kraym will second. And if you take the time to worry about recovering me, you'd better be damned sure the others are already on the way out, because if anything happens otherwise I'm going to be really tiffed. I will take you apart a molecule at a time. Understood?"

The younger woman made no further protest. "Yes, Sergeant. I will take command, Senior Corporal Kraym will second."

"Corporal Kraym?"

"Understood, Sergeant."

"And just for the record, Ariam," said Rett, "you're due for upgrade in a few tendays, Kraym's review is a month after that. You are, both of you, more than ready to take this unit if not one of your own."

"We'll see," the corporal replied evasively. "I don't have to accept the upgrade. You've passed up yours often enough. And as long as you're still around, I'm not too eager to make sergeant *or* platoon leader."

Rett started to laugh, but it hurt too much and only a croak escaped. "I can't say I blame you." She heard noise outside and looked around at her people, trying to reach all of them with her eyes no matter how much it aggravated her body. "I love you guys. Get out of here, okay? That's all I want."

1.14 YIXOLRYN COALITION HQ, CIRCLE
CENTERLAND PROVINCE, NYORFIAS
0535.06.08 (LOCAL RECKONING)

It seemed to Rett that half the enemy forces on Nyorfias turned up to witness her execution. At first glance, the huge auditorium seemed filled with a solid mass of people. *You still with me, Pam? Still interesting? Stick around, you haven't seen anything yet!* thought Rett.

A soft mental laugh tickled Rett's mind.

~Never a dull moment, it seems,~ Pam thought in return. ~I have a question, Rett, I can feel your fear for the others, but don't you ever get scared for yourself?~

Yes, Rett returned. *Shit, I get terrified. And that's putting it mildly. But we can't show an enemy we feel any pain or fear, Pam, so those feelings get redirected into energy or action. And I'm too scared of what might happen to them to worry about me.*

Pam was quiet for a second or two. ~About people thinking you're larger than life, they're right. I'm right here in your mind and having trouble believing people can really be the way you are. No wonder the enemy's taking all this trouble, they wouldn't do that if you were ordinary!~

Rett kept the sigh in her thoughts. *I'm just like anyone else, damn it. We're all doing everything we can. We all do our best. Forget it, all right?*

~What happens now?~

Rett's second assessment of the area was more detailed as the guards escorted her through the hall toward the firing zone. A choke loop ringed her bruised throat, loosely for now, but held by an alert guard.

She supposed she should be grateful to the Leader. His orders to leave her undisturbed had given her a chance to recharge somewhat. And once safely locked in her little room, she'd been allowed just enough range of motion to keep her limbs from stiffening up. She and Pam had enjoyed a laugh that the Leader wanted her looking good for his big moment. Where was the fun in killing someone who already looked half dead?

Still, it would have been nicer to have had a blanket and some water, too. But she wasn't complaining.

What happens now? I'm going to cause a diversion, and what happens after that is anyone's guess. There's always a weak spot. I just hope F-troop can exploit it.

Officers made up the bulk of those Yixolryn Coalition troops present, most armed as usual when not in the field: with a sidearm of typical design or a small stunner. Up front, with an unobstructed view, was her platoon. To a careless first glance, the relatively small space they occupied gave every impression of containing disembodied heads, thanks to the color and light reflecting uniforms.

Rett's glance was anything but careless and she was used to looking sideways to negate the camouflaging effects of their uniform's unique material. There appeared to be a guard for each, and Rett sensed the nervous auras of most of them. The Special Forces combat uniform unnerved many Coalition troops, who, despite their advantage of heat sensitive targeters, still relied on a completely humanoid sense of sight.

I'm surprised they left them uniform at all. Iheolon would have had them off quick enough.

~Don't go there,~ Pam reminded.

None of her people were restrained more than they had been the day before, at least not in any way she could see. That was encouraging. Those long faces and slumped shoulders must have really convinced the Coalition they were truly defeated. But the facial expressions and body language Rett saw from them in no way reflected the energy she interpreted: they were ready to jump. She hoped H'tenneck's interrupt device still worked. She caught his eye and he sent her a brief flick of both eyebrows. He raised his hands slowly as if to wipe at his forehead. Of course the wrist devices were still there, but his action told Rett that F-troop would be completely mobile when the time came.

Relief. Of course, this was a huge gamble. But win or lose, better to go out with a fight, and better to die fighting than to be an enemy prisoner.

They've underestimated us again, Pam, thought Rett with hope. *The Leader should have listened to Iheolon. I'm glad he didn't. The platoon*

103

shouldn't have too much trouble. Hey! These guys are going to be shooting at me in a minute or so and my personal chances aren't that good. What happens to you if I get killed?

~I thought you were the expert on ego-merges,~ retorted Pam, trying to keep her mounting nervousness to herself.

I actually don't know that much about them. There's only been four recorded instances in the past five hundred years—since the first people came here. None of the hosts died during the mergers.

~Well, I don't want either of us to die, in a dream or otherwise. So don't you think this is a good time for your diversion?~

The guard escort backed Rett against the front wall. Only scorch marks and pitting marked the wall—the docking units to which her restraints would be tuned must be below the pourstone surface. If they were going to secure her there, it was going to take a moment or two of deactivation and a physical adjustment of the restraining units.

104

Good, Rett thought, running through several possible scenarios and preparing herself accordingly. They'd have to free up range of motion for at least half, if not all of her, to get her situated. Of course the first thing they'd do was half-strangle her, which, Rett had to admit, was an effective and simple control. *What, Pam?*

~It would ruin my dream totally if you got killed, so don't. And this would be a good time for your diversion!~

Not just yet. They have to give me more scope on these restraints first. For once, added Rett with total honesty, *I really wish both of us were dreaming! Back off now, okay?*

Rett sought out Ariam among those who waited. As their eyes met, the defeated expression on Ariam's face disappeared, allowing Rett to see it composed, calm, ready. Her gray eyes, even at the distance between them, spoke volumes. *Love you,* thought Rett, sending her and Kraym in turn a look of encouragement. Kraym answered with the briefest twitch of an eyebrow. F-troop would be in good hands. All of her people were exceptional.

Deities, she was proud of them.

The enemy sharpshooters took their positions. The whines of powerpacks charging weapons seemed louder than ever in the sudden, expectant stillness. Rett's guard chose that moment to widen the field between the magnetic restraints on her wrists so they could reposition her against the wall. She felt the restriction release, managed to take a huge, deep breath before the loop around her throat began to tighten.

This was it, she told herself. She didn't have to hold anything back. The guard with the control would go first.

She took the split-second opening and rocketed into action like a missile from a launcher.

The foremost trooper's face made violent contact with the rough stone. Rett heard more than the material of the targeting goggles break. One down. Before the guard holding the choke line could jerk it tight, Rett tangled her arm in it and jerked forward, bringing the guard toward her. Her foot slammed into his chest, crushing the light armor and the bones beneath it.

Her old friend Left lunged at her; Rett stuck her hip in his path, her elbow cracking down on the nape of his neck as he fell, killing him instantly. Another caught the full force of another lethal kick, his body becoming a heavy missile of dead or unconscious flesh that took down several more troopers who were scrambling onto the platform.

Rett fought on instinctively, holding nothing back, her frontmost thought to keep going long enough for the platoon to make their escape. Then her world quite suddenly exploded into a shower of bright lights followed by instant blackness.

105

1.1.5 A SEMI-RURAL HOME, READINGTON TOWNSHIP
NEW JERSEY, USA, EARTH
CURRENT ERA

BEEP...BEEP...BEEP...BEEP...

PAM'S EYELIDS FLEW OPEN AND she sat bolt upright in her rumpled sleeping bag. One hand reached automatically for the alarm clock and turned it off.

"Holy freaking out shit!" she exclaimed softly. She was out of breath, her heart was pounding, and her head felt like horses had stampeded across it. Like she had gone out and partied hard for New Year's Eve.

But no, she hadn't. She'd come home right after the liquor store closed at ten P.M. and had spent the time before she fell asleep being creatively challenged. And then that dream.

That dream. "Was it just a dream?"

Both hands rising to her head, she scrubbed fingertips through her scalp and let the heels of both hands draw firmly over her face. Goosebumps rose on her skin.

"I can still remember it all. Every single bit. Every smell, taste, sound." She was shivering. A glance out the partially open window suggested the glittering white, frosty world waiting for her might be, at least, partway accountable for her chill. "If it was a dream, I'll have to make sure we talk about paintball at work more often. What a great idea for a story."

She reached for her glasses and got up, wondering what happened next. Would she have to write her own ending, or would her dream pick up where it had stopped? Sometimes she had recurring dreams that seemed to connect. Not too often, true, but sometimes. She rubbed absently at her left leg as a cramp twisted the muscle there.

"Holy shit." Pam realized it was the exact spot where Rett had been burned in the dream.

No need to get paranoid. It had been a fantastic dream, that was all. She extracted woolly socks, clean sweats, t-shirt and a heavy flannel shirt from the old tack trunk in which she kept her clothes. She resolved to keep thinking about it and write it all down later. For now, she had to get on with her everyday routine: dress, jump in the truck, go feed the horses and muck out the stalls, come back home and clean up for work. It was back to reality.

* * * * *

SHE FELT REMOTE AND STRANGE most of the day, unable to keep her mind on work. Good thing it wasn't busy, far from it. After a while she simply had to tell someone about the dream, though, and found herself talking to her co-worker, Dave Lamposki. She gave just the particulars. Almost like Rett had when she was giving the rather flat report about the battle for Circle. Even as she spoke she had to wonder if Dave missed her usual style—over the top, fully embroidered with adjectives and adverbs.

"I still feel uneasy about it. Like I should have stuck around."

"It was a *dream*, Pam."

"I'm not so sure." *Yeah, right? Stick around, when Rett couldn't wait to get rid of me in the first place?*

"Earth to Pam," laughed Dave.

Startled, Pam jerked her head around to look at him. "I'm sorry—what?"

"It sounds like a good idea for one of those stories you're always writing. You probably thought about it because me and the other guys were talking about the paintball place in the Poconos."

"Maybe you're right. Look, you think you can handle things out here? I should finish entering the invoices on the computer," she said. "There's a stack of 'em three weeks high back there. I have to get all of them in before I could run the year end reports." She sighed. "Boss'll be lucky if he gets them in March. Call me if you get busy, okay?"

Dave chuckled and waved his hand toward the empty parking lot. "You could see for yourself the customers are lining up from here to the state line," he said with amusement.

All that day and the next, the vivid memory of the dream haunted Pam. On the third, with every aspect still crystal clear in her mind, she began to write about it. She added details here and there, rounded out the basics, imagined what was going on in the minds of some of the other characters she had encountered through Rett. It looked good, but she hoped she would have the chance to confirm them. Somehow.

* * * * *

SHE DIDN'T HAVE MUCH TIME to think about her dream the rest of the week. She spent an unusually warm winter Saturday in an exhaustive pre-spring cleaning of the stable she rented. Her friend Jen, who kept her two horses there, helped. While they worked, brushing down old spider webs from the rafters, stripping every stall to the absolute bottom and rebedding, checking all the lighting and wiring for signs of damage that would start a fire and replacing it where indicated, Pam told Jen about the dream.

Like Dave, Jen suggested Pam just write another story. "And I think you need another vacation," Jen told her, laughing. "Don't go to the Rockies this time, go to the shore or something. Maybe then you'll dream about being in the Navy, instead."

"I hate the Jersey shore," Pam muttered. "You know that. Too many people."

"Not in the middle of January," Jen pointed out.

"I can't swim."

"Oh, you. Let's go."

Pam followed Jen up the stairs and around the old silo to the spot they parked their trucks. "It seemed real."

"You and that imagination!" Jen reached into her vehicle and tossed something at her. "Here. Read this and get a few good chuckles."

Pam looked at the cover of the book. It depicted a stunning, long-haired, shirtless, handsome man, locked in a passionate embrace with a beautiful, well-endowed woman wearing a dress just a thread away from falling to her hips.

She groaned. "Not another one. You and your bodice-rippers."

"Why not? You think they're hilarious because they're so predictable. I mean, you're the one who gave me the last two I read. You'll have fun with this one. Not only is it bad—the author gets all the dates mixed up. And has the heroine inventing penicillin and performing surgery with a claymore."

* * * * *

LATER THAT NIGHT, PAM CHUCKED the book across the room. She never got to the end of the first chapter. "Can't these things be a little more original?" she snarled. At least she got some perverse satisfaction as the paperback splatted, melon-breasted heroine first, against the wall. "Ooff, sorry, Princess! That'll teach you to go braless."

Minutes later, the exertions of the day caught up with her and she fell into an exhausted sleep.

1.1.6 UNDISCLOSED LOCATION

SOUTH CENTRAL BRANCH PROVINCE, NYORFIAS
0535.09.06 (LOCAL RECKONING)

"SERGEANT…DAMN IT, CAN YOU HEAR me now? If you don't answer me in five seconds, I'll ground you for a year!"

That was Med's voice. And he sounded tiffed. Why? What did she do now to tiff him?

Rett was aware, but only dimly, kind of like a fading battery light. *Med, I'm okay. I'm just tired. I want to sleep.* She wanted so badly to tell him, yet she couldn't make herself speak aloud. *Don't ground me for a year, Med. Why can't I talk?*

Feeling exploded back into her numbed body and something clicked sharply in her mind. Rett snapped back into reality with a gasp.

~Why? You dope! You were just dead! Or close enough to it. Get real, Rett! Breathe, damn it. Fight! That's what you do best, isn't it?~

Her initial gasp had emptied lungs that had little air to begin with. Then something forced them to expand, causing cold clean air to rush down her bruised windpipe like a cataract of whitewater. The same force, coming from within yet not of her own making, pushed at her again, forcing the air back out with Rett's pained sound of protest. She nearly choked on her voice when her body ignored her and forced her to draw another deep breath. Breathing hurt. But it felt right. Feeling a swift hunger for more of that beautiful air, her next breath was her own.

~Good! Take another breath now, and another. Damned if I came back in time to be in a dead person!~

Pam? Rett gulped in painful breaths and concentrated on the creaking pangs in her ribs, the soreness of her throat, bone-deep aches in her muscles, and the burning pain near the surface. The discomfort increased with fierce intensity, but it helped clear her mental processes and reminded her that she was still alive.

"I think that did it," Med's voice said in relief and was followed by a long exhale. "Yes, she's back. Good pulse now. And, dare we be surprised, conscious."

"Sarge?"

It took a while for the three blurred dark ovals hovering in her unfocused vision to resolve into familiar faces. She cleared her sore throat before attempting to speak. "Hello, Med, Kraym, Ariam. What's up? You guys okay?"

No one said anything for such a long moment that Rett felt a flutter of panic. Wait a second. She was outdoors, in the woods, tall trees rising around her. That meant she was a good distance from Circle, since the land around the city was open and rolling. What was she doing here, with them? She honestly never expected to leave Circle alive.

Compressing her lips in dread and suspicion, Rett attempted to sit up. Med and Ariam held her down. "Someone better tell me and fast, that the rest of the platoon is wherever we are," whispered Rett with every bit of lethal intensity she could muster.

"All here, Sarge," said Kraym, his large hand gently patting hers in reassurance.

"Well, I sent Pip and Jessek ahead to find the rover we left hidden," Ariam clarified. "But we're all accounted for otherwise."

"Then good gods and deities," exploded Rett, not bothering to modulate her volume, "what's wrong?" She managed some volume this time, but her abused throat made her voice squeaky and it disappeared completely on the last words.

Corporal Ariam's face cleared of worry. "She'll be all right now if she can yell like that," she said to Med and Kraym.

All right—now her head was going to blow off her shoulders. Why hadn't she simply asked Kraym to kick it for her it instead of shouting? It would have hurt less.

"Sarge," said Med's voice through the fresh roaring in her ears, "Corporal Ariam did it, and managed to get you as well." The medtech's deft touch helped some of the turbulence in her brain to subside. "Right from under three divisions."

"I didn't do it by myself. We pulled it off together," Ariam corrected Med swiftly, her irritation striking a familiar chord.

That's usually my line, thought Rett to Pam with an inward laugh.

"You had us worried for a while," continued Ariam.

"I'll say. I didn't have time to stabilize you until now. We just came across the river a little while ago and on top of everything else that happened—all that cold water was a bit too much even for your azurium-clad metabolism to handle. So you locked up on me for about two minutes," the medtech informed Rett in a more pleasant manner. He patted a captured enemy SMG powerpack. "I had to jumpstart you. Turns out those low powered stuns are good for things other than incapacitating people."

Rett shook her head, with care since her neck was aching, still feeling a bit confused. At least that explained why she felt damp and a bit chilly on top of everything else. After a lot of effort she managed to press a hand to her forehead. "Is everyone all right?" she asked finally.

Kraym gave his report. "Just some minor grazes. Kaitan has a nasty fracture of the forearm. Gerrale burned her hands. Just about everyone has minor burns, cuts and bruises, nothing life threatening, everyone's mobile. With one exception so far. You."

Rett wrinkled her nose. "I'm fine." She then had to wonder why Ariam, Med, and Kraym started struggling with their facial expressions.

Kraym coughed, cleared his throat, and continued filling her in. "Wish you could've seen it, Sarge. We took them totally by surprise. It was beautiful. In three, four seconds, eight of us had SMGs and started picking off troopers and Coalition officers like targets on the practice range. We were all armed a minute later. Unfortunately none of us managed to get a clear track on Iheolon or the Leader."

"We didn't have time anyway. And the best part," said Ariam, "as soon as they were armed, Worren's group found us an exit route, right to where Iheolon had a couple of nice big armored troop rovers waiting to transport us after the show was over. We sent one off as a decoy and crammed into the other."

"Having the rovers meant we could go back and get you."

"How so, Kraym?"

Kraym adjusted his lenses. "You took out your entire detail. You were wide open for a recovery, but we had some difficulty getting to you soon enough."

Rett was confused as well as suspicious. She felt awful, but not that bad. She'd felt worse. "Is that why, perhaps, Ariam and Med won't let me up?"

"You were just about dead, Sarge."

Rett bared her teeth. "Aside from that."

Med relaxed and shrugged. "I guess that's up to you now, Sergeant," said the medtech in a manner that wasn't too reassuring.

"Why, Med? I'm still in one piece. At least, I think I am."

Kraym made a rude noise. "Yes, all your parts are still attached and vaguely resemble the ones you had yesterday. To say the least."

"Amazing, considering nothing of vital importance was hit," added Med, then helped her sit up. "Easy does it. Among other things, you have some cracked ribs. Don't try to move too fast."

Med was being nice to her now, his tone gentle. Damn. He was only nice when people were dying.

She found out soon enough. Rett winced, gritted her teeth and changed her mind about having ever felt worse than this. She controlled her breathing, told herself she wasn't going to throw up. The planet slowly stopped spinning like a turbofan, the ringing in her ears faded. The blackness in front of her eyes brightened into comprehensible light and color. After several minutes, the initial dizzy, nauseated rush of aching, burning pain subsided to a more tolerable level.

"Med, is this a good idea?" asked Ariam from somewhere above her.

"For now it is," Med answered enigmatically.

When she could see clearly again, Rett pulled herself together and allowed Kraym to assist her to her feet. The big corporal wisely kept a supportive hand on her. Rett leaned into his strong help with gratitude.

After the dizziness subsided, she surveyed the more easily visible portions of herself. Her uniform bore the torn, singed marks of some SMG grazes, her wrists were blistered and arms exposed almost to the elbow; the material of uniform and boot uppers around each ankle totally gone and the skin there scorched as well.

She didn't see any new holes, like the one in her leg. Grazed, burned, broken ribs, a terrific headache, sore neck and throat, some good bruises. "Did I really take that bad of a jolt?"

"It wasn't just one. Don't you feel heat anywhere, Sarge?" Med moved into her range of vision again and tilted his head up to gaze into her face, his worry visible.

"I feel a lot of things everywhere, Med," Rett pointed out in a low, dangerous tone. Playing games with Med was not high on her current preference list.

"Humor me. Concentrate."

Rett closed her eyes, glad Kraym supported her because her action caused her to feel faint. No, better keep them open. The short interval was long enough to winnow out a raging heat across her shoulders, back and hips in addition to something like a general sunburn all over. She didn't want to dwell on what it would feel like without factoring in her state of dampness and the chill that must have pushed her body into "Feels as if I was fried a little in a few places, yeah."

"A little!" muttered Ariam in disbelief. "If you took any more toasting, one good sneeze would've blown you away."

"Can we get to the point, before I pass out?" asked Rett, getting impatient.

"During the party up front," said Med, "if you remember any of it at all, after you decked your fifth trooper, you were tackled. You managed to grab two more and take them back with you and all three of you landed against a powergrid. I think they tried to reactivate those magnetic things at the same time and someone from our end tried to take out the grid with an energy beam. The fireworks were pretty intense. Knocked out lights and alarms in the entire building, communications, too. Made it easier for us to spook out.

"Meanwhile, Worren came back to say he'd secured transport, so Ariam started sending people out, and decided since we had conditions in our favor we were taking you out, too. This is about the time you went back into the grid, like Med said. Lucky Trebor was keeping you covered and gave the heads up. Gerrale reached you first and pulled you out before you were fried to a crunch."

"Is she—" Rett made the mistake of trying to turn her head and neck to check that the stocky squadleader and fourth-up for F-troop was all right.

"She's fine—nothing a tenday of treatments won't fix. Burned her hands yanking those magnetic restraints off you," said Med. "They came open, but they were still hot. I'm glad to hear you definitely have feeling and there seems to be no nerve damage." Med hesitated, frowning now with the weight of decisions instead of grumpiness. "The situation being what it is, if you think you can manage, I'd like you to stay awake and moving as long as you're able."

She had to smile, but held back what wanted to be an urge to hysterical laughter. "This is total turnaround for you, Med."

"Yeah, but don't worry, you'll be right where I want you and in no condition to argue as soon as we get back."

"Let's worry about getting back first," Rett said. Time to concentrate and turn the pain into energy for moving. "Wait a minute, something's not right." She tried to look around at the back of herself, but her neck ached too badly to even point her chin past her collarbone. "I've uniform back there, don't I?" The way her surface felt, chilled, damp, burning, and aching all at the same time, it was hard to tell what was covered by anything, much less distinguishing skin from uniform.

"You do," Ariam said.

"Well, that's good. I'm already halfway out of uniform and I'd really be tiffed if I had to go all the way back and look silly killing Mott and Shamos with my butt hanging out."

The chuckles from the rest of F-troop did more to hearten her. "Let's see if I can stand on my own," she told Kraym, who released his light hold, staying nearby just in case. "Thanks, big guy."

She cast another grateful look to Corporal Gerrale. "Thanks, Gerrale, I owe you."

Gerrale smiled back. "Not a problem, Sarge."

"All of you. H'tenneck, Mikel…thanks, people. Great work! Wait—where are Pip and Jessek?"

"Sent ahead to find our rover," said Ariam quickly. "I'm sorry, I thought I mentioned that earlier."

~She actually did,~ Pam put in. ~Mention it.~

Rett grimaced. She wasn't going to be very useful to anyone on the way back. "Good thing you and Kraym are in command, Ariam. Take us home. I don't care for the idea of going back to Circle under anyone's terms than our own."

"Yes, I still have command. Temporarily. And we were waiting for you." With a nod, Ariam turned and gave the order to move out.

"Want me to block some of that?" Med asked.

Rett gave him a wan smile. "You want me on my feet you're going to have to block a bit more than *some* of it. Just give me a moment." *I'll need you to back down as long as his hands are on me—I have no idea how strongly he can perceive you, but I don't want to take any chances. He can tell when I'm evading.*

~He can feel this? What does he mean, "block" some of it?~ Pam asked in amazement. It staggered her to feel the amount of pain in Rett's body and she just couldn't believe the sergeant was actually on her feet and ready to travel.

He's a healer-empath, Rett returned. *Can't hide pain from him.*

~He can heal you with his mind?~

No—his Talent isn't like that—although there have been a few like that in our history. He just knows exactly where it hurts and how badly; knows when one of us is injured, or if we're not…we're not "right". Even if he's elsewhere. He has a pretty long range with F-troop. Everything else is skill and training—he's amazing, really.

~Oh. Why can't he give you a painkiller?~

I'm allergic to a lot of drugs, including painkillers. Med knows just where to put a little pressure to block off some of the pain. Like he did in that cell. Whenever that was. And just before with my headache.

~Oh! Wow. Well, I'll let him work his magic on you.~ With that, Pam went behind her barrier again.

Thankfully it didn't take long for Med to make some temporary improvements. Rett soon felt more alert; everything was working—sort of. Her combat sense was quiet. Still, something wasn't right; she still felt strange, and it wasn't the result of an ego-merge, SMG burns, cracked ribs, or electrical shock. Rett soon realized her feeling emanated from the fact she stood in enemy held territory, with her unit, on combat alert. And she carried no weapon. She was disabled and not in command, but didn't mean she couldn't be ready to defend herself or F-troop in case of trouble. Even Gerrale, with her burned hands, and Kaitan, with her broken arm, carried a weapon of some kind.

"What's wrong now?" asked Corporal Ariam as she stopped in her tracks. "Do you need help?"

Rett shook her head. "Maybe I will in a while," she admitted, "but for now, does anyone have an extra weapon of some kind? I'm only effective at close range otherwise. And I'm not exactly in any condition for close range."

"She's almost back to normal," Kraym told Ariam.

"Thank goodness for that!" exclaimed Ariam, motioning another platoon member to give Rett a spare handgun and an extra charger for it. "I was getting really worried about having to permanently make platoon leader!"

Since she couldn't muster the energy for a comeback, Rett let that go. But she had to ask Pam: *Still think you're dreaming?*

~Not any more, at least not until I wake up again! Because while I have a great imagination, it's failing to explain how time passed for me on Earth and you here, much less how you're even able to speak or move right now.~

You'll have to tell me more about it later. I mean, you did wake up and everything was normal, right? I think I got that impression. It hurts too much to think very hard right now. But say, in the meanwhile, maybe you can put that imagination to work trying to figure out if that first big shock they said I took knocked you out of me and the one Med did somehow kicked you back in.

~Yeah. Right. I'll mull that over, but I don't think it's something that simple, especially if you told me the local gods were involved.~

They're not gods.

~Deities.~

They're not— Rett hunted for an explanation, but she wasn't up to going into detail. *Let's just say the term "deities" is convenient. It's easier to say than "superparanormal life forms".*

Pam chuckled. ~Okay. But just like you have to check stuff out about Mott and Shamos when we get back, we're going to need to check some stuff about this situation we're in. And Rett?~

Yeah, Pam?

~I'm really glad you didn't die.~

Same here. And I...uh...am actually glad to have you back. And, Pam, Rett added, *once we get past this ridge, you could go ahead and divert me. I think I'll need it.*

~I think I need it, too,~ Pam thought. ~After all, I feel everything you do.~ With that, she settled back and waited to see what would happen next.

117

~oOo~

1.2.0 BEATING THE ODDS

52ND DIVISION HQ
SOUTH CENTRAL BRANCH PROVINCE, NYORFIAS
0535.06.30 (LOCAL RECKONING)

~I THOUGHT YOU SAID IT WAS summer here,~ grumped Pam as fat raindrops pelted down. ~The rain's not so bad, but it's so cold.~

Oh, as if I can control the weather, returned Rett with a grin inward and out.

Combined with the darkness of early morning, the damp gloom painted the compound of the 52nd Division Headquarters in varying tones of slick, shiny grays. An icy wind slanted the rain into Rett's face. She ducked her head, glad of the warm, waterproof clothing she wore.

~Aren't you supposed to be able to handle it?~ Pam asked.

It was easy to tell Pam knew better than that, but Rett answered her anyway. *Yes. But being wet and cold to my bones when I don't have to be isn't only a waste of energy and a distraction: it's just plain stupid.*

She moved over to let a squad of infantry squelch past, their figures bulkier than normal with the addition of extra gear for the weather.

All the same, this much rain is unusual for this part of Main. One of those odd weather patterns is all, ocean currents shift, jet stream takes a jump, and here we are. We're in a huge river valley hammered between two coastlines, a big series of mountain ranges and a giant desert. Weather can't go anywhere else, so it sits. Colonel Evard mentioned the other day that this seems to happen every four decades or so, but he's never seen it last this long this late in the season.

Rain, heavy and unrelenting, had been the norm for the past tenday and a half. A good deal of the compound would have been underwater if the buildings weren't portable. But even though the entire encampment moved to higher ground—again—it was impossible to avoid all the mud and puddles and dampness.

~Mushrooms?~ inquired Pam.

What?

~You're thinking mushrooms. Big, golden brown ones.~

Rett sidestepped a deep puddle. *Well, weather like this usually brings them on,* she thought, trying to be casual about it. Too late.

~Ah-ha! So, yes, she does have a weakness! She will do anything, anything, for a plate of roasted mushrooms!~ Pam thought in mental tones of such comic evil Rett laughed again.

"Found my secret," she said aloud, crossing the last stretch of compound swiftly. "Do me a favor. Don't tell anyone."

~Smartass,~ grumbled Pam.

Ducking under the overhang near the CP's entrance, Rett shook most of the water off and threw back her hood. One hand smoothed her hair and made a tiny adjustment to her headband. *Pam...*

~I'll be good,~ Pam promised. The last thing she wanted was a repeat of the first meeting she had with senior officers in Rett's body. In one way, it was hilarious, but in another, she squirmed with embarrassment every time she thought how she must have made Rett look to those people.

Luckily, things worked out. She had been merged with Rett long enough to know the depth of the Nyorfian's responsibility and commitment to the cause and people for which she fought. Fifteen minutes of making the platoon leader act as if she'd turned completely inside out had been almost fifteen minutes too long. With a tiny shiver of remembrance, she backed into the secure imaginary corner she'd created. She was working on making the corner more like a little studio, but for now it was still a corner. She left herself open enough for comment, but secure enough that a reaction from her wouldn't become a physical action on Rett's part.

Thanks, Pam, Rett sent with genuine appreciation. Then she went inside.

Glancing up from his work with a smile, the division commander's adjutant said, "Colonel wants you to go right in, Sergeant."

"Thanks."

She really liked the new 52nd command staff, especially the new CO, SubColonel Evard. Evard had been part of the planetwide militia since his seventeenth year, and that had been long before the war began. Evard had, just a handful of days ago, turned his eighty-fifth year.

~He doesn't look a minute over sixty,~ insisted Pam.

Rett sent a little mental grin to Pam as that leak of outright amazement came from her place. Apparently there were more than a few physical differences between their species. Barring accident, illness, or war, the average Nyorfian could expect to live an active, useful life well past their first century.

Evard was a native of Centerland Province and had been a crop farmer before turning full time soldier. In the two tendays he'd been in command of the 52nd, he'd proven his capability, organization, and insight. He hadn't wasted any time about it, either, personally and directly plowing right into the middle of the tangled mess that the recently exposed Coalition agents Mott and Shamos had left behind.

Best of all, Evard, along with his staff, remembered to use her real name. She hadn't heard Killer from anyone since coming back from Circle.

Was this meeting about Mott and Shamos? Her thoughts darkened. Maybe the colonel had news about them. She hoped so. Maybe he'd tell her where to find them so she could kick them around a while before she really started to hurt them.

With that hopeful thought, and another reminder to Pam to please keep herself under control, she stepped through the door. "Sergeant Rett reporting…" There was no one behind the desk. At least, no one she saw right away. She focused her ability to interpret the energies put out by objects around her. Dismissing the neutral impressions of

121

inanimate objects, she located her target below and behind the desk, a mass of brown, dark gold, and aqua edged with dark edges of hotter colors she associated with irritation more than danger. "Something I can help you with, sir?"

Evard's gray-streaked head popped over the surface. His weathered face looked a bit more flushed than usual: from exertion or embarrassment, or both, she wasn't sure. But he offered a welcome smile in such a warm manner Rett had to return it.

"Lost my favorite marker under here." He displayed his prize, laid it on the desk, and levered himself to an upright position with the heartfelt groan of an older person who spent most days on his feet and working hard despite the burden of chronic arthritis.

His knee joints popped and cracked as he straightened, and she winced inwardly in sympathy. The weather couldn't be helping him too much, either.

122

"Drag a chair over here, Rett. Did you and your people get a good rest?"

"Yes, sir, we did." It was such a relief to see her people with naturally high energy and in good moods again. Not even the rainy weather could take that from them. "Thank you." She snagged a chair sitting against the right hand wall and placed it near the desk, waiting for the colonel to settle himself first.

"Good. I wish it could've been longer. Sit."

As he took his own seat, his joints popped like rifle shots. This time she saw his brows furrow, jaw muscles tighten, and cheeks darken. His energy aura shifted to match, more of the dark reds and oranges streaking through his normal array.

"Can you guess why I don't go on assignments calling for stealth any more?" Evard let out a forced sort of chuckle and reached for a handpainted earthenware mug, clearly the handiwork of a young and aspiring artist. The bright happy colors glowed like jewels in the militarily drab and utilitarian surroundings. From the morose way he gazed into its depths, she guessed it was empty.

He started to rise again, the mug in one large, gnarled, blunt hand, but she leaned over and took it from him. A flash of irritation crossed his face. "I can get—"

"Please, sir," she said, "I know that. But as long as I'm here, it would be my pleasure."

He gave in. "You're a good girl, Rett." He settled himself with a relieved sigh.

Smothering a grin, she quickly turned to the carafe on a side table. The way he said that made her feel as if she were eight years old. She smiled at the whimsical family portrayed on the mug. Inside, on the bottom, were painted four names inside a forever circle. *Grandfa, Daddy, Tiosheva, Mommy.*

Her smile faded for a second, her motion froze. The names before her mind's eye were different; one of them her own, carved into the bark of an ancient, huge longcone in Treetop. With ruthless force, she shoved that recollection down where it belonged before Pam could pick up on it. Letting out a soft breath, she poured the gold-green tea into the mug, covering the names there just as she had covered her memories.

123

"And you're all clear with Medical now? No lasting damages?"

"Good as new, sir." Rett handed over his replenished mug of tea and settled herself on her seat. Regarding the 52nd's new CO with outward calm, she inwardly wondered what he was leading up to.

"Rett, if your back gets any stiffer I think it'll crack. It would make mine feel better if you relaxed it a bit." His hands cupped the earthenware mug.

Rett *was* relaxed, but apparently she didn't appear enough so for the colonel. So she sat back against her chair and crossed her legs. Evard had already flat out told her that she or anyone in F-troop wouldn't get by trying any of their Special Forces formalities on him when it was business as usual at HQ. He also wanted her to speak up, and out, and give her opinion whether he asked for it or not, let him know how she really felt about things. In other words, he was the exact opposite of Mott.

Mott didn't count any more, she reminded herself. Mott wasn't even Nyorfian, even though he'd been biologically altered to resemble one. How they managed that was still a mystery.

Since she'd developed an instant liking for Colonel Evard, Rett tried to oblige him, but two tendays was simply not enough time to completely break habits built over the past decade.

"All right then, listen to this, and tell me what you think, any way you like. I told you that before." He paused, continued at her nod. "Good. I'll get right to the point, then. It's the Wide River Gap bridge again. We need it, badly, and the city of Circle. You know that would about finish the enemy here on Nyorfias. MainCommand is pushing me pretty hard for it."

"I was expecting we'd get back to that bridge," sighed Rett. "But I think you shouldn't try it without at least two extra battalions: as backup and then to take over and hold the damn bridge once we have it, sir."

"I want you to do it."

"And about Circle, the enemy's backed up, dug in and armed to the eyebrows. Two divisions, plus Commander Iheolon's, unless he shipped out to Epnoce already. I doubt that now, since F-troop took out a lot of officers. They need to keep what's left to make sure the troopers don't slack off. So that makes three divisions…" Rett stopped short. "*What* did you say, sir?"

"I want you to take the Wide River Gap bridge and set up the attack on Circle. I could give you the 415th and the 109th right now."

Rett didn't bother to try her astonishment. "You want me to take the bridge with forty commandos and two infantry battalions, sir? Plus Circle?"

"That's all I have this moment."

You're not fooling around with my head, are you, Pam? Rett thought sharply.

Pam gave every impression of sitting back in her corner with a wounded expression.

"Colonel, I'm sorry, is this a joke?"

The officer's expression answered that. No joke. His impression of affable welcome had faded into a weighty and deep disquiet.

Rett pulled her thoughts and face into better order. "Of course we'll have an advantage in this weather. The river has crested and those underground hides they built are under water, so the enemy'll have to be out in the open, unless they've grown gills. We can also move through the slop a lot easier than they can.

"But it'll take the two battalions just to provide minimum defense for that bridge once it's taken. You know how huge it is, sir. River's five miles wide, bridge is six and a half. And there are heavy weapons emplacements on both banks as well as the bridge itself. Also a lot of open space on both sides, especially the Circle bank. And, without backup troops, if you don't hit Circle and hit it hard right after that bridge is taken, the enemy will just wipe us out. No matter how good people say we are, sir, it's suicidal to even think of attacking and holding the bridge, then attacking Circle, with my unit and two infantry battalions!"

"Can you try?"

"Why me, sir?" She was glad the officer told her she was free to express herself. "I mean, yes, logically we would spearhead an operation like this. But as far as being in charge…you know we specialize in hit hard and let the infantry take over!"

"I want to put you in charge of this. If anyone in two worlds can pull it off, it's you and F-troop. Would you try?"

"You want me to command the attack."

"Yes."

"Sir, I'm a platoon leader. This is a serious target. Deploying more than forty people at a time isn't something I've had experience doing. At all."

"So you divide those two battalions into forty person units and deploy them."

"Colonel—"

"Your rank and job description aren't issues. And quite a few people, including your Special Forces CO, my staff, and infantry commanders, considered this matter in depth. You've as much field experience as most of my officers. Besides, according to Major Yidnar's notations in your records, had you taken your upgrades each time you were reviewed and offered one, you would have a senior captain's rank by now."

"Colonel—"

Again he cut her short. "Everyone agrees we have better odds with you and F-troop calling the shots. As a matter of fact, my other officers made the suggestion you be put in charge."

Rett let a soft breath out through her teeth. "All right, Colonel, let's put the issue of command aside a minute and get to the really important part."

Evard gestured for her to go ahead.

"We're talking of throwing a total of less than a thousand people with no heavy armor and no air support against three divisions that have a good strong defense, including mobile armored units, long and short range artillery, and air support."

Her gesture stopped Colonel Evard before he could take a breath and remind her about the backup units. "Even if you can get those units, unless armored and AirSpacefighters are with us at the jump, all I have is a thousand ground troops against more than ten thousand, including armored and air. The numbers do not account for any losses we may take attacking the bridge. Or count those who must remain behind to guard it.

"So let's just give this scenario a bottom line and say we're attacking Circle with anywhere from four to six hundred people with light weapons."

Rett looked down at her hands, wondering how her fingers became so twisted together. A swift mental apology from Pam, trying to follow Rett's calculations, answered that. Untangling them, her gaze went back to Colonel Evard.

"I have to look at this realistically, sir. The planners and number crunchers at MainCommand may be factoring in troops that aren't available yet, but those of us that are going to be out there can't afford to count people, weapons and vehicles we don't have. And the weather can break any time, so while we can hope for it to stick as long as we need it to, we can't count on it."

He had to nod agreement.

"To go for both targets with those numbers is suicide, sir." Rett blew out a breath. Her own access to Intelligence was fairly top level. Nothing she'd read in the daily reports hinted at the situations being desperate enough for such an unlikely attempt. "I'm sorry, Colonel. I'll not volunteer my unit or myself for that." She paused slightly. "Special Forces isn't above taking huge risks, as you know—that's why we exist. But there's a difference between huge risk and impossible odds."

She leaned forward slightly, her hands on the edge of his desk. "At this point, I'm only refusing to volunteer, sir. Unless you give me a damned good reason why we can't wait for backups, and why this situation is desperate enough for this sort of attack, the only way F-troop will take this assignment is with your order." She felt glad again for the difference between this officer and Mott. Evard would give her reasons.

The older man nodded. "Fair enough. I don't like this either, Rett, I really don't. I want you to take this willingly. Unfortunately, everything you said is absolutely right." The CO made a pained grimace. "But MainCommand wants it done now, before the Coalition can regroup and get more troops and supplies in this system. Like you said, for the moment the weather is on our side. The icing levels of this storm alone have been enough to keep everyone grounded from Branch to Grainland, Nyorfian or Coalition. A high-pressure front is going to push this out in a few days."

"Maybe less," Rett said with a nod, since as a lifetime habit, she kept up with the met reports several times a day.

"So we need to take every advantage this situation presents." Evard paused for a swallow of his tea. "We have to stop the Coalition here and now, get our own troops to Epnoce, and start taking our worlds back. But without the Circle spaceport being ours again," the Colonel's voice was serious, "we may be looking for another ten years to this war, if our people can last that long…and if the Yixolryn Coalition doesn't simply decide to blast this system right out of the galaxy. We're so damned close, either way. We have to take the chance, because we won't get another one."

Rett couldn't disagree, but held back from comment.

He angled his chair and activated the huge screen of the mapping computer behind him. Picking up a pointer, he tapped the display for the latest rendering of the area under consideration.

"Here's what's happening. Our units are being redeployed all over Nyorfias, especially here in Centerland and Branch, aiming to this push. Major Yidnar is trying to get more of his own units up here as fast as he can, too, but Special Forces, as you know, is still spread out all over the place." His wand indicated at least a handful of those places, most to the south and west. "Now, the 5th Division is coming at Circle from the west-northwest." He drew a curving arrow through the lower reaches of the magnificent Branch Range. "They'll cross the river here with a temporary bridge."

Another spot was marked, some fifty miles upstream in the high country. "They can be in a position to help in twenty hours. Sooner if the snow they're hitting lets up. If MainCommand gave me more time I could get half my division backing you up in one day, the rest in two."

Rett shifted in her seat. The 5th was a well-seasoned mountain division and should have no problem—besides the weather and Coalition encounters—getting through what looked like a difficult river crossing. "They've been pushing nonstop through those mountains, sir. What sort of condition are they in?"

"Tired. But their supplies are good and the CO tells me her people are determined." He swiveled his seat to face her fully. "I know this is tough for you to consider, Rett, but think about it, it makes perfect sense. In any scenario, we have to count on F-troop being the spearheading force from our approach. In this operation, your people will have to lend any technique or hints they can to the infantry so they can better assist you. Your people have methods that make up for lack of numbers. As the leader of the spearheading unit, it's only logical you oversee the entire operation in the field. Besides, you and your people know the Circle area and the situation better than any of my infantry officers."

Of course they did, they were just there. "Understood, sir. However, the problem is: we won't have two days. The enemy won't sit around waiting for us while our support and backup units make it in. Once we have the bridge, we *must* move forward, or those three divisions are going to come out and mash us right into that valley. The weather might slow them down a little but it won't stop them." She raked a hand through her hair, wishing, not for the first time, that it still had length enough for really good yank. "At least if we keep moving they'll get suspicious enough to sit in Circle and plan a defense."

"Oh?"

"Yes, sir. They'll never think we're crazy enough to attack them with four hundred people. They'll think it's a diversion for something far larger. When nothing larger comes…they'll move out with a vengeance, clean up what's left of us, and then go get their bridge back."

Feeling a headache coming on, Rett adjusted her position again and tried to relax muscles gone far too tense. The fact Evard had not yet simply ordered her to go and take command hinted at information he had yet to reveal. All this speculation was beginning to irritate her. "I can understand the need for immediate action, sir. I don't understand why MainCommand can't wait a day at least, or until you have more units in position. Is there something else I should know?"

"Yes." As if he'd been waiting for that very question, Evard picked up a folder and handed it across the desk to her, then leaned back in his chair and crossed his arms over his chest. "This hasn't gone out over any regular channels. We're still not sure of how many holes Mott and Shamos left behind them. A courier brought it two days ago.

"First I'm going to tell you the good news. The GTC has finally shown up. We've the Rangers and twenty thousand GTC marines backing our people stationed in space. So hopefully no further influx of Coalition troops or supplies are going to get in…or out. And they're pushing hard to get to Epnoce."

"That *is* good news, sir." For a moment Rett was breathless and her thought processes stuck on a single mantra. *Finally. Finally. Oh good deities, finally.*

From within, Pam dared to come out of her mostly passive state into Rett's conscious mind. ~Not the right time for fangirl appreciation, Rett. I'd feel as giddy as you if you explained why this is good news…~

Rett recovered. *Thanks, Pam.* To Evard, she gave a real smile, since he was looking at her with a mixture of amusement and concern. "That's the best news I've heard in nine years."

It was so good, in fact, that she didn't make Pam wait for an explanation. *We're part of a huge alliance of worlds known as the Galactic Trade Commission. We sent a request for help after realizing the exact scale and nature of the enemy invasion. But we're so far out from anything or anyone else, it takes at least five years for anyone from GTC Central to get here. Plus the Coalition had our regular communications system blocked, so we had to use something slower they couldn't detect. But they're here now—and that means hope, Pam. More than ever.*

"It'll work wonders for morale," Rett said to Evard, "if not for our numbers on this planet. That is, if this is something that can be said elsewhere."

"When we take Circle both the good and bad news will be public knowledge. But not until then." Evard nodded at the folder in her hands. "Now you can get the bad news."

She slid the hardcopy from the folder and scanned the terse contents. Her good feelings vanished and her guts went cold.

...in the past three tendays, the Yixolryn Coalition has landed ten thousand fresh troops on Epnoce...making a total of one hundred fifty thousand...

"Two hundred armored carrier shuttles ready to launch..." she read in a disbelieving whisper.

Two hundred Coalition troop shuttles capable of transporting three hundred troops each, plus all their ordnance and equipment with them.

"You can guess the destination of those troop ships, Rett."

"Yes, sir."

Sixty thousand fully armed and fresh troops. More than four times the present entire complement of what remained of the Nyorfian military, land, sea, air and space combined.

GTC finally here or not, she'd call that a desperate situation.

~You can't be so few!~

Trust me, Pam, we are so few. Rett was too overwhelmed to remind Pam she should be in the background. *Twelve years of war does that, and unlike the Coalition, we've not had a periodic supply of reinforcements.*

"Colonel," Rett said aloud, "we could have saved a lot of time had you shown me this first."

He shook his grizzled head a little. "There were some things I needed to hear from you. If I handed that off to you first thing I would have never had the same feedback. What I heard, to me, justifies putting you in command. So you and F-troop will go?"

"We'll go with a will and give it all we have, sir."

His relief obvious, Evard reached again for his mug. Rett guessed by now any liquid remaining was stone cold, but the colonel drained it anyway. "Thanks. Our citizens on Epnoce have formed a sort of underground resistance force and are doing all they can to thwart the enemy from there. Also, since the GTC showed up, some of our AirSpacefighter ships came back from border patrol in space, and they've been keeping the enemy within the Epnocian atmosphere, at least. We're not sure how much longer they're going to hold out, though."

"Another good reason for getting this done right away," commented Rett with another exhalation through her teeth. Evard had been right when he said they wouldn't get a second chance.

"Need time to get ready?"

"We're always ready, sir. You know F-troop can move out of here with a word. It's the infantry we'll have to wait for."

"You're right," he said with an agreeable chuckle. "That's usually the case, isn't it? But not today. I've been working on this since the dispatch arrived. Everyone's been briefed already. We were waiting on your agreement."

She gave him a nod of respect that came right from the bottoms of her feet. She was going to have to keep remembering—right up front—the fact there hadn't only been a change in the command staff of the 52nd, but a complete and total turnaround on how things were handled.

"Well, then. Can we plan on this operation moving forward in, say, three hours? That will give me time to finalize things with the battalion commanders. Unless you want to meet with them beforehand?"

"Not if it will delay the operation, sir. The weather won't hold. All of them aren't here, are they? Just the 109th. Why detour the 415th when we can all meet in the same place, at the same time, and say things all at once?"

"Better be careful, Rett." Evard looked up at her with a sparkle of warm humor in his eyes. "From what I've heard from you today I'd be hard put to believe you're only a platoon leader. Four hours then. That will give me time to complete with them and arrange transportation for you and the 109th."

She stood. "That sounds good, sir."

"I'll send up my units as fast as I can, as soon as they check in. They're headed to rendezvous as we speak. I don't like this either," Evard said again, almost to himself.

Rett paused before asking to be dismissed and studied the pensive division commander. His gaze was fixed on the file on his desk, his eyebrows pulled together into a single line over his broad nose. "Colonel, don't worry about it. We've had tough odds before. You know this entire system's had tough odds ever since this war began. This operation beats anything I've experienced for bad odds—well, as I said before, almost impossible odds—but faced with the alternative, I'd call them pretty good. Besides, I know F-troop wants revenge at that bridge and I'd like the opportunity to pay my respects to Commander Iheolon and the Leader in Circle. On *my* terms. With all that going for us, my unit alone will do the work of an extra battalion."

"That's what Major Yidnar said."

"Sounds like you've had more direct contact with him in two tendays than I've had in years," she said wistfully. She missed being with the 2023rd, her parent unit, that extended family of Battalion. "And sir, I still want you to log my unwillingness to take the command, but not the job." Rett chuckled. "I'll be looking for those reinforcements. Just do your best, sir, and we'll do ours."

"Thanks, Sergeant." The worry line between his brows eased a little. "Yidnar told me I could always count on you to take anything except a rank upgrade."

"He's right," agreed Rett lightly, not wanting him to go there, either. Her turning down the past three rank upgrades she'd been offered was something Major Yidnar wasn't going to let go the next time a review came up. "I get into enough trouble as a sergeant. Dismissed, sir?"

"For now. I'm sure we'll have some last minute things to discuss."

"Colonel, I do have one more question. How's Captain D'lano? All Medical told me was that he was still critical. Security's been so tight on him, my own medtech couldn't get information. I understand wanting to keep him safe, but we just want to know how he is, if he'll recover."

"I'm sorry. MainCommand gave the order. But I'll tell you that as of this morning, he's conscious again."

She nodded. "Thank you, sir. I also had some thoughts you might be telling me about Mott and Shamos."

Evard shook his head grimly. "Mott and Shamos are still at large—and on planet, since we've been monitoring spaceflight. MainCommand is investigating. I thought that almost undetectable mind monitoring and control device they came up with years ago was bad—but discovering the Coalition has capability to alter someone biologically is even worse."

The force Rett used to tighten down on past memories was so strong Pam nearly jumped from her corner. What had triggered it? Pam wondered. Evard mentioning that mind device?

"I knew they were naturalized citizens," Rett said to Evard while adding an interior warning to Pam. "It's hard…"

"You don't have to tell me that. I knew them, or thought I did," Evard said. "And they were good to the 52nd until a while ago. I'm sure the investigation is going to turn up a lot of little things that add up into something bigger and uglier than what we already know right now."

"I'd like to continue thinking Nyorfians, native born or natural-ized, just wouldn't do something like that…normally."

The colonel nodded in agreement. "Acting against our own people and worlds simply isn't in our nature. I understand the Nyorfian Council and MainCommand are fairly certain an Adept can root out any more of these plants, humanoid or altered. They'll be coming around to verify us all."

Oh, great. What was she supposed to do about Pam? She couldn't block an Adept. What happened when they found she had an entire distinct alien personality in her head? "And D'lano, Colonel? Will he recover?"

133

"Those two left him for dead. He very nearly was after they got through with him. The medtechs tell me the first words out of his mouth this morning was that he found out about the ambush and he had to stop your unit from going in. I understand they had difficulty convincing him that was some time ago. But yes, he'll recover. Medical staff says he's going to be all right now."

Rett sighed in relief. "Thank you for telling me, sir. It'll be good news to all of us. If you would, give him a message we were asking."

"I'll tell him personally," promised the officer. "Later, Rett. Luck and good deities go with you."

Luck all right, she snorted to herself, cocking one eye upward as she exited. *As far as the deities are concerned, they've done quite enough with this ego-merge! Damn it!*

~And here I thought you were over being angry about me,~ groused Pam.

Oh, I am. But I'm not over being scared.

~Maybe if we practice enough, between us we can make me invisible even to one of your Adepts,~ offered Pam. ~Or you can hope that your superparanormal friends yank me out long enough for you to pass inspection.~

I'm glad you're willing to work with me on this. Maybe we'll do both. But later.

1.2.2 UNDISCLOSED LOCATION
SOUTH CENTRAL BRANCH PROVINCE, NYORFIAS
0535.30.06 (LOCAL RECKONING)

DESPITE THE CIRCUMSTANCES, RETT WAS glad to be active again and on a combat mission. If she didn't have to lead the attack force, things would've been almost okay. Not perfect. Perfect would be no war. But okay.

"Gosh, Sarge, I wonder why this looks so familiar?"

She tossed a glance at her seniormost co-second. She knew Ariam was making an attempt at humor, but she wasn't really in the mood for it. "Oh, gosh, Corporal, I don't know," she answered in the same sort of high pitched, bewildered voice. Then she dropped it back into her normal range, her next words biting. "Maybe it's because we all were almost killed here two tendays ago!"

"Hey. Don't blow your headband over it." The younger woman adjusted the sling of her TT-1 and tucked back a stray lock of hair. "We're going to do this."

"Yes, we are. *We have to.* And this time," said Rett in a hard voice, "we'll not be stopped by stun beams or troops underground."

"Nothing's going to stop us," said Ariam with confidence. "We're going all the way or nowhere."

"That's what this mission is, Ariam." She again wished someone else were in charge. "All the way or nowhere."

* * * * *

SOON, RETT WAS POSITIONING HER unit along the top of the ridge, in the same spots as two tendays ago. The infantry units were halted until things checked out. Corporal Kraym, as ready as a medtech's aide, had her VARs in her hand as she reached for them.

She couldn't ask for a better team of co-seconds: Ariam's quick instincts and fire, combined with Kraym's steadiness and attention to detail; together they augmented each other's strengths. Her entire platoon was like that, all superb individuals, and as a team, simply fantastic.

~And you love them,~ Pam thought. ~That's something you can't hide from anyone, inside or out.~

Yes. Unconditionally. Then she began her scrutiny of the partially flooded river valley below. "Looks real busy down there today," she commented to her seconds and touched the zoom control on the VARs.

"Any of them have fins?" Kraym inquired whimsically.

"Hope not. They never expected the water to get this high. Good thing, too."

"Good thing," he said, "or they might've sent in a squadron or so of those amphibious rovers they had around the delta near Hundei Inlet."

"Can't say they haven't, although I don't see any." Rett shivered, and it wasn't from the dampness. She hoped this mission didn't turn into one like that had been. Inside, she could easily see streaks of bright frustration in Pam's energy. *Not now.* Shaking her head, she firmly redirected her attention where it belonged.

"How strong do you think they are?" Kraym asked.

"I'd say the full garrison is there this time." She straightened and handed the VARs to Ariam. "Here, keep looking. And tell me if you see that officer with the tentacles or more like it. It can be a problem." She chewed thoughtfully on her lower lip for a minute, then glanced at Kraym. "We can't afford to lose any people on this, not that we can ever afford to lose anyone. Especially if we're not going to have any help going on to Circle. Kraym, what's your opinion of the smallest unit we can leave behind to hold onto it?"

The big corporal adjusted his corrective lenses, a gesture more habitual than necessary. Rett explained to Pam's inquiry that Kraym, like many other Nyorfians, had to wear his longer than planned. The war and the need to concentrate medical resources on matters of immediacy had put an effective stop to any elective optical surgery beyond the simple correction of near or farsightedness. Kraym's own visual problem, however, with or without his lenses, had no effect on his ability and effectiveness as a member of the 2023rd and F-troop. If it had, he would never have made it past the preliminary screening process.

Kraym spoke, as usual, after careful consideration. "At the very least, two infantry companies and one of our squads, I'd say. Our people can cover the outlying positions toward Circle. Either Trebor's or Worren's squad will do, I think. Worren's people would be my choice. You'll need Trebor on the jump and mobile. Worren knows this country, too, so it'll be easier for him to move and choose his positions. Get him and his sharpshooters up in the trees and I'll be surprised if any troopers get back.

"Once Colonel Evard's units catch up, our squad can meet up with us right before we go for the city. I'd like to leave more behind, Sarge, but we'll need as many people as we can to go forward. We don't know what kind of losses we're going to take either."

Rett nodded, brushing rain from her face as the wind gusted, slanting the icy wetness toward them. She tugged the brim of her hood a little lower over her eyes. "I was thinking along those lines myself. I can't see any other way." She glanced toward the bridge and shook her head, wishing, not for the last time, she wasn't in charge. "Well, it's time we met with our troops."

"Your troops, you mean."

"No," Rett said evilly. "Oh, no. *Ours.* If I'm in command, and F-troop's leading, that puts you and Corporal Ariam as co-seconds of this operation."

"Oh, joy," mumbled Corporal Ariam from behind the VARs.

"Hey, like Colonel Evard said, it's a matter of splitting these guys up into platoons, squads, and patrols. I think that was the best idea I heard all day. Let's hope those infantry officers see it that way. Round them up for me, big guy, we'll meet over by that stand of big spicebush in fifteen minutes. Ariam, talk to me."

"I'd say a good battalion's worth down there. They're all heavily armed, but look relaxed. Expecting the weather to keep them safe, I think. Once they wake up to us we might get a stiff fight, but we shouldn't have too much problem taking the bridge. It's afterward we have to worry about." Ariam paused slightly, looking away from the VARs long enough to glance at Rett. "Kraym should be doing this, you know. He's the expert in tac-survey."

137

"I already heard his report," Rett said with amusement. "You heard him. He took a good long look at the bridge last time and, aside from all of us missing signs of those underground bunkers, he doesn't ever miss or forget a single detail. Besides, you need this experience, Corporal. Get any cross training you can. One day, when you're in front of your own troop, you'll be glad for it."

"As if I've not had command before," Rett heard Ariam mumble in reply.

"I meant your *own* command, not only taking over for me when I go missing or am incapacitated."

"You're not planning on any more of that, are you?" Ariam didn't change her position, but Rett noticed the hard dark orange of tension creep into her energy aura.

"Let's hope it's not needed. From or by any of us. I have a special job for you, though, which is why I have you looking instead of Kraym. You're taking a team from F-troop and the infantry to the other side."

"You're considering attacking the bridge from both sides at once?"

"Yes. Part of your team is going to be sent ahead to keep any troopers from getting back to Circle on the road and any easy access close to the road they might take. Then we'll want to cut and jam communications and disable vehicles. I want you to take out the guardhouses, bunkers, and barracks. Leave the weapons batteries intact if you can, we're going to need them for the new defense. How much a problem do you think that'll be?"

"I'll have demolition and chemical people?"

"Corporal Nitraym's squad and any others, including your pick from any the infantry commanders can provide. Just leave a few for me."

"No problem at all. We'd have to go after dark and we can cross upstream. We came back from Circle that way after we ditched the troop rover we stole, remember?"

"Er, Ariam," said Rett a little testily, "if you care to recall, I wasn't exactly conscious for that part of it. So no, I don't remember, and apparently you left it off the report."

"Sorry, Sarge, but I had a good reason to leave it off. I *am* at fault for not remembering to fill you in."

"Yes, you are. Want to tell me now?"

"When we got back and found Mott and Shamos gone, all our security was compromised. We were told to skip certain details until new protocols went up."

"I know that—but I also know after the new security went up, corrections should have been made. And *you* didn't do that." Watching Ariam in her peripheral vision, Rett saw the younger woman wince. "You know, it's a good thing Kraym covers your ass, but Corporal, I'm not going to let him do that any more. I'll find him something else to do besides your busywork *and* his."

Ariam didn't answer right away. Her expression didn't change, but Rett saw the clear colors of her normal aura start turning gray. "Yes, Sergeant."

"Now tell me how you're going to cross the river."

"Upstream about fifteen miles there's a narrow gorge, four miles across, big rocks, shallow rapids. Water will be higher and faster with all this rain, but nothing we can't handle."

~Four miles is narrow?~ Pam couldn't help it.

On this river it is. It isn't called "Wide" for nothing. Back off! "You'll have GIs to get over it, too," warned Rett aloud.

Not that anyone's Basic training omitted something like this. Basic training, however, was basic, and she wasn't sure how detailed the supplemental six tenday Infantry training had been; didn't know the backgrounds or skill level of any of those troops, or what they'd been doing recently. As far as the latter went, both the battalions Evard gave her had come up with him from the south of Main.

"How many, exactly, are you having me take?" Ariam shifted, wet vegetation squeaking beneath her. As usual she rebounded quickly from Rett's reprimand. Rett supposed she should be grateful Ariam wasn't one to dwell on things: she got over them and moved on.

Unlike me. I've never found it as easy. "Double handful of platoons at least," Rett said. "Probably a few more. Their commanders will pick them individually. Won't be carrying anything heavy because you'll all need to move fast over there."

"We'll get over," said Ariam with confidence. "Having more people will make the crossing even faster. And we won't have to worry too much about stealth there, that's rough country." Ariam grinned. "We

139

know the enemy stays clear. Coalition troops can't maneuver well through terrain like that even in the best weather with that armor and those heavy weapons they carry."

"Let's not count on it, Corporal. They've already proven they can surprise us with some original and creative thinking."

"I won't count on it, but I'm going to hope for it."

"I'd like to keep Trebor with me to keep things organized on this side of the bridge, so you can take Worren's squad," Rett said, swiping a raindrop from her nose. "They'll be staying back here with the bridge defense when we go ahead…at least until we get reinforcements." She tried to stay hopeful about that. "In the meanwhile we'll need Worren between Circle and the bridge, with his best sharpshooters covering any escape routes. We can't let any of the enemy make it back to Circle for reinforcements. You'll need to keep about a third of your infantry with you. Send the rest as far ahead as you can, as support to Worren. He'll know where to put them."

"He should," agreed Ariam. "His farm used to be on the other side not very far from here. So, those troopers'll either end up swimming, or have to get through that line. Since the land is so wet, they'll not stray far from the road, so that shouldn't be too difficult. Especially if we get to all the vehicles first."

Reaching out her left hand, Rett gave Ariam's hood covered head an affectionate shake. "Glad you're with me on this, Ariam. Just make sure once you get over there to remind all the GIs they are only to aim *away* from the bridge." They didn't need people from their own side getting caught in F-troop's crossfire patterns. Nor did they need a well-meant shot from the infantry to accidentally hit one of F-troop.

"No problem," Ariam said. "Can I have Kraym, too?"

Rett took the VARs from the corporal. "I can't break up an unbeatable team, can I?"

"About half a year ago you threatened to transfer us to units on opposite sides of this continent," reminded Ariam.

Rett grinned, remembering the incident. "That's right, I did. Exaggerating details on a report."

"There wasn't one detail on there that wasn't true, and you know it."

"It was a *report*, Ariam, not a dissertation on my every movement long enough to cover the entire seven hundred year history of the Galactic Trade Commission."

At Pam's sharp upswing of interest Rett quickly thought: *Before your time, Pam. Not now.*

"Just a couple minutes ago you came down on me for leaving stuff out. Make up your mind," Ariam grumbled.

"Somewhere in the middle is all I ask. And yes, take Kraym."

"Thanks. I'll arrange it so that the buildings on both sides blow at the same time."

"Good. I want them to think the entire Free Army is ready to jump on them. Hit hard and fast on both sides, make a lot of noise. And I mean we want *noise* here."

"Nitraym and I can whomp up some extra fireworks and hand them around before we go," suggested Ariam. "Bang, flash, and smoke, mostly. We can twist them together really fast."

"Do it. At this meeting, we'll find out who handles the demo on the infantry's side. Get with them and tell them how to make them, too, and see if they have any good tricks we can use. We need to really scare the Coalition troops for this to go down to our advantage." Rett regarded the younger woman seriously. "Are you up for this, Ari? You'll need to be wide open over there."

"Sarge," Ariam said at last, "stop worrying so much. I'm ready. I said before we'll go all the way or nowhere."

"And this mission?" Rett asked softly. Sometimes Ariam's empathic talent extended into clairvoyance, especially when feelings were as strong as she described.

"It'll be hard, but I strongly feel we can pull this off. Everyone is positive, including the infantry. I get a let's do it attitude from everyone so strongly I'm surprised the enemy can't feel us here. Lucky for us they don't!" Ariam looked away, but not before Rett saw the expression of uncertainty darken the younger woman's clear gray eyes. "The hardest part will be when it's over," Ariam said quietly. "All that matters though, Rett, is we're going to do it."

Rett lifted the VARs and continued her survey of the bridge and valley below. She rarely knew Ariam's feelings to be wrong. Everyone

141

was positive, that was good. Helped to have confident troops. Her co-second's sudden aversion from eye contact troubled her. Something was going to happen. What? She had no more time to dwell upon that line of thought, for Kraym came to tell them the infantry officers and platoon leaders had arrived.

The attack was planned out and set up. The infantry commanders surprised her by giving her friendly, attentive attitudes. Rett wasn't shy about asking for suggestions and advice. The response was insightful and encouraging. They thought the breakdown was a good idea. Evard might have only come up with two battalions, but they had to be among his sharpest. So, despite all her misgivings, Rett began to feel better about the ultimate outcome of this seemingly impossible mission.

1.2.3 WIDE RIVER GAP (NORTH BANK)
SOUTH CENTRAL BRANCH PROVINCE, NYORFIAS
0535.06.30 (LOCAL RECKONING)

DUE TO THE CONDITIONS, RETT waited as long as possible before moving her people into position. The water was cold, the mud thick, and the less time they had to spend in it remaining absolutely still and growing stiff, the better. Soon they were ready and waiting; so close to the bridge they could hear what the enemy troopers on duty were saying.

Hunkered down past her elbows in the water, Rett held position with her people. The ready tension of the upcoming battle made it easier not to think about the fact that her water- and cold-resistant uniform had limitations, and just about now the river was seeping in through any available opening.

So far, so good. On one level, she was keen and ready for combat, but on a deeper one, she felt resentment and regret. She didn't enjoy killing, no matter what people thought. She especially hated knowing that most of the enemy soldiers who would die in this battle had no desire to fight in the first place. That they had been ripped from their planets of origin after they fell to a Coalition invasion, and forced into the enemy's ranks, kept there and made to fight only by a combination of severe mental conditioning, drugs, threats, and promises.

~Then no wonder your people are pushing them off Nyorfias~, came from Pam.

Rett's response to this came like the floodwaters from the Wide River: as a torrent of thought, a current of deep passion and near desperation surfacing as Pam interpreted the flow.

They are being pushed back: at a great price. The Yixolryns and their close allies are still convinced of their own superiority, even after all these years. That's what makes them so dangerous, and yet, easy to predict. That arrogance you saw from the Leader is pretty typical. I think the fact we've learned how to exploit that has been one of the reasons we're starting to gain some ground. At least until we run into more new officers, more new species like that tentacled officer who thought enough to plant the ambush underground.

Pam offered some silent support on that. Rett had taken that over-sight, not to mention the fiasco of Yixolryn agents Mott and Shamos, personally.

No matter where they come from, the troopers will fight, because they fear the Coalition more than they do us. There's still more of the enemy, a lot more now, in this system than there are Nyorfian citizens. If we fail here, Pam, the chances of losing are guaranteed. If we succeed here and take back Nyorfias, we still have to take Epnoce.

Pam felt the deep-rooted dread in Rett's next thought so strongly her mental essence got goosebumps.

And we've heard what happened on other worlds that put up resistance or challenged the Yixolryn sense of importance. If they feel really threatened, they just might decide to open up some clear area in this little corner of the quadrant. All it would take is a tiny antimatter missile from space, or a wipe to both our planets with thermonuclears and other weapons of mass destruction.

Rett's own shiver was not entirely from the frigid water in which she crouched.

They have that capability, we know that. We're just not sure if the enemy forces already in this system have those weapons. It's a fair guess they don't, or they'd have made threats already. They didn't expect the resistance we gave—and still are giving. Possibly, they're waiting long enough to get that ordnance from whatever part of the galaxy they came from.

~But now those guys are here, the GTC, whoever they are, it won't,~ Pam thought. ~Right?~

We're hoping so. Rett stifled another physical shudder, glanced at her chrono…few more minutes. *Your world isn't a member of the Galactic Trade Commission?* she asked then in surprise.

~Shit,~ Pam thought. ~I don't even know if we're in the same universe. You'll have to tell me about it later. But if they have such extreme technology, why haven't they simply used it already? You guys are fighting them with…such low-tech weapons.~

That'll make their purpose in coming here in the first place nonexistent. They want our resources—intact. We have everything here. Pure water. Minerals. Wood. Food. People as slave labor to work for them. Bodies to fill ranks in the military for the next system on the list. Our system makes an ideal way station—a rest stop in the middle of nowhere where ships can refuel, take on water and food. They're not going to ruin that unless they absolutely have to. They'll hold back on a total wipeout as long as possible. Rett shifted a little, her movement barely causing a ripple. *But there's no way to really predict anything, is there? What will come, will come. The only thing we Nyorfians know is we're not giving up.*

Overwhelmed by both the strength of Rett's commitment and what clearly was the conclusion of the longest explanation of anything the Nyorfian had yet to volunteer, Pam didn't push her luck to try for more. ~Thanks for letting me know all this. I'll try not to screw it up. And…good luck.~ She pulled back to allow the sergeant to prepare for the battle ahead, making the careful adjustments she had had plenty of opportunity to practice since being merged. Just enough to see and understand.

Rett checked her chrono again. Those charges a demolition patrol had set earlier would go off…now. Her team ducked momentarily as debris from the bunker, guardhouses, and barracks on their side of the river fell among them in its own type of rain. Great splashes of water sheeted over them, glittering lurid oranges and yellows from the flares of explosions; helping to obliterate their movements. They whipped into action.

The night was no longer peacefully quiet. In those precious first minutes of enemy surprise, F-troop emerged from the downpour and gloom. Rett had time to think how strange it was, for once, not to engage in combat with the typical silence the enemy often found so unnerving. With the others she yelled and shouted and whistled and made any sort of noise she could think of. She was sure Pam helped her think of a few. Behind them, the infantry units waiting for their signals added to the din. Those boisterous sounds, combined with the river's own rushing flow, amplified by the damp and rain, and punctuated with the distinctive crackle and *bbrrBBRRIPP!* of small arms fire, reverberated across the once sleepy river valley.

* * * * *

AFTER A FEW MINUTES, WHEN the shocked enemy troopers started recovering their wits, bolts of SMG lightning stabbed deadly glowing pathways in the night.

The enemy officer now in charge of bridge defense was in a hot panic. The gelatinous mass of its body quivered with such violence the humanoid subordinate thought the alien might lose cohesion. "Call Circle for reinforcements!" it yelled at the subordinate. "The entire Free Army is out there! Didn't someone say there were three armored divisions, too?"

The subordinate never thought he would miss the massive Unethi, Captain Thip. But since Thip had died in one of the first explosions, this useless alien was in charge. Thip hadn't been a pleasant commander, but it never lost its reason and never, ever panicked.

"Four, sir, and com is destroyed! Short-range links are being jammed! Sensors too. There's no way to tell how many or where they're coming from."

"Try to round up some troops. We have to try to get back and…" The officer's speech ended in a shivering wail and the wide-eyed subordinate watched as the thin membrane keeping the jelly-like flesh of the alien in place burst. The armor meant to deflect pulses or beams from energy weapons did nothing to protect anyone from Nyorfian bullets.

The subordinate barely avoided being splashed with the noxious remains. He took one look at the puddle and dribbles of gunk dissolving whatever it touched: armor, metal, everything—then ducked out and ran.

* * * * *

RETT AND THOSE WITH HER loped and splashed through water thigh-deep in most spots to make sure the infantry units covered the mostly flooded out weapons emplacements and bunkers on the riverbanks. There was no doubt they caught the enemy totally by surprise. Trebor's people were already near the middle of the bridge span.

Once their side of the river was secured, she whistled up her group. They went to back up Trebor's squad, now encountering stiff resistance as the enemy, most of them on the far side, began to realize they were about to get caught in the middle of a major disaster. She guessed the threat of failing and having to face the wrath of the Leader in Circle was all it took to motivate most of these troopers, since they started throwing themselves into fighting with uncharacteristic self-sacrifice.

* * * * *

CORPORAL ARIAM COMPLETED ARMING THE small explosive charges attached to enemy transport vehicles parked some distance from the bridge. The mud-crusted condition of them indicated why she didn't spot them here on a scan earlier. They were probably being used for patrol, or running back and forth from Circle. On seeing them, she'd left her core group with Kraym to take care of these problems herself.

Everything was going according to plan and well ahead of schedule. *Nothing like a good surprise,* thought Ariam. Keeping an ear to her pcom and a wary eye for any troopers intent on escape, she finished her work by touch alone. Her attention fixed on the bulk of another vehicle about thirty lengths to her left. What was it? Certainly not a rover. Another something not present in the scans earlier.

Ariam grimaced, a mental reminder she'd set alerting her that Worren hadn't commed her yet. He should have been in position by now, despite the large loop his group had to make.

Pushing away from the vehicles, she slithered back through the cold muddy water and stayed low until she was clear of them. As she straightened, she spotted figures splashing through puddles and mud, just off the road, racing hard for the cover of brush some two hundred lengths distant. Cueing her pcom, she warned the Nyorfian GIs of her intention and before the fleeing troopers could reach that line, Ariam snapped her weapon to her shoulder and fired into the group three times. Three figures dropped, the other four angled away, hearing the loud fierce yells from the infantry units waiting in that cover for just such an occurrence.

"That direction won't help you guys much, either," murmured Ariam, moving for a better position. Behind her, the five troop rovers exploded. She didn't want to get any farther from the bridge and things happening back there. That was the place she should be in right now. But what was keeping Worren?

"Fang two, this is Fang Six, we're live."

Finally. Good. She acknowledged. "Confirm live, Fang Six. I want to hear about what held you back later. Right now you've four targets heading your way."

"Sorry about that, Fang Two." His voice held a ripple of wry amusement. "Sufficient for the moment to say what delayed us is no longer an issue. Targets acquired," The junior corporal paused. Ariam heard four quick shots from that direction. "And down."

* * * * *

SMG FIRE RICOCHETED DANGEROUSLY FROM quartzite bridge construction, especially where previous scores melted the crystalline stone to glassy patches. Rett pcom'ed a warning to alert her people as she jumped back to avoid such a burst.

The number of enemy troopers on the bridge declined rapidly as commando crossfire caught them in the middle. She had no worries her people might hit each other: they trained specifically for work like this. She left the infantry units off the bridge assault for that particular reason.

The SMG fire over here was heavy enough and dangerously concentrated due to the narrowness of the structure and tendency of the energy beams to reflect off the glossy patches of melted quartzite or enemy armor. The infantry units already on the Circle bank had orders to fire anywhere except directly toward the bridge. The others waited for a signal to back up if they were needed; if not, take over when the position was secured.

A flare of energy to the side brought her weapon around to pick off a trooper as he leaped from the bridge. The armored figure jerked before disappearing into the swollen river. Maybe she did him a favor: armored troopers didn't float very well, and that water was fast and cold. She knew she would prefer being dead instead of drowning in panic. She caught a brief glimpse of heavy energy weapons fire from the far side of the bridge and heard terse pcom transmissions from the infantry units and a few of her own people on that side.

Good deities, she thought, listening in as Worren told Ariam what delayed him. With the flooding, the Coalition bivouacs had moved back farther, one of them so far back Worren's squad had intercepted it. The troopers there had not been anywhere near their weapons. Eighty troopers taken and secured, no shots fired, no casualties. A few wanted to die of embarrassment from getting caught so...unexpectedly, but that didn't count.

Ariam pcom'ed an officer from her infantry detachment to send a patrol back to the spot as a guard, and things continued.

Despite everything else going on, Rett had to allow herself a chuckle. She couldn't wait for the full version. Then realization dawned. They were doing it. Despite the odds, they were going to get this bridge. But the real battle will be for Circle, if they held this bridge long enough to move forward there! She focused her mind fully back on business as she twisted aside and slammed the commando ahead of her out of another reflective burst that almost caught the both of them.

149

"Careful, Ewayn!"

He sent her a quick, tight grin, brushing at a sleeve. In spite of the heavy rain, that area of his arm was scorched and smoking. "Thanks, Sarge!" He moved ahead.

Then Med began reporting casualties.

* * * * *

SHAKING HER HEAD A LITTLE after closing com with Worren, Ariam turned back to her end of the bridge. Then she stopped short, skin crawling, realizing she was within reach of the unusual vehicle she'd spotted earlier.

East Ocean Province. Hundei Inlet. The location popped into her mind as soon as she recognized the threatening shape. No mistake at this range. She swallowed. She'd been told about vehicles like this.

Kraym, Rett, Trebor, and Nerrah had personal experience with them. All of them had said they hoped not to be on the firing end of one of these ever again.

They probably brought them in when the river crested. But how many? If there were more of these things, they were in trouble. These rovers were nearly impossible to breach or blow up. The only way to make them vulnerable was to flip them over, and that was tricky enough.

Big, armored, and low profile, the amphibious rover squatted close to the mucky ground and seemed to stare at Ariam with the same wary intent she regarded it. There were people inside. She briefly touched at least ten minds enough to know they were very aware of her.

Had it been out, like the others, or has it just come in from Circle, or was it camouflaged somehow in the daylight? Or, thought Ariam with a swallow, were they able to block it from being detected, the same way she heard this thing was capable of bouncing off any type of weapons fire?

None of that mattered right now. What mattered was the amphirover's slow, silent advance on Ariam's position.

Shit, move! She jumped, but the damage was done already: to Ariam's night-adjusted vision. Before she could avert her gaze, eight blue-white little suns flared with stunning brightness, searing into her wide-open pupils. She couldn't see a thing.

Listening intently, tensing for action, she knew the vehicle stopped. Heard the sliding swish of a well-lubricated door opening. Sensed the threat of a small group of troopers closing in on her. Physically blinded, but ready, she concentrated every ounce of her combat sense and empathic awareness on the enemy. Even as her body geared into close combat mode, she found a second to curse herself for her carelessness.

No time to tiff about it now! Ahead, eye level! her mind ordered.

Ariam's rifle butt crunched into a trooper's face and she felt and heard the dull splintering of bone and plastic. She reversed the gun's direction abruptly and felt it solidly connect under the jaw of another. Ariam spun out of the way as that one fell. She shoved the muzzle of her rifle forward until it met resistance and then squeezed the trigger. Another went down.

Something hard slammed her arm, causing instant numbness from shoulder to fingertips. A heavy, savage tug on her weapon almost threw her off balance. She didn't try to hang on. Instead, Ariam instinctively lunged forward, knife in her good hand, extending the compressed blades in a smooth reflex. She whipped around and planted the long blade with a twisting motion; felt the metal grate against bones; felt hot blood gush over her arm. The trooper screamed horribly as her wrist jerked downward, slicing with ease through armor meant primarily to deflect energy beams. She backfisted another with the same hand, the hilt of the knife adding the unyielding force of a hammer blow. A garbled sound and a thumping splash behind her told its own tale.

Ariam tried to maneuver for a more secure position. Those troopers—and parts of troopers—scattered on the ground made the already wet footing even more treacherous.

How many more? At least four were out of action, dead or disabled. She sensed six, maybe seven others. It was hard to tell, some of the more alien minds or more unemotional ones didn't make as strong an impression as others. Her body whipped aside to avoid a blow from behind and the unfortunate trooper went down hard as Ariam's own reverse roundhouse kick solidly connected in the open space between chest armor and hips. She followed through with her long knife.

* * * * *

Corporal Kraym had seen the low-slung vehicle's rack lights flare and caught sight of Ariam in the brightness. A stab of worry flashed through him. Worren's squad was too far to assist, so was the infantry covering the woods and road. He had all he could handle right here. Here, where Ariam was supposed to have rejoined their group to cope with the remaining troopers on the riverbank.

Normally he'd only be worried about those people stupid enough to attack Ariam. The platoon second's graceful, slender appearance fooled quite a few people. She was about as fragile as half a ton of solid steel.

That thought did little to reassure him. But as much as he wanted to go, he couldn't. His job was right here, and he had to see it through.

* * * * *

ARIAM FELL FORWARD AS A leg sweep caught her behind the knees. She attempted to roll out before they pinned her down. Her numb arm was recovering some sensation; however right now it was still more handicap than help. She scrambled to get back on her feet, to keep moving.

She lost the knife in the attempt to regain her feet and again her legs went out from under her. As Ariam blindly fought for her balance and her life on the treacherous, slippery ground, she knew she wasn't going to recover.

Ariam cursed, rolling away only to find another trooper forcing her back. Time to call for help. The sensitive pickup on her pcom immediately connected with the softest of voice commands. "Com connect—"

A foot crashed into her chest. Any message Ariam intended to send went with the breath forced from her lungs.

1.2.4 WIDE RIVER GAP (SOUTH BANK)
NORTH CENTRAL CENTERLAND PROVINCE, NYORFIAS
0535.06.30 (LOCAL RECKONING)

KRAYM FELT SOME RELIEF AS individual commandos and GI patrols started pcom'ing in with all clears; things were quieting down rapidly. He was busy fielding pcom transmissions for several minutes, somewhere in the back of his mind hardly believing they'd been successful, as well as internally lamenting the reports of injuries and losses taken on this side of the bridge.

He heard no news of casualties from the rest of F-troop yet, but knew there had to be some injuries, at least. The fire had been hard and thick, he'd taken a few handfuls of grazes himself. Made him glad for the sheeting rain: at least it cooled the burns, making them easier to ignore.

He remained hopeful. Once he heard the platoon leader's all clear and started the unit's check-in procedure, he'd know the status. Only then would he relax a bit.

There. The welcomest sound he'd heard in a long night of sound of every description and then some. The long awaited all clear whistle was followed by another signaling the rest of the infantry to move up.

Then he heard a rush of static over his pcom receiver. Someone tried to connect and activated the general frequency, but either changed their mind or—

Ariam.

"Com connect Fang two!" Kraym told his pcom. "Fang two, this is Fang three. Status!"

Not even static answered this time.

"Kraym!"

He turned toward the bridge, in the direction of his platoon leader's voice.

Sergeant Rett squished through the rain to his side. "Well, we did it. You only gave me a partial clear on this side, I couldn't get Ariam just now, I think she's having some trouble—*Hey!*"

She instantly slapped a clip of explosive rounds to her weapon and brought it up. Finally spotting what his platoon leader had targeted, Kraym swiftly forced the muzzle down, causing Rett's shot to go wild.

"No, Sarge!"

"Shit, Corporal, what under the flaming sun are you trying to do? That vehicle can run mud, water, or road! Get past everything we set up over there!"

"You couldn't dent it anyway."

"They can be flipped," grated his platoon leader, and reminding him just how strong she was, shook off his grip and took aim once more.

Kraym clamped his hand over her weapon with determination. "Sarge, they have Ariam, I think."

"They have *what?*" Sergeant Rett relaxed her aim so fast Kraym almost lost his balance. By that time, the speeding amphirover was well out of range for anything save a SMG shot to be effective. The sergeant cursed savagely again, rounding in on him with a snarl. The flat of her hand shoved into his chest and gathered a fistful of jacket and uniform.

Kraym had seen the full force of the unusual strength his platoon leader possessed unleashed only in combat. Now it was turned on him. Only his toes touched the ground. Combined now with her fury, it chilled him to the bone.

"I hope you said that amphirover was full of kids and babies, Corporal. Because that's the *only* excuse that's going to keep your ass out of trouble."

He took a breath. "I'm sorry, Sergeant, I said I think they have Ariam. I'm not sure. I think you're right about her being in trouble. I couldn't get a response from her on the com."

"Well, damn it then, Corporal, *make* sure." Voice low and deadly, she emphasized her anger with a hard shake. "And when you're finished, I'm going to kick your ass from here to Epnoce!" Kraym's heels squelched back into the mucky ground as she released her hold. "Com connect Fang four!" the sergeant snapped. "Take over check in."

"Fang leader, take over check in confirmed," replied Trebor's deep voice. "I'll report back shortly."

She cut her com. "Move it, Corporal Kraym!" she ordered harshly, then abruptly turned back to the bridge, already back on com, this time with Med.

Under other circumstances, his leader's level of tiff would have frozen Kraym solid instead of merely causing a chill. He'd been out of line, Ariam captured or not. In this sort of situation, any of them were expendable and they knew it.

But he had to be sure.

Kraym bolted in the general direction the transport had been. He sensed no danger, kept his weapon ready anyway, and as he ran, switched on his powerful handlight, sweeping the beam over the wet ground.

His beam froze on the site of violence. Then he moved the light over six dead troopers, including one that had been neatly eviscerated. Stopped again on a black headband, still dry enough to float in a mud-clouded puddle. A few feet away lay a TT-1 automatic rifle. Over there in the sodden grass, a water-filled depression showed where the heavily armored amphibious rover had rested before moving out. His gaze followed the flattened path through the waterlogged growth. They had been moving fast. Even if he hadn't seen them, he knew a rover's turbofans didn't leave a path like that through dry or wet terrain unless running hard.

A quiet whistle alerted the corporal to the platoon leader's presence, then Rett moved up to stand next to him.

"Kraym," she said softly.

"Sarge, I—"

There was great weariness in the sergeant's voice. "Can't change what happened. Just tell me you didn't see that vehicle until I aimed at it."

Kraym adjusted his lenses. He wasn't going to lie about it, not even to avoid getting into trouble. "I saw it earlier, stationary, about twenty minutes ago. It flashed the lights and I saw Ariam nearby. We were hot then, so I couldn't pay attention to anything beyond that. But no. I didn't see it again until you took aim at it."

"I missed," she said then. "Sorry for jumping in your face like that."

Sensing this was not the time to argue, Kraym just asked: "F-troop call in clear?"

"No." Her voice was tight. "Three dead, five serious and going home for good if they make it that far, ten minor that will be out for a while, and everyone else has something scraped, burned, or grazed but is still good to go. Except for one. Med says Gerrale won't make it. She wants me. I'm going to need your help."

Kraym closed his eyes for a second and shook his head. He knew that Gerrale had gone down, but didn't know it had been that bad. "Sarge…"

"We had a tough fight, Kraym, you know that. If that SMG fire was any more solid we would've been able to walk on it. The infantry lost thirty-eight. All in all, it's pretty damn amazing we didn't lose more."

She gripped Kraym's arm, then her hand slipped off his sleeve as if suddenly weakened. Maybe it was, or maybe it felt that way because she left his side and went to scoop up Ariam's headband. Kraym adjusted the width of the light on his shoulder, enough to see the rain or the puddle hadn't yet removed some red streaks and blotches still spreading on the material.

The sergeant cursed softly and shoved the headband in her belt. She went to pick up Ariam's weapon, sparing a brief glance at the grotesquely sprawled bodies of the dead troopers before tossing the TT-1 to Kraym. Then she reached for Ariam's long knife, still embedded in one of the dead, wrenching it free with a sharp, savage motion. She swished it in a puddle, wiped it on the grass, tucked it into her shoulder harness.

Finally the sergeant spoke. "We can't worry about Ariam now."

"I know that, Sarge."

"Let's go, Kraym," she said, her voice heavy. "We need to get back to the other side. I have a rover standing by with some of our other casualties Med wants to see."

"He just doesn't seem to trust other medtechs, does he?"

The sergeant just shrugged. "Come on. I'm…going to need time for Gerrale. And we don't have much before we have to move on."

* * * * *

WISHING SHE COULD PRESS HER hands against her throbbing, pounding head, Ariam hunched forward, willing her brain not to explode. Her wrists were bound behind her back with the webbing from a weapon sling, and if she kept them from retying her, she could work free in a few seconds. First, she had to clear her head and get her breath, or nothing would work.

Very much aware of the five enemy weapons aimed in her direction, she didn't move. Her breathing produced the only movement in her body. As she started rerouting the pain into different avenues and forced her mind to sharpen, her level of tiff rose. All the possibilities and should-have-beens crowded into her head, making it pound harder.

Well, she wasn't going to waste time with the "if onlys". She was here now, and she had to find a way out.

"Someone got a light? Let's see exactly what we caught," suggested a voice.

Ariam straightened up, then blinked her still-sore eyes in the dim light that turned upon her.

"It's one of those damned commandos!"

"We should just kill her right now," said a female voice harshly. "Killer's people are nothing but trouble."

"We should take her in. She's a senior corporal, so she's either one of Killer's squad leaders or a second. Might be important to us," a third voice said reasonably.

"I'd just as soon kill them off, before they kill us!" insisted the woman's voice.

"Yeah," agreed the first trooper. "Look what happens whenever we think Killer's out of action. Less than a month ago—"

"No, Pym's right," said someone else, with authority in her voice. "We'll take her to the Leader. Commander Iheolon should be interested too. They might get information about that attack from her, as well."

"I'd like to know where they came up with so many people," said someone else. "They must've had a couple divisions hidden somewhere.

Didn't think there were that many left, let alone in this zone. At any rate, since we're bringing back a warning and one of Killer's people, we should get some kind of reward!"

At the mention of Commander Iheolon, Ariam's stomach clenched. She could hardly make out the five faces behind the handlight. The blood trickling into her eyes didn't help, but she held still. Maybe they'd think her too badly hurt or scared to make trouble. Under the cloak of a passive, injured appearance, she alertly watched for her chance to make a break for freedom.

The trooper holding the light moved closer.

"Careful, Pym. She—"

"Be reasonable, Curter. Just keep me covered. I want to look at this cut, just to make sure she doesn't bleed to death before we get her back."

"Yeah, you know how Commander Iheolon likes them, alive and kicking, so to speak!" said the authoritative female voice. "We'll have to tie her up better, too. What do we have? Anyone have manacles?"

"You," said the one named Pym to Ariam, "just keep still."

Ariam detonated into movement like one of her explosive charges. Sliding her wrists free, she rammed into the big trooper, knocking him back into a tangle with three of his comrades. She used the rebound motion to launch herself toward the half open rear hatch of the amphirover. Lightning struck. She knew she went down hard because she heard the thump, but didn't feel a thing as she went down a handspan from her goal.

* * * * *

RETT'S SOUL QUIVERED AS MED turned toward her. The expression on the medtech's normally sour face had been replaced by one of terrible, bitter regret. He gave her a succinct list of Gerrale's injuries and concluded simply: "I'm sorry, Sarge."

Knowing his admission that nothing could be done for Gerrale was, on a level for Med, the same as surrendering to the enemy without a fight, Rett could only give his shoulder a brief touch of appreciation. She had no words for Med. He turned back to the figure he knelt alongside, and with a gentle, loving and final gesture of farewell, Med took himself off to tend to the other wounded she and Kraym had brought from the other side.

Feeling as if every move she made was hampered by thick, invisible mud, she took the last two steps forward. She forced all emotion from her thoughts. There were several methods she could employ for what she had to do. The preferred technique was silent, involving no fire-arms discharge. But in Gerrale's condition, conscious and already in unimaginable pain, the stunner would be more merciful. In the right location, a direct shot, even from a stunner, would cause instant death.

Gerrale lay in the position the blast had left her, half-in, half-out of a cold, shallow puddle. The debris that had broken her back, ruptured internal organs, and crushed everything else from the hips downward, had been removed.

How long has she been here, like this? Rett had commed her once, received a reply from Gerrale herself that she was injured and not able for movement. But that was all.

Rett settled her length alongside her dying comrade, making as much contact as she could without causing more discomfort. Carefully, so, so carefully, she gathered Gerrale into her arms, feeling the wounded woman's response to her presence with every pore: relief, acceptance, and a curious sensation of concern.

Rett kissed her, whispering, "Gerrale, I'm here."

Gerrale's lips moved. *I know.* Gerrale swallowed and tried to speak again, a twist of worry tightening her features. *Steffi...?*

"Steffi's fine. I'm sorry she isn't here. What should I tell her?"

I'm sorry. I love you. Be happy.

"I'll tell her," whispered Rett, smoothing a strand of damp hair. "I'll make sure she's all right, we all will." Her eyes burned, but she forced them to remain dry.

Corporal Kraym's large, reassuring presence, just behind her, was close enough that Rett felt the heat from his body. His silent support gave her the strength to do what she must, if Gerrale still wanted it so. "Gerrale, you asked me for help, I'm here to give it. I need to be sure this is what you want."

Gerrale finally opened her tawny eyes and locked gazes with Rett. Peaceful now and beyond exhaustion, her face showed nothing except ultimate confidence and trust. Rett forced her free hand to her weapons belt, unholstered her sidearm, and brought it within Gerrale's range of vision.

Gerrale, in too much pain to speak, nodded, a tiny motion of affirmation. She relaxed in acceptance and profound relief as she felt the muzzle of Rett's hand stunner in close, cold, firm contact with the skin above her left ear.

Rett's mind locked onto her mission, shutting out all outside interference, all her other thoughts and emotions. All she saw was Gerrale's face, right in front of hers.

Her gaze locked unwaveringly with that of her sister-in-arms. "Are you sure?" she asked her again, gently.

Gerrale managed to smile slightly, encouragingly, with another slight nod and expressive look that went beyond pain. Her reply was verbal, but more of an exhale than a spoken "yes". Gerrale relaxed even farther into Rett's supporting embrace.

"I love you, Gerrale," Rett told her softly, "we all do. You'll always be with us. Thank you."

Rett kissed her again and Gerrale closed her eyes peacefully, the small smile on her face unforced, her head resting into the cold contact of Rett's weapon. *Do it now,* said Gerrale's lips soundlessly.

Her left hand steadied her comrade's head and her right forefinger touched the firing switch.

She held Gerrale closely afterward, dimly aware of Pam with her, in full support, yet also aware of barely suppressed...shock? Regret? Something unidentifiable, yet understandable.

Something Rett silently appreciated Pam's holding back.

* * * * *

KRAYM FELT THE THICK SENSATION of time slowing to a crawl. After he heard her weapon discharge, a shudder rocked him from heels to head and his skin puckered with chillbumps that had nothing to do with the cold wet rain or the puddle in which he knelt.

He could imagine that, for his platoon leader, it must have felt as if she spent ten years instead of two minutes in that puddle with Gerrale. Now it was over, that time stopped cold. Still, he waited another agonizing minute, kneeling in silence, taking deep breaths. When he felt calm and composed, he reached out to help his platoon leader stand.

"Come on, Sarge." His grip on her arm was steady. She didn't resist; didn't really help him either, standing in a sort of trance as he took her sidearm from her, returning it to the holster on her belt.

Extracting a wipe from a utility belt pocket, he cleaned her left hand, then examined the right. Already the blisters were forming from the ends of her long fingers to her forearm: one of the hazards of making such a close range shot with an energy weapon, even a small one. She stood passive as he found some burn spray among the medical supplies in his utility belt and applied it to keep the swelling and blistering down. She'd need to use that hand for other things. Then he started walking her away, all the while reminding her of the duties still awaiting them both.

By the third step Kraym felt the tautness return to her muscles and was able to drop his supportive grip. He kept close nevertheless. "You back?"

She kept walking and didn't look at him. "Yes. Thanks."

"Sure."

"Let's wrap things up here."

1.2.5 YIXOLRYN COALITION HQ, CIRCLE
OFFICE OF THE LEADER
0535.06.31 (LOCAL RECKONING)

THE LEADER EYED ARIAM WITH keen interest. Here was one of those Sergeant Killer commandos. More virulent than plague, the lot of them. What should he do with her? He let his gaze travel slowly over the young corporal, noticing she appeared soft and fragile, the opposite of Killer. Yet, this woman killed six troopers, wounded three more in close combat, and almost succeeded in escaping on the way to his headquarters.

Like her platoon leader, she stood straight and tall despite her battered condition. Unlike Killer, the younger woman's large gray eyes seemed dazed and clouded with uncertainty. Killer's dark eyes had been clear and cold, cold enough to give the Leader chills just thinking about the comparison. Back to this one. Her general expression was the familiar, emotionless one he'd come to expect from his Nyorfian prisoners, at least at first! Maybe she would be easier to persuade than the others, despite the fact she endured her initial interrogation in a stoic silence.

Should he turn her over to Iheolon's man, Jaq Pym? Sure he was a Zetinorian and having him in the same room, even at the far end of this large office, was almost unbearable. But the humanoid trooper had quite a reputation for inducing conversation from reluctant Nyorfians, especially females. They just couldn't seem to resist his good looks—well, the humanoid standard of what passed for good looks—and his famous approach of wanting to help them, wanting to defect. And when that didn't work...

The Zetinorian had other methods, methods more subtle than those of his superior, Commander Iheolon, but just as effective and ultimately devastating. Iheolon even had to admit he had no idea exactly what Pym did, yet he always got results.

Fury heated his belly as the Leader remembered the humiliating escape by Killer's platoon some two tendays ago. Just when he'd had them all in his grasp! His glance went from Ariam to the data display on his desk.

Now he would find the details concerning this young woman. After that, he'd decide his course of action. Good thing his agents, the ones the Nyorfians knew as Mott and Shamos, had managed to send him these files on Killer and her platoon before making their escape.

"So you are one of Sergeant Killer's valiant—and resourceful—troop," said the Leader finally. Picking up Ariam's ID discs from his desk, he detached one from the chain and slid it into a drive slot.

"Ah, yes. Ariam, Corporal." He stopped short, a sharp sense of satisfaction replacing the angry heat of moments before. "Yes," he said, hissing out the word with extreme pleasure. He glanced quickly over the basic information the small ID disk offered, then spoke her ID number to bring up a cross-reference file. "And here's your file, very interesting, indeed. An expert marksman, demolition a specialty. Hmm. I see here your father is yet another who is fairly high on our list of most annoying Nyorfians. That's good to know." He looked up to see if she reacted to that, but she stood as if frozen. Not what he expected from the person who most likely effected the mass escape that Commander Iheolon had tried to warn him about. It had grated on every nerve he had to admit he should have listened, but maybe he had a chance to turn things around now. "And you're psi talented—high empathy rating...very valuable."

＊ ＊ ＊ ＊ ＊

THE LEADER HAD THEIR FILES.

Ariam forced her expression to remain the same. She had been afraid that this was what happened to the 52nd's copies of F-troop's command level files. In field units, such information was kept on DSUs instead of being stored on centrally accessed networks. Colonel Evard said F-troop's data storage unit was missing. They thought that maybe Shamos and Mott destroyed it along with most of the records that might have contained incriminating evidence or lead to other Coalition agents among the Nyorfian population.

But this was worse than any of that. Certain information on individuals wasn't released on publicly available records, like those even the Coalition could access from an ID disc or normally secured Omni. But the command level records went deeper—not as deep or detailed as their full records only the Special Forces kept, but deep and detailed enough. Ariam felt a little queasy thinking of the implications.

The Leader looked up. "Sergeant Killer's second-in-command, with Corporal Kraym. You've been in Special Forces a little over six years, two years with this platoon. Excellent record. I fail to understand the Nyorfian policy of allowing so much choice in matters of advancement." The Leader leaned back, flicking at his data display with a finger. "Both you and your platoon leader would have made formidable officers by now. Like your father is. Have you ever stopped to think your refusals hindered the goals of the Free Army?"

If they needed officers to kick their asses into action like his Coalition troopers did, then yes, thought Ariam. But the Nyorfian military didn't operate that way.

"What are the plans now, after the bridge? An attack on Circle, perhaps?" He laughed in derision. "What does your psychic awareness tell you about that? Your people should realize by now it's impossible to keep fighting. We have a virtually unlimited supply of troops and your tiny little population is half that it was ten years ago! No matter how many personnel you've got out there, we have more. Your petty victories are meaningless!"

Ariam stared on a spot in the wall behind the Leader's thinly haired head and said nothing.

"Trooper Pym!"

"Sir!"

"Stay where you are," the Leader said quickly, and Ariam saw something that looked like a grimace cross the repulsive gray face of the Yixolryn.

"I'm going to let you have this one. Take some time to read over her records and then see what you can get out of her. Don't bruise that pretty face much more than it already is, you know we want them to be identifiable. And keep any other damage minimal. I have plans for this Nyorfian corporal." He smiled obnoxiously. "*Big* plans." His tiny eyes fixed on Ariam and his voice turned perversely pleasant. "Commander Iheolon tells me Trooper Pym is quite the expert at starting up a conversation."

For a half second, no more, Ariam thought she wouldn't mind talking with the big trooper. She didn't allow her expression or focal point to change, although she was tempted to take another look at him. She distinctly felt there was something worth knowing about Trooper Jaq Pym. And what she was getting from him was anything but the emotions she'd expect from someone who was going to torture or rape or whatever else to break her composure.

She stifled such a ridiculous idea as quickly as she thought it. He was the enemy and Ariam wasn't telling anyone anything worth knowing. No matter what happened!

1.2.6 WIDE RIVER GAP (SOUTH BANK)
NORTH CENTRAL CENTERLAND PROVINCE, NYORFIAS
0535.06.31 (LOCAL RECKONING)

RETT SENT HER REPORTS OVER to the 415th's battalion clerk who'd been designated to handle this operation's clerical needs and slowly replaced her Omni in its belt holder.

Infantry had thirty-eight killed, two hundred and thirty-six wounded. Among those, twenty would be permanently off active duty and sixty were in serious condition. All the infantry casualties had been the selected few, about three hundred and fifty in all, who had participated in the actual attack on both sides of the bridge. Most of them were treated and released, the rest would be out anywhere from a matter of days to a month or so. Thank all deities. And they had fought well by all accounts.

Three of her platoon had been killed outright taking that bridge. One given mercy. Five hurt badly enough to be off Active for good. Eight more who should have been out a few days at least, but Med and Rett both knew would be too hot to restrict until this operation was complete. Those eight had to be satisfied with being allowed to go on in a limited capacity, but going on was what they wanted.

Out of forty-one individuals, twenty-two of them had some sort of graze, burn, muscle strain, or bruise. Such things, however, in F-troop's opinion, were normal, minor, and they were good to go.

Only Corporal Worren's people had escaped any real injury.

And there was one missing in action.

Rett felt ten times her age of twenty-eight Standard as she resolutely completed each step between now and the next phase of the mission. Her duties kept her mind focused. Personal thoughts weren't allowed to interfere. But she was running out of things to do. As her list dwindled, her agitation increased.

Feeling the direction of Rett's thoughts, Pam eased from her corner. She didn't care if Rett yelled at her now. That would be a good thing. Better than heaping all this undeserved guilt over things out of her control on her own head. And then, later, shoving it all with the seething accumulation of other ugly things buried away in a festering mass that would never go away. No, it would just sit quietly like a cancer and wait for an opportune moment to grow and kill her from the inside out.

Feeling Pam's thoughts surface, Rett took a breath and thought sharply, *This is* not *a good time, Pam.*

~Oh yes, it is. It's the best time. And I'm in a pretty good spot right now, Sergeant. If it's going to take a dimwitted alien mindforce to kick you in the ass, then I'm going to do it.~

Pam's firm thoughts still echoed the fear, dark sorrow, and grief Rett was keeping buried firmly beneath her dwindling task list.

~Look. Like you told me, this is a war. You can't change what happened, or stopped it from happening. I'm sorry people you love were killed, hurt badly. I'm sorry Ariam is missing, but she's alive, so there's a chance you're going to get her back. And about Gerrale, you should be counting yourself damned lucky you had time to communicate with her at all, to tell her thanks and goodbye, much less be able to give her what almost anyone would like to have in the same situation. No one wants to suffer.~

Rett clenched her teeth hard and glanced around in case she had a reaction that was going to betray her. On one level, she knew Pam meant only to divert her. No doubt Rett craved diversion, which was why she was starting to panic as her tasks were completed. And there was no denying their shared sense of loss and tragedy.

But her response thought was sharp and angry and fueled with a bitter need to retaliate at something, anything. Even if she hurt herself to get at it. Namely Pam.

You don't understand, Pam. It's the first time I've ever lost anyone from F-troop, dead or to the enemy. And the first time I've ever had to do what I did before! I've never had to give mercy—I've only backed up the person doing it, like Kraym did for me. For my old platoon leader from C-troop, for a few others, more times than I want to remember. That was hard enough.

Pam dug in firmly, letting Rett's unfiltered backlash crash over her like a wave. She didn't back off on either the sympathetic support or unyielding fact that Rett had to push onward with present responsibilities.

Rett felt this, but still lashed out with venom.

Just back off. After two years, eight hundred and forty seven missions with F-troop with no one killed—hurt, yeah, out for a while, yeah, but not killed—it's kind of tough to take now, okay? These aren't just people under my command and they're more than people I'm responsible for. More than my friends. They're my family. You've never had to...

For a brief instant, Rett felt something from Pam that paralleled her feelings of before. A brief flash, barely coherent; enough for Rett to know.

This time, it was Pam who firmly shut off her recollection.

You did. Rett's bitter anger faded as swiftly as it had come. *You...*

~Forget that,~ Pam thought, her mental tone rough as she jerked aside her own pained memories.

It doesn't matter he wasn't humanoid. You were friends, and you loved him.

Pam cut in sharply. ~The situation has no comparison. I'm sorry. You're right, but you can't blame yourself. You can't blame Evard. You can blame the war. That's where it should go. So yes, you can tell me to back off and I will, now. But that was all I was trying to point out.~ Pam's by now familiar mental voice echoed the helpless anger, pain, and loss of Rett's own thoughts. ~And don't fuck with me, Rett, because I'm right here and I know what you feel!~

I know you do, Rett thought back, gently now. *Thanks for grieving with me. And for being there—for being here with me. I'm sorry.*

~No problem, Rett. That's what friends are for.~

Rett paused, considering, knowing of all the labels good and bad she'd ever used for Pam, she never had applied the one of "friend". Until now. She smiled a bit ruefully inward and out. *Thanks, Pam.* She kept it simple, knowing Pam would understand. From the warm feeling that came to replace the hurt, cold ones, Rett knew she did.

"You okay, Sarge?"

She composed her face before turning to greet Kraym, checking him carefully with eyes and energy sense. In the brief interval they had here, he'd taken the task of collecting the personal gear of F-troop's dead. Later, she would have to sort it all out for shipment to the victim's families, adding whatever official documents, commendations, and other personal gear that was stored at 52nd HQ. But that would be later, much later, when this mission was complete. "For now, yes. And you?"

"Nothing time won't cure," he said with his usual truthfulness.

She nodded to the Omni in his hand. "You've news?"

The corporal handed her his device. "I just came from the Ops rover. This came in as I was dropping off the gear they're holding for us."

"It's about Ariam." Rett guessed in a flat voice.

"Read it," Kraym said shortly. "It's from our biggest admirer next to Commander Iheolon, the Leader."

Rett took the device from her co-second. " 'Sergeant Killer,' " she read aloud, "'we will return your Corporal Ariam, unharmed, in exchange for yourself. You have ten hours to contact us'…Ten hours. Why so much time?" She shoved the Omni back at Kraym.

Soon her personal Omni was in her hand, the latest met report in brutally graphic detail. She pushed the display into Kraym's range of vision. "See that?"

"Another storm system. Great. Maybe we should ask for part of the Western Fleet and some dive teams instead of more infantry."

Reminding herself not everyone grew up ingesting climate data and weather reports as often as meals, Rett took a breath. "This isn't just another storm, Kraym. We've been sitting under a stationary front for two tendays, growing mold. This thing is shooting up the Wide River from the south like a log down a flume. And over here is an area of high pressure coming off the Western Sea, bringing back our wayward jet stream; dragging yet a third system with it. I know this seems a bit off the track…" Rett held up a warning hand. "But it's important. The weather has as much impact and influence on what's going to happen here in the next five to thirty hours as the Coalition does. Maybe even more."

Frowning at the display on her Omni, her co-second waited in silence for her to go on.

"I'll put it in plainer detail then. We're going to be right in the middle when these systems collide. Lightning, thunder, hail…hail enough so you'll think you're in a rockslide. Wind, strong enough to flatten forests. The wind alone…" She shook her head. "Microbursts or sustained straightline gusts, strong like the percussion from an explosion. Only it doesn't stop as quickly. More rain. A lot of it in a short time. Maybe tornados. You've experienced storms like that."

Kraym nodded.

"All this in a handful of hours, and gone. Like that. Summer is back with the jet stream. That means aircraft can fly, Kraym." Rett shook her head. "We can't wait ten hours. We can't even wait half that. This storm is going to be here in five, six hours, tops. If we survive the initial impact, it'll give us maybe five hours of good cover before it starts to break up. And then it's hello, sunshine, and we'd already better be in the city. Oh, give me that." She recovered her Omni from the big corporal and slammed it back in its belt pocket.

Rett raked a hand through her hair, wishing, as usual, there was enough to grab for a good yank. A ten-hour delay would be a disaster, especially if it meant the Leader was hoping to get a few of those reserves from Epnoce! "Well, she's due for upgrade in a few days and we both know she's more than capable to replace me as platoon leader."

"Wait a minute, Sarge! You can't—"

"Have to. Damn it, Kraym, enough of us have died in the past few hours! Delaying the attack is not an option. And I can't let them…I just can't. They won't kill her, you know. She's Talented. We can't let them have her." Gritting her teeth, Rett stopped right there. "If they want me that badly, they can have me."

Rett was well aware her usual self-control was in critical condition. But at this exact moment and space and time she didn't care what she said, how she said it, and had enough presence of mind to be glad Kraym was the only physical body within range. She needed to vent or explode.

Kraym pulled her about sharply to face him. "Sarge, we're all ready to die for this system if we have to! And any one of us would be proud to die for you. Plus, you can't do this. We've the attack on Circle on the line and it's just not—"

"I understand, Kraym." Her tone gentled slightly. "But you don't get the complete image. Remember our command level files disappeared?"

"Yes." Her normally good-natured co-second made an excellent physical example of one of those big, unstable supercells continuing a relentless advance on their position. "However, I fail to see the significance."

"Think about it. The Leader must have them. That's the only reason he's making this sort of demand."

Kraym became so tight in the mouth his lips went colorless. "He has our command level files?"

"Yes. Our family connections, certain of our higher level skills, special training that might have been left off public records."

"So he'll know she's Talented. So he'll know how to hurt any fam—oh, good deities. What else can go wrong?"

"And right now when it's obvious where we're headed next. And that...*person*..." she said for lack of a better word, "knows he has me in the middle of a logjam on the rapids. I can't refuse, it's impossible. He knows that and I know that. So, I won't let him, or Ariam, down. Simple enough?"

The corporal's hand tightened on her arm. "No. I don't under-stand. I need more specifics. You might know everything in those files, you have access to them. I don't." His voice became hard, grip harder. "Damn it, Sarge, tell me!"

If anyone else had been squeezing her arm and threatening her, Rett might have chosen either to retaliate or walk away without another word. But Kraym and this crazy situation presented an altogether dif-ferent case. It was common knowledge in F-troop that Kraym and Ariam, an unbeatable team whether on regular duty or in combat, were a pair off duty as well. It was apparent that no matter how close he had become to Ariam, he hadn't an idea in two worlds why Rett was so affected by the turn of events.

Locking her gaze with his, Rett looked deep into his frustrated brown eyes. *Kraym deserves to know,* decided Rett. *And it's no use to keep it a secret any more.*

From inside she felt a rush of understanding surprise from Pam as well, and took a second to congratulate herself on keeping that big of a thing from her ego-merge friend until this moment.

"Kraym," she said, her voice soft, "Ariam is my sister."

The huge young man's arm dropped limply to his side.

"And I made a promise to protect her with my life long before I ever made a commitment to Special Forces. Specific enough?" One corner of Rett's mouth quirked up slightly at his reaction of astonishment. "I'm sorry I didn't tell you before now." Then she spun on her heel and started away.

* * * * *

KRAYM STOOD ROOTED TO THE spot in shock. Years. How many? He and Ariam had come to F-troop at the same time, from different units, just a bit over three years ago. And he never knew, never guessed. Ariam? *His* Ariam? Sergeant Rett's *sister?* They were so different looking…as different as twilight and daytime. The Sarge so tall, built as strong as an armored rover, dark skinned, dark eyes. Ariam fair and slim. No one would make a connection based on looks.

But good deities, now things made sense.

"Sarge?" he called. Now he knew why the two women were so close; why they seemed to think on the same wavelength. Why…why everything.

He had to admire them both all the more for keeping that relationship from interfering in their interaction as platoon leader and second-in-command. Major Yidnar certainly knew Rett and Ariam were related when he assigned Ariam as F-troop co-second. Whenever the Major matched people as commander and junior, from the squad-level on up, he always had a reason. Hoping for…what?

Hoping for all of them to team up and mesh exactly the way they had, of course.

He added in the average Nyorfian's usual disregard of family names. So many people had the same family name: there were only a few hundred of them still existing from the original settlers. No new ones had been created. There was never a need. And since so many were the same, and the people who had them were not usually that closely or directly related, they went unused for the most part. The native-born Nyorfian was proud to have a unique name of his or her own, a name no one else ever had, and those were the names they used for almost everything.

"And those names aren't used except for the most detailed records. Civil and military. Including…command level records." Kraym sucked in a breath with another rush of understanding. "Shit. Sarge, wait a minute!" He moved quickly to catch up with her and paced alongside his platoon leader.

"I suppose we should be relieved not *everything* is on the command records." The sergeant spoke as if he had never left her side.

173

"Like your energy sense?"

"And just how *much* Talent Ariam has. Among other things people outside Special Forces don't need to know."

"I guess." Kraym wiped a smear from one of his lenses, only making it worse.

"I'm only worried they plan to pick off Ariam before she gets clear," said the sergeant said, giving a tug to her weapons belt. "You could be damned certain they don't plan to let her walk off unharmed…that is, if she even is unharmed beyond what injuries she took fighting. From the files they know you and she make an effective team, which is the reason Major Yidnar initiated F-troop's co-seconds in command situation. They could easily figure that even if I'm gone, both of you will keep up this unit's effectiveness."

She paused to look earnestly at him. "As one half of an effective team, do you have any ideas, Corporal?"

Kraym pushed up his glasses and tried to find words. "Well…"

The platoon leader's Omni chose that moment to beep softly, in the three-toned signal that heralded a non-verbal command communiqué. She took her unit and activated the display, angling it so Kraym could see it, too.

Will have three more battalions for you by 0900. Good job on the
Gap bridge. Good hunting at Circle. The 5th is ahead of schedule
and will be in contact with you to coordinate attack time of the
city. Am in the process of relocating the rest of the division to
back you up. Keep both eyes on the weather.___Evard___52nd

Kraym, like his platoon leader, read the dispatch silently. He took special notice of the time it was sent: a few minutes before the message from the Leader.

The sergeant started shaking her head.

"What's the problem?" he demanded.

"Timing."

What? The timing of the messages? Then he then realized what she meant. "So we go in with the—"

"Kraym, stop. We can't do that."

"It was a stupid idea," he admitted, "but right now I'm feeling pretty stupid, Sarge."

"They'll waste her double quick if there's any show of force. I'd better get another met update. I'm not just worried about conditions clearing for aircraft now. Weather or no, if we go in force they'll see us, *and* the 5th, before we could do anything. You know it's impossible to hide a group of any large size."

He had to agree. "And the enemy troops in Circle are probably already aware of the 5th coming at them. No matter how stupid they seem to act, they could certainly guess we're on the way, too."

He followed the sergeant's glance from Omni to the sky. No longer a formless grayness spitting rain, it was now a multi-shaded range of grays from pale blue-gray to dark violet as layers of clouds became visible.

"Keep in mind this new storm can act against us as well as for us." She sighed deeply. "And of course we both know standard procedure calls for us to let Ariam take her chances. Especially with this attack ready."

"But you're not going to, are you," Kraym said savagely. "Despite operational procedure, despite orders. You're going to set everything up and then leave command of this strike force, give yourself for her anyway, no matter what. And I'll go along with it, Sarge. Despite myself and all I know better. But only if you have a plan that has a chance in two worlds of working out to get both of you back. Because, if you don't have something with a chance of working... as much as I love Ariam and you love her, duty comes first. If you come up with an idea that I don't think will work, I'll do whatever is necessary to stop you."

"Understood. But the enemy doesn't seem to know that."

"No," agreed Kraym. "From the message they seem to think you'll drop everything and come to Ariam's rescue."

"They didn't miss that target by much," muttered his platoon leader.

Her words confirmed that she was already firmly committed to taking a drastic action. "If we screw this up, Sarge..." He let a breath out through his teeth. "Best we could hope for is to pull it off, take Circle as well and hope all we get is a reprimand." 175

* * * * *

Rett thanked all deities for Kraym's unswerving loyalty. Now all she needed was a solution. "I know that, Corporal. So, let's try to think of something. You know we take any chances we're given, even slight ones."

~I have an idea...~

"What is it?" she asked aloud.

"What, what? I didn't say anything." Kraym looked puzzled.

"Let me think!" snapped Rett, then touched his arm in apology. "Sorry, Kraym. Didn't mean to bite. Just let me think a minute, okay?" *Okay Pam, I'm desperate. What?*

For no more than a second Pam considered shutting up. Oh, so Rett, who had trouble using her imagination and was in a time crunch, had be *desperate* to listen to an idea from the dimwitted alien mindforce?

All right, so maybe Pam was overreacting, but the events of the past day had left her a bit edgy and shell-shocked. But it was too late to rein in the bitchy feelings that had risen so quickly. Rett was responding even as Pam tried to back down, the sergeant's right hand raking through her hair in that habitual gesture of frustration.

Pam, I'm sorry. I really am. I'm not thinking too clearly at the moment and on top of everything, this has become entirely too personal. I'd appreciate any help or ideas you might have.

~First, I need a point clarified,~ said Pam, deciding that maybe some unexpected bitchiness from her was just what Rett had needed. ~The Leader left the time of the exchange your call, didn't he? He just said "within ten hours"? Did I understand that right?~

Rett took Kraym's Omni from his surprised hands and flipped back to the message from the Leader. *You have ten hours to contact us,* she read, having forgotten Pam couldn't read her language and knowing from her ego-merge experience, so far, that thought-impressions, while more accurate than speech translation, still got misunderstood.

You're right. I read it the first time as contact him in the tenth hour, she admitted to Pam, *but your impression of it was closer. We have no more than ten hours, so anytime between now and then.* "That is a good thing." she said aloud.

And Pam launched into her idea.

Pam, forget I ever said you were dimwitted, okay?

Rett was aware of Kraym watching her, arms across his chest and head cocked a bit to one side. The position reminded her all too well of the time he and Ariam thought she was going off the steep end, back when the ego-merge first started and Pam had taken her over completely.

Right now, she didn't care. "I've an idea. Just give me a moment," she told him, and gave her full attention to Pam, her Omni, and the idea that was growing more feasible by the second.

"It's so simple," Rett mumbled. "Simple enough to work. They'll never expect such a straightforward action."

Kraym cleared his throat. "Care to clue me in?"

Her fingers flew over her Omni's touchpad and screen, but she took a moment to glance up at him. "Just another moment." And then, letting out a breath, she tucked her Omni back into its pocket, brushed rain from her face and gestured for him to walk with her. As she hastily outlined the plan, she saw the shift in his energies from frustration to astonishment.

"So at that time they'll not be expecting a damned thing in Circle but rough weather!" Rett concluded, and stopped walking to regard him expectantly. "What do you think?"

Kraym poked at his lenses. "There are quite a few bugs in that idea, but I think it might work. And here I am the specialist in Tactical and Survey." He chuckled. "They'll never expect *you* to deviate from the conditions. But you're right, they never honor their bargains and they're not just going to let Ariam walk away. I'd feel a lot better if you had a backup…"

Pam added a thought. ~I just think it may help more if you can get some air support…have them up at the first crack of good weather…~

"…even if they only act as decoys if your ground troops or backups are still moving into position," finished Kraym. "And if they can go beyond that, so much the better." 177

Rett would not have believed she had heard Pam's thought in her head and the spoken words from Kraym mirror each other so closely. For a moment she was uncomfortable and wondered if there was a chance she betrayed the secret of her ego-merge.

~Hey, Kraym's pretty smart. And as we say on Earth, great minds think alike,~ came in a rather lofty manner from Pam.

The comment forced a laugh from Rett. "Good idea. Maybe we can get some remote controlled fighter drones up, I'll have to check it out!" She grinned at him. "Made up for that move back at the bridge, Kraym. Especially if this works. If it doesn't…I can't help either one of us."

Kraym returned her grin, although not with much humor. "We'll both be on jobs for the rest of our natural lives that will make the methane in Bolle's Marsh smell good, so we'd better hope it works or we die trying."

1.2.7 YIXOLRYN COALITION HQ, CIRCLE
CENTERLAND PROVINCE, NYORFIAS
0535.06.31 (LOCAL RECKONING

THE TROOPER GAVE ARIAM a firm push into a room and closed the door behind him. He pointed to a chair. "Sit there," he ordered.

The chair and something that looked like a medical exam table bristling with restraints were the only objects in the small room. Wondering what to expect and prepared mentally and physically for the worst, Ariam shrugged and sat down. She kept up her attitude of cool withdrawal.

"How's your sister doing?" asked the trooper.

"Don't know what you mean."

"You *do* have a voice! Sergeant Killer, your sister."

"Sergeant *Rett*," Ariam corrected pointedly, "is my platoon leader. Everyone knows that."

The trooper adjusted controls on his restraining unit. Ariam felt the magnetic field between the manacles on her ankles contract. Each of his large hands shaped themselves to the contours of her shoulders and at least two-thirds of his considerable weight came down through them. The combination of his weight, hers, the back of the chair and the metal wrist units generated real concern inside her. Two broken wrists weren't needed right now.

"We know Sergeant Rett is your sister, Corporal Ariam. Those records list you both as having the same family name, the same parents. And your father, Colonel Reve. Of the famous 21st Division. What a catch he'd make. Why do you think you're not getting the usual treatment? Not that you would, being psi-able…it would be a little different since they'd need you for breeding or providing genetic material. The Yixolryns are hot to get those abilities into their own genetic makeup. They haven't had success with it in the lab, yet. So, they'd be trying harder to keep you alive and relatively whole until something works out, but nothing much else would change. Think about it."

The trooper's words finally sank in. Use her to bait a trap for Rett? And maybe for their father afterward?

"You understand me now?"

"For an asshole you don't understand shit. Her first duty is to her people, Nyorfias and the Free Army. She won't do anything," Ariam said flatly. On the inside, she knew better. If Rett could find a way, any way, Rett would. Her sister had promised her long ago that nothing would ever stop her from coming to Ariam's aid, and Rett, without fail, always kept her promises.

And deities help anyone who got in Rett's way.

"Even is she wasn't your sister," the trooper continued, straightening, "Killer would still come for you, just like your platoon always tried to come for her. That's the way your people operate whenever they can. I've found that much out in my research."

Ariam refused to comment. She fixed an insolent stare on him and straightened in her seat. She flexed her fingers and wrists.

"I wasn't going to break them, I just had to get your attention," he said. "I'm not going to hurt you. I want to help you get out of here."

He pushed back his targeting goggles. Ariam struggled with her composure for a second. Good gods and deities and everything in between, he was hot. Probably the handsomest humanoid male she had seen. She'd never seen a skin tone like his: a slight but definite rusty red that was definitely a natural color and not due to being excessively overheated. His breathing was too even, his skin too dry, for that to be a factor to his features. His eyes were a startling, vivid shade of blue, even the very depths of them as clear as pure water. She forced her focus aside before she was sucked right down and drowned. At the same time, she wanted to take the advantage of such an open window to his soul. But not yet. Not yet.

He simply stood there and studied her in silence for a long, long minute. "Not too much family resemblance, is there?" An unconscious sort of half smile formed on his utterly sexy lips. "Then again, there is, maybe not as sharp and defined, but the jawline, the chin…cheekbones, even the same size and tilt to the eyes. I can see it now."

Ariam allowed the tenor of her outward expression to change from insolence to contempt. On her inner level, her feelings were confused; turbulent. Her gut instincts were warring with her trained ones, and those both were fighting with whatever she had to show on the surface.

When did he have a chance to notice that kind of detail on Rett?

"You're going to make this real hard for me, aren't you? And you're the empath. So, what am I doing that's not getting through that talent? Or did your head injury cause something to block it? Let's start over. I want to help you. And I want you to help me, too. I think between the both of us we can—"

"Do you think I'm some kind of idiot? You can do better than that, I hope. Why don't you just go with the usual program? That would be easier than listening to your pathetic attempts at getting me to sucker up and trust you," snarled Ariam.

She was trained and schooled quite thoroughly in many capture situations: how to act, what to do, what to say or not to say. Her verbal venting now might earn her more trouble. But it helped adjust her mindset more firmly so she could clear and redirect any deep fear and pain into a ready mental control.

She was ready for anything. Ready for anything but this pathetic guy she almost wanted to believe. Gut instinct told her he was telling the truth. It also kept her from extending her talent beyond a certain range to verify her gut feeling until she was sure he wasn't an enemy Talent trying to lure her into a trap. She didn't remember hearing about the Coalition having any psi-able troopers, though. And if they did, they wouldn't use them this way. She reminded herself not to take anything for granted. After all, for thirty years the Yixolryn agents Mott and Shamos had lived, worked, and fought alongside people who trusted them. And look where that went. Of course they knew she was an empath, so whenever she was around they were really careful not to get her suspicious. So she never pushed on them, she never had a reason to. But now...

* * * * *

THE NYORFIAN'S STEADY, COLD, STEEL hard eyes cut through him like a knife and Jaq Pym sighed. All right, the head injury. He had to take that into consideration. Her injury was blocking her talent. Unless, of course, her talent was weak, or one that relied exclusively on a physical touch. Those kinds of details weren't available. Damn it, he had hoped for a little more, someone who could truly verify his intentions.

For the past six years of his life, Jaq dreamed of someday escaping from the Yixolryn Coalition. His world, Zetinor Prime, fell to Coalition troops almost twenty years earlier. Twenty years that he physically remembered, anyway. All he was certain about was that he had been fifteen years old the day he was "recruited" for military service. His family had been killed in front of him, and next thing he knew, he had been packed aboard a troopship, pumped full of drugs, and shoved into a cryogenic unit. They hadn't pulled him out of it until two years before the Coalition invasion fleet reached this star system. That was when he discovered all he remembered about his family was that he had one, and they had died.

He obeyed Yixolryn directives because compliance meant his survival; however, Jaq hated them. Especially when he had been told, shortly after his reawakening, that his homeworld of Zetinor Prime, after being totally stripped of anything useful, served as a testing site for Yixolryn Coalition weapons.

His survival also depended on him providing a service no one else could perform better, because most Yixolryns, even part-Yixolryns, were unable to endure being near a Zetinorian for a prolonged period of time. So he bided his time, learned all he could, developed valuable skills, and watched carefully for his chance to break free of his forced service. In the meantime, he performed the tasks that kept him alive: his ability with non-Standard languages and his ability to get along with people—specifically, in Coalition viewpoint—his ability to get along with Nyorfians.

He had constructed a reputation as an interrogator over the past year and a half, based on fabulous, fact-based lies he'd invented after his sessions with Nyorfian prisoners. Whether the Nyorfians believed

181

him or not, most of the time his actions kept the prisoners he'd "questioned" valuable and safe from the standard torture, gang rape and/or mutilation that was characteristic of Commander Iheolon's usual routine.

He couldn't count on his luck holding out much longer. One of these days, Commander Iheolon would realize what he was doing. This would be his last chance, especially since the Leader had preferred him to his commander for the task. Iheolon already barely tolerated him. The Leader's insult to Iheolon by choosing Jaq for Corporal Ariam's initial questioning would give Iheolon a good reason to put up with Jaq for only as long as it took to get him somewhere out of the way and have a weapon malfunction.

Or worse. Especially if he couldn't convince this Ariam to work with him. "I'm dead serious. I want to—"

"Is this what makes you so good? You should make yourself want to puke!" the Nyorfian shot back sarcastically. "Do you give this crap to everyone? Or just females?"

"Corporal Ariam, I've been looking for the right combination of circumstances for a long time now. I have to get out of my situation, and you have to get out of yours. But if you're not going to give me a chance…I can't help either one of us."

She remained still and silent, staring at him with an expression Jaq had seen other Nyorfian soldiers pay dearly for at the hands of Commander Iheolon and his cohorts.

Jaq wanted to make his new home here. For however long that would last, hours or years, depending on the outcome of the war and if he lived to see that outcome. Most of all, Jaq Pym wanted somehow to link up with Sergeant Killer and F-troop and maybe, just maybe, get to know the sergeant a little bit better.

Much better, in fact.

A curse, if one could call it that, of his race was the absolute and positive knowledge of discovering an opposite to lifemate with. Sometimes without even seeing them in person. A rather bad image taken by a surveillance recorder was all it had taken before he felt destiny grab hold of him with a ferocity that had all but knocked him from his chair. Since then, he knew his life was linked with the

Nyorfian woman the Coalition called "Killer". Deep down, he guessed such an event was impossible at best. Why would she want anything to do with him, anyway? He was the enemy, for now at least.

But he had to try. The compulsion wouldn't let go of him unless he made the effort.

He tried to help the sergeant before, a few years ago. He thought by disengaging the devices keeping her awake, she could slip into that strange and untouchable deepsleep mode the Nyorfian Special Forces were trained to use as a last resort. Most of the Coalition believed it was for suicide, and maybe it was, but she was already dying. He knew, for sure, that Commander Iheolon was going to prolong the process for as long a period as possible.

But she was so far gone, the transformation had been so swift and abrupt, he and everyone else thought she had died. Even Commander Iheolon. It was all he could do to control his glad relief when he heard later that hadn't been the case. He'd come so close to giving himself away that time.

"Okay." Jaq shrugged and let out a long breath. "You know what? I'm tired. I'm out of ideas. I'm at the end my resources, and my luck. I was trying to be straight up front with you, Corporal Ariam. But you're not listening. On any level." He heard the undercurrent of desperation in his own voice and didn't care.

He didn't have too much time before they checked his progress. Iheolon grudgingly allowed him to work unmonitored because some Nyorfians sensed outside interference and flat out refused any sort of communication. With this woman's training and ability, the only reason she spoke at all had to result from knowing nothing left this room. Other than that, he was sure Corporal Ariam would've maintained the same stony silence she'd kept from the moment they captured her.

Commander Iheolon invariably inspected his progress at intervals, and Jaq had no doubt the Leader would be with him.

"So you tell me, Corporal. What do I have to do to convince you? I'll do it, here and now."

"Deactivate these restraints, give me a weapon, and stand aside. Then I'll believe you. Maybe." Ariam shook her head in exasperation.

Minor flaw in that plan, thought Jaq with real worry for her. "You'll be killed before you clear the door. There are guards all over outside. The Leader's not taking any chances with you. You're Killer's sister. You're psi-able."

"Then at least I'll die fighting! Beats being talked to death by you, any day, you oversized pile of—"

* * * * *

THE BIG TROOPER MOVED, AND quickly enough to surprise Ariam, who'd been about just ready for anything. She suddenly found herself thrown to the floor, with him standing over her growling something in a threatening tone. Remaining calm, she met his gaze, tensing muscles to absorb impact from a blow. But in his eyes she saw only desperation and sheer pleading that convinced Ariam to act, make it good, and just in time.

The door opened to admit the Leader and Commander Iheolon.

"Oversized pile of what, bitch?" The trooper directed a kick at her that somehow never connected and Ariam rolled with it as if launched from a missile pad. She assumed a doubled over position and turned her face into the floor to hide a rush of amusement. Maybe she could start to believe this guy. Finally using her empathic talent, Ariam felt his honesty as clear and true as the amazing color of his eyes.

Still, her conviction needed boosting. His dumb act could be covering something else. Maybe this trooper was also an empath and able to hide his true feelings from her. Maybe his reputation was well deserved!

"Anything, Pym?" demanded Iheolon, striding over and pushing Ariam onto her back with his foot.

Ariam was glad of the bruises and cuts gained in her fight earlier. They still looked fresh enough to be convincing.

"These commandos are tougher than most, sir."

"Has she said anything at all?" The Leader joined Iheolon and peered down at Ariam.

"My Leader," said the trooper respectfully, "you told me to keep the damage minimal. I'll have to use a lot more…ahh…force, if I may. Then we may get somewhere—past the arrogant posturing and insults I've been getting so far."

The Leader of the invading Yixolryn Coalition forces hesitated. But Iheolon reached down, twisted his hand into the uniform material between Ariam's breasts, and hauled her up. He slammed her onto the table so hard the impact forced a grunt from her. Even as her injured shoulder and arm went numb again, she thanked all good deities for it. Had Iheolon slammed her like that directly on her back, she'd have both arms injured and no hope for making any attempt of getting herself out of this situation.

"I have some very interesting devices and chemicals I've been anxious to try," Iheolon said.

As his hands began exploring her body, Ariam didn't change her face, retaining calm indifference. Diverting her attention from his physical touch was easy, a minor detail. The hard part was being an empath. His intent was clear and strong. The physical contact intensified it. He'd pick up with Ariam where he'd left off with Rett, with the added bonus of extracting revenge for Rett's failure to submit to him.

He leaned close, his breath warm on her face. With detached assessment Ariam noted it actually was fresh smelling, quite the opposite of what she expected. Iheolon was only half Yixolryn, and this close she had a good view of his bladelike jawbone and the way his skin stretched over it. He wasn't exactly gray-hued as the full Yixolryns were, like the Leader. Rather he was mottled, a more common tannish humanoid shade with grayish patches.

"It would be interesting to see if you'll maintain the same silence as she did for ten days. If you lived that long." His brutish features twisted into what was supposed to be a smile. "Then again, I would make sure you did. I've made improvements on my little devices since using them on your sister." Trailing a fingertip along the side of her face, he added, "Better yet, maybe I'll be able to make a side-by-side comparison. Perhaps your father will be there to watch."

Ariam blinked, a simple, natural reflex of her body, as if she heard nothing but the sighing of the wind. As anger at her indifference flared in the Iheolon's small, deepset eyes, the whiny, nasal voice of the Leader became louder as he moved closer.

"Just try to keep her looking reasonably unhurt," the Leader was saying as his shadow fell across Ariam's line of sight. "Please, Iheolon. You'll have your chance if Trooper Pym fails. But *without* your toys. We need to keep her viable and intact. For now."

"And if not?"

"You'll get what you want, within the parameters I've set, as we agreed."

Iheolon gave Ariam a look that froze her guts solid. He wanted that trooper to fail. The commander's glance flickered to the side where the big trooper stood, then came back to Ariam. Good gods and deities, Iheolon hated him. He wanted him to fail. Why? What did the ruddy-hued trooper ever do to him?

Ariam switched her awareness to the Leader, trying to gauge his feelings as well. She didn't like "touching" Yixolryns with her mind: full or part-blooded didn't matter, they left her feeling sticky. The Leader didn't like the trooper either, but it wasn't hate. The Leader thought the trooper was from an inferior race, and didn't like being around him for some reason, but he didn't hate him. Interesting.

"I'll look forward to it. Either way." Iheolon reluctantly released his hold on Ariam and turned aside.

"Carry on, Trooper," said the Leader.

"Thank you, sir. May I ask that no one disturb me unless I call for assistance?"

"You have two hours, Trooper. Possibly less."

"Yes, sir! Thank you, sir." The trooper let out a breath of relief once they'd gone. "Sorry," he told Ariam, a pale line around his lips. Without effort, he plucked her from the table and returned her to the chair. "That was close."

His large hands felt cold. They froze her arms right through the material of her uniform. It felt good on her right arm, which was regaining feeling with every agonizing second. Nothing was broken or dislocated, but it would be very sore and a possible handicap. In a few more moments Ariam realized the hand the trooper kept on her injured arm wasn't holding her stationary. Instead, his big fingers were carefully probing her upper arm and shoulder, probably for the same assessment she'd already made. "Nothing out of place," he muttered.

This situation was getting more interesting by the minute. She opened herself a little more, taking advantage of the physical contact. Was that sensation of nausea his, or hers? Ariam was hard pressed to tell. Where was his coming from? Ariam didn't want to think about what had caused hers. So, rerouting the direction of her thoughts, she allowed her indifferent expression to flow into the sarcastic insolence of before.

"You could continue to pull this dumb shit act you're putting on me. I'm not falling for it. There's only one thing that'll convince me. And I already told you what that was."

As she spoke, his hands left her arms. Straightening, he turned aside. Before Ariam's next word came out, his weapons belt landed solidly in her lap. He touched his control unit, releasing the magnetic field between Ariam's restraints. The control device then joined the weapons. His helmet, with its built-in comunit, came off next, landing on the floor near her feet.

187

Ariam's mouth closed with a snap. Wow. Time to fall back and regroup.

"You want more? I'll go get them. This is all I have at the moment. Well, there's my uniform, but it would be way too big for you."

Ariam slid the weapon from its holster and made certain it held a full charge. It was nothing more than a glorified hand stunner, larger and heavier to accelerate the energy pulses it generated. No matter. The important thing was: the weapon was operational and in her hands.

When she looked up at the man again, it was over the gun's barrel. Her left hand coded the device that would open the metal bands on her wrists and ankles. The bands opened and fell to the floor.

His humanoid, yet exotic, good looks were only augmented as the hair, flattened from the helmet, crackled up with a life of its own. A rampant central band of pale gold, like the crest of a wave, ran from just above the center of his forehead to the nape of his neck, where the hair disappeared under his collar. The rest of his long wild locks were every possible shade of brown broken only here and there with streaks of pure red-gold.

"What race are you?" Ariam asked, having never seen a humanoid like him before.

"Zetinorian."

She was full of questions, but ruthlessly shoved them down. Now was *not* the right time to satisfy her personal curiosity.

His staggering blue eyes were darkened, but calm. He didn't look bothered, only deeply disappointed. He spoke in a low voice that echoed the disappointment on his face. "If you want to die now, that's up to you. Your sister will never know. She'll come to the exchange point and the Leader and Commander Iheolon will get her anyway. They'd prefer to get their genetic material from you, but hers might do, now they know that psi runs in the family. So go ahead, Corporal. Just make sure you kill me, not just knock me out or disable me, okay? Or I'll be facing the same sort of deal you would have with Commander Iheolon. He doesn't allow race or gender to make a large difference in his methods, not among humanoids anyway."

"Back up," she told him. "To the wall. Stop when I tell you."

He obeyed.

"Stop. Lean back. Don't touch the wall with your hands: I want your arms crossed in front of you. Brace yourself with your head and shoulders only." She stood, looped the belt over her shoulders, and approached him.

"You really are serious, aren't you?" She nudged the angle of his body to the wall even wider so he had to concentrate on not falling flat on his back. His new position almost put his head on a level with hers, and it wasn't an easy one to hold, either. "Thanks for the gun. It's been very nice chatting with you, but I have to go now." She leveled the weapon at the trooper's face.

She had left his hands and arms free to move for a reason, and waited for him to take advantage and try an attack, but he didn't move them. Moving in closer, Ariam searched him with both her eyes and mind. Resignation for his own fate; regret for hers. A faint awareness of queasiness lingered between them and she knew this time it was his, left over from whatever Iheolon had said or done to trigger it. His ruddy color faded a little, but not once did his eye contact or expression waiver. That finally removed the last of her doubts and convinced her that the Zetinorian was sincere.

Letting down the protective mental barrier she had erected between them, her weaponless hand reached for the pulse beating in his throat. The coldness she made her face show kept him frozen in place as three of her fingers made a firm contact with his flesh and the pulsing artery beneath it.

He didn't move, but she felt the confusion leap to the surface of everything else he was feeling. Making certain her face showed only her dispassionate intention to kill him, Ariam held her gaze and her aim steady. Her injured arm screamed protest, but she ignored it. She'd get her answer soon enough.

She took a soft breath and allowed the hitherto unwavering barrel of the weapon to move slightly. The man couldn't help squeezing his eyes halfway closed or gritting his teeth, but anything else he felt didn't change. Regret. Resignation. Confusion.

When she suddenly reversed the weapon and held it out to him, she thought he was going to pass out. His breath expelled with a whoosh, and any underlying color on his ruddy skin faded to pale rust-pink. Ariam's free hand quickly moved to the neck opening of his armor to steady him when he almost lost his already precarious balance.

His eyes weren't half closed now. They were wide with shock and disbelief.

"Oh, stand up straight." Ariam had to shove into his body a little to help him out; he was too big and heavy for her to steady him any other way. His home planet had to be a heavy gravity world. From what she felt, he was twice as heavy as he looked. "Take it. I'm convinced. But you still won't get any real information," she warned. "Do you have a plan?"

Chuckling aloud at the new expression on his face, Ariam stepped back as the Zetinorian found his feet. She had to close his cold and nerveless fingers around the weapon's grip. "Maybe you'd better sit down," she suggested.

But the Zetinorian was recovering. The deep rusty shade she assumed was his normal skin color returned. The pupils of his incredible blue eyes normalized and he was no longer staring, but watching her; still confused, but definitely relieved. There was a new emotion rising in him now too—hope.

He sucked in a breath and let it out slowly. "Thank the One…you *are* an empath."

"You mean you had doubts?" Ariam tilted her head and crossed her arms.

"And quite a good actor."

"Yes, I'm proud of myself."

"That's good, because we'll need to put it to a harder test." Then he smiled at her with such warm brilliance Ariam thought her knees melted.

"On second thought," she said, feeling faint, "maybe *I'd* better sit down." She did, right there on the floor.

The trooper came down to that level, too, setting his gun aside, leaning forward with a tangible new energy that zinged right into Ariam's soul. "You don't have to tell me anything real, just enough to make up something they'll believe. We don't have much time. And I do have a plan. It's flexible, it'll work as long as Killer shows up and is as fast on her feet as always. She might even come up with something similar."

Ariam cocked her head to one side and reached toward him, with her right hand this time, ignoring the pull and burning pain of torn muscle. *A few hours and I'll wish it were numb again,* she thought, touching all five of her spread fingers lightly to his face.

He blinked and flinched slightly but didn't move.

"Think that again," she said.

"What?" Bafflement gave his face an endearing little boy expression.

"What you thought when you said 'she might even come up with something similar'." Her smile grew with the clarification. Jaq Pym wanted more than just to defect to the Free Army. She also redefined a few impressions she'd experienced earlier. Now she understood their significance.

Torn between amusement and sympathy, Ariam shook her head and dropped her contact. Everything he felt was right up front. She didn't have to strain any mental talent to sense his feelings.

"I think we should introduce ourselves properly, Trooper." She offered him her hands, palms upturned. "Ariam, Treetop Province, Nyorfias. Will you give me your name?"

And proving that he had indeed established contacts with native Nyorfians before, the Zetinorian didn't hesitate to cover Ariam's upturned palms with his. "Jaq Pym, Zetinor Prime."

Ariam couldn't quite get her fingers completely around his hands for a reassuring squeeze, so she smiled instead before pulling them back. "I've changed my mind, Jaq Pym. I'm going to give you some *real* information. Important strategic information."

"No, you don't…"

"Yes, really. You're going to need all the tactical advantage you can get."

"If things go wrong, they'll get whatever you say out of me for certain. I really don't want to—"

"Shut up, or we'll go right back to where we were a few moments ago."

His mouth closed. A deep crease formed between his eyebrows.

"Now listen. There's one essential thing you should know about my sister, if you ever want to get on her good side," Ariam leaned toward him, gesturing that he should lean a little nearer as well. She lowered her voice even though she knew no other ears or devices were listening. "Rett *hates* being called 'Killer'. *Loathes* it. She might not show it, but when you show up—whatever way that will be, preferably at the same time I do—she's definitely going to notice you're a good-looking guy. If you smile at her the way you did at me, she might not need to sit down, but she's going to lose some balance. But if you call her Killer just once, it's all over. So, don't blow your chances by making that mistake. Now let's get down to business!"

1.2.8 UNDISCLOSED LOCATION
CENTERLAND PROVINCE, NYORFIAS
0535.06.31 (LOCAL RECKONING)

"THIS IS AS READY AS it's going to get."

Rett blew a breath out through her teeth and studied her Omni, finalizing her checklist, releasing certain password protected areas so Kraym could access them with his code, since her Omni would be staying behind with him.

She mulled things over, trying to find any detail she might have missed and still had time to correct. Her portion of the attack force was now paused at their last checkpoint, only some ten miles from the city limits.

Colonel Evard had come through, whomping up two extra battalions from somewhere, so instead of the original three promised, five more battalions of the twenty that comprised the 52nd had come in. Rett had sent them to the east flank.

He also contacted AirSpacefighters personally instead of going through channels in MainCommand. Whatever he told them got results. The personnel- and equipment-challenged flying arm of the Free Army managed to scrape together a drone squadron and two human piloted fighters, which would carry backseaters to control the unmanned craft. These waited for the first opening in the weather, which was unquestionably ominous.

Another squadron was being rerouted from far to the east near Azurebay, which was experiencing the third tropical storm to make landfall on the east coast in as many tendays. Whether they came in time to be useful to the attack or not remained to be seen. Evard hadn't even been able to secure a departure time, much less a definite ETA.

All that mattered was that the squadrons were coming. Whenever they arrived, and if the attack was successful, they'd stay on permanently as part of the new Circle defense.

Corporal Bhayorn escorted two young and enthusiastic representatives from the civilian resistance defenders in Circle, identical twins of a gangly seventeen. How they had slipped safely though the tight net of sophisticated devices the enemy had around the city was anyone's guess. Rett didn't take the time to ask them, instead giving them her full attention as they gave their report.

"We're going to have the most important places marked so you can target them first—"

"—with this," said the other, leaning over to take Rett's Omni right out of her hands so he could trace the symbol on the screen.

"It's a chewie bird," explained the first twin. "We use its call to signal, too."

"There—" started Rett.

"There's no chewies around here," the second one said right on top of what Rett had been about to point out. "But the Coalition doesn't know that. So they don't pay any attention to our whistles."

Rett managed a nod. "I—"

"Our uncle's group at the spaceport has a plan, too," said the first eagerly. "They have access to the main power supply. There's a technician there who's tapped into their scanning and tracking systems—she's put false signals out there for them before. She can put scanner echoes everywhere, blur their signals, set off their alarms. She's ready to do it again so their attention can get diverted elsewhere—"

"—and everyone who isn't going to shelter is going to cause as much confusion as they can."

Rett finally got a word in the breathless recital. "This all sounds great. And those going to shelter? Families with children, others who may be disabled? Do they have enough time?"

"Most already are, due to the storm warnings. Several live tornados and a few potential ones are being tracked, and the Coalition makes them go to shelter first thing." The first twin pushed hair off his face. "There's been a lot of trouble caused during storms."

Both of the twins grinned toothily, leaving Rett no doubt the storms didn't cause as much damage as the resident underground did.

"I'm glad you guys are on *our* side," Rett told them both, returning the grin. "But I don't think you should try to get back just now. You..." Rett hesitated as the twins exchanged worried glances. She was going to have them stay with the infantry support units rather than risk weather and Coalition guards to get back when the attack was imminent. They wanted to get back to their city and their loved ones, that much was plain.

They watched her, the uncertainty whether they would be allowed to contest her decision clear. They were young, yes, but they weren't children anymore. They were considered responsible enough to leave Circle and get this information safely past enemy lines. They were the same age as she was when she went off to Basic.

She liked what she saw: that loyalty and determination. "You probably know the best way to get back. Thanks for the update, it'll make all the difference in two worlds. Good luck."

"We'll be ready," they promised in the same breath, and she watched them race away with the same undaunted energy they'd arrived with.

Shortly afterward, the 5th Infantry Division contacted her and was ready and waiting just southwest of the city for the signal to move up in final positions. The portion of the 415th and 109th Battalions still with Rett and F-troop were going directly for the north entry of the spaceport. Any of Evard's latecomers would be coming from the river approach. From there, they could split easily, going into the city itself or the spaceport, wherever they were needed. So, she didn't worry too much about that.

She'd sent her answer to the Leader of the invasion forces in Circle. A little less than two hours from now, all this would come together. Or, as Pam said, "the shit will hit the fan". Whatever that meant.

The only detail that waited for the last possible minute was the exact location of the exchange for Ariam. As Pam pointed out, that way, Rett would be fairly certain of one ambush, and that one would be from her own people. With odds that were tough enough already, she felt better having that little bit of insurance.

1.2.9 YIXOLRYN COALITION HQ, CIRCLE
CENTERLAND PROVINCE, NYORFIAS
0535.06.31 (LOCAL RECKONING)

NAKED, COLD, SORE, AND WORRIED, Ariam brooded alone in the interrogation room. She sat on the floor, in a corner, with her knees drawn under her chin, again closely bound by the electromagnetic restraints. Her right arm twinged just a bit, but she could use it if she had to. Jaq Pym had dosed her with some anti-inflammatory, saying he was aware she could probably handle pain well but she was going to need her concentration for other things. She had to agree. She also had to be glad in that moment that she didn't inherit the same metabolic intolerance for drugs as her sister.

The Zetinorian had made up a wonderful fiction based entirely in fact to tell his superiors. A short time later, a gloating Leader informed her that Rett agreed to the exchange. Ariam, artfully disheveled, the dirt on her body rearranged, some fresh blood encouraged and smeared here and there, had called upon every bit of her dramatic ability to act like she had been crushed into submission by an expert who'd known exactly what threats to use.

The Leader had fixed Jaq with an approving stare. "As much as I detest Zetinorians," he announced pompously, "I admire skill when I see it. You've just been transferred, Trooper."

"My Leader?"

The alien nodded. "To my personal staff. I want you to train others in your methods. I'll have plenty of Nyorfians for you to use as examples once we've dealt with this…attack their pathetic little army is attempting. Don't," the Leader warned Iheolon. "You'll get what you want. You don't need the Zetinorian, his skills are wasted since you prefer your own methods."

Commander Iheolon hadn't been pleased, but he didn't dare argue.

Ariam had hated giving the Leader this impression with her own example. She hoped with all her heart that some good would come of it. Better yet, she thought savagely, that the Leader and Commander Iheolon were taken with the city of Circle!

Her snarl faded as quickly as it came, reversing into a smile as she thought about Jaq. How did someone like him survive so long in the Coalition without losing his mind? Once she had dropped her barriers of doubt, she sensed not only his honesty, so much like Kraym's, but also his deeply caring and kind nature. Such a strong part of him to hide for so long. She realized now, too, that he'd tried to give her a chance to get away back in the rover. She had to wonder if he helped make things easier for them almost a month ago in Circle.

And without a doubt, he was the trooper who helped Rett almost two years before, in her first horrible experience as a prisoner of Commander Iheolon. His reaction of gut-churning nausea earlier had been from his own memories of that. She had asked him flat out if that impression was true. He had not answered with words. He didn't have to.

She shivered. If she wanted to retain any sort of control over herself, she couldn't think about any of that. If she got out of this, she vowed, as long as it was within her power, that she'd keep Rett from getting into that sort of situation ever again.

That some unknown Coalition trooper had taken a chance on giving her some help, giving her time to go into deepsleep, had been the only detail of that particular capture Rett had voluntarily shared with any of them. She used the example as a point to illustrate the Nyorfian policy of not killing enemy soldiers unless in hot combat or immediate defense, if possible.

The Zetinorian's infatuation for Rett could also prove very interesting if things worked out. She showed her knees a wistful smile, gladly taking this new track with her thoughts. Rett needed someone special in her life. Someone who knew what she'd been through and wouldn't be afraid to love her. Someone who could begin healing those horrible mental scars Rett had buried so dangerously deep.

She hoped Rett would give him a chance. Maybe, once they came to know each other, Rett and Jaq could become better than friends, like Ariam was with Kraym.

Kraym. How she longed for him right now, so much she felt tears threaten. She wanted his warm arms around her and his moustache tickling her ear. She wanted to hear him tell her that he loved her in that way that always made everything all right, no matter how bad things really were. So many times a soft word or a special glance from him in a free moment had kept her head cool during situations that varied from simple tension to commanding F-troop during Rett's more dangerous solo diversionary tactics.

She comforted herself with thoughts of him now. Her interest in him had been purely professional at first, since he wasn't really the sort Ariam usually found attractive. She was the one who'd discovered Kraym's natural ability to buffer negative moods: something of which he'd been unaware. She'd helped him develop it to the advantage of a needful F-troop where stress ran high. Everything else had just fallen into place naturally.

She considered her situation and options and decided she could allow herself the luxury of a moment's sniffle. Having swollen eyes and some tears on her face would only add validity to her enactment. "You know," Ariam remarked to her knees after swiping her eyes on them, "this waiting around really bites."

197

Shivering, she hunched closer together. Freezing in here. She'd be lucky not to come down with some virus from being in all that mucky water, and now sitting around in her skin. If she survived long enough to get sick. She wrinkled her nose.

She didn't have to wonder why Rett would take the chance of hanging up the entire mission for her. No—Rett would make sure the mission would still go, just that it would go without her. She'd be in huge trouble, even if she pulled off a miracle. But Rett wouldn't care about that. Ariam sighed. Did she even have to wonder?

Rett's looking after Ariam had begun long before their mother and brother were killed in the Yixolryn Coalition attack on an unarmed shuttle to Epnoce preceding the invasion of their homesystem. But since then, and ever since their father had been called to full active duty with the Free Army, twelve long years ago, Rett hadn't only been her older sister, but every other role left unfilled by the death of their mother and brother and the absence of their father.

Three and a half years younger than her sister, Ariam followed the same pattern into the military: enlisting shortly before she turned eighteen. After she completed Basic, she made it into Special Forces.

After spending four years among other units, she received a new assignment. It had been right after the ill-fated battle for Azurebay. Nearly four Special Forces units had been completely wiped out, and those who survived were formed into a new platoon designated F-troop. Ariam and three handfuls of others from various units were sent in to bring the new unit to full strength. She had no idea Rett would be her superior and her sister had no prior warning her newest group of transfers included Ariam until they had come face to face and Ariam had handed over her orders.

She'd always known that it wasn't unusual for family or close friends to serve in the same units, but such assignments were usually requested by both parties, and then sent through an approval process. What made things more complicated was the fact that Ariam had been assigned as platoon co-second-in-command. So she and Rett had mutually decided that it might be better all around not to advertise that they were sisters, and to forget it altogether when working as commander and junior.

It was just as well that people would know now, she decided, scratching an itch on her nose against her knee. What wasn't good was that the *wrong* people knew, and that they knew other things that could hurt the entire platoon.

She blinked as the lighting in the room brightened. The door opened to admit a Coalition officer and five troopers, including Jaq Pym. She felt the release as the force on her leg restraints nulled and all five troopers had weapons leveled on her.

"Let's go, Corporal," ordered the officer.

But she didn't move. What she really wanted to do was jump out of her corner and explode like a bomb in the middle of the guard detail. Instead, she squeezed herself tighter into her corner, made a small noise and pressed her face into her knees. She and Jaq Pym had agreed that she stood a better chance if she remained in character as someone who'd completely broken down under his pressure and threats. Her bruised and disheveled condition, her nudity, the artfully ripped clothing thrown to one side of the room, all attested to the fact the Zetinorian had done his job well.

The officer sounded disgusted. "I thought these commandos were tougher than that. What'd you do to her, Pym? Get up, you!"

Ariam turned a growl into a whimper when a boot nudged her hip. Only her knees saw her snarl and bared teeth. She composed herself swiftly as the officer's hand twisted in her hair. She thought about how she'd feel if she never saw Rett, Kraym, her father or anyone she loved ever again.

"Pathetic." The officer started into her face a moment, then let her go. "Never mind, we'll find out later. I was told you'd be giving us all lessons. Come on, get her clothes and hurry up about it. I don't want to get caught out in the weather and something's going to break any time. Let's go," the officer told them.

For a minute, Ariam thought she was going to start laughing. She held onto that thought as the troopers, despite the urgings from their superior, took their time shoving her into what remained of her clothing.

1.2.10 UNDISCLOSED LOCATION
CENTERLAND PROVINCE, NYORFIAS
0535.06.31 (LOCAL RECKONING)

RETT WAITED AT THE MEETING place. As required, she was in the open, in plain sight. She seated herself on a big flat rock, her headband and weapons on the ground and to the left, at a distance specified by the agreement. That the distance was well within her ability to cover in one jump didn't seem worth pointing out.

Overhead the sky had turned a threatening hue with several layers of cloud moving at various speeds and not all the same direction. Thunder rumbled. Lightning flashed frequently, glittering through the sodden growth above, below, and around her.

Hidden in this cover, yet out of sight and sensor range, waited a select group of volunteers from her unit. As Pam had suggested, "Screw this alone and unarmed crap!" Especially since the possibility the enemy would keep to the agreement was so small, Rett would need to set her VARs in full zoom mode to find it.

Rett had asked for five volunteers after explaining the possible repercussions of her action. Of course, she had a lot more than five. All that was left of able bodies in F-troop, matter of fact. Deities, she loved them. She left command to Kraym and Trebor, secure knowing if things didn't work out, both men were more than capable. At this point, besides F-troop, no one else knew of her intentions. F-troop had clear, strict orders. The few people with her would leave at the first sign of any major trouble and get back to Kraym and the attack on Circle. Rett and Corporal Ariam would take their own chances with the Yixolryn Coalition troops here.

She was aware of Pam with her, grateful now for the alien—no, grateful now for her *friend*. Pam remained still and quiet, waiting with her. It was nice not to feel so alone.

Composing herself, Rett relaxed her body and sharpened her other senses. Her thoughts matched the turbulence of the atmosphere, and getting one under control just brought another worry to the surface.

What condition would Ariam be in? Her muscles clenched as she thought of her own experiences as a prisoner of Commander Iheolon. Then she reminded herself it wasn't Iheolon who had Ariam, it was the Leader. Even so, she pushed any notions back down where they belonged.

Eyeing the sky, she accepted the fact she owed as much of her inner tension to the living energy of the approaching storm as she did to the situation. It was hard to factor out the huge discharges between sky and ground from her energy sense. The lightning made huge yellow explosions over all the other things she was trying to scope. She took the opportunity to practice screening it out and in a few minutes felt reasonably pleased that it no longer overwhelmed everything else.

The wind had died down and the world was eerily quiet. Only the soft dripping of water from branches and leaves broke the stillness. No birds. A mutter of thunder that went on and on, the sound waves vibrating the ground below like tremors from a distant earthquake.

Damn, why did she have to think of that? Now, watch, they'd get a quake. The entire length of Wide River and the land it crossed straddled a growing rift in the Nyorfian main continent, which was one reason no Nyorfian settlements were anywhere within twenty miles of the river and bridges infrequent. There hadn't been a tremor for months, but still, earthquakes were not strangers to this land. She didn't like earthquakes. Not one bit.

She let out the breath she'd held with the wind, in the last of the stillness catching the sound of a rover in the distance. They were sending a big one. Probably that amphirover, or something in the same class.

No time for other thoughts now. Not even the rising breeze or the purple-white flash of a lightning bolt striking something just a few miles away. Or the sky darkening with every breath she took. Rett's vision inside and out focused on the direction from which she'd heard the rover.

Soon, the detachment came through the trees. And Ariam was with them, yes. She didn't quite have a clear view, but the familiar aura, the tangled golden hair, the height of the head it crowned, and Rett's connection to her as a sister told her it was so.

A headcount was automatic. Fifteen troopers, one officer. Sixteen, unless there was a driver or a guard left with the rover. Already standing, hands in front and fingers open to show she held no weapons, Rett paid close attention to the detail. She saw nervous glances skyward from the troopers. Heard low, harsh reminders to pay attention from the officer. She held position, bracing herself a bit against the gusts now rattling the tree branches. Rett tensed as Ariam, still obviously bound, was hauled into the front. If they left her wrists shackled that would complicate things only a little.

She'd feel a lot better if they took off those mag-restraints.

A blinding lightning flash and almost simultaneous boom made the entire detail flinch. Rett took the opportunity to take a long, unnoticed step closer, a lethal heat replacing the cold dread inside her. The flash had given her a much better view of her sister, and a low growl rose in her throat. Unharmed, her ass! What did they do to her?

Ariam chose that moment to glance toward her. The cringing terror that her sister was showing to her guard detail vanished from her face instantly, halting the movement Rett had been about to make. Thank all deities she was putting it on…but she still had a reason for it. And she had been injured. Then Rett saw Ariam's lips form a single word.

Wait!

Released finally, the younger woman stumbled forward with a good shove from behind. Rett locked gazes with her. Ariam was trying to tell her something, with everything she had, a swift and silent exchange of information that used every subtle nuance of expression; motions slight enough to go unnoticed or be mistaken for natural movement, and empathic projection.

Rett's bond with Ariam had always been strong. Even as children they were each quick to accurately read the other, their thoughts picking up where the other left off. Fake getting hit? What did that mean? Did she read her sister's lips the wrong way? *What?*

Fake it. Friend. Ariam's signs were unmistakable.

Rett understood now, and moved her head ever so slightly in agreement. Ariam had somehow managed an ally. Doubts rose strong, but Ariam would have thoroughly vetted whoever it was before trusting, especially after the Mott-Shamos situation. So Rett would play along with whatever scheme Ariam had going. She only wished she knew exactly what the game was. And which one of them she wasn't supposed to kill.

They were all taking chances here, though.

In her turn, she continued to indicate with tiny body motions that there were rocks strategically placed in the grass, that the bio safeties on her weapons were enabled for Ariam to fire them.

* * * * *

Feeling a little better, Ariam took an unhurried step toward Rett's discarded weapons. She had heard that chilling growl from her sister even through the rising wind and thunder. Now things depended on Jaq Pym. She hoped he'd been able to make the switch with the power cells of the ML-12s. He told her it was his job to inspect and replace the power cells before his unit went anywhere and he would change them all out to training cells, which only fired a beam of light and mild heat.

Or so Ariam hoped.

She knew there was also a very good chance the Zetinorian would be killed in this. He knew it, too, but he was willing to risk whatever he had to.

"Damn it, let's move!" shouted the Coalition captain as a series of earth shattering booms followed four blinding flashes of lightning. The wind turned bitter and a sudden fury of fat, wet snowflakes whirled out of the sky. Ariam's unhurried movement turned into a blur as she scooped up Rett's TT-1 and weapons belt, throwing the belt over her shoulder and her body aside as the SMG strike came.

The sound's all wrong. Like anyone in F-troop, Ariam was more than familiar with the range of sounds from Coalition weapons, from the charging whine of the powerpacks to the release and passage of the energy discharges themselves. Jaq Pym's powerpack switch had been a success.

Coming around firing, Ariam dropped the officer in charge of the detachment even as she saw Rett take a direct hit from one of the ML-12s. Ariam fired off two more killing shots and saw Jaq Pym swing to cover her...

The beam of light energy hit her square in the middle of her stomach, leaving a spot of warmth. Thankfully, heat was all she felt. Ariam went with the pantomime of getting hit as much as she dared, making sure she stayed off her sore right arm.

Still clutching the weapon, she remained unmoving, lying in apparent death a few feet away from Rett. Ignoring the wet puffy slap of the snow, she sent a mental feeler toward her sister. Of course, no matter where she was on the planet and maybe beyond, she would know instantly if Rett were dead or badly hurt. But this time, even from up close she had doubts. Rett's more than convincing manner of hitting the ground, combined with this position of absolute boneless-ness, was so realistic she had to double-check. Only the absence of smoke told the truth. And the weather and the situation would cover that neatly enough.

"Shit! Move it, hurry up!" Taking over for his slain leader, the second-in-command of the detail urged his troopers. "Get the bodies and let's go. Pym, get the rover ready to go!"

Ice, not snow, started pinging off their helmets and armor. It stung as it hit Ariam's face. She kept it still, but mentally extended a push for urgency to the humanoid minds around her.

Hands grabbed her. *About time.* The sleet was changing to hail and hitting like shrapnel. It was getting too hard to remain motionless and pretend she didn't feel it.

Her sister moved first, with the deadly, blinding speed she was noted for. The sounds her sister's boots made hitting Coalition bodies were lethal. Knowing attention would suddenly switch to Rett, Ariam counted to three and made her own move a heartbeat later. She rolled over and fired point blank into the trooper over her, the shot passing completely through the humanoid's armor and into the trooper behind him.

Reaching with her left hand for Rett's long knife on the weapons belt, she drew it free of the scabbard and tossed it to her sister. It smacked into Rett's ready grip with a solid sound. Both of them were on their feet now and the remaining troopers were dumbfounded, but reacting. Unfortunately, the reaction came much too late for them. In minutes, they all were down.

"Damn it, Ariam," yelled Rett, rounding in on her. Ariam cringed, remembering a few times in the past when Rett would give her a good shake. Instead, Rett put her fingers to her lips and whistled.

"You brought backup?" Ariam couldn't believe it. "You?"

"Shut up. Just shut up." Now Rett grabbed Ariam's shoulders, her grip hard.

"Don't shake me," pleaded Ariam.

Rett eyed her up and down anxiously. "Let's move. There's a tornado the size of Cadie's Peak about three minutes from picking up where this left off. Are you all right?" She didn't wait for an answer. At Nerrah's shout, she propelled Ariam toward the Yixolryn low-slung armored rover.

205

Ariam dragged her feet. "Wait, where's Jaq Pym?"

"We *can't* wait."

Ariam's forearm and hand rose to protect her eyes. Her gaze, half slitted against the assault of the elements, ripped through the clearing counting bodies, looking for a big form even a short acquaintance had made familiar. "I have to know what happened to him, Rett!"

But Rett had a good grip on her. There was no way Ariam was going to get free, even with a major struggle.

Jessek urged them on. "We're clear, we've one left over, let's *go!*"

"One what?" shouted Rett.

Ariam stopped resisting at his answer. She hoped with all her heart the "one left over" was the Zetinorian, who'd risked everything to get this far. Then more clearly, she remembered hearing the second-in-command of the detachment telling him to go and get the rover ready to move. Thank all good deities.

"If we don't move now the only way we're hitting Circle is as debris, even in this armored beast!" yelled Ewayn from ahead. "Come on!"

The wind strengthened and Ariam heard a smack as if fist had hit flesh, followed by a hissed curse from Rett, who all but threw Ariam into the shelter offered by the amphirover and dove after. The rattling of hail now the size of baby fists deafened even the explosions of thunder and the rising shriek of the wind. The vehicle shot forward, only the ready hands of their comrades preventing Rett and Ariam from tumbling out the still open hatch as quickly as they had tumbled in.

For a minute, the sisters remained in a tangle of arms and legs, then Rett extracted herself. Kneeling, her hands again moved to grip both Ariam's upper arms, sitting her up so they faced each other. That was, if sitting up was a good way for Ariam to describe having her upper body vertical, her butt three handspans from the floor, and her legs going forward along the floor, one to each side of Rett's knees.

Sometimes, she forgot just how strong Rett was. Just how much she held back. "Rett, I'm fine." Getting her own legs tucked beneath so she too knelt, she lifted her gaze to the terrible anxiety in Rett's dark eyes.

Her sister scanned her up and down with complete, swift assessment. The grip on Ariam's injured upper right arm relaxed almost instantly, Rett's hand going flat there, a light of apology and concern surfacing through everything else.

"I'm fine, Rett, just roughed up. Arm's hurting, yes, just a good bruising. Most of that happened in the fight before they knocked me down. Most of this damage to my uniform was for effect. Looks worse than it is. Honestly. I'm all right."

Rett shook her head and hugged her close and hard, face tight against Ariam's neck and shoulder, her breathing rough. Ariam's own arms hugged back just as tightly; the hard shudder running the length of Rett's long body was echoed by her own.

"Who did we lose at the bridge?" asked Ariam softly when Rett finally let her get a good breath. She pulled back slightly so she could see Rett and glance around at the others with them. Ariam had felt several of those tiny "fingers" she kept on all the platoon members go cold and disappear, but she hadn't had time to dwell on them.

Ariam felt a sharp sense of pain from Steffi, who was behind her; saw the raw agony in her sister's eyes before they closed. Rett had to swallow a few times before giving Ariam a terse update.

"We won't forget them," her sister concluded quietly, "but I'll be eternally grateful you weren't among them, Ari." Rett gave her another hug and released her, the normal businesslike demeanor and face settling into place to become Sergeant Rett again. "Jessek. Update?"

Jessek was ready. "We're clear of this tornado for now, Sarge. It's headed right to the spaceport. Our units that were ready to jump there are holding back. It'll track right down the main runway from what I'm seeing. Attack started right before the first shot fired in that clearing, right on time. Coalition was watching the sky instead of us, so all units report no initial resistance.

"I've read one report all communication is down within the city," added Jessek, eyeing his Omni, "but it's not confirmed. Hail, rain, and gusts causing some problems in places, but our units are proceeding with caution where they can. A few more tornados are being reported here and there but nothing touching down yet."

"Good work. And this trooper we picked up, where is he?"

"Well, if he's not back here," Ariam said brightly, "he must be with Nerrah up front. Probably driving."

Rett groaned. "I should have guessed. I know Nerrah couldn't make one of these go so fast the first time driving one...I don't think any of us in this group can." She slid her headband over her wet hair and cued her pcom. "Fang Six, we're going to stop for a few minutes. Bring that leftover trooper back here."

Ariam leaned toward Rett. "Rett, he wants to join us. He's a good person. If it wasn't for him, things would have been very different for me so—"

One of Rett's fingers pressed into Ariam's lips.

"I understand, Ariam. And I know you've had some rough handling and it's easy to forget, just coming back, that we're not going to treat out prisoners the same way."

"Pris—" Ariam stopped her protest when Rett increased the pressure slightly.

"I trust your opinion, you know that. If you say he can be trusted and he's a good person, I believe you. Especially after that arrangement you and he came up with back there. But you know the procedures as well as I do. Defecting, escaping, whatever you want to call it, until he's cleared Major Yidnar and MainCommand's security checks, he's a prisoner. Understood, Corporal?"

"Yes, Sergeant." And wasn't she the one to tell Jaq Pym the very same thing a few hours ago? She'd gone and taken her speculation about the trooper's personal interests in Rett so far that she forgot.

Seconds later Nerrah and the trooper, minus helmet, armor and weapons, were in the back with them. The space that had felt roomy before was diminished: Ariam realized the Zetinorian was just as big without his armor as with it. His hair defied the weather, the wayward strands refusing to be beaten flat despite the water dripping from them.

Nerrah swiped rain from her elegant face, expression serene as always. Ariam felt bright amusement bubbling just beneath the surface of Squad Two's second, and there was a glint in her tilted black eyes.

"Report." Rett, on the other hand, wasn't amused.

"Sergeant, he's given his name as Jaq Pym, planet of origin, Zetinor Prime." Nerrah handed the platoon leader her Omni. "Says we can call him Jaq."

For a minute Ariam wondered why Rett didn't use her own Omni. She must have left it with Kraym. She would have, just in case things didn't work out. She needed Nerrah's to access the command net to let them know what's going on.

Listening to Nerrah's quick report, Ariam shivered. From the sound of it, Jaq had come close to death several times. Nerrah and Jessek had both had him targeted, and had Rett not given them a signal to hold fire, he wouldn't be standing her now.

"It was hard to hold fire when we saw you and Ariam go down," admitted Nerrah, "but we really knew something was up because the sound of the SMG discharges was wrong. Once you made your move, Sarge, Mikel and I decided we would need the rover more than they would, so we left the others to cover and went to secure it. That's when we ran into Jaq Pym. No trouble, no fight, didn't even look surprised. Said 'Take me, I'm yours.'" Nerrah shook her head. "Never had a trooper say that to me before. I think he's sick or something!"

Ariam, studying Jaq since his entrance, smiled. Jaq certainly had an incurable case. Not even Med's formidable skill would provide a remedy.

The Zetinorian's handsome face was as calm as Nerrah's and his gaze was locked onto Rett. The sergeant had yet to look up at him, busy with logging notations into Nerrah's Omni.

"Thanks for what you did, Jaq Pym," Rett said, addressing Nerrah's Omni more than the stranger. "You took a big chance and we all appreciate it. You won't be restrained while under guard, but any sudden moves will be regarded as hostile and met…with…force." Rett punctuated the end of her statement with stabs at the Omni's manual entry keys.

"I understand," he said.

No doubt, thought Ariam, Nerrah had given him the standard options when he'd given his name and had been disarmed.

Rett nodded, still not looking up. "Good. We're going to have to leave you in a while, and when we do you'll be secured, but we'll make sure you're safe. When we've the time, I'd like to know how you switched the power sources on all those ML-12s without anyone noticing. Among other things. But we're in a bit of a rush right now, so…" She looked up finally, and either lost the ability to speak or forgot what she'd been going to say.

Ariam had to bite hard on her lower lip to hold back a laugh. Was it coincidental, she wondered, that at the moment they had eye contact a thunderclap detonated so loudly outside it shook the rover? From the peculiar expression on Rett's face, one would think the lightning had hit her.

The look in his gorgeous blue eyes and the slow smile spreading across Jaq's lips would have melted the Scobey's River Glacier. But Rett cleared her throat, and Ariam could almost hear every extra shield her sister had slamming into place. "Right. Anyway, we've—"

The Zetinorian's smile increased a few degrees. "Whatever you need to do is fine, I'll cooperate," he said, interrupting her. "And I'm in love with you, Sergeant Rett."

"If it were *me* he was looking at like that I'd be flat on the floor about now," muttered Jessek to Ariam. "Take me I'm yours, indeed." He let out a low, soft breath.

"Now, now," Ariam murmured so Rett wouldn't hear. "Mikel might not appreciate that."

"Says who? I'd share," another voice behind Ariam muttered. She gestured for Mikel to be quiet.

Meanwhile, Rett pinched the bridge of her nose with a thumb and forefinger, shook her head, and let out a short, explosive sound that might have been a laugh. "You're right, Nerrah, he's ill." Extending a pacifying hand toward the Zetinorian, she said, "Look, Jaq Pym—"

"Jaq," he said.

"—don't worry, we'll get you to a medtech as soon as possible." Her other hand and arm went toward Nerrah with the Omni. "Good deities, I don't have time—mmn!"

Ariam's reflexes and muscles reacted to deflect Rett's offense as, just as he did back at the Leader's headquarters, Jaq Pym proved he had the ability to move quickly. As Rett stepped back, he closed the gap, took her face in both his hands and kissed her. Gentle, yet solid, the kiss landed firmly on her mouth, stopping her words midflow.

As the Zetinorian made contact Ariam wrapped her entire body around Rett's left arm. From the other side, Specialist Jessek threw all his weight around the sergeant's right arm, which was already starting to move toward Jaq, Omni and all. Thank all deities, Ariam managed to think, that Rett was so surprised he invaded her personal space, much less made contact! Or Jaq might have discovered just how far she would have rammed Nerrah's Omni down his throat before she and Jess grabbed her.

Ariam wondered if she had thought too soon, because at that point both her feet came off the floor. From the anxious expression she caught on the sharpshooter's face, Jessek's feet no longer had contact with the floor, either. Maybe they'd both end up getting stuffed down Jaq's throat with Nerrah's Omni. If Rett decided not to back down, it would take a full stun to change her mind.

"Back down, Rett," Ariam said softly, extending every scrap of her empathic talent into calming the retaliatory fury that had overtaken her sister.

Rett growled. She didn't fight them, but neither did she show any indication of retracting her anger.

"If you're done with this, Sarge?" Nerrah reached for her Omni, still gripped in the clenched fingers of the sergeant's right hand.

"Yes. Quite. Thank you." Rett spoke through her teeth, her face a breath away from Jaq's. Other than a warm flush of deeper color in her brown cheeks and blazing fire in her eyes, her face was devoid of emotion. "Take your hands off me and step back, Trooper Pym."

Ariam watched the Zetinorian with her eyes and mind. He flinched slightly at Rett's form of address, but overall, he looked pleased with himself and entirely unrepentant. He slowly let his hands and fingertips glide from the sergeant's stony face and took a half step back. He stood quietly as Rett shrugged off Ariam and Jessek's restraining holds.

"And that happened because…?" Other than tilting her head in inquiry, Rett didn't move.

The Zetinorian hit the sergeant again with a smile, this one not so brilliant and devastating, but soft and a bit wistful. "Because I've waited a long time to do that and don't know if I'd have another chance," he said. "It was worth it," he added.

Ariam went on full alert with Rett's sharp exhale. Again closing both hands around her sister's left arm, she whispered, "Let it go." The hard muscles under her fingers quivered with restraint. Ariam was glad to feel that much, because if Rett landed one punch on the Zetinorian without controlling her force it would probably kill him, built for a heavier gravity or not. "Rett. Let it go," repeated Ariam calmly, softly.

* * * * *

"All right." Rett took a deep breath, letting it out slowly. She had to calm down. She had a job to do. She would be professional. The poor guy was mixed up in the head, but he wasn't intending harm. Her fury subsided, leaving only annoyance. "All right then, hotshot, since you can get some real speed out of this rover, I'd like for you to get back up front and drive. Ewayn, Nerrah, you're up front with him. If you would cooperate and show them some of the finer points of this vehicle, it would be appreciated."

"Be happy to," agreed the Zetinorian peaceably.

Rett nipped back a few more sarcastic, useless and rather childish comments that started rising to her lips, and bit the inside of her cheek instead. What happened shouldn't have bothered her like that at all. It was minor, trivial and shouldn't have triggered much more than her reaction to redirect a possible offensive. With minimum force, although the verbal warning they gave always implied the opposite. Like she'd reminded Ariam: Nyorfians didn't treat their prisoners like the Coalition did, on any count. Had this Jaq indeed been intent on violence, he would have merely been neutralized and restrained.

She was emotional about it. Why? Why? There was no reason for it! She had nearly lost control over it, too. She might have killed him, and that would have been inexcusable. "Jaq Pym," she said, stopping his exit from the rover, "I apologize for an entirely too hasty assessment of your intentions." She forced her voice to one cool, distant, professional.

"Sergeant Rett," he replied, his voice altogether too warm and personal in contrast, "I was fairly warned of the consequences. And I thank you for a very gracious response, in spite of your warning."

And just what did he mean by that? Knowing he didn't refer to her intentions of dealing him a permanent disabling injury as he smiled again, Rett's pulse and body temperature shot up.

~You kissed him back,~ supplied Pam, matter-of-fact.

I didn't, did I? No. I… Feeling her temper start into the danger ranges again, she fell back to counting.

~You did. I'm right here, and trust me, I felt everything. Sure, you got mad he surprised you and invaded your space, but that was after you kissed him back.~

Forget it, forget it, forget it, she chanted in between marking the seconds it took to calm her mind and body. Finally, she forced an indifferent and cool show of teeth in response. She had more important tasks demanding attention. Time to get at them.

"Nerrah, Ewayn, when we get to where we're going, make sure he's in a relatively safe place and secure him. We won't be able to leave anyone behind to watch you," she explained to the Zetinorian. "They'll make sure you're not uncomfortable and I'll have my medtech take charge of you as soon as he's able."

"Sure," agreed Jaq cheerfully, giving Nerrah a friendly smile.

Rett didn't want to believe her ears. Nerrah hadn't giggled, had she? The ever serene and elegant Nerrah, who'd been, like Trebor, one of those left from C troop, had been with Rett a long time. Enough for Rett to know she did not giggle. Ever. At least, not where Rett could hear her.

She just hoped they all held together until this job was finished.

Shaking her head, Rett snapped out, "Move out! Let's go!"

Turning to the rest of her group, she realized forgetting what had just happened any time soon was an impossible dream. The Zetinorian's audacious action had already earned him five more admiring supporters beside Ariam. No doubt the sharp and observant eyes of her handpicked group had seen entirely too much from various angles and were trying not to turn inside out with the burning need to compare notes.

And all too soon, the whole of F-troop would be in on it. Forget them finding out Ariam was really her sister. After this, she could tell them Ariam was really another Yixolryn agent and they would still be more interested in the Zetinorian and speculating on if he was going to try anything else between now and the time they turned him over to Major Yidnar and MainCommand.

The sooner they did that, the better. Once he was gone, she'd have to live with the teasing for a while but like anything else, time would cure it. Besides, even though it had been a long time since anyone teased her, she'd grown up with worse. At least she knew F-troop's teasing came from a good place.

But the four smirks she saw at this moment in time were four too many. "Wipe them off, people!" she snapped.

They tried, she had to admit that. Their efforts to look serious almost brought Rett's own sense of the ridiculous to the surface and her lips twitched in response. Flattening them, she glared around, assigning Mikel and Steffi to keep watch and for Jessek to assist her with Ariam.

As they made quick repairs to Ariam's injuries and uniform, Rett silently thanked all good gods and deities, and the ex-Coalition trooper driving the rover, that her little sister's condition was no worse. Ariam had plenty of minor cuts and bruises. The head wound looked painful. The nasty bruising from right elbow to shoulder blade was a handicap. Ariam insisted, however, that she was good to go. She would be more so once the new dose of anti-inflammatory medication went to work.

Rett didn't have the heart to disagree. In Ariam's place, she'd be saying the same thing; having the same driving need to work what had happened out of her system.

"Maybe we should leave some of these rips alone," Rett muttered darkly after seeing Ariam's amusement had yet to fade. "Once the rain lets up we might need a decoy, so I'll send you out. It might stop at least part of the humanoid elements of enemy traffic long enough for us to get something done."

Her words did nothing to dispel her sister's smile, or the ones creeping back to the others with them. And she'd bet everything she had that Ariam knew he was going to do it. Rett snarled in her thoughts.

~Little sisters. Gotta love 'em.~

Rett ignored Pam for the moment, quite certain that if she could see Pam physically right now she'd have an asinine smirk on her face just as big and wide as Ariam's had been.

"Sure," Ariam was answering in a careless manner. "A few were pretty impressed before, and I think I'd be a lot more fun for them to watch than a tornado. Might work if you want to try it. I'll go out starkers with just my rifle and headband if it'll help."

The snickers from Jessek, Mikel, and Steffi were ill contained. Even Rett chuckled, thinking about enemy reactions to that scenario.

"Won't work all that well from any distance," commented Mikel lightly. "With all the dirt and bruises, they'd just think you were wearing infantry camos instead of our gear."

"Still might slow a few of them up enough for a second glance," grinned Jessek, applying another section of camo tape to the last rent over Ariam's hip.

"But what do you think about Jaq, Rett?"

Trying not to, thanks, she thought, pointedly ignoring Ariam's nudge.

"He's gorgeous," sighed Jessek, busy with Ariam's hair.

Ariam swatted him. "I didn't ask *you*."

He laughed and gave a playful tug to her hair in response.

"Well, Rett? And he kissed you," Ariam added.

If Rett hadn't known Ariam since birth, she might have thought her sister was jealous instead of thrilled to death and merely trying to rile her with teasing. Ariam was at her dramatic best, reminding Rett of the performances she used to put on as a child to get her way. Her second wore a perplexed frown as she adjusted her headband around the hair that Jessek had quickly smoothed, braided, and secured in her usual style.

Giving a final small adjustment to the way the black strip of material covered the neat bandage on her forehead, Ariam went on. "And with everything we did to make it look like he went at me, he might have well been Med." She managed, quite well, to increase the appearance of injured rejection to match the bewildered annoyance in her voice. "Absolutely starkers and never a look or feel. All he could talk about was you!"

"Are you finished?" Rett wanted to know.

"Not quite." The glint in those gray eyes was anything but finished. Ariam had an appreciative audience and she was enjoying pushing Rett's limits.

Eyeing Ariam's right shoulder, Rett calculated the amount of force she needed to apply to cause some serious long-term damage. Maybe that would shut up her garrulous younger sister.

"I've heard some interesting things about Zetinorians," commented Jessek, giving Rett a sly, sideways glance.

"You have? I've not heard of Zetinorians at all until I met Jaq." Ariam leaned toward the young sharpshooter. "Enlighten us."

"For one, once they're sighted in on someone romantically, that's it. Whether the feeling is mutual or not, they're stuck—they're already mated for life in their minds. And…they're supposed to be great at sex."

Rett gritted her teeth and said nothing. Again, the heat grew in her face. Shooting Jessek a glare, she made it perfectly clear if he kept it up he was getting tossed out the back of the rover on his head, one of her best sharpshooters or not.

Instantly his face flattened into cool neutrality. He didn't try to hide the twinkle in his eyes, though.

Pam started to insert her take on the matter, but Rett cut her short.

Oh, and yes, I suppose you've something else to say about...about that, thought Rett before Pam let her thought surface. *And before you ask, I'm allowing her to go on with this because it's blowing off a lot of tension for her and for them. But before you go off on teasing me like everyone else here, just let me say thanks.*

Pam's mental smile was huge. ~You're welcome. I'm glad things worked out. You play the outraged princess very well, too, by the way.~

At first, Rett didn't get the reference, having no idea what a "princess" was. Pam added some mental illustrations.

I did not!

~Oh, yes, you did. I was right here. Come on, admit it, you liked it. You thought about it ever since he hit you with those gorgeous blue eyes. You're still thinking about it now!~

Once more Rett denied it. She had doubts about the situation... and the implication the Zetinorian had made that she responded.

~Maybe not consciously,~ Pam was thinking, ~but your body sure did. And I don't mean that truly magical moment when you tried to ram Nerrah's Omni down his throat, either. Face it, Rett, he kissed you, you kissed him, and you liked it. You still feel it, huh?~

As a matter of fact, a warm tingle was still lingering on her lips. Rett felt the heat in her face deepen. *That's enough, Pam.*

~Good thing Ariam and Jessek had such a hold on you, or you would have overbalanced and fallen on him.~

Catching a knowing glance from Ariam, Rett gritted her teeth so hard she thought they'd crack. *Shut UP, Pam.*

~Sure, Rett. I think I've said it all for now.~ And laughing, Pam withdrew, making herself small again.

1.2.11 CIRCLE SPACEPORT
CENTERLAND PROVINCE, NYORFIAS
0535.06.31 (LOCAL RECKONING)

"MY LEADER, SHOULD WE PREPARE to withdraw?"

The Leader spun around and fixed his subordinate with a cold glare. "Withdraw?" His voice rose. "With an exhausted division and a paltry eight battalions attacking our superior forces? We outnumber them! By three full divisions!"

The officer cringed. He decided not to point out the fact that certain key elements of defense were experiencing severe problems from sources unknown and unrelated to the weather. Hail had destroyed more than half of their air cover on the ground at the spaceport. Some of the hailstones were the size of humanoid heads. A massive tornado had followed immediately, causing even more damage. Accompanying wind gusts had reached five times gale force. Defenses there had been scattered. A great deal of what remained had taken other sort of damage: more hail, more wind, and lightning, or so claimed the civilian technicians.

The officer had doubts about that, too. And to make matters worse, communications were being misdirected and garbled. Guidance and targeting systems on their larger weapons were being jammed into uselessness by conflicting signals coming from many directions and heavy atmospheric interference.

Of course, they still outgunned and outnumbered their attackers. To the subordinate, however, all that was of no consequence right now. One message had come through all too clearly. In his opinion, it was the only one that mattered.

He got right to the bottom line. "The word is," he said delicately, "that the plan to either kill or bring back both Killer and her sister failed, and the detachment that was sent is dead. Sergeant Killer and her unit have just breached the north gate of the spaceport."

Or, what was left of said gate. No matter. He and the Leader now stood near the southeastern portion of that very same spaceport in case a hasty retreat was called for, and Killer's unit was entirely too close for comfort.

The Leader's face darkened to the color of the swirling storm clouds boiling overhead. His tiny eyes flamed and threatened to start from his head. "I've had enough of that Sergeant Killer!" he screamed in a rising tone that ended in a near shriek.

A deafening clap of thunder punctuated his statement. "I want her shot! On sight! Is that understood? I want her dead body! Fifteen million credits to the trooper who brings me her ID discs!" He almost deafened his subordinate, his fleshy fist rising into the air as a vivid streak of purple lightning detonated somewhere across the wide landing strip.

"Yes, sir!"

218

"Then we'll gather the troops and regroup—to attack on all fronts!" screeched the Leader. "No mere female from an inferior race is going to make me look like a fool!"

The subordinate thought his Leader did look like a fool at that moment, but he prudently turned and fled.

1.2.12 CIRCLE SPACEPORT
CENTERLAND PROVINCE, NYORFIAS
0535.06.35 (LOCAL RECKONING)

THE BATTLE FOR CIRCLE LASTED three days and part of a fourth. The enemy tried to regroup and counterattack, but failed. Like the violent thrust of the storm front itself, the unexpected momentum of the initial strike, the fighting fury of the Nyorfians from almost any direction, and the cunning actions taken by the citizens within the city had the three enemy divisions reeling in confusion as if struck by a sharp blow to the head.

And now, on a sun-drenched afternoon on that fourth day, the weary men and women of the Free Army strike force wanted no more than the opportunity to drop in their tracks and take the time to breathe. When the remainder of the 52nd Division and other fresh… well, *fresher*, troops caught up with them that morning, Rett and the infantry officers of the strike force began turning over command operations to the new arrivals. More units, supplies, and equipment were being flown in from the military bases in Branch and Centerland, now that the skies were safe.

Rett couldn't remember when she had been more drained. It wasn't exhaustion, really. She didn't want to sleep, although she truly needed to. She was empty, and just wanted to sit and do absolutely nothing but breathe. Just for a while.

First she had to finish making her preliminary reports. Fortunately, Colonel Evard had sent her a handful of clerks, so all she and the other unit commanders had to do was talk.

Which she'd better start doing again. She straightened and gave the patient clerk a nod.

Even after the last of the thunderstorms rumbled away that first evening, and the stars shone brilliant and clear for the first time in over twenty nights, the enemy forces failed to recover. Scattered like leaves and branches torn from the trees, they lacked the cohesive strength of numbers that was their own best offense and defense.

Pam, I am not performing a drama reading here. I am trying to give a report. Now, come on. I appreciate your help, but if I start talking like you're thinking, I won't be talking to a clerk any more, I'll be talking to a psych med. You're as bad as Ariam.

~Yeah, but you're putting the poor clerk to sleep. It's okay to insert adjectives and adverbs between the nouns and verbs, you know.~ Pam pulled back with a big mental sigh.

The deployment of the attack forces as smaller, individual units sliced the city and the enemy troops within into neat little sections in which the primary targets were Yixolryn Coalition unit command posts, communications, and officers. The troopers within the sections were systematically destroyed if they tried an offensive fight; or held at bay if they went for a mild defense.

The next day was clear, starting out cool and turning warm. Rett had adjusted tactics to fit the weather change.

As Rett went on with her dry report, Pam thought to herself that while many hadn't noticed the change of weather due to the intensity of battle, the kids of Circle must have known it for sure. Through Rett, Pam knew that all families with children under a certain age had been sitting tight, safely underground or in a secure interior until the shooting stopped. Pam imagined what might have happened if those long- rainbound children and their stressed parents were turned loose on what remained of the Coalition troopers in the city. It was definitely a concept she'd have to remember later.

"The enemy troops still able to move and fight pulled back to the spaceport," Rett was saying. "The Leader's best troops were there, including several special units from Commander Iheolon's division. All made up from allied races, not assimilated ones."

The huge spaceport, almost covering the same amount of area as the city itself, was the scene of the most vicious fighting. The Yixolryn Coalition's elite forces were truly fanatical. They dug in and held out, and finally, half of those troops had launched a suicide offensive in the attempt to allow the Leader, his staff, Iheolon and the remainder of his forces to escape on one huge troop shuttle that had been spared both the wrath of the storms and sabotage of the civilian spaceport workers. What few AirSpacefighters and anti-aircraft weapons the Nyorfians had were unable to bring down the heavily armed spacecraft and they had to let it go. After that, as the enemy in and around Circle found themselves unsupported, most troopers gave up. The elite troopers didn't. There were no survivors among them.

Having delivered the basics, Rett expressed gratitude to the clerk. She knew she'd have to get into details and numbers later. But thanks to the help of this alert and meticulous scribe now, her job later would be far easier.

"Colonel's orders, Sergeant Rett—" the clerk informed her. "Find a place to sit back and wait for him to contact you."

* * * * *

RETT FOUND THE REMAINDER OF her spent commando platoon sprawled, in all the various positions exhausted bodies could assume, toward the sunnier end of an access path between spaceport buildings. Rett had thought to take them to a better place—there was a nice, grassy, tree-sprinkled hillside not too far away. After taking a look at them now, she didn't have the heart to make them move. Maybe here was as good as anywhere until Colonel Evard contacted her.

She leaned against a sun-drenched wall. The sight of a further reduced F-troop produced a dull ache. Twelve dead, nine going home for good. The rest of them a little worse for wear, but still good to go.

Half. The names and faces were seared into her heart. As much as the ache gnawed at her, she was too drained to feel much more at the moment. She saw Steffi, head on Ariam's shoulder, Ariam's arms around her.

She was glad Ariam was giving some time to Stef. Just as Med's Talent was priceless to those physically wounded, Ariam's helped soothed those who were grieving.

Ariam, in turn, leaned against Kraym, whose head was tipped back and corrective lenses slightly askew. So she was pulling from his gift as both buffer and amplifier, which accounted for the sad, tired, but relatively peaceful energy auras Rett managed to interpret for the rest of them.

No, she wasn't going to bother any of them for the moment.

221

Rett checked her Omni for the status on the injured: unchanged, but at least this time the message added that her visit would be allowed. *As soon as I settle these guys, I'll go.* And Colonel Evard had mentioned they would be in Circle for a few tendays or so at least, so once the mission details were wrapped up, they would honor their dead.

Thought was becoming a chore. Rett didn't feel like speaking, moving, or even taking a deep breath. The bone-penetrating warmth of the sun felt good. Her body didn't resist the pull of gravity and soon she sat against the wall. The Omni that had been in her hand had fallen to the cracked pourstone surface in the shadow of her right hip. She heard it hit the hard surface, but didn't care. She closed her eyes but kept a very small part of her attention on her pcom for Colonel Evard's call.

She never expected that communication to be so soon, or physical.

"Sergeant Rett!" a voice snapped out, a thoroughly familiar voice of command. "On your feet!"

Her muscles reacted to that voice, bringing her from a boneless sprawl to the absolute perpendicular so quickly she felt dizzy and nearly knocked the pair of officers flat.

The first face she focused on was SubColonel Evard, but this was not the voice that brought her upright.

What in two worlds? She didn't know he was within five thousand miles of Circle! For the second officer, in Special Forces combat garb, was Major Yidnar, commander of the 2023rd Special Forces.

"The rest of you, as you were," the Major told F-troop.

Rett heard her people settle back. She couldn't have stood taller if she'd tried, and she was trying. Her body and brain were wide awake, and painfully so. She rerouted with subconscious gratitude because the pain would take her a lot farther than her brief spurt of adrenaline had.

She kept her eyes front and reminded herself things could have been worse; much worse. No civilians had been killed or, aside from one report of a broken arm and a concussion from a large hailstone, even injured. That was the bottom line and all that mattered. In the light of that, the blistering reprimand she expected for her blatant disregard of procedure, leaving command of the attack forces to recover Ariam, would be nothing. She'd had that report prepared before she'd gone out to get Ariam back, and on her return, had kicked it back to Evard. She had no doubt it was the reason both he and Yidnar were here right now.

The results were worth the risk. Besides, not even a public reprimand from Major Yidnar could make her feel much worse at the moment, since her freshened energy reminded her there was more than a double handful of F-troop she'd never see again.

"Sergeant!" snapped Major Yidnar.

"Yes, sir!"

"The Colonel tells me he put you in charge of these attacks on the Wide River Gap bridge and Circle."

"He did, yes sir!"

"Casualties?"

She gave him the numbers and breakdowns for both sides and they sounded far larger now she spoke them aloud.

"Your own?"

"Twelve dead, nine serious, twenty minor but good to go, sir." She barely kept the pain from her voice. Those twenty, including her, stood or sat here now.

"I'm sorry for your losses," the Major said quietly. "They'll not be forgotten."

The gentle undertone in her commander's voice brought a fierce ache to her throat, which she swallowed down ruthlessly. "Thank you, sir."

"You have anything you want to tell me, Sergeant?" said Major Yidnar after a minute, his voice strict again.

"Yes, sir," Rett said honestly. "The jobs done by the civilian population of the city, my platoon and the rest of the strike force were exemplary, as indicated in my reports. But I feel my own performance, especially in the situation involving Corporal Ariam, was unregulated, inferior, and held back the operation."

Major Yidnar cleared his throat and when he spoke, a faint note of surprise was in his voice. "You do?"

Rett's back muscles started cramping from the effort of trying to stand taller. While she fidgeted inwardly, she never allowed her outward expression or position to change from the correct attitude expected of her.

"I do, sir," she answered.

"You've done one damn job for sure," said the Major in a half growl.

"Yes, sir," said Rett, wishing she could close her eyes and disappear.

"One damn *good* job, Sergeant," the Special Forces commander amended. "You're lucky you pulled everything off. Only for that are we willing to forget about your, shall we say, detour? I've been hearing a lot of stories and rumors lately, so I figured it was time I came up to check on you myself. At ease, Sergeant."

Rett relaxed into the position gratefully. *Good job, my ass,* she thought inwardly.

~I know the price was high, but you and the others did get the job done,~ Pam pointed out so quietly that Rett didn't protest the intrusion.

"Thank you, sir." She looked questioningly at her commander, relieved and comforted to notice his rugged features and lean rangy figure were the same as always. It had been two years since she'd last seen him in person. Perhaps there were a few more silver threads in his jet-black hair, maybe an extra stress line or two around his eyes, the dark metallic color of blued steel. But none the worse for wear.

"The 2023rd's pretty proud of you and F-troop, Sergeant Rett."

"We just try to keep up the battalion's reputation, sir."

Major Yidnar put his fists on his hips and regarded her with pained exasperation. "So far," he told her, in a perplexed tone, "we've run ragged trying to keep up with yours."

Rett felt her face get hot. "I wasn't alone, sir. And the weather helped." Her gaze dropped.

"Look up! If I were you, Sergeant, I'd be damned proud. No one could have pulled this thing off but you. The weather was a bonus, not the deciding factor. It was confidence in your reputation, and in your unit's reputation, that added motivation to this attack in the first place.

That's a fact, not luck. And in the light of things, even if it was luck I'll take it. So will the rest of Nyorfias and Epnoce. May I have your headband, Sergeant Rett?"

Rett's throat closed in panic. One's unit commander only asked for the headband if one were getting a new pcom, suspended on a disciplinary action, discharged, or promoted. She couldn't be getting promoted: she turned down the junior lieutenant's upgrade she'd been offered—for the third time—several months ago. He wouldn't do that to her and make it an order, would he? No. And her pcom worked fine. So she had to be in trouble.

Steeling herself, Rett reached up and lifted the black, blue-banded headband from her head. The Major's face, eyes, and even his energy aura didn't offer her a single clue. Fueled by adrenaline and nerves, she pulled everything she had into scoping him. Nothing. A normal array of blue, aqua, and gold. He could have been kicking back with an ale and preparing to tell one of his fishing tales for all she could figure.

225

The rangy man took her headband and spent some time examining it as if he'd never seen one before.

* * * * *

ARIAM LEANED FORWARD, HER INTEREST sharpening as she focused her tired talent on the Major. He was enjoying every single second of Rett's agony. Inwardly, Ariam grinned. The Major wasn't above putting on a dramatic act every once in a while himself. His training offworld with the GTC Rangers had left him capable of bluffing even Adept level talents. Yidnar's skill at not letting anyone know what he was thinking or feeling was legendary, and the subject of a lot of betting pools in Special Forces. Most of the time he had a good reason for putting on an act, but today she guessed he was merely enjoying watching Rett try not to turn inside out revealing her own inner feelings.

He finally reached into a compartment on his utility belt and started affixing something small to the headband.

Rett's shock and dismay flared so brightly against Ariam's wide-open senses it nearly made her gasp aloud.

"What?" Kraym nudged her in concern. "He's not sus—"

"Hush," whispered Ariam.

Ariam saw Rett's composure break for a moment into an expression of stunned protest. Then it disappeared into the cool, unemotional expression reserved for the most formal of occasions. The only problem was that the grayish undertone washing out the warm brown on Rett's face was a shade Ariam usually associated with nausea. Since Med was halfway to getting up, Ariam knew whatever Rett was feeling at that moment was anything but good.

Major Yidnar took a moment to admire whatever it was he had put on the sergeant's headband. Then, looking up, he said: "On recommendation of the citizens of the Nyorfian System, the Planetary Council and the staff at MainCommand, plus unanimous approval from F-troop and the infantry officers and troops under her temporary command as well as those senior to her, for actions over the past ten years Standard but especially for those most recent, Senior Sergeant Rett is awarded our system's highest recognition. As is my right and privilege as her acting commander, I am honored to present Sergeant Rett with the Freedom Star."

Ariam and the remnants of F-troop were on their feet now. They'd been trying to get Rett the Freedom Star for a few years now. The agreement had to be unanimous, and no doubt Mott and Shamos had somehow managed to hold it up previously. Now was the perfect time. Ariam's entire being swelled with pride and love for her sister; her platoon leader. She wished their father were here for this.

The Major settled Rett's headband in place upon her head, carefully keeping his fingers on the material instead of Rett's hair as he made minute adjustments. Ariam couldn't hear what he said to Rett, but whatever it was, it didn't change Rett's frozen stance, the set of her face, or the sick and chaotic feelings Ariam was still getting from her.

"It's about time," Ariam heard Pipano say softly from somewhere behind her.

* * * * *

"THANK YOU, SIR." RETT DIDN'T know how she managed to force the words out, or return the salute given her by both officers. She had recommended the award for several members of her platoon after the

Wide River ambush; just recently for her dead and wounded comrades, endorsed more commendations for the people under her command. The thought of receiving such an award for herself had never entered her mind. *All I need to do now is puke. That would finish me.*

~You're blushing again. And you've stopped breathing. Breathing is a good thing. Remember? Don't make me take over!~

The thought of Pam taking over at this moment was so terrifying that Rett recovered her aplomb instantly. She gritted her back teeth, forcing the heat on her face to go elsewhere. *I can't contest it,* she thought back. *I can't refuse, or protest, or give it back. I'll have to wear it as long as I wear a uniform.*

~Then wear it. Didn't you tell me once that what you want for yourself doesn't matter? Looks like what you've been doing has mattered to a lot of people, and they want you to know that. Wear it for them.~

Thanks, Pam. You're right. It is for them. For those here and those gone. Rett took in a deep breath and let out her personal discomfort on the exhale.

Major Yidnar addressed all of them. "All other commendations and a general memorial for those lost from the entire attack force will take place upon completion of this assignment. And of course…now that I'm here I'd like to be present when you send those from F-troop onward."

"We'd be honored, sir."

He nodded. In another moment, his serious expression transformed into a grin. "Oh, and incidentally, Sergeant, after that young Zetinorian, Jaq Pym, is debriefed, he'll be assigned to your unit as a technical consultant. He's a very valuable source of skill and information, not only technical, but tactical. You'll take care of him for us, won't you?"

Rett's expression froze. Everything else suddenly became trivial, even the threat of Pam taking control of her words and actions. "The Zetinorian? To *my* unit? An ex-Coalition trooper as an advisor…to a *combat* unit, sir?" A note of dismay crept into her voice.

She thought she heard a muffled snort of amusement from somewhere among her platoon. Nerrah? Rett couldn't believe it. First giggling, now snorting. Nerrah needed some time off. With Trebor. She'd arrange it as soon as possible. She modulated her expression and locked it down since what she was feeling inside was perilously close to taking over her face.

"You have a problem with that, Sergeant?" Major Yidnar's mellow tone bordered on the dangerous.

Fuck, yes! Rett shouted in her mind. "It seems highly irregular, sir," she said aloud, and no matter what her body and face said, she had no doubts the Major knew exactly what she was thinking. If only Colonel Evard not been there Rett would have felt free to argue her case a bit, but... *"if onlys" waste time,* she reminded herself and Pam with a deep mental sigh of resignation.

"It is. But that's the deal he wanted, Rett, and as far as I'm concerned—for what this man knows, I'll let him have what he asked for. And so will MainCommand. We'll go over the details later."

"Yes, sir."

"Any questions?"

"No, sir." Rett followed the Major's glance a bit anxiously at it roved over what was left of her grimy, scorched, ragged platoon. They looked just gorgeous to Rett. There wasn't one thing for which he could fault them.

Then from the corner of her eye she saw one of his thick black eyebrows elevate.

Ariam, Rett thought with a mental groan. The repairs Rett and the others had done to Ariam's uniform had held on for the past few days, wind, rain, and all. But during the past ten hours or so, it had all but gone missing in action. All of them were rather threadbare...but Ariam was down to camo tape and bandages. As Pam had observed earlier, good thing the weather turned mild.

"Sergeant?"

"Sir?" Rett answered innocently.

He cleared his throat a bit. "Try to make sure your second-in-command is wearing something more than med bandages and camo tape by tomorrow morning, Sergeant. You know it wouldn't be an issue if it were within our Battalion, but…" he shrugged. "As the only Special Forces unit here, F-troop has to try a bit harder to keep up appearances."

"Yes, sir," answered Rett.

"I'll be around, like I said. We'll take headbands off and talk later," promised Major Yidnar in parting.

He means we can talk like real people and not like commander and juniors, Rett told Pam swiftly before her ego-merge friend could ask.

Colonel Evard smiled at her. "You and F-troop sleep yourselves out, and we'll have the full debriefing at your convenience after that. If you and yours can make it as far as the new Battalion HQ," he gestured to the right and mentioned a thankfully short distance, "someone will fetch up F-troop's personal gear and show you a place to clean up and rest. It's a lounge area for spaceport crews—all the amenities. Lots of hot water, I promise."

Hot water…bathing tank. Rett wanted to kiss him. She settled instead for a grateful smile. "Thank you, sir. We'll take advantage of that." She accepted the large folder of hardcopy correspondence he handed her.

He walked away with Major Yidnar, and Rett was glad to notice Evard didn't limp too badly. She hoped the warm dry weather held for a while.

Corporal Ariam was the first to speak after the officers left. "Rett, turn around. I want to see how it looks!"

"What? Oh." Rett turned, frowning. "You know I—"

She was interrupted by concerted sound of approval from her people.

"Looks good on you, Sarge," said Trebor, pride in his deep voice.

~I want to see how it looks, too,~ complained Pam. ~Really see it, not see it from you imagining it.~

Later, Pam. Won't be long. "Look, you guys, I—"

"Face it, Sarge, we've been trying to get this thing on your head-band for a long time." H'tenneck had a deep look of satisfaction on his ebony features.

H'tenneck's only been with us for a year. I suppose when I was eighteen, a year seemed like a longer time, too. "Fine. Can I—"

Corporal Kraym cut her off this time. "You have to let people show more appreciation up front, Sergeant."

Rett crossed her arms, dangling the folder full of correspondence from her right hand. "Anyone else?" She cocked her head to one side and waited. "Can I say something now? Good."

She awarded them all a smile and put every bit of what she felt for them in it. "Thank you," she said. "I couldn't have done it without you. All of you." She knew better than to say anything else to them. She could stand up naked and unarmed to a battalion of Coalition troopers better than she could take even half of F-troop coming down on her for something as simple as gracefully accepting a compliment. Rett uncrossed her arms and gestured with the folder. "Letters."

Mention of news of friends, home and family energized them and it didn't take long for Rett to distribute the communication.

~What's up with this? Can't you get e-mail—I mean, messages from home—on those Omnis?~ Pam wanted to know.

Sure. But not during combat operations. Anything personal stops at a central point, gets hardcopied, and sent by courier. It's complicated, but it works. Heh heh, look at this. I've been waiting for this one for a while. Rett reached out and snagged a straggling lock of Ariam's hair when her sister started to walk away with Kraym. "Wait, Corporal. This came in for you." Rett handed over a thick little packet that bore seals from MainCommand and the 2023rd Special Forces.

"What in two worlds..." Ariam opened her packet. New rank patches fell into her hand. They carried the three circles of a junior sergeant followed by the half diamond of a platoon second.

"Congratulations. You've lived to make sergeant. You needn't have anxiety attacks about it any more. Do you accept the upgrade?"

"I accept the upgrade." Ariam's face glowed beneath its coating of dirt and dust. "Does this mean we can start arguing in public again?"

"Just don't get carried away. You've still four more circles to earn before you catch up with me, Junior Sergeant."

"And a Freedom Star," added Ariam. "Not that I want one, seeing all you had to do to get yours."

Rett swatted her. Ariam laughed and then hugged her so hard Rett grunted. "I love you, Rett."

"I love you more." Rett disengaged Ariam and stepped back. "Be careful with that arm. Come on, F-troop," she said to the others, "Colonel Evard says we're to go the Battalion HQ. He mentioned something about cleaning up."

She had everyone's attention now. Wearing days and days worth of dirt, sweat, blood, and bits of stuff best left unmentioned from any number of sources was fine when you couldn't take time out for personal grooming. But not one of them ever passed up an opportunity to clean up. Ever. "And then we can crash."

Ariam turned to Corporal Kraym. "Corporal!"

"Yes, Sergeant! Anything I can do for you?" Kraym snapped out a salute in his best style.

"As a matter of fact, there's a lot you could do for me," replied Ariam. "Some of my camo tape's coming loose."

"Yes," said Kraym. "I've been keeping both eyes on it."

"I'll bet," muttered Rett. From inside, Pam's mental snickers threatened to spill out of Rett's throat.

"What would you like me to do with it, Sergeant Ariam?" Kraym took two long steps and stood a fingerlength away from Ariam.

"Well, it's going to have to come off sooner or later," she told him, tilting her head and letting her lips form a mischievous, teasing curve.

Rett groaned and raked a hand through her hair. After what they had all been through, she was ready to forgive a certain lapse in the usual behavior expected in public, or even among each other, but this had the potential to go a little bit too far. "Save it for when we get to this place Colonel Evard has for us, Junior Sergeant, or Corporal Kraym will end up wearing all your tape before we get under cover. You do have an appearance to keep up, you know."

"You remember that when Jaq Pym starts working with us," Ariam said sweetly in reply.

"Shut up, Ariam," ordered Rett. She felt the heat bloom in her face as her sharp-eared platoon picked up on the new junior sergeant's comment and made sounds and whistles in response. "Let's move out!"

~oOo~

1.3.0 THE FOREVER CIRCLE

TREETOP LUMBER
FORESTRY MANAGEMENT AREA 010N
TREETOP PROVINCE, NYORFIAS
522.10.18 (LOCAL RECKONING)

T HAT OLD TREE WASN'T THE biggest longcone in this part of the forest, but it was the oldest. And it was Rett's. The ancient conifer had been standing for centuries, even before the first colonists came to Nyorfias four hundred years ago. But Rett, even though she was fourteen and old enough to know better, was convinced the tree had waited all that time for her. And she would do what she could do to make sure it was still standing for centuries to come.

It was a popular spot: the lower quarter of the tree was a natural magnet for all the children who lived near Treetop Lumber. Several stout limbs extended over a sheltered pool in the river for endless hours of splashing wet fun—provided a few adults were within shouting distance. Since the only time the pool was deep enough for such antics coincided with the steelhead run, having a few adults on hand was never a problem.

She shared the lower reaches willingly enough, but the upper parts were her true domain, her escape. The tree was almost her best friend. She smiled to herself, thinking of one of the secrets she shared with the tree. Today, she would share it with Ariam and Tovadan.

It was autumn, and the air was crisp and sharp. No swimming today. Rett and her siblings had spent the morning foraging and playing games, and it was time for lunch. It was Ariam who had suggested That Old Tree, since she only was allowed to go there with both Rett and Tovadan. As she came around a bend in the trail, Rett dropped her full forage bags, hitched up her shoulder pack, and ran. Her last running stride took her right up the side of the trunk. Then she made a leap for the first low branch.

"Come on, you two, I'm hungry! Don't drop your lunches."

Tovadan tried to imitate her. But even his most valiant effort fell short of reaching the lowest branch. He clung like a scale to That Old Tree's trunk; fingers and toes finding more than enough holds in the deep fissures of the bark. Rett turned to watch Ariam. That stubborn, familiar pout came on the younger girl's face, followed by a long, measuring glance. It wasn't hard to guess what her sister was thinking.

234

Ariam had been sick for such a long time, a strange condition that weakened her blood and bones. This past spring the doctors had said she was cured, but she still tired easily. They shouldn't be climbing now at all, after the day they had. Rett frowned. Ariam was going to be very sore that evening. Rett hated to see her sister in pain like that, but they all realized that the occasional day of overexertion also had the benefit of making Ariam stronger.

Never mind that, because stronger or not, Ariam was no way strong enough to try the stunts that she and Tova did so easily. Wrapping her legs around the tree limb, Rett dropped head down, extending her arms to their fullest reach. "Come on, Tova."

Tovadan, already more than half the way up to Rett's branch, grabbed hold of her forearms and scampered up her body with the ease of a longcone kurra.

"Ari—come up." Rett thanked all deities that Ariam didn't dwell on the running jump. Her little sister was excited enough to be allowed to climb the tree at all. By the time she was high enough to reach Rett's ready grip, she was flushed with exertion and breathless, but her eyes were shining. Ariam clamped her hands around Rett's wrists and hung there.

"Come on," Rett encouraged. "Like Tova did. You can do it."

"Swing me up!" demanded the little girl in a breathless giggle. "Swing me up with you!"

The light of pleading and hope in Ariam's small, pale face brought a swift reconsideration to the instant negative response that had been ready to leave Rett's lips. She weighed the frustration of her sister at always being left behind, being left out of normal boisterous games and activity. She had a hard hike today, but she didn't complain once.

"Please, Rett."

"All right. Just this once. You're getting too heavy for this," Rett grumbled, changing her grip. Inwardly, she doubted Ariam would ever be too heavy for her, but giving in to her little sister's whims without a protest would only encourage more begging later. Ariam was nothing if not resourceful at taking every advantage of those who fell prey to her wishes.

Still hanging upside down, Rett checked the path her body had to take to make certain sure it was open.

"Ready? Are we cleared for takeoff, Flight Control?" Rett called to her brother.

"You're cleared for takeoff and landing, Pilot!" called Tova from above, already moving into a position to catch and steady Ariam if he had to.

"Here we go—full power launch!"

Ari's delighted shriek frightened a curious flock of chewies into a complaining, multicolored whirl. The brightly plumaged birds had been following their progress ever since Rett and her siblings had left the yard around the sawmill.

Rett liked chewies. Some people thought they were pests, so naturally nosy, always feeling a need to be personally involved in the affairs of humans and other animals they spotted. Not to mention the pesky avians were always hoping for a handout. But Rett liked their bright colors, curiosity, playful antics, and the way they communicated everything from changing weather to the presence of predators. Like That Old Tree, they belonged here.

That particular flock wouldn't be back any time soon, though. Rett guessed that shrieking humanoid children flying about in the trees were just too much for even a chewie to handle.

The branch that Rett led them to was as broad as a table. At the point it emerged from the longcone's huge trunk was a soft thick mat of old needles, twigs, lichens and moss.

"This is a good spot." Tovadan unslung his shoulder pack. He threw his arms wide and gazed up into the shadowed heights of the ancient longcone, a greeting ritual every local in the area used to salute the tree. Ariam did the same, adding a few soft pats to the tough bark that supported them. Then they all got comfortable.

Out of their shoulder packs came water bottles and lunch: crunchy orange starflower bulbs, fruit, and slightly squashed grain rolls filled with a mixture of smoked steelhead and mashed bitternut pulp. The well-named bitternut's large seed was inedible, but the pale violet pulp surrounding it was rich and smooth. Rett took a big bite and closed her eyes. Food always tasted better up in a tree. She was happy. Today was a holiday from work and study, and life was good.

"I've never been this high up." Ari brushed the crumbs clinging to her fingers and to the front of her overall and watched as they fell to the forest floor below. Changing her position to stretch out on the limb, she gazed in delight at the new vistas offered by their perch. "I think I can see all the way from Cadie's Peak to Scobey's Glacier."

"You can if we go up another thirty lengths," Rett said, glad of the healthy color that exertion and fresh air had brought to her sister's cheeks.

"If we go up another thirty lengths, we'll have gone higher than any kid in Treetop." Tova gazed into the upper branches speculatively. "Except you, of course," he added to Rett.

"If we go any higher, we'll be in trouble," Ariam pointed out. "And we're already higher than any other kid has been in this tree but Rett. Too bad no one but us will know how high you've really been."

"Can we go anyway?"

"Sure, Tova. Later. Two or three or four years from now." Rett made a face.

Ariam sprawled lazily over the wide branch, her shining golden hair spilling over one side and wafting in the breeze. "Is it really very windy at the top, just like on top of a mountain?"

Rett nodded. "Most of the time, in good weather. But you know as well as I that a mountain peak doesn't whip around like a fishing rod with a big blueback on the line."

"Or a bug on a grass blade," said Tova.

"That's a good way to put it." Even so, Rett had to fight back a deep longing to dig her fingers and toes into the friendly rough bark and run to the top that very moment. It was as close as she could come to achieving flight and that sensation demanded sharing. One day, she promised herself, they would. When Tova and Ari got a little older, and Ari stronger.

"Is this your secret place?" Tova let the papery husk from a star-flower bulb drift off into the air and took a loud bite of the crunchy vegetable.

"One of them," she answered, glad Tova and Ari didn't push the subject of climbing higher. They still needed to climb down and finish the hike home, where they'd have to sort and store what they had foraged before falling like a pack of starving growtus on one of their father's enormous dinners.

They'd all sleep solid tonight, no matter what. Glancing skyward, Rett eyed the clouds. More storms or not.

"Is it still a secret now that we know?" Ariam rolled to her stomach and propped her chin on her fists.

Rett washed down the last bite of her roll and capped her water bottle. "It's our secret now." Leaning her back against That Old Tree's huge trunk, she said, "I brought you here for another reason. I've surprises for you both."

Her hands dug beneath the soft cushion of lichen, moss and old needles, her eyes never leaving the curious, eager faces wondering what sort of treasure she would show them.

Fisting her hands around the mysterious objects, she withdrew them from beneath their cover. She extended one arm to Ari, one to Tova.

Ari bit her full lower lip as it quivered in restraint and suspense. Tova leaned forward so far Rett thought he might lose his balance. Deciding she had prolonged their agony long enough, she turned her fists so her hands would open palm up and lifted her fingers. A sunbeam chose that moment to flare into brightness across her open hands. The resultant blaze of rainbow glitters flashing from the center of each of her hands astonished Rett as much as it awed her brother and sister.

"Good gods and deities and everything in between," breathed Tovadan. His dark eyes were huge and his voice cracked into a tone almost as deep as their father's. "Not for us?"

"Yes." Rett smiled. "They're not poisonous, you know. Take them."

"That's azurium."

Rett pulled her hands closer to her own body for a moment and peered closely at the crystals as if she'd never seen them before. "It is? I thought they were cones from a blue pine. Wait, I better put them back. I know those cones are under here somewhere."

Ash gray and charcoal dark eyes widened even more with her words, but Rett only made a token show of returning the crystals to their mossy nest. Then, with an exaggerated sigh, she wrinkled her nose and rolled her eyes. "I know they're azurium. They're for you. One for each."

"But that's the most important stuff in this sector, next to vichroxite and timber. Isn't that what we supply to the GTC, and what those other people trying to get us to trade with them want? You can sell them."

Rett noted that despite Tovadan's words, his covetous stare never left the glorious, rich color of the crystals in her hands.

"Why? It's just a rock. A couple little pieces. And this is their home, same as ours. Now you can take a piece of home with you wherever you go."

"Rett!" squealed Ariam. "They're the same. I mean, both of them are from the same stone. It's cracked in half. Did you…?"

"Good eye, as usual, Ari. I found it in the river." Rett waved vaguely upstream. "I thought it was one rock, but when I picked it up, the halves fell apart in my hand." She tilted her palms a little, watching the sunlight catch on the flat, sharp planes of the fracture the river hadn't had time to polish. "One for each," she repeated, stretching her arms longer than they already were. "I'm going to drop them…"

Tova and Ari both slowly reached for their gifts, taking them in careful and reverent hands. Azurium might be one of the most precious and expensive resources Nyorfias had to offer the galactic market, but the expressions on Ari and Tova's faces were beyond price. Rett leaned back against That Old Tree's friendly trunk, padding her head in her hands. She again eyed the deceptively peaceful looking stratocirrus clouds drifting overhead, enjoying the warm, satisfied glow filling her.

Inactivity didn't suit what she felt. Slapping a hand to the utility knife most Treetop residents carried since they were old enough to walk, Rett tossed a "Stay here, I'll be back" at her siblings and dropped off the big branch to some of the thinner ones below. She found the spot she wanted on the trunk and leaned her forehead against it for a moment, imagining she could feel the life pulsing beneath the thick armor of bark. *Tree. You didn't mind when Dad and Mother marked you. Would you mind this?*

That Old Tree wouldn't mind a bit.

Still smiling, Rett wrapped her legs around the branch she sat on and flipped upside down like before.

"What are you doing?" Ariam called.

"You'll see!" Rett swept aside her shoulder-length hair with an impatient hand as the breeze playfully pushed it into her eyes. *I should have used a hair tie.* In a few more seconds, her annoyance was forgotten and her short, sharp blade was busy against the outer layers of bark.

When she returned to Tova and Ariam, she had to nudge them awake. "Come on, we're going home."

She was careful to assist them—going down was harder than going up—over the spots their shorter lengths had the most difficulty. And she kept within arm's reach of Ariam. But for the most part, Rett let her brother and sister find toe and handholds in That Old Tree's deeply corrugated skin. That Old Tree wouldn't let them fall if they were careful.

Of course Ariam was the first to notice the fresh inscription on That Old Tree's rough face and slithered to a spot where she was able to get a better look. Then she reached out with her slender fingers to touch the marks Rett had made.

"Ari, Tova, Rett," Ariam whispered, and traced the forever circle enclosing them. "Forever together." Standing on her toes, she touched the older mark just above the new one. "Reve and Tonia. Oh, Rett, I didn't know this was here. Mother and Dad used to climb up here, too?"

Rett hid a smile in her sleeve. When she first found the mark on her own, she began to suspect the reason she had such a deep personal attachment for That Old Tree was due to the fact her parents had liked to linger in its secret places just as much as she did—although they probably didn't spend their time the same way. "They still do sometimes."

The three of them stood for a moment longer, Tova and Ariam both fingering the inscriptions. If they were getting anything extra from them with their empathic talents, Rett had no idea. Nor was she particularly interested: there were some things that were just enough to know without going in to detail.

239

Rett swung to the lowest branch on the side away from the river. "Come on. I'm for home and a bath."

Once her siblings were on the same level, she jumped the five lengths of distance to the ground.

"Why don't we just swim right here? I'm that hot," complained Ari. "The water isn't that cold yet." Instead of waiting for Rett to help her, like she was supposed to, Ariam slid her body over the branch and dropped.

Too startled to even gasp, Rett leaped to catch her before Ariam's feet touched the forest floor. Clutching her sister close, all Rett could hear for a moment was the pounding sound of her own heartbeat. Getting her breath back and swallowing hard, Rett opened her eyes and glared at Ariam.

"Next time you do that, I might not be here to catch you!" Rett scolded as she gave Ariam a shake. She added another for good measure before setting the little girl gently on her feet. "You remember what the doctor said about your bones! They're getting stronger, but it'll be a year or so yet." Only when she saw Ariam wince did she realize she had again forgotten to hold back the force of which she was capable. Rett's stomach clenched and she loosened her grip. "Do you want a broken bone? Or to have to stay home all the time instead of come with me and Tova? Or worse...do you want to be dead?"

Ariam dropped her head penitently and sent Rett an unhappy glance from her huge gray eyes. "I thought I could do it. I'm sorry."

"Hhmph." Rett gave Ariam a final rough shake and turned to watch Tova's descent. "No, we can't swim. It's getting dark and it's getting cold. Come on then, sport," she told her brother.

Tova hung and dropped, too. Rett didn't worry about him as much. His longer legs and stronger bones withstood the jolting landings he gave them. They gathered up their forage bags and started on the homeward trail.

Ariam lagged behind. Not even Tova's encouragement brought Ariam to walk with them. Rett ignored her for exactly ten strides and decided she didn't have the heart to be cross with her any longer. Telling Tova to go ahead, Rett halted and waited for her sister to catch up.

The quick hand the little girl ran over her eyes didn't remove the telltale tracks of tears in her flushed and dirty face.

She was so sensitive. Rett felt like a monster for making her cry.

"You scared me, Ariam. I'm sorry I yelled but when you let go of the branch, I wasn't ready. I was afraid I'd miss and you'd be hurt. And I'm sorry for hurting you."

Ariam flung herself into Rett's open arms. "I'm sorry for not listening. But, oh Rett, I'm tired of waiting for my bones to be strong. I want to do what the other kids do. What you and Tova do. It doesn't make sense that I'm strong enough to pull myself up, or swing, but I'm not allowed to jump, or even run sometimes, only where it's smooth. I want to go rock climbing with you and slide through all those slippy weedy rocks on the Blueback rapids…and I c-c-can't!"

"Shh, shh." Kneeling, Rett hugged Ariam close and then dried her tears with a clean corner of her shirt. "You will. I promise. But you have to be patient. I promise next year when Tova goes to Epnoce, I'll take you as high to the top of That Old Tree as the weather lets us go. Just you and me."

"Really?" Ariam sniffled, but the clouds in the gray eyes were giving way to stars.

241

"Have I ever broken a promise to you or Tova?"

Ariam sniffed again and wiped the back of her hand across her nose, smudging more dirt across her face.

"Oh Ari," sighed Rett, giving into a chuckle. Digging into her pack for her water bottle and a wipe, she started cleaning the smudges and streaks from her sister's face. She repeated her question.

Ariam's long hair swung as she shook her head. "Not ever."

"Well, then." Rett stood up and held out a hand, closing it firmly over the small thin fingers that extended so trustingly. "Let's go home."

"Yeah. I heard Daddy say he was roasting mushrooms, and you know what happened last time you were late…"

Rett dropped her sister's hand and growled. "You better run, because I'm going to get you for that."

The younger girl half-screamed, half-giggled, and started running.

~oOo~

1.4.0 LEAVE OF ABSENCE

52ND DIVISION HQ, CIRCLE SPACEPORT
CENTERLAND PROVINCE, NYORFIAS
0535.07.26 (LOCAL RECKONING)

A FLICK OF HER FINGER SAVED the selected portions of Intelligence and tactical reports to her personal file. Rett might need to pull up those bits later, for other assignments. F-troop had been going on sporadic missions since Circle, cleaning up pockets of remaining Coalition forces here and there. The rolling hills of Centerland Province—and some interesting new shielding devices that even now were being altered to use against their enemy—had hidden a surprising number of small Coalition bases. Those bases were guarded by enemy soldiers better trained, more motivated, and willing to hold out at all costs while waiting for the reserve troops on Epnoce. That very few of these troopers turned out to be of the more humanoid variety—most of them were from the Yixolryn core worlds and their earliest allies—was not a surprise.

~You guys really stepped up. Smaller numbers, lower technology, and all. Kicking major enemy butt.~ Pam sounded awed.

Well, we are defending our home. And hopes are high now. We can't lose sight of the fact that there were still more Coalition troopers in the system than Nyorfians. Or, that the protection of those GTC support forces on the borders in space could be breached by a determined offensive from outside the system.

But look at this, Pam. Rett tapped the screen of her Omni. *Not only did they make it to our space—they've made insystem, and got through the Coalition defenses around Epnoce!*

~They? Who? You know I can't read your language,~ Pam complained. ~I'm still trying to work out how it is that I can only understand what I see and hear through you when I'm...~ She hunted for a concept. ~When I'm more forward.~

Sorry. Rett didn't understand how Pam's perception and understanding through the ego-merge worked either, so she skipped right to the part she did understand. *It says here that a special task force of GTC Fleet, Rangers, and Nyorfian Spacemarines have managed to get inside Coalition defenses surrounding Epnoce.*

~Anything about Mott and Shamos?~

No. Rett kicked a stone from her path, perhaps a bit harder than she intended, for it ricocheted from the side of one of the temporary buildings she passed and she had to jump sideways to avoid it whanging her in the knee. *You know I check on that a few times a day. I think they managed to get offworld. That, or they're very well hidden.*

Rett didn't hold very much hope that they would find any traces, given that Mott and Shamos could have turned into anything by now. That they were born three-quarter Yixolryns and somehow made to pass for full humanoid, humanoid enough to fool medical scans, was mind-boggling to Rett. It gave her a major headache just thinking about how it was possible. So she stopped thinking about it and trusted the more scientific minded of the Nyorfian population would figure it out. She'd rather expend thought energy into figuring out how to find them. Although if those two had any real brains, they'd be far, *far* offworld by now and never return.

I'm busy right now, Pam. So if you don't mind—?

* * * * *

FROM WITHIN RETT, PAM HAD reached the absolute end of her forced patience. This pattern had gone on for almost three weeks…well, for a bit over two tendays, as they reckoned time here.

No matter how one counted it, it had gone on long enough.

Understanding what Rett's job entailed and how incredibly busy her host truly was didn't make it better. Pam endured wrapping up of details, briefings and debriefings one right after another, the endless reports, all without one single leak of thought to interfere. Through F-troop's memorial, where the recovered dead were sent onward in fire, through the more generic but no less moving service given for all those dead from the attack forces, Pam had simply offered silent support.

Oh, she wasn't entirely sitting back in her "corner" during those times, only holding that complicated balance that allowed her to comprehend everything that was going on without interfering. She'd been a little more forward in Rett's consciousness than that. But she had been quiet. And Rett had been very aware of her then. It was as if the Nyorfian needed the reassurance that she wasn't as alone as she felt making those personal video calls—and even a few local visits—to the families or friends of those in F-troop who'd been killed.

The few times she had crept forward, like just now, Rett answered briefly, and then asked her to withdraw again.

Pam had had enough of it.

She wasn't only feeling rejected and overlooked: she was worried. Rett had been going non-stop since Colonel Evard had put her in command of that chancy mission. She had a good idea why the sergeant was so driven, but there was no excuse for such extremes.

And damn it, she wasn't about to stand here as part of Rett and not stop her from killing herself from the inside out. Pam kept her personal thoughts well below the level she and Rett used to communicate directly. It was getting a lot easier with all the practice she'd had lately, Her host was running on fumes, and that just wouldn't do. Everyone had been after her to slow down a bit, from Ariam and Kraym, to

Med, Colonel Evard, even Major Yidnar. Pam knew the Major wasn't kidding around when he had taken Rett aside before he left and told her she had to start turning over more work to her juniors.

Well, all Rett's chores were completed now, so there were no more excuses. And from what Pam had been able to understand from Rett's reading, things were going to be quiet for a while. F-troop had just been placed on conditional standby, which meant they were on free time but restricted to the base. The "base" was the new 52nd Division HQ, which now occupied the southeastern end of the Circle spaceport.

F-troop had a very comfortable bivouac there. From Rett, Pam knew it beat anything the Nyorfian had experienced in field conditions, if it could even be called that, in ten years. When not on active assignment, they were still staying at the transient shuttle crew quarters, with real bunks, real bathrooms—the Nyorfian equivalent of them, anyway—and one thing that Rett looked forward to every chance she had: unlimited hot water.

Eating, sleeping, and hanging out; recharging physical, mental and spiritual batteries for a few days by doing absolutely nothing was just perfect for most of Rett's platoon, especially lately. Perfect for everyone except Pam's host, who now walked along in the shade of the building housing the 52nd CP staring at the display of her Omni as if her life depended on it.

I'm going to have to learn to read this language by myself soon. Pam then focused on her plan to get Rett to take another nap, like she had managed a few days ago.

* * * * *

CHECKING HER TASK LIST ON the Omni, Rett realized there was absolutely nothing else that demanded her attention for the next several hours.

Nothing. At all.

"Then where am I going?" She came to a stop about ten paces before the front corner of the building, more than a lack of chores on her list prompting her. The combat sense and ability to scope energy auras that training and years of experience had developed in her encouraged caution: there was a group of people right around that corner. Normally she might have kept right on going, but lately she had taken to making sure she knew who she was going to find before being surprised. Only part of that was due to a recent confrontation with well-meaning Nyorfian news correspondents after the Coalition had been ousted from Circle.

Rett pushed her awareness forward. Someone had stuck a table and a few benches out there a tenday or so ago. Many stopped to linger since it was nice and sunny in the morning, shady in the afternoon, with a nice view of the rolling green fields of Centerland Province rising around an arm of graceful cityscape.

She exerted only enough focus on the personal energy auras of those present to feel the general mood of the group. No threat.

The breeze skittered around the corner, bringing with it the dark rumble of male voices and a deep chuckle or two. Rett eased a little closer, a smile growing as she identified several of them: H'tenneck, Trebor, Nitraym, Colonel Evard. And deities, was that Med? Yes. The discussion seemed lively and she was tempted to see just what it was about when another voice from the group stopped her mid-step.

"Well, far be it from me to interrupt," she said under her breath.

~Chicken.~ The single thought surfaced with a single explanatory image and about ten billion levels of tiff. Some strange mental noises followed.

Pivoting smoothly one heel, Rett reversed course, her conscience twinging for not responding to Pam. She had things to do yet. The missing task from her list, for example.

Jaq Pym. Ex-Coalition trooper, new F-troop tech advisor. Definitely another item she'd have to deal with eventually instead of doing almost everything to avoid him. Like it or not, he was part of her unit now and she was, technically, his boss.

Major Yidnar had spent several extra days after the Circle details were wrapped up, for the sole purpose of debriefing the big Zetinorian. Now Jaq Pym was verified—by a Master Adept, no less—who said there was no doubt of the Zetinorian's sincerity or intentions. Things were then set up: he was registered, sponsored personally for potential citizenship by Major Yidnar, and other details made all nice and neat and legal.

No doubt he and the Major were now the best of friends, thought Rett a little sarcastically, still tiffed over having the Zetinorian forced on her.

The Major himself had delivered Jaq to her before he had to leave. He had chatted with them both, going over exactly what Jaq could and could not do before, during, and after the security clearances and set- tling in processes and everything else. Rett had to feel some relief that he wouldn't be going with them on combat missions—at least not yet.

And all the while, the implicit warning in the Major's gunmetal blue eyes told Rett in no uncertain terms that she'd better suck it up and deal with it. Properly.

248   So she had, temporarily, anyway. She'd seen to kitting Jaq with uniform and gear, ordering them from quartermaster services. As an advisor and with his special status, he wasn't going to be carrying weapons, so she had to make sure he was capable of defending himself in other ways. She designated Pip and Bhayorn to see to that. He was supposed to share knowledge with them, so she stuck her new technical advisor with F-troop's more technically minded. Jaq wasn't allowed to go on assignment with them yet, so when F-troop was away, he had to wait it out at the 52nd Division's Ops center where he worked on projects for MainCommand. In addition, Jaq had an entire schedule of daily duties just like anyone else.

So far, it worked out just fine for Rett. Especially since when people were off duty she hardly saw Jaq or his new best friends anymore unless they all had their heads together over something.

She couldn't keep avoiding him like this. It wasn't right, or fair, and it was too easy to get stuck in a habit if she let it continue. Sort of like she'd been doing with Pam. A twinge of guilt rose from her toes. It wasn't like her, acting like this. So why was she?

~I can offer a few ideas,~ thought Pam in a black grumble without budging from her corner.

Why don't you start by telling me what a chicken is? returned Rett. She failed to understand the significance of the fat white bird creature Pam imagined.

The smokescreen disintegrated, but the black sulk stayed with Pam and her mental "voice" retained a definite note of accusation. ~Well, where I come from, not on all parts of Earth, but in my country, when someone calls someone else a chicken it's because someone else is scared to do something—usually something there's no valid reason to be scared of in the first place.~

You mean about Jaq Pym. Well, then you're hitting the target pretty close there, Pam. But I think I have a valid reason.

~You think he's good looking?~ asked Pam.

Good gods and deities, I might be a chicken, but I'd be the last person to say he wasn't in the top handful of best looking humanoid males I've seen. And all right, while we're at it, he seems nice, honest, and likeable; most of the platoon's in love with him in one way or another. Major Yidnar has all but adopted him. You've seen how he looks at me, though—

~Oh yes.~ Pam's thoughts turned very dry. ~Would that be the "Hi there, I'm Jaq, and I'm attracted to you and want to get to know you" look, or the one that strips you naked and makes you feel like slime?~

He doesn't look at me like that, Rett shot back, a bit startled at her own vehement defense.

~My point exactly.~

I didn't really want to discuss Jaq. "But come to think of it," she finished aloud, "that gear I ordered in for him hasn't come in yet. I know I was sent a confirmation on it..."

~You really do the evasion thing well. Maybe you should write a manual on it.~ Pam went seething back to her place.

Rett checked her Omni, frowning. Yes, there was the confirmation. Growling, she made a notation to follow this up with a voice call. Good excuse as any for her change in direction.

~Chicken.~ More odd mental noises followed.

Rett sighed. *Pam—*

~Will it be "Later, Pam, when I'm not so busy?" again, or do you have a new excuse?~ queried Pam with exaggerated politeness.

One side of Rett's mouth curved into a lopsided grin. *As a matter of fact—*

"Sergeant RETT! In my office now!"

Colonel Evard's cheerful bellow was probably heard loud and clear all the way to the Wide River Gap.

~Busted!~ came from Pam with an evil little chuckle.

Rett felt anything but amused. The only way Evard could have been alerted she was nearby was from Med. And Med normally didn't vector in on individuals unless something triggered his talent as a healer empath.

~You've been getting warnings from everyone to slow down.~ Pam didn't have to add the "told you so" implicit in her thought.

Then why would Evard call me, and not Med show up right in front of me like he always does, ready to drag me off to his lair? Rett ran a hand through her hair, raking her headband off with the gesture. Smoothing the short, thick growth on her head, she slid her headband back in place. *What is it? I feel fine.* She flicked imaginary dust off her uniform and checked the lay of her headband. Her frown grew as she retraced her steps and came around the corner she had avoided only seconds before. No one sat at the table now.

I don't like this, thought Rett uneasily. She felt like she was walking right into a trap of some sort.

Letting out her breath in a soft sigh, she shook her head and went inside as usual. *I'm being ridiculous. Evard's always wanting to talk to me about something.*

She greeted Evard's adjutant with a smile. As always, he was busy, but never busy enough not to grin back. With his usual, "Colonel says to go right in, Sergeant," she went past, stepping through the open doorway into Evard's office.

* * * * *

"CLOSE THE DOOR AND DRAG a chair over, Rett," said Evard. He leaned back in his chair as the tall woman silently complied, closing the door behind her without a sound, a long strong arm snagging a chair from the selection against one wall. She sat, giving him a smile, waiting in silence for him to speak.

He liked to have a comfortable relationship with people under his command, temporarily or otherwise. Gaining such a relaxed familiarity from F-troop's leader had been a battle worth fighting, and he was more than satisfied. If he hadn't jumped on her right from the beginning, she still would have saluted him before sitting down so stiffly he would have to think her body was composed of right angles.

Sure, the Special Forces formality was a shield, but let her, and the rest of them, use it elsewhere. Not with him.

Studying her in silence for a minute, he thought if any branch of the Nyorfian defenders needed such a strong shield, it was certainly Major Yidnar's 2023rd. The Special Forces wore no armor and carried few weapons, but due to their inflexible training and code of conduct, they were the best fighting people in the system. Rett's unit had proved that beyond a doubt barely three tendays ago, during the battle for Circle.

The sergeant sat patiently under his scrutiny, her posture relaxed, but alert, her attitude one of polite inquiry. Evard didn't waste time in small talk when he finally spoke.

"How'd you like some personal time off, Rett?"

"Not really, sir. Not right now."

He leaned back in his chair, his expression thoughtful. "According to your records, you've been managing to pass up personal free time for three years now. Started when you were still in C-troop. Passing it up as often as rank upgrades! Don't you want to go home for a while?"

The sergeant's face hardened slightly. "Coalition burned down most of it, sir."

Evard had heard about that, of course, but he didn't think it had harmed her home or the town of Treetop. Even so, he supposed he wouldn't want to go home on a short visit to see the landscape and the home he loved destroyed, either. It wouldn't give someone much to look forward to, that was for sure. Unless…"Friends and family?"

"My friends are in the military, sir; as for family, Ariam's already here."

The way she stressed it gave Evard enough warning not to bring up any mention of Colonel Reve, Rett and Ariam's father. Junior Sergeant Ariam had forewarned him that the platoon leader and her father didn't get along. He couldn't help wonder why, especially since Ariam hadn't indicated she felt the same way.

"Nevertheless, I've noticed Sergeant Ariam doesn't pass up her personal time off. Nor does anyone else from your platoon. Sure, they asked for delays when things were hot, but they all went." Evard looked at her earnestly. "Since Circle, you've arranged for everyone but you to have at least a few days break. It's your turn to get away for a while. Change of scenery."

Evard felt some regret as her relaxed posture began straightening. The openness in her face faded.

"What have I done wrong, sir? Have I slipped up? Made any mistakes?"

"I have no issues with your performance. But you're looking a little run down lately. Four tendays off, away from here, would do you all the good in two worlds, I think."

He'd only seen this sort of incredulity on her face once before, when he first proposed she lead the attack on the Gap bridge. The way Evard saw it, about right now Sergeant Rett was wishing to find herself facing an entire armored division of Coalition troopers, unarmed and in a corner, than hear him suggesting she take a Standard month off for herself.

"Four tendays. You want me to leave for *four* tendays!"

"That is a lot less time than the total of all your passed up days, Rett. I could make it longer, if you want," remarked Evard, knowing he was playing with a potential tornado saying that. It had to be said. He was ready for her to push the issue that she or her unit wasn't technically under his orders. He hoped it wouldn't come to that, but started getting the feeling she wasn't going to go peaceably. "How about I arrange someone to go with you? Would that make it easier?"

"How about the entire platoon, sir."

"Can't do. What about that young Zetinorian?"

A flash of pure tiff flared in those dark eyes. "I don't think so. Colonel—why?"

"You can't keep going the way you are. Mott and Shamos had been purposely running you and F-troop into the ground, and this Circle campaign nearly wiped you out. You've never had a chance to recover *completely*—" he stressed the word when he saw her ready to argue that point, "—and sooner or later, it's going to catch up with you. Then you'll probably be forced on disability. Even worse, you'll get all your people killed because of some careless mistake."

The sergeant closed her eyes for a moment, no doubt remembering the disastrous ambush at the Wide River Gap Bridge. They were lucky that time not to lose anyone. Not so much when they went back to take it. That hit her hard.

"Sir—"

He cut her short. "I've spoken at length with your medtech and Major Yidnar about this, Sergeant. Especially with your medtech. In case you didn't already guess, he was the one who tipped me off you were right around the corner."

She gave a short nod to indicate she'd figured that out.

"You know you have to give your body a break from the regulators, leave it function normally once in a while. If there's any thought of children in your future you know you have to."

"Yes, you're right, sir, but we're almost finished here. I could take time before we—"

Evard shook his head. He could wait and try to argue her into agreement for a tenday without going anywhere, so it was time to pull out his heavy artillery and fire for effect. "No, Sergeant. You know how it goes. Something else will come up later. The right time is now, when we have things well in hand. Your seconds are competent, well proven, and able. I didn't want to do it this way. I'm making it an order."

"With respect, Colonel, I—"

He waved a hand. "I've been duly authorized by Major Yidnar to take whatever action I think is necessary in this case." He lifted a notepad and turned it for her view. "I'll send a copy of this to your Omni, you can look it over when we're finished here."

Her brief flash of shock was masked so quickly he couldn't be sure he'd even seen it. "I know you don't like that I did this. I didn't like having to do it, either. But my order is better than a Medical suspension. And your medtech is threatening one. So you'll leave tomorrow; I'll have a rover waiting at 0700. Wear standard grays, like anyone on leave. You'll go to Branch, from there you can go to whatever other secure area you like."

Evard swore he heard every shield the sergeant had slamming into place. Her demeanor changed to the very one he'd worked so hard to avoid: distant, polite, emotionless. And, he noted sadly, sitting as if her body was composed of right angles.

"Yes, sir. Thank you, sir." She stood. "Dismissed, sir?"

He kept a weary sigh in his thoughts. Special Forces wasn't the only branch that practiced keeping expressions on or off their faces. "Only to make arrangements with your seconds' in command, have a visit with your medtech so he can pull your implants, and pack up."

"Yes, sir."

And as quietly as she had entered, she was gone.

* * * * *

FOUR TENDAYS! FORTY ENTIRE DAYS! *One Standard month. What'll I do? Nothing? And you just shut up!* she flung at Pam.

Pam protested. ~Damn it, Rett, it's not my fault! They're right—you know they are. Everyone's been telling you to slow down and you just wouldn't listen. Not to mention you were headed for a meltdown before I even got here. You can't run and hide by working yourself to death.~

With a mental and physical snarl of rage, Rett tried to slam up a wall between their consciousnesses. She felt something come between them, but knew it had been Pam who kicked closed the mental door. And kicked it hard enough to set off an instant tension headache, which only added to Rett's present level of tiff.

She ignored the unasked for alien presence in her mind. She knew she was being unfair, since Pam never asked to be merged either, and always had Rett's best interests at heart. But at this moment, Rett was too angry to care.

Focused as she was on her enforced vacation, she barely avoided a collision with Corporal Kraym as she exited the CP.

"What's up, Sarge? We have an assignment?"

"I'm leaving in the morning."

"On assignment? Just you? That's pretty strange."

"Major Yidnar gave special authorization to Evard and he's ordering me on leave for *four* tendays," Rett clarified savagely.

"I'm sorry he had to make it an order." Kraym said nothing else for a while, and Rett seethed. *So Kraym is in on this too. Ariam. Everyone, probably.*

~God, Rett, they care about you. They want you at your best. Isn't that what they're supposed to do, just as you do for them?~

Shut up, Pam.

"But I think that's great, Sarge," said her co-second. "You know you're way overdue for some personal time."

Rett snorted. "What's so great about it? What am I supposed to *do* for a month?"

"Wouldn't hurt if you slept the entire time." Kraym kept pace with her as she made a sound of exasperation and headed off. "Look, Sarge, maybe you'll find out it's pretty nice not to have people shooting at you all the time. Maybe you'll meet some people you know, or meet some new people and make friends. Who knows? You might even have *fun!* Ho! Isn't that frightening!"

"Yes," Rett said, finding it impossible to stay furious in Kraym's large and reassuring presence. Something about him just absorbed and nullified any negativity she threw out. He had that effect on a lot of people. Ariam had discovered his aptitude and helped Kraym turn it into as strong of an asset as Rett's ability to mentally interpret energy auras from living or inanimate objects.

"Fun and fear do go together sometimes." He adjusted his corrective lenses and grinned at her. "You can go and be scared and, when you come back, we can have fun hearing all about it."

Rett stopped short. Kraym went a stride past her and turned, widening his teasing grin. She knew everything she felt right now was in the open and from the way his brown eyes sparkled, it amused him to witness the war of indecision she fought. Right now, the battle to decide if she should slug him or laugh with him was even.

She gave up. She chuckled, smiled, and shook her head, in amusement now, letting her tense body relax. "If you didn't do so much to keep Ariam in line, I'd have no idea why I keep you around at all," she grumbled. "You're just a great big flaming useless mass of muscle."

"Well then. That answers it," Kraym said. "You need me as a second-in-command because between strength and brains, I've the brains."

256

This time, Rett smacked him.

"Where are you going? To Branch town?" He rubbed the arm she had swatted as they resumed walking.

Rett nodded.

"Hey, there are a lot of great places in Branch."

Rett shrugged. "I heard that, but I've only ever been at the Base."

"You haven't seen any of the town, then. It's still a logging town, no matter what, and trees are the biggest thing going next to fishing. I like going there, and Ariam says the area is a lot like your Treetop. Just bigger."

"Trees and fishing, hunting in the fall. What more is there?" She gave him a one-sided smile. "It does sound like Treetop."

"I have a friend stationed there right now, he's with the military police." Kraym chuckled. "Old Newi and me, we were called the terrors of Bolle's Marsh at one time, especially after we almost blew up the methane collecting plant. I think the locals were relieved when we left for Basic. We were so wild and irresponsible as kids that even after we settled down and became good citizens, they weren't sure how long it would last."

"You? Wild and irresponsible?" She found it hard to imagine. Kraym was always so...so organized.

"Oh, yes, Sarge. I guess I've grown up a little since then."

"We all have," sighed Rett.

"Anyway, I could tell Newi you're coming. He'd show you around. He's a nice guy. Like me," added her co-second with a wink that increased the small smile on her face. "Want me to com him?"

"No, that's okay." At least Kraym, while encouraging her to have a personal life, never pushed the touchy issue of Jaq Pym on her. At least, not when or where she could find out about it.

"Look, Sarge, don't stress over it. We'll still be here when you get back! And maybe, so will the enemy. Although at the rate we've gone lately, can't say we'll have any left in a tenday or so."

Rett sighed in resignation. "The enemy I don't care about, but you'd all better be. None of the troop better get in trouble while I'm gone, either. This unit's the only family I have, besides Ariam."

"What about your father? Colonel Reve?"

"He doesn't seem to share that feeling, so I don't either," she said 257 flatly. "Don't bring him up, okay?"

"Deities, Sarge. I'm sorry, I didn't realize, I mean, Ariam—"

"Sergeant Ariam is my sister, and in many…non-physical ways we are similar, yes. However, she and I are two very different people, Corporal."

"I'm sorry, Sarge."

"Don't worry about it," she said. "It's my problem. *I'm* sorry for snapping like that."

"Could I ask you a personal favor, Sarge?"

"Sure. Anything for you."

"Promise me you'll try to enjoy your time off," requested Kraym, adjusting his glasses. "Give it your best shot."

"I'll try."

"Promise me, Sarge. And I'll make sure Ariam does her share of the reports and filing, don't worry."

Rett gave him a half smile. "I'm sure you will—but when it comes to working with *you*, she's never had a problem." Since they were in a fairly public area, Rett glanced around quickly, then turned and hugged Kraym tightly in appreciation. "I don't know what I'd ever do without you, big guy. I promise!"

Kraym hugged her back. "I'm not going anywhere." He turned her loose and they both stepped apart. "Not without Ariam, anyway."

Rett gave him a shove. She would love it if one day Kraym and Ariam made their partnership official. "Then you'd better go find her and break the news she might actually have to do some real work." With that, she went off to find Med, wondering if her medtech would keel over in a dead faint at her showing up for his services under her own power, if not at her own free will.

He didn't faint. Of course not. He was waiting for her. Thank all deities he spared her a lecture. Instead he simply extracted her implant and warned her that her menstrual cycle would start within one to four days, and to be very careful about getting into situations that would upset or anger her for at least a tenday until her body chemistry resynchronized.

Rett was tempted to say she was in one of those situations now, but knowing Med, he'd add two tendays of Medical leave on top of the four tendays she already was getting sent away for.

"Easier going on these hormonal implants than going off them. And how long has it been for you? Do you even remember?"

"No, I don't think about it."

"*Four* years. When it should have been at least once every year. You want to have kids, you'd *better* start thinking about it." He handed her over a small package. "Do you even remember how to use these?"

Rett sighed. "Yes, Med, I think I can remember."

"And take this. No, don't open it, that'll activate it. Wait until you need it."

"What is it?"

"A heating pack."

She wrinkled her nose, wondering why he thought she'd need one of those. "I haven't been that sore. What do I need this for?"

"Have I ever given you anything you didn't need? Medically," he added hastily as she started to retort. "Oh, and here's more of that moisturizing salve you should be using, not that you've really had time. But you will, so use it every day without fail, especially after bathing." He added several more containers to her pile.

Rett eyed the pile, then reached for her utility belt and extracted a small gear bag. She barely got everything into it, even with the stretch capacity of the material. But she wasn't about to stay here long enough to repack it because Med would for sure find several other items for her to take meanwhile. "Thanks, Med. Take care of them for me, all right?"

He didn't have to ask what she meant, and his normally sour face actually made it into a grin. "I will, Sarge. Get lots of rest. And have fun," he called after her as turned to go.

Rett thought about the queasiness, mood swings, and various other maladies she was expecting in the next tenday, glanced at the stuff in her hands, and sighed. "Right."

1.4.2 UNDISCLOSED LOCATION
0535.07.26 (LOCAL RECKONING)

"WE HAVE TO GET OFF this planet. Out of this system." Moving back from the video pickup so his gesture would not be missed, the heavyset humanoid smashed his fist into his palm for emphasis. "They're getting closer to us every day. They've already found ways to penetrate our screening shields."

"Tell me, Motuk." The leader of the Yixolryn Coalition's invasion forces sat back, remaining carefully casual. He shuddered inwardly as Motuk's all-too humanoid pinkish-tan face came close once more. He'd known Motuk before his change, when he still looked normal, like a Yixolryn. It disgusted the Leader to look at him now. "How do we get you and Sclamuse Iheolon off-planet when we're presently so disadvantaged?"

Motuk bared his teeth. "I don't care how you do it. All I know that is if you don't find a way, we'll go to the Nyorfians—unless they catch us first—and tell them everything we know. Everything."

"Are you threatening me, Motuk?" Of course they couldn't afford to leave these two behind. Although some of the members were only three-quarter and half-blooded Yixolryn, the Iheolon family was held in the Coalition's high regard. These two had given up much—much of their former lives and any physical shred of their Yixolryn blood. They wanted the rewards they'd been promised. They didn't want to hear any excuses and were desperate enough to carry out their threat. Motuk and his sibling were clever and mercenary. They would make sure that if they had to go down now, after all this time, the entire invasion went down with them.

"If that's what it takes," snarled Motuk.

As much as that thought broke the Leader into a nervous sweat, at the same time, he had to admit the notion was in line with Yixolryn standards.

"And you think they'll listen to you after your exposure as spies and enemy agents among them?"

"These people are softhearted." Sclamuse Iheolon stepped into the visual range of the communication device. His humanoid coloring was darker than that of Motuk's, reminding the Leader somewhat of Sergeant Killer. A sneer twisted Sclamuse's thin face. "It's sickening! They offer leniency for cooperation. They offer *citizenship* to our troops who defect or to prisoners who show a desire to renounce their ties to us! Haven't you noticed the defection rates increasing?" Sclamuse made a noise of disgust. "We certainly saw enough of that over the past few years. And it's not only the humanoids."

"Those traitors will be dealt with when the takeover is complete," the Leader promised darkly.

"If we're caught—or turn ourselves in," Motuk pointed out, "there will not be a Coalition takeover. No Yixolryn victory."

The Leader hid his flinch behind an angry frown. And if the unthinkable happened and they did lose, they would all undoubtedly be hoping the Nyorfians didn't turn the survivors over to the GTC. They knew very well that the Galactic Trade Commission levied a harsh, immediate justice against those who attacked their member worlds. It took the remote location of the Nyorfian system—on the absolute fringes of GTC space—and almost a century of careful planning to get the Coalition effort this far.

"How long will we have to wait?" demanded Motuk. "Twelve more years? There will be no people left. We've lived among them long enough to know. The defense will not end with the eradication of their military. They will fight to the last toothless old one and the smallest child. And when there is no one left, then what? How will the Coalition get what it came for then?"

"I'm telling you," muttered Sclamuse, "more examples should be made of civilians, rather than the military. The civilians aren't helpless; they're just the last line of defense. They've certainly caused enough damage in occupied areas, or do you believe when your commanders report malfunctions that it is actually faulty equipment? I say we start hitting them where it really hurts."

"The High Command forbids it. You were taken to task once already, Sclamuse, with that little degenerative disease you started spreading to their children. They managed to find a treatment and preventative for it quickly enough, but you might have left us lacking for able bodies. We still want as many of the inhabitants as possible, and we want them reasonably cooperative."

"Those in the High Command are blind fools," Sclamuse said heatedly. "I'm telling you, I've lived long enough to know. Their families are what's most important to them—any of them. I don't just mean their immediate relatives, I mean *any* family unit. If we took a few of their precious families and made public—"

"You know nothing!" The Leader's snarl was so menacing that both agents were silenced. "If we start in on their families and children, it will increase the resistance, not decrease it. Those incidents where commanders forgot themselves or troopers failed to obey have already proven it! The natives would rather see their loved ones dead than see them under our rule. No, we go on the way we have been. Our orders stand firm."

"Get us out of here." Motuk brought them back to the topic of the communication.

"It was not my fault that you failed to rendezvous with us in Circle," retorted the Leader. "You know they have a net so tight around Nyorfias now that it would be impossible to sneak even our fastest scoutship in to pick you up. You must try to get to Epnoce. With all the troops they will undoubtedly be moving, your only chance is to try to hide among them."

Motuk had to concede to that fact. "They have our bio patterns now," he remarked. "We try to board any ship leaving this backwater mudball, we'll be discovered."

"So change them, as you did when you first took this assignment. You still have the means? I know you can't make any large changes, but you should be able to change yourselves just enough to get by any monitors they have set up. It is the only way we can help you. Once you get to Epnoce, Tyndal Iheolon will find a way to pick you up. He has family loyalty enough to already have inquired about your welfare. He would undoubtedly arrange a recovery. Already we have communicated too long. Out!"

* * * * *

"AND WELL HE SHOULD," MUTTERED Motuk, slapping the Nyorfian end of the com channel closed just as an alarm light flashed on his device. "That was too close."

The Nyorfians had tagged their transmissions a few times before, but were as yet unable to pinpoint or decode them. Sclamuse, as skilled as he was in manipulating computers and com devices, barely managed to stay ahead of those who would detect them. It would be only a matter of time.

"Well, we'd better change. Let's see, for you, some darkening of skin tone. Good thing you've lost weight. That will help. For me, a lightening is in order. A bit of adjustment in the DNA structure for both of us…another adjustment wouldn't hurt our ability to reproduce any more than the first."

"Do we risk it? Even a slight change might be too much," Motuk said without turning to his partner, who was once known to Nyorfians as Major Shamus.

"Well," drawled Sclamuse. "It seems we either take the chance of using it or stay here forever."

Motuk didn't find this as amusing as Sclamuse did. He turned toward his brother with a shiver. Sclamuse glanced up briefly from the device that would make the necessary adjustments to their physical forms.

"Stay here. Stay here? On this backwater mudball on the way to nowhere? I'll take my chances with the device." It had been long enough. Motuk hated Nyorfias, hated Nyorfians. Only the hope of seeing these insufferably stubborn, self-reliant, yet pitifully softhearted people brought under Coalition domination had kept them both focused. "Then we'll have to find two unfortunates to assume the identities of."

"That shouldn't be a problem. Circle is full of choices. I made enough back doors into the top levels of military records. They couldn't have found them all. With luck, by the time they find out anything was amiss, we'll be gone. So, do you want to go first?" inquired Sclamuse, gesturing with the device.

Motuk stripped to the waist and presented his back to Sclamuse. This situation was Killer's fault. How he hated her. Those two years he'd had to deal with her as the commander of the infantry division to which her platoon had been assigned had been all but intolerable. Especially when at every turn, she and her unit managed to live through ambushes, escape countless traps, succeed on forays arranged to fail. Even those few times she'd actually been captured—three times during those two years—had ended in failure. Their own cousin Commander Tyndal Iheolon had her for a tenday and failed to kill her...then again, he hadn't been trying to kill her. Tyndal simply enjoyed torturing people, and his obsession with Killer resulted from the fact she failed to give him any satisfaction from the process.

Damn her! Damn her for living through what would have killed anyone else. He could understand his cousin's obsession with her, and the Coalition's imperative that Killer and others like her be dealt with permanently and publicly. Such heroes undermined Coalition attempts to break the will of the people.

He cursed now for his own failure to deal with her permanently. Events in the field aside, all his attempts to get her in trouble, called out in disciplinary actions, none of that had worked, either. She had scraped by on technicalities: she knew all the obscure loopholes the average soldier would never think to use. The separate rules the Special Forces observed while working with the infantry covered her, too. And when the other angles didn't work, that insufferable Special Forces commander Major Yidnar pulled her ass out of trouble with every connection he had at his disposal. He'd get his due, one of these days. Tyndal had Yidnar on his personal most wanted list, too, right after Killer.

Motuk was frustrated he hadn't been able to take advantage of the many opportunities he'd had to do physical harm. There had been so many. But for fear of blowing his deep cover, he'd been helpless to act. "Tyndal should have killed her instead of playing with her the way he did."

"You're thinking of Killer again."

"How could I not when she was responsible for this?" Motuk threw out his arms to indicate their present situation. "Are you going to get on with it, or what? What are you waiting for?"

"It's finished. Careful, brother. You do not want to develop our half-blood cousin's all-consuming obsession."

"You're right. All I truly want to do is get back to a civilized planet. You're finished?" Lowering his arms, Motuk reached behind his back to finger the lower third of his spinal area. It was painful now, that was certain, the area around the punctures already beginning to swell. Before long he would undoubtedly be feeling the effects of transition.

"And, as I recall," Sclamuse pointed out, making more adjustments to the device before handing it to Motuk, "It was the liaison officer, D'lano, who first blew our cover. Killer was merely a pain in the ass." He shrugged off his shirt so that Motuk could apply the device to him. "Pity we didn't kill him sooner, before he got his message off to MainCommand."

"We didn't kill him," reminded Motuk. "He recovered."

"Recovery. A singularly annoying habit of these people. They are impossibly resilient. All those clever little plagues I set loose the first decade or so. All failed."

"Which is another reason the High Command wants to preserve them—that and the psi talent potential the race has."

"I can see the need for healthy workers. But haven't we proven they cannot be turned for anything else?" Sclamuse flinched, grabbed the damp rock wall for balance, and let out a sharp breath as Motuk pressed the device firmly against the lower back.

Motuk watched dispassionately as more than twenty slender probes slithered between the sharp, knobby bones of the spine, into the core. Blood welled up around the punctures through skin and flesh. He kept the pressure steady even as the warm red rivulets streaked over his fingers.

"I don't care anymore. Let the geneticists worry about that. All I want is to go far, far away from here and enjoy the rewards we were promised." Motuk abruptly withdrew the device when it beeped.

Sclamuse slid to his knees, then turned to sit on the floor of the cave. He looked very ill. His hands were shaking as they fumbled to replace his shirt.

Motuk placed the device carefully in a pack with several others. He adjusted his own clothing and snatched their blankets before settling himself on the floor alongside his brother. Just in time, too. His head was spinning.

"I'll have to agree with you," Sclamuse allowed finally, managing to wrap a blanket around his quivering form. "Killer is not our problem any more."

1.4.3 TOWN OF BRANCH
BRANCH PROVINCE, NYORFIAS
0535.07.27 (LOCAL RECKONING)

RETT SLUNG HER KITBAG OVER her shoulder and reached to rescue her weapons case from the driver. The tiny, silver-haired reservist was trying to drag it from the cargo hold of the rover, both her feet leaving the ground as she strained. The case probably weighed just as much as the woman trying to lift it.

"I have it, you can let go." Rett didn't want her gear causing someone's great-great grandmother an injury. "Thanks."

"You're welcome, dear. Enjoy your stay."

The logging town of Branch was also home to the largest military base in the north central part of the Nyorfian main continent. Rett was glad Branch wasn't a large city like Circle. It reminded her of Treetop town, but with more traffic. Of course Treetop town didn't have a huge military base adjacent to it. A base that was the central headquarters for all military branches on planet.

Rett headed toward the checkstation. Like any Special Forces operative, her plans were subject to change without notice, on or off duty. There was always a chance that she would be called to jump into something completely combat ready. Consequently, all her personal gear and her entire personal arsenal traveled with her. Military personnel on leave, though, were not supposed to carry firearms or like devices in Branch. So, she had to leave her cache here at the checkstation with the military police.

She knew she was leaving her gear safe, and they'd have it ready to go with her on a moment's notice. All the same, she felt uneasy about it. Couldn't do anything about that, though. Like everyone else on leave, she had to comply with the rules.

* * * * *

N'WESSAR KEPT HIS EYES ON the soldier as she approached the checkstation. He'd started watching her the minute the rover had stopped in the unloading area. At first, it was a routine glance, idle curiosity to see if the next person old Bretthe brought in was anyone he knew. Then there had been something else that caught his interest. It wasn't the Special Forces headband—there were enough of those around here. Maybe it was the way she glanced around, getting her bearings. Maybe the way she walked, confident of the ground beneath her feet, yet still somehow a bit uncertain of her direction or, for that matter, her reason for being here at all.

"Best first guesses, how many years since the last leave for this one?"

"Bit over two," said his assistant promptly after a glance out the window.

"I say two as well, neither over or under," guessed the MP N'wessar had relieved ten minutes earlier, after glancing outside from the reports she was still filing. "Never been to Branch town before either."

"I'll go for three myself, for first guess." He and his comrades would have another guess before checking the records, but only later, after the soldier left them. He nodded in greeting as the soldier entered. "Welcome to Branch. Have any trouble on the trip in?"

A brief headshake answered him. She handed over her ID, leaving her kitbag balanced over one broad shoulder. Her other hand was occupied with the weapons case. N'wessar slid the ID into his Omni and noted her name, rank, and branch of service. "You can disarm, Sergeant. I'll take the rifle, you can put whatever else you're leaving here on the counter."

She indicated her compliance with a nod, and he wondered if he was going to get any words at all from her. No, it wasn't required, but he'd never had a problem getting at least a hello out of anyone before. He considered revising his estimation.

Her kitbag went down to the floor, so did the case. Then she handed over a well worn but scrupulously maintained TT-1 automatic. Next came the weapons belt with sidearm, ammunition and various other peripheral devices, gear that had obviously become as much a part of the newcomer as the clothing she wore. As each item was detached or extracted and lined up on the counter in front of him, he thought he was lucky that she wore the same working grays as any military person on leave. Had she been clad in the color and light reflecting combat uniform that made the Special Forces become all but invisible, he wouldn't have been as able to appreciate the view as much.

He started registering the items on the counter. All in all, it still wasn't a quarter as much firepower as some of the Spacemarines he checked in usually carried. Then again, the Nyorfian Special Forces didn't weigh themselves down with equipment. Deities, they didn't even wear the light body armor other ground troops wore, much less the fully self-contained unit the average Spacemarine mated to his or her body for combat.

"That's it?" N'wessar asked, handing off the last item to his assistant and making notations on his Omni.

She reached for the long, semi-rigid weapons case at her feet and set it on the countertop, unlocking it for his inspection. Backup weapons, no doubt. Yes. Two more TT-1s, a bit newer than the first one she'd handed over. An assortment of smaller weapons, extra ammunition, chargers. Everything showed signs of wear, but like the rest of her gear, clean and ready to use. Deities, but she was strong—she'd picked up the case in one hand as if it had been empty. He snapped the lid back down, locking the case.

N'wessar's glance went to the knife still on the sergeant's utility belt. She was quick to put a hand on it, but to protest its removal or expedite it, he had no idea.

"No—it's all right, keep it if you prefer. I just need to make to make a note of it. Everyone in this town carries a blade of some kind, between fishing and foraging. That one doesn't explode, emit harmful radiation, or shoot projectiles at high speeds? Er, under normal conditions, that is."

He liked his rotation on leavetime check in. In addition to keeping observational skills sharp, it was one of the few times his job allowed him to interact on more personal levels with other people. Some insightful higher-up made the excellent observation that the Nyorfian troops coming in on leave were invariably stressed. So part of his job was to not only relieve them of their weapons and give directions, but also to see that they left his station in a reasonably good frame of mind.

269

He had to admit, it helped his off duty social life as well. But what was it going to take to get this serious, silent Special Forces sergeant to crack even the smallest smile?

"No, nothing like that."

So she did have a voice. It was low and almost curt, but was that a little easing of the tight line of her jaw, a bit of light coming into those gorgeous dark eyes?

"Hopefully you shouldn't be needing it, unless your meat's really tough or you need to hack your way through the Sixthday Salad Fest at Jilytra's. We try our best to make sure Branch is safe!"

* * * * *

As Rett reached to retrieve her ID and the small DSU that was her gear retrieval token, the MP gave her a friendly grin. She kept her face still, unsure what to make of the situation.

She sensed Pam's inner exasperation and didn't have to exert the slightest bit of imagination to guess her interior companion was rolling her eyes. Well, in her own defense, she'd been out of social contact for a long time. Okay, so he was just being friendly. She wasn't used to MPs being social, most of them she met recently had serious and sensitive duties. They never smiled, laughed, or joked around on duty. So it was a bit unsettling to be confronted with one who, right now, was acting the complete opposite way.

As if he read her mind, his voice took on the near monotone of one of those more serious types, mimicking exactly the manner and routine speech of a guard at a high security gate. His face became non-animated, as perfectly impersonal as his voice. But his eyes never lost their sparkle. "Directions to the hostel, a map of the town, recreation opportunities and points of interest I've made available to your Omni, just use the access the code on your token. Have a nice time."

Was he mocking her? Or just trying to get her to lighten up? She was way too tense. It wouldn't kill her to be friendly. She wasn't even the one on duty.

"Thank you, Sergeant." Deities, that was lame, she thought in disgust.

At once, he reverted to his former manner and when he spoke, a warmer, more personal undertone was in his voice. "You probably won't be lacking for company or things to do, but if you are, a lot of us off duty hang out at the Old Mill Pub. No tough meat there, I guarantee it." He added a warm, questioning smile.

She chuckled finally, feeling an intense personal relief his interest wasn't in her name, her reputation, or her unit. Not that any of that meant he had to treat her any differently from anyone else. In fact, she preferred if he wouldn't. But now she simply didn't know how to react to him.

His charm lay entirely in his manner rather than looks. He was slight-statured, had light brown skin, and a nice smile. She had to admit that she liked the soft western Centerland accent that rolled beneath his words. Reminded her of the landscape of the province she had just left that morning. She also liked the way his red-brown hair escaped the confines of the neat braid that dangled below the deep violet cap all MPs wore. Her practical side noticed the length would be easy to grab in a fight.

"Thanks," was all Rett had to reply, but she warmed her tone. The MP was appealing and friendly. In fact, she realized, feeling suddenly bewildered, the way he glanced at her was similar to the glances she received from Jaq Pym. There was a lot more in Jaq's eyes she didn't understand, but this part of it was the same. She dismissed that thought with an internal headshake, as a far more familiar association rose to the forefront of her mind—the MP's accent.

"Hey, do you know a guy named Kraym?"

His smile grew. "Kraym! Who on the entire eastern half of Centerland Lake doesn't know him? Or me, for that matter. Can you say notorious? We were practically raised together, the terrors of Bolle's Marsh! Then we grew up. He became organized, that lunkhead, enough to get into Special Forces. And me? Somehow I ended up on this side of law and order."

He indicated the proof of the uniform he wore with a roll of his eyes. "Kraym's with…" the man's gaze dropped to his Omni and back to her, the smile at its widest possible point.

271

"He's with your unit, isn't he, Sergeant?" His lean hand extended over the counter toward her, palm up. "N'wessar, from Bolle's Marsh. My friends call me Newi."

"Rett, from Treetop." She covered his hand with hers for a brief instant. "My friends call me Rett." She added this tartly, but then gave him a real smile to make up for it.

His entire face lit up in response. "So, wow, you *can* smile! I thought I was losing my touch for a moment. It goes on my record every time people leave my station without one."

"You probably never had to work so hard in your life." Rett chuckled and reached for her kitbag, slung it over her shoulder. She smiled at the pair of soldiers who'd come in and stood behind her.

"You're almost right, but from the minute you walked in here I was working more on getting you to loosen up and smile than making any connections, as obvious as they might have been." He laughed. "Imagine that. Kraym's platoon leader right in front of me, and all I'm thinking of is getting her to say *yes* to an ale. Well, now, in the light of things, we really should get together and trade stories at the Old Mill!"

Feeling lighter and better about the entire situation, Rett decided it wouldn't hurt. "Maybe I'll check it out sometime. What's the best time to go there?"

He told her. Rett moved on, aware the glances of both the MP and the new arrivals followed her out the door.

Rett found the hostel after a ten-minute walk from the MP checkstation and left her personal belongings there. After a quick wash and a change to plain, loose fitting off-duty fatigues, she went for a look at the town's layout. She'd never been in Branch itself, only the MilitaryCentral Base. And that visit was only for a few hours while she and F-troop had waited to transfer to another jumper when her unit was first loaned to the 52nd.

It didn't take long for Rett to become aware that being in a plain uniform with no markings was a guarantee of anonymity. She felt stares hitting her as sure as she sensed being targeted by enemy fire. Overheard a few whispered comments. She kept an amiable expression on her face, but even the few people who met her with eye contact looked more awed than friendly. She heard, and saw, the words *Sergeant*

Killer from more than one pair of lips. The hated nickname made her grimace even in her thoughts. She was just a person like everyone else, damn it, doing her best fighting the war. Just like a lot of other people!

It must be because those correspondents caught me in Circle, she thought. *I knew I should have brushed them off, but I was in a public area.*

She groaned, having detested the meeting so much she didn't even want to think about it. She had tried to talk about the operation, how all the different units pulled together, about how the civilians in Circle played such a huge supporting role. But all they had wanted to hear about was her and her reputation with their enemy. So now as result of that interview, people were recognizing her without her Special Forces uniform and headband…but not as Sergeant Rett. As Killer.

I guess Colonel Evard's period of command already spoiled me… made me think everyone forgot about Killer. At least Kraym's friend back there treated me normally.

273

Then the familiar sounds of big machines and power tools drew her in the direction of the river and the main sawmill that was still Branch's primary industry, despite the war. As she drifted closer, she could smell the fresh, resiny scent of new lumber and hear the unmistakable, earsplitting whines of big saws ripping wood. Taking a deep, deep breath of the familiar smells, Rett smiled, a flood of memories surging through her mind.

She'd grown up in Treetop Province, three thousand miles to the west. Rett was proud to call herself a logger and had explained to Pam some time ago what she and other Nyorfians in the timber industry did entailed a lot more than "cutting down trees acres at a time and grinding them into paper."

Rett snorted. Pam's mental images of clearcuts and denuded mountainsides…it couldn't be that bad, could it? And making paper, paper that was thrown away, from wood! What sort of wasteful, backward planet was Earth?

A sense of outrage rose from Pam's corner, making Rett instantly guilty.

Good gods and deities, thought Rett, *Pam. Why do I always take my bad moods out on YOU?*

Pam's barrier went down and she made a mental gesture of flinging her arms wide. ~Because I'm a wide-open stationary target. Nailed flat to this wall in your head. I can't go anywhere, so here I sit, ready, willing and damned convenient. But what the hell, that's what friends are for. And you never gave me a chance to explain anything about Earth, it's not all bad. It's just different from here.~

Rett let out a breath. She'd treated Pam badly. Beyond badly. *I'm sorry. I haven't been as much of a friend to you as you have been to me. Especially these past few tendays. Do I have a chance of making it up?*

Pam was silent for a time, giving every indication of giving the matter of forgiveness serious thought. Rett squirmed, but no matter how she looked at her overall behavior toward her ego-merge companion, it had been bad, and she'd been a solid azurium bitch. Or whatever metal Pam always referred to in that manner.

Pam pronounced her judgment. ~You can continue making every attempt to untangle your nerves and have some rest and fun on this vacation. That cute MP was a good start. I hope we see more of him. If anything, he can make you laugh.~

I already promised Kraym I would, Rett thought. *And I've never in my life have gone back on a promise. So yes, I will. But what can I do for you?*

~I'll let you know as we go along. For now, tell me more about Nyorfias. You were just thinking about Treetop. Home, right? That's a good place to start.~

I think you made me dream about it a handful of days ago. Didn't you?

Pam disagreed. ~I didn't make you dream, Rett. I admit I'm guilty of encouraging you to sleep. But I didn't make you dream. You have to remember: when you're asleep or unconscious, so am I. I'm not sorry for pushing you to sleep. How many years has it been since you dreamed?~

Rett couldn't remember. *I stopped dreaming about a lot of things, awake or asleep. Until you came.* With a small shrug outward and in, she traced the patterns in the low stone wall between her and the mill yard.

All right. Treetop. I haven't been back there since right after I completed training for Special Forces. A sharp twinge of regret made her look away from the yard and the thickly forested mountains beyond. *Last I heard, Coalition SMGs fired most of the forestland in our management areas, and it spread over a good part of the district. It wasn't deliberate, since the Coalition wants those resources too…wood and wood products are more valuable than azurium, vichroxite, or transuranics in some parts of the galaxy. They tried to put out the fires just as hard as our own people. But hundreds of thousands of square miles were totally destroyed.*

A loose piece of stone came off beneath her fingers. *Treetop town and Treetop Lumber didn't burn, but the fire came close. I don't know what's left up there…and I'm not sure I'm ready to find out, at least not yet.*

Rett sat on the wall, pulled one leg up, and tried to relax. Watching the crews work in the busy yard, she tried to find some happier memories to share with Pam.

275

1.4.4 MILL YARD, BRANCH
BRANCH PROVINCE, NYORFIAS
0535.07.27 (LOCAL RECKONING)

RETT'S ATTENTION WAS DRAWN TO a trio of teenagers operating a ripper. The furtive glances in her direction, the heads coming close for conversation, alerted her that she was either a target or topic.

~That boy can't be any older than twelve. They put kids to work early here?~ Pam wanted to know.

Kids start as soon as they show an interest and can follow basic instructions, explained Rett. *Oh, there's plenty of free time for kids, if that's what you're worried about. And if you don't show an aptitude or interest for the family trades—there are other options. But we all know we need to help out our families, whether it's foraging, or household chores, or doing a few hours a tenday at the family business, or helping take care of siblings. Don't kids help out on Earth?*

~Some. People…think a little differently. In my family, we had to help in the house and with our siblings. So tell me more.~

You're being evasive.

~Hey, I'm the one who was being ignored for three weeks…or tendays…whatever you call them, it was a long time. Always being told "later, Pam". Besides—the more you tell me, the better I'll be able to put comparisons with my society into perspective for you.~

Hello…I've been spotted, and by someone other than the kids.

~Can you get in trouble for hanging out over here?~

Rett almost chuckled aloud. *Hardly. I'd be more likely to get in trouble for* not *coming through and asking for a tour—or inquiring about the best local fishing spots.*

~Then why is that guy looking at you so strangely?~

I don't know. He's the Ops manager, see that symbol on his helmet? He's probably, like everyone else around here, wondering why Sergeant Killer's staring at his yard.

As the man moved closer, Rett could see the expression on his face went a bit beyond recognition. *He knows me.*

~And you don't know him?~

I'm trying to remember. We had people from different outfits across Main come in once in a while...but...

The man's grin was growing with each forward step. "I can't believe this. Good gods and deities. It's Rett, isn't it. From Treetop? Reve and Tonia's eldest."

"Yes," Rett confirmed. It was his voice, not his features, which finally triggered the memory. "Lans?"

He nodded, both his hands extending in greeting and welcome. "I didn't think you'd remember. It's been almost fourteen years. I'm a lot older now. And so are you—I don't think I would have even recognized you with the short hair without seeing your face on the newsnets recently. But I never thought I'd see you *here*."

"I remember your visit. The Forester's Guild meeting was in Treetop that year." Rett kept her grimace inside and returned the open handed trust shown by Lans. Their grips met with equal firmness.

She didn't mind the mental sniff from Pam, or the comment ~See, not everyone thinks of you as Killer first!~   277

"When I first saw you back then," said Lans, "you and your kid brother and sister were working in the yard, just like my three over there." He gestured to the teenagers, his smile broadening. "Well, maybe your little sister wasn't working very hard, she was just getting over that odd bone disease that had her down a few years, do I remember that right? She was supervising, I think."

Rett chuckled. "Probably."

"How's she doing now? Ariam, right? Bones strong again?"

"Fully recovered and very well, at least when I last saw her."

~All of six hours ago,~ thought Pam without any rancor.

"Good." Lans shook his head, eyeing her up and down. "I still can't believe it's you. Last I saw you, you had hair down to here and were all legs from the armpits down. You sure grew up, Rett, big and tall like your dad. But you look like your mother. No mistaking those eyes."

She didn't think she looked at all like her mother. But she was all right with being told she had her mother's eyes. They also had the same type of hair, space black and thick and impossible for most warm-blooded people to grasp with an uncovered hand, but that, like her energy sense, wasn't something most people needed to know.

"Heard what happened to Tonia and Tovadan," Lans was saying. "I'm very sorry. Nyorfias and the Guild both lost a lot of good people that day. It must have been rough on you girls and Reve."

She dipped her head, acknowledging his condolences. "Yes, for a while." Then she relaxed, shoved any animosity she felt about her father aside for the moment, and opened herself for some friendly chitchat. "I think I remember you mostly because you're one of the few people in two worlds who dared to argue with Reve. About delaying the floats because of unusually heavy rains. Reve didn't think the rivers would crest as high as you did. You two stood in the yard and yelled in each other's faces for the better part of an hour and you didn't back down one fingerlength."

"Yeah, Reve was never one to admit—" Then Lans stopped and stared at her.

Rett could guess his thoughts. The noise from his mill was loud enough that both spoke with voices raised already. Rett, Tovadan, and Ariam had been working in almost identical conditions.

"You *heard* us? Over the machines?"

"No. Couldn't. But we learned how to read lips early. The three of us were close anyway, with Ari and Tova being Talented...so I guess it happened naturally. Not to mention that kids have to keep ahead somehow and unless you were on a more important job, you just got the helmets with the hearing protection and not the coms."

The operation manager laughed. "So Reve really was a little tight with the credit sometimes."

"Yes, he was, but not without reason," Rett had to admit. "We thought being able to read lips was a fun thing to do. Besides that, Tova and Ariam sure knew without looking when people expressed conflicting opinions."

"So," Lans said, longcone-green eyes twinkling, "if you're here for a job, you're hired."

Rett hesitated, the black specter of her forty-day exile looming large. "Do you mean that?"

"Of course I didn't." Lans guffawed and shook his head. "No, you're obviously here on a break, not to work. I *am* inviting you to lunch with the family, though. I visited with Rafe and his family not too long ago, once the Treetop area was free of Coalition occupation and open to travel again. Finally had a chance to see that big old tree of yours, but only because it was on the way to Rafe's favorite fishing hole."

Here Rett brightened. She quickly updated Pam that Rafe was Treetop Lumber's longtime operations manager, and after Rett's father went to full active duty, Rafe had kept a paternal eye out for Rett and Ariam, easily including them among the seven daughters he had already.

"I can give you the latest gossip from Treetop."

Rett held out a hand. "Wait," she said. "That Old Tree…the fires didn't come that close?"

"No." Lans shook his head, his cheerfulness fading. "But not far from there."

"Don't tell me anything else about that. I've kept up, but I didn't dare ask about my tr—I mean about That Old Tree. It's as much a resident of Treetop as anyone else, you know."

"So I was told. All right. Now about lunch. It's a half holiday, but we—"

"I'd better not stay any longer, then," Rett said reluctantly. "I was just having a look, Lans. Thanks, I'll get out of the way, now."

"You're not in anyone's way. Don't be in such a rush. My kids will kill me if I tell them you were here and they didn't get to meet you! You're a real hero to Fortlan and Farley. Or did you have other plans?"

"As a matter of fact, Lans, I just arrived and I'm kind of at a loss for things to do."

Pam!

~I didn't do a thing, sweetie. You said that on your own!~ said Rett's mental companion in a thought of exaggerated innocence.

Well, maybe so, maybe not, but Rett had spoken the words and it was too late to back out gracefully now.

Lans looked as pleased as a longcone kurra with a nestful of nuts. "Good. I knew we'd need that load of mushrooms the kids hauled home the other day."

"Mushrooms?" she repeated, hoping she'd heard correctly.

"Beautiful ones. Tree ears, browns, shells…we've had so many this year, especially after all that bad weather. Then it's settled?"

"Yes, thank you. It'll be my pleasure. But only," added Rett, "if you'll let me help your kids finish up that job. Looks like something I might remember how to do. I could earn my lunch at the same time." She tried that appealing expression she'd seen Ariam use so effectively, combining it with her best smile.

Lans reacted as if she'd sideswiped him with a low-level stun charge instead of a sidelong glance, appearing to lose his balance for a heartbeat. "Of course—" he agreed instantly, then thought about it, started to say something else and gave up when he looked at her again. "Just like your mother," he muttered, then shook his head a little, smiling. "Of course. Come on, I'll get you a helmet. With a headset," he added with a chuckle.

* * * * *

THE CUTTING WHINE OF THE ripper blade died into silence as Lans brought Rett closer. The youngest boy, who'd been operating the blade, stared at her.

"Don't stop. I just brought over some help. Sergeant Rett, my oldest, Kentrez; my daughter, Farley, and Fortlan, up there on the blade, is the youngest. Looks like cutting is about done, but you'll still need to stack this lot before quitting time. And don't forget the spacers this time, all right?" The operation manager left them to continue his job of running the yard operations.

In wordless surprise, the three young people nodded politely to Rett. But all of them had identical expressions.

Pam took her best guess. ~I'll bet they're thinking: Good deities, someone famous like her wants to do this boring stuff?~

Shove that famous shit up back your invisible butt, Pam. Rett roughed up her short hair and settled her helmet over it.

~I still can't get over how someone's hand can slide right through your hair without getting a grip, but other stuff stays right on it,~ thought Pam. ~I'd think it would stay as slick as a horse's hide after you put too much show polish on them.~

I told you my mother was from offworld—

~Yes, you did tell me that much.~

It's a throwback to when their race still lived more in the water than on top of it. The slick hair kept them from being lunch to a number of other warm-blooded creatures that lived there, too. Remind me to explain more later. Right now I have to talk to these kids, okay?

~That's one excuse I'll let you slide with,~ said Pam with a mental smile.

After some adjustments to the padded webbing inside that would keep it in place, Rett activated the comunit built into the ear protectors. She grinned at the seemingly frozen teenagers. "Okay, I'm the new guy on the crew, so just tell me where you want me."

She couldn't have asked for a better activity to settle her still-agitated spirit. And the kids were a bonus, she loved kids of any age, always had. But she had a certain soft spot for those in the sometimes difficult transition between leaving childhood and becoming adults.

Her manner seemed to dissolve their shy reserve. The eldest, Kentrez, recovered his authority as chief of this small crew. "Uh, we are nearly done cutting. Stacking's what we need to get started on. We'll need a pallet set up. They're over by the maintenance shed, Sergeant. Fort'll go with you and help bring it back since it looks like we're not getting a floater anytime soon."

"It's Rett, Kentrez. Just Rett. No problem on the pallet."

"Just call me Kent," the lanky youth said, giving his younger brother a little push as he took his place at the blade.

"Kent. And you're Fort. You have a short name, too?" she asked Farley, who shook her brown-haired head without saying anything. "Well, Fort, it's you and me. Show me the way."

She shortened her stride to match the steps of the nervous twelve-year-old. She didn't try to make conversation and after a minute, his tension seemed to ebb. His head came up, his shoulders went down. "Over there." Fort pointed. He had a husky voice, not quite deepened, but when it did Rett guessed it would be deep and resonant.

"Hey, good thing there's two of us," Rett told him. She didn't need help carrying the big frame, so she nodded toward the bundled rolls of spacers "If you can get one of those, I can get this."

"We almost would have forgotten again," said Fort as he hurriedly reached for a bundle of spacers. "But, Ser—"

"Rett."

"Those pallets are really heavy. It usually takes two big grownups to carry one. We were supposed to get the floater Naidrera's group is using and they were supposed to be done with it an hour ago, but they're purposely keeping it longer so we don't finish in time."

"You have some sort of score running with Naidrera and her team?"

"Always," sighed Fort as he heaved his bundle to a sturdy shoulder. "She's the Boss's daughter, and has six older kids on her team. We're only three, and until last tenday, we were running even. But now..." He sighed. "Oh well. Are you sure you can get that...never mind."

Rett, having the matter well in hand—or, on her head—grinned at him as he turned. She shifted the balance of the frame a little. "I hate carrying big things out in front of me, don't you?"

He adjusted the load on his own shoulder. "Yeah, it's easier on your back with the weight up high."

"Come on," Rett said. "If you've a time to beat as well as a job to finish, then let's get at it."

"You mean you'll help? I mean—"

"I know what you mean."

"But isn't that like cheating?" The boy stared up at her with an earnest frown.

"I honestly don't think so. Aren't they holding back your floater, when you were scheduled to have one? Giving you my help is simply evening the odds." Rett started back, balancing her pallet. "So—if you think of me as replacing your floater—just another piece of equipment you were supposed to have, it's not cheating at all. You've just happened to acquire a floater that can also stack."

Fort's round face lit with gleeful hope. Like two old friends, they headed back to the others and went to work.

* * * * *

LUNCH WITH THE OPERATION MANAGER's family was a very informal affair. The easy rapport she'd formed with the kids carried over to the roomy kitchen, which took up most of the space on the house's ground level. She and Kent were given charge of cleaning and slicing the mushrooms. Since it turned out Kent was as crazy for them as she was, they both shamelessly snitched at the varieties that didn't require cooking as they worked.

Fort and his father whacked away at several other kinds of vegetables while Farley made forays from cutting boards to cooking unit, tossing ingredients into pots with the carelessness of a master cook. Restalya, Lan's partner, nursed their ten-month-old baby while she set the table, adding a big plate of rolls and a large pitcher of fruit juice.

The conversation covered Lans' visit to Treetop in more detail, then moved to logging, local fishing, and schooling. Restalya was a teacher at the Branch primary school and had plenty of funny, warm stories about her students. Rett guessed the topic of the war was deliberately avoided. For that, she was grateful. Things were cleaned up, put away and soon she found herself relaxing in the common area with the family.

~I think this is great for you,~ Pam dared to comment. ~You're happy. You feel normal.~

Rett couldn't deny it. As much as she still would prefer to be with her unit, she *was* comfortable and happy at the moment.

Fort carefully settled himself to one side of her, eyeing her knife. "That's pretty big."

"Yeah, it is. It's more than a just a tool, like you should usually use knives."

"May I look at it, Sergeant Killer?"

Rett closed her hand over the sheathed blade, studying the young face that had suddenly turned so shy and formal again. "Only on one condition."

"Oh, I won't touch it."

Rett shook her head. "No, you can handle it all you like, Fort, I don't have to worry that any logger's kid doesn't know how to handle edged metal!" She leaned toward him a bit. "The condition is this: my name is Rett. In here, like in the yard, like just before. No difference. Just Rett, okay? The Yixolryn Coalition gave me that other name and I don't like it. I hate it, to tell you the truth."

He dropped his gaze, not sure how to respond.

"My friends call me Rett. *Never* Killer."

Fort's eyes widened. "We're friends?"

"Well, we've worked together, shared a meal together, and are sitting around being very friendly right now, so what do you think?" She reached out and tousled his straight hair.

"I mean, for always. Not just for now while you're visiting?"

"Yes, I'd like to think so." She withdrew the knife from its sheath. Extending the blade to its full length, she offered it to Fort hilt first.

The blued metal blade reflected dully in the overhead light as the teenager received it with a careful reverence better suited to fragile works of art.

"It's not magical or anything," Rett said dryly, "and it's not going to break."

Fort laughed. The last trace of his moment of shyness vanished. "But why do you need one that's so big?"

"Most of the time I haven't needed the extra length, but the few times I did I was glad of it. Not all our enemies are normal sized, or even humanoid."

"I thought all your equipment was camouflaged." Kent leaned over his brother's shoulder to examine the blade.

"When we're on combat alert it is," explained Rett. "Nothing is left to shine or reflect. But when we stand full gear inspection, or are sent on leave, or perform maintenance on our gear, all the camo paint, tape, shields and covers are removed. Have to do that occasionally, or we may overlook stressed or damaged areas on our equipment."

~Even the human equipment like you,~ added Pam from inside. At first, the change in uniforms had made a slight difference in the nearly constant, ready tension she'd grown used to in Rett's body. A very small one, yes, but a difference all the same. Then this visit had made that tension vanish completely. At least until Fort had called her Killer, which made Rett remember she'd just left her headband in her kitbag back in the hostel, not retired it for good. But it was great while it lasted. Rett needed more of it.

After her knife made the rounds and its merits discussed, Rett accepted its return. As she returned the blade to the sheath on her hip, she noticed the time display on her chrono and let out a soft exclamation. She'd been here for almost six hours.

"What is it, Rett?" asked Restalya in concern.

"I've imposed on your time too long, I'm sorry." Rett stood up.

Lans and Restalya laughed. "Imposed?" they said together.

"After I practically dragged you in and put you to work?" Lans shook his head.

"Don't be ridiculous, we all had such a lovely time. I hope we didn't keep you from doing something." Restalya looked worried.

Rett put on a serious expression. "You have. You've kept me from going completely out of my mind on the first day of my first time off in three years."

Rett laughed at the relieved faces around her. "I've had a great afternoon, but I really should get going. Thanks—all of you. You've brought back some nicer times for me. Farley, whatever you call that stuff you made, it was the best lunch I've had in…years," she decided. "Years. I don't know how many. That thing you did with the mushrooms, I hope you can duplicate that?" At the girl's nod, Rett asked: "Would it be asking too much for you to note it down and send it to me?"

Farley beamed. "Be happy to."

Lans draped an arm around his daughter's shoulders. "Farley's ambition is to have her own public house and cook to her heart's content. She's vowed to give Jilytra's some real competition one day," he said.

"I just might have to relocate to Branch then. Deities, thanks, Farley. You just have to put my name on the recipe and send it to MilitaryCentral. They route all our mail."

"Come back any time," said Lans, a mischievous twinkle in his green eyes. "I'll put you on the payroll. I could always use an experienced hand in the yard."

Rett leaned down to tickle the baby. "Maybe I'll take you up on that. But I was hard put to keep up with this crew." She nodded at the kids.

"You're kidding," exploded Kent. "I still can't believe we moved and stacked it all in time."

She threw a conspiratorial wink at Fort and leaned toward him. "Amazing what you can get done when you put your mind to it."

Fort grinned. "And your back."

Rett then started for the door, then turned. "I do have a thought, Lans. When this war is over, Treetop Lumber is going to have crews with time on their hands. Maybe you could help file them into temporary positions with other outfits around the area?"

The Branch operation manager nodded. "We'll work out something," he agreed. "We're all going to be shorthanded and having a contingency plan now will just ease the transition for a lot of people when this is over. I'll mention it to the Forester's Guild at the next meeting."

1.4.5 HOSTEL, BRANCH
BRANCH PROVINCE, NYORFIAS
0535.07.29 (LOCAL RECKONING)

RETT RETURNED TO HER HOSTEL and slept for two solid days. On the third, feeling violently ill and clutching her cramping belly, she awakened and staggered into the lavatory to discover her first menstrual cycle in three years had arrived with a vengeance. Rett had never had a difficult period before. She felt truly grateful for Pam for assuring her that no, she wasn't going to die from cramps, that this was typical for many women—at least those Pam knew.

~You know, if you weren't allergic to painkillers, a couple of ibuprofen would take care of this in about a half hour.~

"Don't you think I wish I could take something? Shut up, Pam. Just as well I have nothing to do," mumbled Rett as she curled up on her bed and hugged Med's heating pack to her abdomen. "I think I would kill the first person who looked at me the wrong way."

~On Earth, we have a name for this— ~

"I don't want to know about it," snarled Rett to her pillow.

~Only most women get it before the period starts,~ continued Pam. ~I'm one of the exceptions, like you are at the moment. I call it PPPMS, for Pre, Present and Postmenstrual Syndrome.~

"And you put up with this *every* cycle?" Rett groaned and tried to find a better position. "I think I felt better after getting kicked around last month after we were ambushed. I know I did. My back didn't hurt this much then. Shit."

~Poor baby. We'll feel better tomorrow,~ promised Pam with all the authority of a wise old grandmother.

Pam was right, but Rett wasn't taking any chances that her long repressed hormones weren't going to get her in trouble. No wonder Med had told her to watch it. Good advice. Even after her cramps had passed, she stayed within the hostel facility, leaving her room only long enough to pick up a meal.

Best of all, her room, though simple, had the most beautiful accessory Rett could ever hope for. Even better than a comfortable bed. A

287

huge bathing tank in which she could stretch her full length and then some, with every possible variety of therapeutic aids. Rett indulged herself and Pam by trying them all out. Between sleeping and soaking, Rett started to feel humanoid again. She spent so much time bathing that Pam started teasing her that she might revert to the water dwelling form of her mother's ancestors. But all that water therapy had good effect: Rett actually *noticed* her body ached less and felt better than it usually did.

Finally, she realized if she stayed inactive for another minute she was either going to grow gills or kill something, so she emerged one afternoon into the open to find a breezy, beautiful, late summer day.

* * * * *

Rett was window-shopping, another Earth term she learned from Pam, and having a lively internal conversation with her internal visitor about the GTC and Nyorfian trade.

We've had nothing from offworld for thirteen years. And with the Coalition still occupying Epnoce and parts of Main, most everything you see is local made.

~You said a lot of you wood products go offworld, but if offworld trade is stopped, why was the mill still operating?~

They're operating, but at very reduced levels. A lot of what was getting cut back there at the Branch mill was for building—or rebuilding. There are some stockpiles that will be ready to go as soon as trade opens again—and we'll need it.

She had become so focused on her internal conversation that when Rett felt a hand touch her arm, she reacted as if jolted from a trance. Before she thought twice about it, she had whoever it was by the throat and immobilized, his legs trapped beneath her left leg and his upper body in a bone threatening, backward position against her left knee.

Pulling her ability to sense energy auras into hard focus, she targeted a second person slightly to the right and behind her. She reached back with her right foot, hooking it around his ankle and yanking him off balance. *He won't stay down long. He's already up. I've got to drop this one—what am I doing?*

Her brain and vision caught up with her reflexes and Rett straightened, apologies rising to her surface like fish to a hatch. "I'm sorry—" She dropped the man she had by the throat at the same instant she recognized him. "Good gods and deities!" She reached down and hauled him to his feet again. "Evetez!" Rett glanced around to the second one, blowing out a breath. "And Semage. You guys should flaming well know better. Evetez, I almost broke your back!"

"I think you did," gasped Evetez in a squeaking sort of voice. He was a tall, lean, blue-eyed man in plain gray fatigues like hers. He pressed a hand to his back, groaning, the other hand gingerly checking his throat and neck. "Ow!"

"I think you'll live," she told him, still rather breathless with surprise for seeing either one of them. "What in two worlds inspired you to such a..." Words failed her. She settled for a dark glare and rounded in on Evetez's rusty-haired companion. "That bubbleheaded moron can be excused," Rett said, stabbing a finger in Evetez's direction, "but I thought you, at least, would have more sense, Semage."

"We had to make sure it was really you," explained the shorter man, swatting the dust off his backside.

"And how many hundreds of people are running around impersonating me in Branch?" she asked sarcastically.

The bubbleheaded moron smiled broadly at her, a familiar merriment dancing in his eyes. "Haven't lost one bit of your speed! Hi, Rett. How're you doing, anyway? I thought you were still on loan to the 52nd. How's F-troop?"

"Troop's fine...those who are left."

Semage threw an exasperated glance at his companion. "I guess the moron forgot about that. I'm sorry, Rett. I heard it was tough."

"I didn't forget," Evetez protested. "Well, maybe I did, but only because I didn't expect to see you."

"It's all right," Rett said. "And it's not exactly something to bring up the first few minutes when we haven't seen each other in so long, anyway."

"Are you here for the recall?"

"I'm here on leave. I can't believe you're here now too." These were her very first and best friends in two worlds, right in front of her, alive and well. Her stare went from one man to the other, not missing anything this time. "How long has it been this time? And I heard about your upgrade, *Lieutenant* Evetez, sir."

She didn't wait for a response, turning instead to the other man, a senior sergeant and platoon leader like herself. "Semage, how's B-troop? Deities, how I miss you guys!"

"We've missed you, too, Rett. Or is it Sergeant Killer now?" Semage grinned at her sour look. "And our hero, no less. Major Yidnar told us about your Freedom Star and from what I've been hearing—now, come on, kid, don't be embarrassed." Semage laughed and hugged her, lifting her right off the sidewalk, his husky arms threatening to crack her ribs. He spun around with her once and kissed her soundly. "From what I've been hearing it's about time people knew you went over and above."

"I'm not the only—" Her friend's arms squeezed the words into oblivion. She again felt the firm warmth of his lips meet hers for an instant, than Semage turned her loose.

"And stop calling me kid, will you? I'm not seventeen any more."

"Could have fooled me," he said. "In any case, I'm still older."

"I've missed you," they said together.

"Hey, me too," said the lieutenant, pushing in for his own hug and kiss, one that was more than friendly and started a long forgotten tingle. At least, thought Rett limply, if she fainted from lack of oxygen Evetez would keep her from falling down.

~Or maybe he'll just drop you on your butt the way you did him,~ came filtering in muzzily from Pam's direction. ~But while that was definitely hot, it's not anything like you felt with Jaq Pym.~

Rett felt instant heat leap into her face at the reminder. The lieutenant's merry blue eyes twinkled when he released his embrace and he kept a supporting hand on her until she found her feet. "I see you *really* missed me too, huh?"

Far too late to worry about any sort of public dignity. Besides, in this light, she didn't care. Rett smacked his shoulder. "You wish."

"How long you in town?" he asked.

"Long enough," replied Rett, glumly now. "Almost three more tendays."

~I take it these guys are a bit more than your best buddies.~

Rett had to chuckle aloud. *At one time, we didn't know where one of us ended and the next one began. We went through Special Forces training together, the same trainee squad. I'll say I know them inside out, same way they know me. And to what you allude...yes. I'll give you a quick overview, but don't expect me to go into detail—at least not now.*

Both men had been a lot of fun off duty and all three had shared a deep and close friendship, despite their fierce competition during individual training. Evetez was always looking for trouble and company to share it with. He'd been involved in his family's Wide River shipping business before the war.

Semage was a quiet, sensitive, warm person—when not in combat mode. His prewar career path had been in marine biology and oceanography. Rett recalled their past times with warmth, and despite her gloomy expression, felt pleased to see both her friends again. More than pleased. Aside from some scars here and there, and looking older and careworn, they were alive and well.

Evetez draped an arm over her shoulders and squeezed her. "Damn if you didn't grow another inch taller," he told her, although as long as Rett could remember, she'd stood eye-to-eye with the wiry, golden-haired man. "Let's go get a drink or ten and talk over old times. What d'you say?"

"There's a place right down the street," added Semage, "where most of us off duty or stationed at MilitaryCentral hang out. The Old Mill Pub. Some really good people sing there in the afternoons."

Pam didn't need to encourage Rett. Rett grinned at her friends and said: "Someone else told me that was a good place. Let's go!"

The public house was nice, if slightly smoky from whatever they were cooking on the open grills. It smelled good. Maybe Rett shouldn't have been surprised it reminded her of the public house in Treetop. After all, Branch was a logging town, too. The woodwork was exquisite and far more intricate and detailed than anything Rett had ever seen before. She could spend several hours in silence just looking around, and made a mental note to come back and do just that when she found herself lacking company.

Business was good for a working day's afternoon. As Semage and N'wessar, the MP who had originally checked her in, had mentioned, the majority of customers seemed to be Free Army personnel, off duty from MilitaryCentral, or on leave.

A musician, playing a gentle tune on a stringed instrument, looked up with a welcoming smile as they entered.

Rett and her friends found a table near the back commanding a view of the entire room.

"Look at us," sighed Rett in disgust. "Not one of us has our back to what's going on in here. We'll never be normal, I guess."

"I know I'll never be able to turn my back on a roomful of strangers," agreed Semage. "Like old Sergeant Regor used to tell us—"

"'What you don't take notice of has a nasty habit of sneaking up and planting a knife in your back!'" Rett and Evetez said together, laughing.

Evetez grinned at Rett. "What really concerns me, Rett, is if you're going to attack everyone who comes up to you on the street!"

"Only bubbleheaded lieutenants with smartassed sidekicks who grab me from behind."

"Sidekick!" Semage looked offended. "*Sidekick?* Excuse me, we're not even in the same unit."

Rett made a face at him. "Give me a break. I've been here less than a tenday and I've slept most of that time."

"Small wonder you're wired," said Semage, "between that, coming off constant alert and kicking off the hormones. I had my hands full with B-troop for a few days when we first got in, but at least my medtech made certain we were all unwound before she let us cut loose!" He shook his head.

Male or female, they all knew what that was like for each other and how it affected emotions otherwise well controlled. Despite the knowing, sometimes reactions caught them totally by surprise.

Evetez nodded agreement. "2023rd Medical made me wait a few days too." He sent a look to Semage. "And 'Mage here's been trying to keep me out of trouble!"

"Yeah. Good thing we didn't meet any earlier than this. I might've flaming well killed you, 'Vetez."

"Like you never wanted to before," he countered.

Semage guffawed. "I can recall Rett confessing to me that she wanted to cause you severe and painful injuries from the first second you both met. Not that I can blame her, for the first six tendays of Special Forces training she was always getting called out for something *you* did."

Rett changed the subject. "So—what's up with the 2023rd? We're being recalled?"

"Most of us are all here, at the Base. A few splinter assault groups like yours still on remote here and there, but we're all supposed to be shipping out to Epnoce in a couple tendays, soon as they get enough escort to get us through, and room on the ground enough for us to land."

"I hear the GTC Rangers are at it. Between our people, the Rangers, and the GTC fleet and marines, we're getting control of our own space back at least."

Evetez nodded again. "A Ranger unit from that task force is going in with a special ops team Major Yidnar put together and a group of our own Spacemarines soon to make a grab for the main spaceport. They'll either take it completely or hold it open long enough to get what troops we have on Epnoce inside. After that, it'll be our turn, which is why we're here waiting."

"A group from the 2023rd is going in?" Rett hadn't read that anywhere. She leaned over the table.

Semage nodded. "Word is," he said in a low tone that didn't go past them, "we already have a Tac-survey scout team there."

Rett's glance went to Evetez. Since training, he'd been in Tac-survey and assigned to of one of those small units that often went in far behind enemy lines for extended periods of time. He nodded. "I wanted to go, since I was told I'd be reassigned after my upgrade, but I was told there were other plans for me." He shrugged. "The Major's had his special group training in simulated heavier gravity for a couple months now. They're hot to go. There's some rumor about an infantry division or two going as well, but no way we can sneak that many people out."

"Didn't you and F-troop get recall orders yet?" asked Semage. "Isn't that why you're here?"

Rett shook her head. "Not yet," she said, troubled. "And I'm the only one from F-troop here." If the rest of the battalion was going to Epnoce, didn't that include her unit? "Maybe the orders are late," she added hopefully. "I really wish we'd get them, soon. I like the 52nd, now they've put real Nyorfians in command."

"Still can't believe that those Coalition agents pulled one over on us for so long," Evetez said with a half-snarl. "That burns me as much as it scares me. I'm glad to know they haven't turned out anyone else yet, but those verifications aren't over with yet, either."

"Were you verified yet?" Rett dreaded her upcoming meeting with a Master Adept. Not that she was a Yixolryn spy or agent—she simply had no idea how she was going to hide Pam when that happened.

"All of us currently on the Base were." Semage shrugged. "It wasn't a big deal. He was in and out—went through B troop in just over an hour."

"That fast?"

"I had the same reaction. He said no one's been able to measure the speed of thought before, and laughed. But it was obvious the effort took a bit out of him, too. He's off Base somewhere now."

That was good to know. "I like the 52nd's new CO. People don't come much finer than Colonel Evard."

"Wasn't he supposed to leave field service and serve at MainCommand?"

It figured that Evetez would know that. "I've no idea. I just know what's on his record. He'd be perfect for that, of course—he's a sharp operator and knows what he's doing. But he loves being in the field, working directly with the troops. He'd be good in the upper levels, but he wouldn't be happy."

"You really like him, don't you," said Semage.

Rett had to smile. "Yes, even though I was tiffed at him a few days ago. But being with the 52nd isn't the same as being with the 2023rd."

The server brought them drinks and the snacks of the day, Evetez paid, and they fell to conversation in earnest until the first singer of the afternoon was persuaded to leave his cozy table, friends, and drink for a round of song.

The singer was a middle-aged infantryman with a mellow tenor voice. Taking the instrument from the regular player, he started on a ballad of his own composition about life as a fishing boat captain on Centerland Lake. The sun, wind and storm, the love of the freshwater sea, was conveyed to his rapt listeners with heartfelt emotion.

Tash was from Centerland Lake, she'd just got her fleet certification when she enlisted.

After that thought, Rett just let herself get lost in the story being told.

Now this is another good thing, thought Pam privately as, without the slightest prompting from her, Rett started using her own long-repressed imagination to visualize the story in the song. The next step would be to get Rett dreaming again on a regular basis, normal sleeping dreams and daydreams. Dreams that didn't consist of endless Omni screens of Intelligence data or tactical maps or weather forecasts. Dreams in which a beautiful river valley bordered by dramatic mountain peaks was a setting for something other than an enemy ambush.

Confident that would all come within the allotted time, Pam settled back in her corner with a contented sigh and was soon enjoying herself as much as Rett. As drastic a step as Evard's order had been, Pam had to admit the old man's timing was perfect.

Rett had always enjoyed music, but never knew it could be so consuming. She sat, entranced, almost forgetting to applaud as the song ended.

"Tash would have liked that," said Semage softly.

"I was thinking about her, too," Rett and Evetez said at the same time.

She was in the same training squad as the three of us, thought Rett in response to Pam's gentle inquiry. *Tasheesh was killed eight months after her first assignment.*

The infantryman, encouraged for an encore, began another tune. This one was a song handed down from the original Nyorfian settlers and he was joined in the refrains by a young alto Spacemarine and a magnificent bass who wore the deep sky violet-blue and black of AirSpacefighters.

~Why aren't those guys in plain fatigues?~ Pam wanted to know.

They're on free time, but they're not on leave.

~Oh. But Evetez and Semage aren't on leave, and they're in plain fatigues.~

They're off duty for a while, or have been, probably a few days.

Pam subsided to mull this over.

"What about you two?" Rett asked her friends. "Will you sing?" She remembered Evetez and Semage sang excellently together, tenor and bass, especially songs of the sea and shore.

"We'll sing if you sing with us," Evetez said, daring in his merry blue eyes. "I mean, we had Tash for the third voice. Maybe you can fill in."

"Deities forbid!" Semage set his mug down, his freckled face a study in remembered pain.

Rett laughed and shook her head. "No way, Evetez, you know I can't sing, not even if someone's life depended on it. Not when I'm sober at least." She grinned at him. "Maybe later, if we're here long enough."

Semage made a strangled noise. "Please, Rett. Don't. I'll give you *anything* you want if you promise you won't do it."

"She's not that bad," said Evetez, but even he looked doubtful.

"Anything," repeated Semage earnestly.

"Even your lucky shell?" teased Rett.

"Even that."

"Then I won't sing."

"Thank all deities." Semage slumped back in his seat, patted the spot on his chest where his lucky shell rested on the lanyard next to his ID tag, and took a long pull from his mug.

~Are you as awful as he thinks?~ Pam wanted to know.

Worse, admitted Rett with a laugh inside and out. *I can whistle like any bird on this planet, but I can't reproduce anything remotely resembling music. They've both heard me.*

Since she was still alert to the comings and goings in the public house, the arrival of the dispatch courier didn't go unnoticed by Rett. At first she didn't give the courier a second thought—it was common enough for messages to be hand delivered in certain areas. Then, as the courier looked around the place carefully, she started feeling uneasy, almost the same way she started feeling when she was about to be targeted. Her instincts were confirmed when the courier made eye contact with her and approached her table in the far corner.

"Shit," Rett said under her breath, any good feelings vanishing.

"Communication, Sergeant Rett. From 52nd HQ." The woman handed Rett a sealed dispatch.

"Thanks." Rett's uneasiness increased. She stared at the missive for several seconds before tearing it open.

> *Rett: Corporal Kraym took serious hits in heavy fighting for that supply dump in sector 215G. I do not have all the mission details yet, but as soon as I do, I will inform you. Medical is getting him ready for transport. As soon as I get a jumper ready to fly, he'll be at MilitaryCentral for further treatment. I wanted to let you know as soon as possible—I know how you are. Don't worry, Sergeant Ariam is handling things well and you'll see Kraym when he gets there___Evard___52nd*

"Rett." Semage touched her arm gently.

For a second or two Semage's voice sounded like it came through a long tunnel: tinny and far away, yet echoing. His touch brought her back, but her own voice, when she spoke, had the same faraway, odd quality.

Not Kraym. Rett's throat tightened in panic. *Not Kraym.*

Promise me something, Sarge

Sure. Anything

"Hey, Rett. Something wrong?"

None of you better get in trouble while I'm gone

We'll still be here when you get back

With Evetez's firm grasp of her forearm, Rett snapped to the present. "One of—" She took a breath to steady the tremor in her tone. "One of my seconds caught it good. Not even a damned tenday and this has to happen!"

Pam's shock from within mirrored Rett's, but it was quickly phased to support. ~Let's hope for the best, and not the worst.~

Evetez released his grip, reached over and skillfully slipped the dispatch from her hand, scanning the contents swiftly. "CO says he should be okay. Look, Rett, it wasn't your fault. Before you know it, you'll all be back together again."

"'Before I know it' is just too ambiguous a period," Rett said, her hand going to the Omni on her belt. "I have to get to him." She quickly composed and sent a message to 52nd Division headquarters, directly to the attention of Colonel Evard. She signed off with a priority reply request and stared at the machine in her hand, wishing she could yank a reply from it with her will alone.

She didn't have to wait very long. Colonel Evard's text reply was direct.

> *Stay exactly where you are. I'll send someone for you when the med ship arrives at MilitaryCentral.*

She was unaware how tightly she held the Omni until Evetez remarked she would certainly crush the device if she squeezed it any harder. He leaned over to glance at the reply Evard had sent, then covered the display with his hand, causing Rett to look at him.

"Hey. You're not going to change what this says by staring at it," Evetez said gently. "He's right, you know. Even if your CO said to come back, Kraym would probably still be on his way here to hospital and you'd miss him again."

"In the meantime," added Semage, "you're not helping anything by sitting there being miserable. Even though there's no other way you could feel about it right now. Even if you were there with him and your troop." His own voice was soft with understanding.

Promise me you'll try to enjoy your time off

I'll try

Promise me, Sarge

Her friends were right. Evetez and Semage also knew what it felt like to have friends from other units and branches, or people under their direct charge hurt, missing, or killed in action. That had been the pattern of their lives as well as hers for a long time now and the helplessness hurt more than the impact of a physical wound.

And here, in Branch, where things were fairly safe, there was no running from it. No work to bury herself in. No troop to run drills with, or assignments that took every bit of attention and concentration. Here she had to face her helplessness and accept it.

~You can't run and hide by working yourself to death.~ Pam's mental voice was soft and echoed the worry Rett tried to keep contained.

Evetez broke the silence. "In the meanwhile, we're here for you. We'll help the time pass." His blue eyes sparkled once more and he poked Rett lightly in the arm. "Ow! Loosen up, Rett, look at you, you're as tense as a reinforced pourstone block wall!" He glanced at Semage. "We still any good at busting up those sort of walls, buddy?"

"Breaking things without using explosive was more Rett's thing than ours. But we can try...we'll have to get her outside," replied Semage seriously, starting up from his chair. "We don't have enough credit between us to pay for damages to this place. At least outdoors we just have to worry about getting picked up by the MPs, but we could probably take them on, too—"

Rett pulled him back down. "Point taken," she told them, smiling in spite of herself. "You two were always able to snap me out of my moods, whether I wanted you to or not!"

She paused, her glance going from one to the other. "I'm really glad we ran into each other," she told them. "Really glad. Okay, divert me."

"We still have a lot to catch up on. Do you realize it's been just a bit over three years since we saw you last, Rett?" said Evetez. "You were still platoon second for C-troop; Semage just got his command; and I came to the assault group sent to help C-troop and the 88th as Tac-survey scout."

He didn't have to mention that barely two tendays later, there wasn't any more C-troop. The platoons that made up the assault group, E and L troops, had also been decimated. And barely any of the 88th had made it, either. But they'd held a corridor open long enough to finish evacuating most of the civilians not already behind enemy lines before finally pulling back in defeat, leaving East Ocean province entirely to the enemy.

299

~You served longest with the 88th and C-troop, right? I'm not going to push,~ added Pam swiftly. ~You just have so many thoughts of them. You clamp down on most of them.~

With good reason. Please don't ever push me about that. If I start telling you, I'll start telling you, but promise never to push me.

~I promise.~

But yes, I was sent to C-troop right out of training. And I was with them right up until after that last battle—F-troop was initially formed up with the survivors, and I made platoon leader.

"I think I recall your scouting more than enemy positions," Rett said aloud to Evetez, with a final inward plea to Pam to settle back. At the same time, she was trying not to remember that Kraym came to F-troop from one of the 2023rd's Tac-survey detachments, too.

Evetez responded with an exaggerated show of innocence.

"He still does," Semage assured her, rolling his eyes. "But the last news we heard of you after you were assigned F-troop was that you were teaching Coalition troopers how to fall out of trees. Now how does a mountain-bred logger's kid like you, who used to practically live in trees, happen to go falling out of them?"

Rett raised an eyebrow. "Heard about that, huh?"

"Heard about your co-second spooking F-troop right out from under the noses of three divisions, too," said Evetez. "And now the Leader's put your bounty up by at least ten million credits."

"Not funny," said Semage, frowning at his friend. "Commander Iheolon's—"

Rett interrupted. "The Leader's so full of his own shit, he thinks it's as precious as azurium. You would think he might have learned something from all that, but he hasn't. Not enough, anyway. No matter what he'll never completely accept any underling's advice, not even Iheolon's."

"It's a good thing for us then. Also that most of their regular troops are kept so stupid or scared between drugs and threats."

"We're starting to see more sharp officers among them, though," said Rett, "so we can't take them for granted, either. I think since we killed off a lot of those more of the Leader's mindset, we're getting more former middle-management types that actually have minds and know how to use them."

"Like that Unethi at the Wide River Gap," said Evetez after a swallow of his ale.

"What?"

"You reported a big alien officer, three tentacles? They're called Unethi," said Evetez. "Not many of them, thank all deities. I hear there's several on Epnoce, and they're very loyal to the Yixolryns. We're still trying to find out more about them. In the meanwhile, I still want to hear how you fell out of that tree."

"I discovered that no matter how many cones fall to the ground, I'll never again do kurra imitations to cover for it when bored and hungry enemy troopers are on patrol."

"*That's* what happened?" Semage started to laugh.

"First time in my life I ever fell out of any tree," admitted Rett, embarrassed.

"She always was cute when she blushed," said Evetez in an evil tone, nudging Semage.

She narrowed her eyes at the pale-haired man. "I suppose getting shot out of a tree is a little better than you going backward off a transport that wasn't even moving. *Without* a shot being fired to help you on your way."

It was the lieutenant's turn to flush and look uncomfortable.

"I remember that," Semage grinned. "He was scouting one of those sharpshooters who came with you from C-troop, what's her name, Nerrah?"

"Nerrah and Trebor." Rett picked up her ale. The three of them were all that had been left of C-troop after the battle for Azurebay. She pushed the memory down, now was not the time. "Nerrah pushed you off, Evetez?" Rett took a mouthful of her ale. "I can't imagine you would even raise one of her eyebrows, much less her interest."

His color deepened. "No, she didn't," he admitted. "And she never gave me any notice. But someone did and I still hurt when I think about it. I never saw that coming!" He rubbed his square jaw reflexively.

Rett laughed without sympathy. Evetez liked women, all women. He had a very healthy libido and liked variety. Between training and medical supplementation, he managed to keep himself under control so that it wasn't a distraction, but it didn't stop him from being an outrageous flirt at any opportunity. She liked the way he tried to come on to the girls, including herself. His exploits had become a never-ending source of entertainment to them in training.

"It must've been Trebor. He's been with Nerrah a long time and he can move like lightning. I always wondered how you broke your jaw falling from a rover onto your back, Evetez!"

"I can't say I didn't deserve it, that's why I never even asked what happened after I woke up in Medical," Evetez admitted, then laughed.

"You're lucky he punched you. If he would've shot at you, you probably wouldn't be around to laugh about it." Rett leaned back a little. "He's the best shot in this system, if not in the entire quadrant."

302

"I've a couple good people in B-troop I make the same claim for," said Semage. "Sounds like we'll need to arrange a competition."

"I'll tell you right now who'll take it. Trebor, Ariam, and Jessek."

"You willing to bet on that?" challenged Semage.

"Whatever you want of anything that's mine to give," Rett said.

"All real, done. Same here. You heard that," Semage said to Evetez, who sat back laughing at them.

"You sound like parents trying to upstage the other with their kids," said the lieutenant in explanation. "Last time I was home, that's all I heard. Who was walking first, or getting teeth, or saying Mama." He shook his head. "All right, your wager's been noted and logged, and I'll see what can be done to arrange something. Trebor, huh? Deities, I remember him from more than Special Forces, he was a neighbor of ours in South Point, taught over at the university." Evetez shook his head again. "Can't get used to being younger and ranking some of our newer people!"

"And now you're a junior lieutenant and he's a senior corporal," added Rett, leaning over a little closer and lightly fingering the sunny hair above her friend's black headband. "Are those gray hairs, Lieutenant? This must be why you think I grew taller. Old age is supposed to shrink your spine right up, or so I've heard."

He swatted at her hand. "Is that the reason you and Semage keep delaying and passing on your upgrades? Just to make me feel older? I thought it because you were both happy with your commands."

"I get into enough trouble as a sergeant," grumbled Rett.

"And I'm already older than either of you," reminded Semage with a droll roll of his hazel eyes.

They continued their animated conversation and were later joined by a few more members of the 2023rd Special Forces. The topic of discussion went to the upcoming battalion transfer to Epnoce, sister planet to Nyorfias. The newcomers were surprised F-troop hadn't been recalled from duty with the 52nd yet.

Despite that and her concern for Kraym, Rett was having a good time. It was great to be with old friends, catching up on old times. She relaxed and felt pretty mellow from the ale, but not to the extent of being totally off her guard. She still worried too much about Kraym to allow that.

She spotted the MP sergeant who had checked her in almost eight days ago and he, upon scanning the room, saw her and smiled in a questioning and hopeful way. Before she could respond to his look, the flicker of an aura recently imprinted as familiar triggered a momentary shock, echoed by Pam.

Rett's friendly response to N'wessar faded abruptly when her glance went to the entrance. Just inside the public house stood her new tech advisor, ex-Coalition trooper Jaq Pym.

1.4.6 OLD MILL PUBLIC HOUSE, BRANCH
BRANCH PROVINCE, NYORFIAS
0535.07.36 (LOCAL RECKONING)

"TROUBLE, RETT?" EVETEZ FOLLOWED RETT's glance. "Hey, he isn't Nyorfian. Isn't he a Zetinorian? They all have that odd crest of hair."

"Yeah. Major Yidnar assigned him as my new tech advisor," Rett said sourly, wondering just how many Zetinorians Evetez had met. From what she understood, they were an endangered species. "Came to our side at Circle after saving Ariam's ass from the enemy. Then again, you probably knew that, like everything else, huh, 'Vetez?"

"Not as much as I'd like. Yet."

"He's the one, huh?" Semage said thoughtfully. "Didn't hear where he was from."

304 "He knows everything about Coalition technology and he also thinks he's madly in love with me and never leaves me alone for a minute. But that's not the issue right now—I think Evard may have sent him with Kraym on that medjumper. He did say he'd send someone for me."

"Better go check it out," said Evetez.

"Right." She stood.

Semage touched her arm lightly. "Want us to come?"

Rett gave her two friends a grateful smile. "No. But thanks. Look, are you guys going to be around town a few days, or back at Base?"

"Don't worry, we'll find you, Rett," promised Semage. "I hope Kraym's okay."

"Thanks. Well, it's been great." She stood and went around the table to quickly hug first Semage, then Evetez. "Thanks for being here when I needed you," she told them both seriously. Then, on a lighter note, she added, "Don't strain your eyes over that redhead, Evetez." She whispered this advice into his ear just enough to raise a seductive wriggle in response. "She's with that Spacemarine and they both just might pack as quick a punch as Trebor! I'll see you later." She made her farewells to the others who had joined them and made her way to the exit.

She paused long enough to speak amiably to N'wessar and regretfully tell him she had some business. *I won't mention Kraym to him until I'm sure what's going on.*

~I think that sounds like a good idea,~ agreed Pam.

Rett didn't see Jaq again until she stepped outside. Astonished, she found full night had settled on the little town of Branch.

"How's Kraym?"

"I'm glad I found you, Rett," Jaq Pym said, sidestepping her query just as she tried to sidestep past him. He caught her arm.

Rett controlled her impulse to jerk away. "Tell me what's going on. Did Evard send you here with Kraym, or to check up on me?"

"He sent me here, yes, but not to 'check up' on you and not," he paused slightly, "with Kraym."

Ice gripped Rett's guts at the change in his voice. "Damn it, what's up?"

Jaq's hand tightened on her arm. "He sent me to tell you," Jaq's voice was gentle, "that Corporal Kraym died a few hours ago, right after the Colonel sent that last message. I'm sorry, Rett. Kraym was very badly hit."

Rett froze for a long minute.

Kraym? Gone? Dead?

We'll still be here when you get back

Kraym—who'd made her promise to enjoy her time off?

Promise me, Sarge

Kraym, always ready with the VARs, always ready with the reports and compwork? Always ready to back her up no matter what? Never to have his huge, strong, comforting presence?

And Ariam…what would she do without Kraym?

Don't know what I'd do without you, big guy

She broke out of her startled shock and savagely shrugged off Jaq's grip. "Why did he send *you?*" she snarled, then caught a breath and turned away to stare blindly down the street.

She choked back a sob, swallowing hard to ease the ache in her throat. She was getting tired of this—having her friends hurt and killed. She was still hurting over the twelve killed at the Wide River Gap and Circle. On top of that, now Kraym…

"Rett, are you crying?"

She straightened and faced the ex-Coalition trooper squarely. "What do people think I am, Jaq Pym? Really? Some kind of robot? Do they think I don't have feelings? They're wrong!"

Her voice shook. "Now you can tell them. 'Guess what, people, Rett does have feelings, just like us!' Sure, sometimes I have to hide feelings, or act a certain way. And I'm not allowed to show pain or fear to an enemy. I have to pretend I don't feel any emotions.

"I can love and hate and laugh and I can cry. I can feel pain. Too much of it. I can be hurt and I do get scared, a lot. Some kind of superhero, huh, Jaq Pym? Yes. I am crying, okay? Just leave me alone!" She whirled away and made herself disappear into the shadows, leaving him standing there.

~I'm sorry,~ came from Pam softly.

Rett ran a hand across her eyes. *He was like a brother to me.*

~I'm going to miss him too.~

I wonder how Ari is taking it, thought Rett after a minute. *They loved each other. They were even talking over ideas for making a permanent commitment when the war ended. I'm not there for her. And I wasn't there for him, either.*

Deities, he'd always been there for her, for almost three solid years. The one time she should have been there for him…

~It's done, Rett. It can't be changed. And I think Ariam will be fine, with time. She's strong. Stronger than you give her credit for. And…~ Pam's mental voice remained soft and apologetic, but took a firmness that bespoke personal experience. ~And Ariam is more willing to ask for and accept help for stuff like this when she needs it.~

Like I remember telling someone not too long ago, Ariam and I are very different people, Rett thought back.

~And there's nothing wrong with that. But there's someone down there who wants nothing better than to give you some support. You don't even have to ask for it. You should at least talk to him, Rett. He cares.~

And since you know him as well as I do, how do you know this?

~Good grief. You do know it. And Ariam told you everything and you trust her feelings. On top of that, you know it in your guts and don't tell me otherwise.~

Rett glanced into the street, where he walked. It hadn't taken him long to start after her. But the Zetinorian was completely unaware the object of his search had taken to the rooftops of Branch and was following him, instead. As much as she wanted him to leave her alone, she was responsible for him, and he wasn't supposed to be wandering about on his own. Not yet.

~Off topic but I really need to know,~ thought Pam. ~With all the space and land around here, why are these houses so close together?~

What? Oh. Winters, Rett explained, the jump in subject bringing her movement to a halt. She sank onto her heels and hugged her knees, watching the Zetinorian's progress down the street. *Winters are rough. Easier all around to be snowed in for half the year if things are close. A lot of people in mountain areas have their winter homes in town, especially families with kids.*

Satisfied with that explanation, Pam jumped right back to where she had left off.

~Imagine how he'd feel if you dropped down smack in front of him right now.~

Rett thought about his reaction and had to stifle a watery, hiccupping sort of giggle through her remaining tears. Pam was right. She had to face him sooner or later. Sooner, she decided and dropped to land some four feet in front of a suddenly speechless Jaq Pym.

"I'm okay. Just wanted to let you know. Thanks for being concerned."

Despite knowing that duty required her to escort him, she turned to let the darkness swallow her once more. She tried to ignore Pam's mental hair pulling and ~No, no, NO, no, NO! Arrggh! Chicken! Idiot! STAY!~

Rett forgot about leaving as his energy fluctuated alarmingly and took a step back toward him. "Are you all right?"

"Wait a minute," he said after a quick breath and swallow. His energy settled into a more normal range. "Where did you come from? I had no…" He reached to his head, pulled his cap off. "I knew I shouldn't have worn this. Where were you?"

She shook her head. "Sorry, trade secret." She backed off as he stepped closer to her.

"Stop, Rett. Please. Are you afraid of me?"

She forced herself to remain where she was. She didn't reply.

"Why do you back off? I just want to talk to you and make sure you're okay." He stuffed the cap into his belt.

She hesitated and then decided to get it all out. "Because now we have to work together. I know you're attracted to me, you've made that clear from the very beginning. I wouldn't be honest not to admit that I find you attractive, too."

"But?" he prompted.

Rett couldn't go on, so he did.

"Now that you mentioned it, I do want to discuss that. Sometime. Not just now. Let's put that part aside, all right?"

She couldn't deny his candor and nodded. "All right."

He spoke after a deep and heartfelt sigh. "I'm really very sorry about Kraym. Colonel Evard sent me because he didn't have anyone else to send. He told me that he would have preferred to send Ariam, if not all of F-troop, because you would all want to be together. I'm sorry I had to bring the news. And I'm going to miss him—in the short time I was with your unit, I really started to know the man. He was a very special person, and he loved you. Not in the same manner he loved Ariam, but maybe just as strongly. Like a sister."

She looked away, fighting back more tears.

"And Ariam is taking it better than you think. Yes—she's hurting, but she's coping; she's focused. She even told me to tell you that Kraym wouldn't want you to worry about anything."

Yes, Ariam is fine—for now. Like me, she'll keep doing the job she has to do. Once we get back together, we can let it out. Rett twisted aside, unable to turn back the emotion closing her throat. "Thank you for telling me." She hardly heard her own voice.

A large hand rested on her shoulder with feather lightness. "Ariam's got the rest of F-troop to support her now, but you don't. Let's worry about you. You may not like me very much, but I'm a good listener. And Evard asked me to make sure you would be all right. Who listens to you when you need to express? You're so busy taking care of everyone else. All I meant to do earlier was to ask if you're all right. I wasn't implying anything else. Sometimes it's just easier to cry with someone who cares."

The deep warmth of his tone, the caring words caressing her like a loving touch, made Rett heat up, shiver and get fresh tears in her eyes at the same time. Her mouth opened, but the words took a half-minute to emerge.

"I'm sorry for assuming...wrongly. I'm fine," she said. Clearing her throat, she continued. "I would have preferred to be there—with him if possible."

"It would not have changed him being alive or dead," he whispered.

"I understand that. But I would have been there," Rett said simply. "Did Med say anything?"

"Med said to tell you he shut down and never regained consciousness. It took a while to get to him." He swallowed. "I was there when they brought him in, Rett. Evard had the jumper ready to go. Med made me come to help, to try to keep him awake. I couldn't. And then his heart stopped. Med had this terrible look on his face..." He took a deep breath. "And then he got up and walked a few feet away."

"Med doesn't like to admit there's nothing he could have done," Rett said in a low voice. "I need to walk."

* * * * *

JAQ FELL IN STEP WITH her, stretching his legs to keep pace with her agitated strides. He hoped she knew where she was going. He hadn't had any time to look at a map or get his bearings. He had to explain his reason for coming to town, after which one of the MPs at the checkstation had offered him a lift directly to the Old Mill public house. *"It's one of the few situations where we can give people rides,"* the woman had said, *"and with your status, and it being dark—well, if I were you I'd take being safely delivered."*

He walked alongside Rett in silence for a while. Turning a corner here and there. Following an aimless zigzagging pattern as far as he was able to tell. The night was warm and velvety dark; the lighting on the walkways bright enough to keep one from tripping, but subdued enough not to dim the twinkle of stars overhead. They were no longer in the business district. The buildings were becoming more residential, with a small office here and there, less lighting. He began to wonder if everyone went to sleep early in this town. There wasn't a lighted window in sight.

Then again, many of the homes and businesses on Nyorfias were empty now, the former owners casualties of war, or evacuated to a safer area, like the families with young children. He had been impressed and amazed when he was told that—with a few exception for approved alternate circumstances—no Nyorfian parent, civilian or career military, with children under the age of fifteen was allowed to go on combat active status. Instead, they filled the non-combat and support positions and everything possible was done to keep the families together and safe.

"No families, no future," Major Yidnar had explained. *"People are our most precious resource, Jaq…"*

He had learned more, so much more. The rangy Special Forces officer had been as candid with Jaq as Jaq had been with him. And when he had expressed his desire to live here, in the Nyorfian system, Yidnar had sponsored him. And this had been *before* Jaq started telling him and other officers and technicians from MainCommand what he knew of Coalition technology.

That Yidnar also supported his interest in Rett, encouraged it, gave him some advice, and wished him luck had only cemented the firm, fast feeling of respect, love, and loyalty to the man that had started in Jaq from the instant they'd met. Maybe he hadn't undergone the Special Forces tough training and earned one of those black headbands. And maybe he was just an auxiliary, an advisor, not intended to go into the thick of combat. But in his feelings toward the Major, Jaq felt he was no different from any other member of the 2023rd.

He just wished Rett would see him that way, at least to start with. Her platoon members accepted him enthusiastically enough. If only she would just let him in, just a little way.

He angled his head toward her. She was talking, finally.

"Kraym was much, much more than a friend and junior. He was like a brother to me. I loved him as one. And as a friend." Rett's voice, still pitched low, almost went unheard.

Jaq swerved a half step closer so he wouldn't strain his ears. He saw her shoulders tighten a bit, but she didn't move away or change her stride.

He made a sound of agreement. "Your entire platoon's like a big family. I expect them to call you Mother sometimes. Rett—"

She checked her forward motion and swung her body toward him. Feeling hopeful, Jaq reached out to rest a hand lightly on one of her strong shoulders.

* * * * *

"I DON'T WANT TO GET close to anyone." Rett spoke abruptly and sensed his entire being freeze for a second. The spot of warmth on her shoulder disappeared. Feeling as if she slapped a child, she managed to stand her ground even as more tears threatened and guilt burned in her stomach, threatening to turn it inside out. *Far too much pain,* she thought miserably, *for someone who wanted to avoid being hurt.*

~You have to stop running first,~ said Pam.

"Anyone else, you mean," Jaq said his tone neutral.

"Yes," she admitted, making herself meet his gaze. "That's the trouble. We're supposed to be close. To know each other so well we can think and act as a single entity. Someone begins a thought or task, the next person picks it up and completes it. It makes us a good team. It's how splinter units like mine are taught to work. But the drawbacks are as great as the advantages. And despite any amount of training, when someone is killed, it hurts. Too much. I'm tired of hurting."

The Zetinorian made a soft sound of understanding. "I've seen how close F-troop is. How you can practically read each other's minds. The love and respect you have for each other. I even asked Major Yidnar about it. He told me that people who fight with and for people they love have more power than any technology in the universe. The Coalition's totally opposite." He moved close to her now and slowly reached out to touch her shoulder again. He paused again, his face troubled. "They're...we're...all so damned twisted. I—"

The naked pain in his tone turned Rett's focus to him. Here was something she knew how to respond to. She didn't pull away from the light touch on her shoulder. She tried, instead, to communicate a supportive feeling as his distress painted bilious streaks across his normal energy aura.

~As long as it comes from someone else?~ nagged Pam, not unkindly. ~The doctor can give the medicine, but not take it?~

Rett dismissed her ego-merge companion's comment with a firm: *This is different, Pam. This isn't grieving. This isn't about loss. This is... cultural,* she said for lack of a better word. "It's not your fault, Jaq Pym," she said then.

"When I think about how we've abused—"

"No," Rett said. "It's not *you*. It *wasn't* you. And you're not one of *them* anymore."

"I never did anything they believed that I had done—"

"I know that. Your debriefing with Major Yidnar has been verified. I read the report on that a few days ago. And Ariam told me everything you did and said to her as well." It was her turn to grip his arm. Under her concern, she managed to be impressed at the girth and density of his biceps.

"How could you be so understanding when it comes to atrocities like that, Rett?" he asked in bewilderment. "I know you've experienced what the Coalition does, given the chance, to Nyorfian military prisoners, especially Special Forces." His tone turned savage. "I know what was done to you! I was...How could you be so calm about it!"

"I'm not calm and understanding about things like that," she told him. A strange current flowed between them, alternating strength and weakness, giving and need. Flashing behind her eyes was an image of herself and the Zetinorian on either side of a deep gorge, each urging the other to come to the other side where it was safe. And as they stretched, straining to touch, the gorge became narrower, until it no longer existed and both stood on the same ground, inches apart.

A hard shudder ran through her body, through his. She felt it through their fingers that somehow tangled together.

"Any soldier, female or male, in the Free Army knows what could happen if caught by the Coalition and none of us want it to happen. But in this war, it's a necessary risk. We're told, in detail, right up front what might happen. Of course, no one could be fully prepared for the some of that stuff, but I have to bury that, put it away.

"I'm speaking for myself, understand. It's something I'll never forget, but I don't allow myself to think about it. I'd be totally crazy if I did."

"You can't bury it forever, Rett," he said in a gentle voice.

"For as long as it takes. I have to." She swallowed, took a breath, controlled her shiver. "Just as you have to. And you must stop thinking of yourself as Coalition. I'm sorry I've not made it more apparent, but you are welcome here. My people are open—we don't have many prejudices. We understand how the Coalition forces people into serving them with threats and drugs and brainwashing. Nyorfians hate waste, in any form, and war is a big waste of people's lives. But we have to defend what is our only reason for existence."

She raised her hand from his upper arm to his shoulder, then touched his face gently. "You will always be Zetinorian. We'll never take that from you. But here—" she touched his chest, "you're Nyorfian, and have been for some time."

The Zetinorian didn't have anything to say. For a moment Rett thought he'd taken offense at her words, but the shift of color in his physical energy denied it. Rett couldn't explain the shift, which was probably why she didn't react when he suddenly leaned forward and down slightly. She let out a soft breath when his lips met hers but didn't move. It was the simplest of touches, fleeting, feather light, non-sexual, but so full of feeling Rett staggered back a step as if grazed by a stun beam.

"Jaq Pym, I need to—"

313

"Hmm? You don't have to explain anything else. Explanations aren't important." His voice, now very quiet, deep, and warm, touched off portions of recently suppressed memory.

She looked up at him searchingly. Something in his voice was familiar. She never wanted that memory to fully surface again, yet...

"Take it easy..." the voice told her. "There's not much I can do. I'll try to help—I don't have much time—"

She was totally unaware of anything outside her body. Jaq, Branch, even Rett's more surface sorrow over Kraym...all that disappeared. Rett's focus and attention was inside, fighting to contain her recollection while releasing just enough to know. *I can't. It's too much. I can't...* The darkness sucked her in like a vortex. *I can't do it, I can't go back there, I can't...*

Pam's mental presence flared within her, uncertain what to do, anxious to help. ~Give me your hand,~ demanded Pam, her uncertainty giving way to solid action.

I don't have one here!

~Imagine you do! Imagine *I* do. Give it to me now. Trust me. I can help.~

Don't let go of me, Pam. Rett reached out with a mental hand like a person drowning, putting her trust and life into the strong, firm grip that caught hold of her.

"Take it easy," the voice said again gently.

At first she hardly realized something had changed. The constant zing of electrical shock and sensations caused by other devices had stopped.

"I can't do very much, I'm sorry." The warmth and concern in the low voice was a bright lifeline. As she focused on it she felt the return of control, the recession of the feeling of complete helplessness. The physical discomfort was nothing compared to that.

Small things. Such small things. Soon she could think again. What was his game? Was this all some trick?

"I can't do anything else. I don't have much time left. Your people are supposed to be able to put yourselves into deepsleep. Can you do that before I have to replace these devices?"

Rett would have opened her eyes wide as she realized what he offered. She didn't have any hope of escape, much less survival, but if she could reach deepsleep mode there would be no way Iheolon or anyone else could make a difference any more.

For the first time since her ordeal began, she broke her voluntary silence asking the unknown trooper for his name.

"Hmm? It's not important."

"It's important to me," Rett had replied.

"Never mind that," he said, his voice going even deeper, almost in a whisper, "just don't throw this away now. Can you do it?" An undertone of urgency colored that soft, warm voice.

"Rett, what is it?"

Echoes of that same urgency snapped Rett to the present. Breathing hard, bone deep shudders rocking her from heels to head, she leaned toward the Zetinorian for support. Without Jaq's grip hard and firm on her arms, she would have been on her knees in the street, unable to stand, to move, to escape.

And without Pam's help in her mind, Rett didn't even want to think about the results. Pam had helped her hold back the details, concentrate only on the voice and what it meant to her back then and right now. *Pam, thank you.*

She swallowed and felt Jaq pull her close, heard the thud of his heart under her ear. His hand smoothed her hair, his voice reached to calm her, asking her again what caused her upset.

She struggled to control her breathing, gather her wits. "It was you." She raised her head to study his face, her expression becoming wondering. "It was you, wasn't it."

"Me? What?" He sounded puzzled.

"You helped me. You helped me go into deepsleep when Iheolon—"

He didn't say anything, but the expression on his face told her she was right. With Pam's help she forced her recollection back where it had been, buried deep. And although it had not surfaced enough for Pam to get more than a hint, her ego-merge companion conveyed her understanding that this was one memory that had to stay as tightly locked as Rett wanted it to.

315

She gripped his upper arms, seeing his face tighten with the force she exerted. "Why haven't you told me who you were, what you did? You wouldn't tell me your name then, but I never forget a voice. I've repressed a lot of that, just as we were talking about. But your voice… when it went so low and soft…I made the connection."

"I thought you had died. Although it was a better option than what Commander Iheolon had in mind—I was very glad to find out it wasn't so."

She shook her head. "I should have died. That was my intention. But I didn't have much control and instead of shutting down completely I just went deep over anything at that moment. I shut down enough for almost anyone to think I was dead without a really close scan." She looked away for a moment. "I have to admit that I'm glad I didn't die, either."

"Rett—"

"Damn it, you should have told me sooner. If you hadn't given me that chance…"

"I didn't want that to influence how you felt about me."

"Not only do I owe you for what you did for Ariam, and for doing what you could before that, when the entire platoon was caught. I owe you for that. For my life. And how many other Nyorfians? How many other times? Other lives? After what you did, how can you still align yourself with the Coalition by saying 'we' instead of 'they'? You took more chances than I ever did! You were never one of them, not once, not for a minute. No matter what you said!" Tears threatened her again and her voice shook. "Damn it, Jaq Pym. I owe you and here I haven't even been giving you the time of day!"

"Don't talk about it any more. I know everything that happened. *Everything*." He emphasized the word, leaving no doubt in Rett's mind he'd even discovered what happened after F-troop had recovered her "dead" body.

A shiver went through her again. "The Major told you." She didn't care to recall the period after her retrieval either.

"Yes. I asked him how you came out of that. You were…not in good shape. Every time I look at you I'm in awe that you weren't permanently handicapped."

She shook her head slowly, needing him to stop. She didn't want to think about that any more.

"I'm sorry to remind you of that, too, but I had know to complete that event for myself. And this brings us back to the beginning, doesn't it? Letting go. It's hard, to let go of friends or family or events that leave scars so deep they might never be erased. But we can still let go. *That* part of both of our lives is over. We make a completion, let go, and it's time to look forward."

"Are all Zetinorians as wise as you?"

He made a noise that might have been a laugh. "I imagine so, since there's a good chance I'm one of the only ones left."

"I've heard rumors of a few others. We'll find them for you." She took a deep breath. "I'm glad you're here." This time, Rett meant it. "I appreciate that you were able to come and tell me about Kraym in person, instead of me just getting a message. And for coming after me."

He offered a lopsided smile that slowly changed into something else. 317

Rett found herself unable to say anything and unable to move. Even in the half-lit darkness of the street, his smile took her breath away. In his incredible blue eyes was a calm and steady promise of forever. And that he would wait for her. As long as he had to.

"What you said before, about not wanting to get close to anyone else because we have to work together. Does that mean I just may have a chance to at least be your friend?" he asked.

More tears blurred her vision. Even after taking cover behind closed lids the truth of his eyes, his soul, washed through her, softening the topmost crusted layers of scarring. Without any effort on her part, the impression of his aura, the pure crystalline blue-violet of Nyorfian sky, registered in her mind. The predominant color flowed into a full spectrum of blues in every hue from nearly white to nearly black, reminding her of the heart of an azurium crystal.

So fitting, she managed to think. He was something as rare and precious as azurium.

"I think that's not an issue any more," she whispered.

"Not just because of—"

She shook her head. "No. Not just because of that. Gratitude has nothing to do with it, Jaq Pym."

"You don't have to call me both names. Jaq would be fine by itself."

"Jaq." She felt different when she said it. Bewildered, she peeked up at him with a sideways glance, wondering just what in two worlds just happened to her.

He laughed softly. "Not too long ago, a filthy, bruised Nyorfian commando was squished up against me in the back of a troop transport. She was exhausted. So much so, that she fell asleep against me. I wanted to do this back then…" his fingers brushed again at the tears lingering on her cheeks, "with the mud. And then there was a piece of grass stuck to your forehead, right here." Another light caress smoothed the tense knot between her brows. And I wanted to do this, too." His arms went around her and suddenly Rett knew what she needed. With a sigh, she leaned into him, her tense muscles relaxing from scalp to toes.

318

* * * * *

THE WEIGHT OF HER HEAD on his shoulder was soft. She was trusting him to support her and he did gladly, gratefully. He spoke softly near her ear, feeling her shiver a bit as his breath fluttered her short dark hair. "I'm not going to push you, Rett. What direction things take is up to you. If this is all you want from me, this is fine."

Her arms slid around him and she nestled closer. "Thank you," she said, a bone-weary, sad, and somewhat relieved tone in her voice. "I'd like you to hold me right now."

She was crying again, silently so that only her uneven breathing and the dampness growing against his shoulder gave her away. He wished he could do more. He pressed his cheek to her hair, feeling the alien slickness of it. He had noticed that before, how he could stroke his hand through the strands but not grasp them. The sensation against his skin was mesmerizing, as was her scent. The motion seemed to calm her, for her breathing steadied and she became still.

He dared to let out a long soundless sigh of relief and satisfaction. *A beginning,* he thought. *When the time is right for more, then more will happen.*

She'd come to him of her own free will. She needed support and Jaq was content to supply it. He couldn't ask for more at this point, since only a few tendays ago this was an impossible dream.

Her head moved against his shoulder, seeking a more comfortable spot. Her ragged sigh fitted her body more closely against his. *I can't believe this is really happening.* Almost sleepy in his own contentment, he held her and wondered again just how someone so tall, solid and strong could feel so light.

The change came over her so abruptly he wondered if he'd done something wrong or threatening he was unaware of. He was pretty sure all he had been doing was holding her. At once, the trusting, pliant body, which had molded to his with a fluid bonelessness, solidified. As if flesh turned to metal, her body temperature dropped, muscles swelled and whatever space between them filled now with a deadly dangerous, ready tension.

Jaq hissed in surprised pain as her fingers tightened on his arms, adding fresh bruises to the ones he was sure she had given him only a double handful of minutes earlier. A solid, unstoppable force sent him reeling, stumbling into the alley between semi-residential buildings.

319

1.4.7 DESERTED RESIDENTIAL AREA, BRANCH
BRANCH PROVINCE, NYORFIAS
0535.07.36 (LOCAL RECKONING)

He understood why a split second later, as glowing energy beams streaked through the street, where they'd just stood, like bolts of lightning. The quiet of the evening shattered with the sounds of a localized, ground level thunderstorm. Jaq found himself being lifted to his feet and urged forward.

"Get going!" Then Rett grabbed him again and flattened them both against a wall as more SMG beams sliced by so close he felt the heat and heard the air sizzle even before the thunderous crash of sound exploded the superheated air.

Less than a heartbeat after that, his body was relocated a third time. Before his feet touched the ground, he was yet again changing position and location.

He put a name to the unstoppable force he experienced seconds ago. Sergeant Rett.

By the One, he thought, *it's all true.* Every word he'd heard about the Nyorfian commandos' combat sense wasn't just idle talk. It was virtually impossible to avoid SMG strikes. The shots traveled faster than any projectile. Rett was keeping them out of the way with more then reflex. Some kind of supernormal instinct guided her.

"Go. Stay down, think cold."

"I'm sticking with you."

"No you're not!" she snapped, her tone low and hard. "Neither of us stands a chance if I'm too busy moving both of us out of..."

* * * * *

Rett had to scramble and use force to flatten the Zetinorian flat to the wall again, her words turning into a hissing, soft curse as a tingling line of heat kissed her shoulder. She thanked all good gods and deities that was all she felt. That one was a stun, she noted clinically. *Don't want to set the town on fire, do we?*

"Deities, Jaq—flatten!" Her elbow drove into his stomach, deflating his lungs. That shot left a wisp of smoke rising from the scorched material above his belt. That definitely wasn't a stun. This was crazy.

He sucked in a breath, found his feet. She let him go, pressing her back firmly into a wall behind them. Damn. Catching her breath, willing her heartbeat to slow, she listened with her entire being. *Where did they go?*

"It's blacker than space out here," Jaq muttered with a soft curse, echoing her thoughts.

"Yes, and you, of all people, Citizen Tech Advisor, should know that in darkness they have the advantage." Well, advantage over most people. She pulled her energy sense into full focus, thanking all deities for it now.

"I wish they'd decide on stun or kill levels," muttered Jaq.

She and F-troop had been surprised to learn that even after handling energy weapons for years, the Zetinorian had never paid attention to the subtle change in sound the different power settings produced. According to him, neither did anyone else on the firing end. At least no one he'd ever been around.

"I'm glad to note those lessons F-troop's been giving you are taking hold," said Rett from between her teeth. "But at this point it doesn't matter. Stunned is good as dead, sometimes worse."

With eyes and mind, she swept the alleyway for some way out. Being boxed into a corner by more than a handful of individuals intent on her destruction was not an acceptable option.

Boxed into a corner, however, appeared to be the situation. She noted, at the same time, that nothing appeared to be burning. Not many options. The flat gray energy resonance from building material told her enough to form a rough outline of her position, a hint at the locations of windows or doorways, little else. No breaks at ground level. Walls and doors were solid. Most windows were shielded. She could go up, of course, but Jaq wouldn't be able to follow.

She needed to see, if not that, feel. But the shadows were too deep, the lighting from the street too dim. She'd have to go look.

"You're in a good spot for the moment. Will you stay put, or do I have to knock you on your butt? I have to check out this access."

"Rett—"

She growled. "Just stay here, control your breathing, and shut up!"

Then she ducked out. If only she wore her regular uniform, and as quickly as the thought came, reminded herself as usual that "if onlys" wasted time. She went low, to all fours, body close to the ground. It didn't take long to check the alley. She couldn't hear anything, didn't sense anyone in the immediate area. No. But they were about to come a lot closer, and there was no way out that Jaq could follow.

She went as fast as she dared back to him, but not so fast she would raise the body temperature she had forced down below normal. Jaq gasped when she straightened alongside him and her hand was quick to stifle him.

322

"Looks like I'm stuck with you. There's no way out. No way you could follow me, anyway, and I'm not leaving you alone. You're not only part of my unit, you're valuable to Nyorfias and, to them, a deserter."

"But—"

Her hand covered his mouth again. "No more," she breathed. "Moving in."

After feeling certain he understood, Rett's attention turned to exploring the wall behind her. A length or two further in, the wall gave a different impression. She slid toward the anomaly, grinning as her hand encountered something cool and smooth.

~Glass!~ thought Pam. ~But thick.~

All that matters is that it's a way, returned Rett, trying to determine the dimensions and strength of the window; hoping to find a sliding panel or opening. Nothing. *And a way that is closed can open with the right incentive.*

~I hope you aren't planning to drop kick this thing.~

I've a little more finesse, and sense, than that.

The azurium-alloy blade of her knife soon pressed hard into the glass, scoring deep lines in several places with silent obedience. Then

Rett leaned back hard, steadily increasing pressure, concentrating every ounce of her weight and strength into her upper back and shoulders. She heard a *chink* and a soft *snap*, but it wasn't enough.

-Well, you're standing next to someone from a heavy gravity world,- Pam put in. -You think getting him to lean on it with you would do?-

Just where I was going. Rett swatted his arm. Blessedly quick on the uptake, the Zetinorian added his dense mass to the cool, smooth expanse.

With a hollow, dull crack, the glass split into several large sections and fell inward. She flinched, waiting for the noise, but there wasn't much. A carpeted floor, then. She urged Jaq inside and rolled her eyes as one of the large, thick shards split and splintered under his feet. So much for the advantages of carpet. She hoped he wore good strong footgear and cringed to think of the damage if he didn't.

Then she followed, managing to avoid the broken glass by catching the dim reflected light from outside.

Her senses aimed at the Zetinorian first. His aura showed no sign of injury, although grayish, muddy striations of stress and orange combat tension marred it now. She let out of soft sigh of relief before turning her attention to the room they had entered.

An office of some kind. But it was too dark to make out details and not the right time to care. She flattened close to the wall just inside and to the left of the window and gestured Jaq to take a similar position opposite.

He obeyed, but a flare of puzzled color indicated he didn't understand.

Didn't matter as long as he just stayed there. This time when Rett took out her knife, she extended the blade fully. She heard a soft intake of breath from Jaq. He understood now.

"Make sure you're on low power this time, damn it," she heard a voice snarl outside. "Stun first, then we'll finish her outside of town. We don't want more attention. Come on, hurry, the MPs are probably already coming. They went in here. You guys, go around the other side."

323

"No one's going to believe we saw Killer all wound around some guy," said a second low voice with amusement.

Wound around him? Rett wrinkled her nose. She was leaning on him, but she didn't remember being wound around him.

"Hey, it was luck we saw her out here tonight at all. But you're right, didn't think she was like that! I've always heard she was an icicle."

All they'd been doing was standing there.

"It didn't slow her reactions any," said a third in a tone of awed respect. "I've never seen anyone move so fast."

Only three? Yes, three energy auras, right outside, bleak, dark red and focused. They were out to kill, and nothing else. She nodded to herself. Helped to know that if she failed to get Jaq or herself out of this, they had nothing worse to worry about.

And they didn't recognize Jaq Pym, so they weren't after him. That was good, too.

"Go in and check, Ruoss," said one of the snipers. "I'll watch the street."

"Glass all over," commented the first man to come in through the window. Rett met him as he pulled his second leg in through the opening. He died silently, but the weight of his body shattered and crunched the glass into smaller bits than before.

"Clumsy idiot," hissed the second voice. "What did you trip over?" The second sniper swung into the room, placing his feet carefully, and bent over the inert form of his comrade.

Rett watched him, ready to strike. He started to turn his head to tell his companion the first man was dead. At that moment she grabbed him, clamping one hand firmly over his mouth as she broke his neck. She let him down quietly and moved back to the window, crouching directly beneath the opening.

"Ruoss? Thory?" The third leaned farther inside, his finger ready on the firing stud of his SMG rifle. "What's going on? I know glass didn't—"

Rett thrust her body upward, her head ramming into the sniper's gut. His body flipped over, his weapon dropped, and Rett slammed herself atop him as his back hit the floor. He yelped as her weight drove his body into the glass shards on the floor, but became still and silent when she let him feel the sharp edge of her knife on his throat.

"Talk, or you're dead," Rett ordered, voice lethally soft. "How many more out there? *Tell me!*"

The man opened his mouth, but not to give Rett any information. She felt him draw a deep breath for a loud yell. "Shit." She let the blade bite deep. The sniper's deeply drawn breath exhaled in a froth of blood that splattered over her upper body. She ignored it and stood up. "Jaq. Get an SMG, cover the window."

Rett found a handgun on one of the dead men, then went to the door, listening intently. She spun suddenly toward Jaq. "Down!"

She threw herself at him, but not before a SMG found its mark. Jaq grunted as the glowing pulse intercepted his head. *No. No, no, no. Damn it.* She was in time to catch him as he fell, managing to redirect his landing to a portion of the floor clear of the dangerous remnants of the window. "Jaq!" She felt for a burn mark, found nothing except a hot area; felt for a pulse, and realized he caught a stun beam.

325

"Great," muttered Rett. "Well then, I suppose I should be grateful that at least you won't get in my way. Don't move." Giving his unconscious shoulder a pat, she let him go and picked up one of the heavy SMGs, pushing the powerunit harness over one shoulder. She hated the bulky energy weapons, but right now, she couldn't afford to be fussy.

What first? Window, or door? There were the threatening glows of two more bodies moving quickly into the alleyway…and five more thinking about coming in through the door!

Focusing her ability, she decided she felt no threat from those outside the door. The energy from these people were collected, red edged and copper-orange with combat readiness, yet they were clear, without dark spots or edges of malice. The intensity of the danger signals from the window above her head set off stronger alarms.

She had to move fast, or get caught in a crossfire. Or risk those others she felt were a non-threat getting injured or killed from those who represented real intent to harm.

Rett felt for the power level setting on the SMG unit and found it charged and on full power. She stood up and fired instantly at the auras she sensed outside the building. She heard bitten off screams from two men. Then swung to cover the inner doorway—just to be sure—as the portal flew open and the room flooded with light.

"Military police! *DROP IT!*"

Five MPs moved inside quickly, weapons trained on her. After a moment, their hard expressions altered into looks of confusion.

Rett had already dropped her weapon, straightened up and moved away from the window. Other than that, she stayed perfectly motionless and made sure her hands were in clear sight, fingers open. The MPs all had fingers on triggers and Rett didn't want to take the chance that one good sneeze on her part would give them cause to fire.

"Identify," said the patrol leader, closing his mouth with a snap.

Blinking to adjust her eyes to the brightness, she complied. "Rett, sergeant, 90674SF." Rett saw recognition in his eyes as they went to her face, but didn't move from her position. "You're a bit late," she told them.

"What in two worlds is going on, here, Sergeant?" demanded the MP patrol leader, his aim not wavering by the width of a hair. A few words and motion of his head sent various individuals on his team into motion. Three went out of the room, one went to check the bodies, and another started toward Jaq.

"That's what I'd like to know," Rett said. Her muscles tensed as the MP near Jaq made a motion as if to push him over with her foot. "Don't."

The MP froze and looked to the lieutenant.

His hard eyes were as level as his weapon. "The Zetinorian was with you?" asked the lieutenant sharply.

"Yes, sir. He's part of my unit. I can provide any identification and verification for his being here if you need. But I won't stand by and see him treated in a manner he doesn't deserve."

The lieutenant conceded the point with a nod and significant glance to his subordinate. "I'll get your statement in a minute. She's not going to hurt him. We saw him earlier, he came in as we were headed out. Can't mistake that hair. We just needed to make sure he was the same one—with Yixolryns having the means to genetically change themselves, we can't be too careful."

Rett wasn't going to argue with that. Although it would take a gutsy Yixolryn to take the form of one of the races they absolutely couldn't stand to be around.

"He is, sir," said the MP near Jaq, crouching down and carefully turning his face to her view. "This is the one Massithe took to the Old Mill earlier." The she looked at the left palm of Jaq's hand intently for a moment before putting it down. Whatever unspoken message went from her to the lieutenant Rett couldn't interpret. She was going to find out.

"These others are dead, sir," said another of his group. "Coalition troopers." Seconds later, a voice on the lieutenant's comunit announced finding the bodies in the alleyway and their identification as troopers, too.

327

Only then did he lower his weapon and gesture for the others to do the same, "You can stand down, Sergeant," the lieutenant told her.

Rett then noticed, for the first time, the would-be assassins were dressed as Free Army infantrymen. *No wonder the MPs were more than tense,* she thought to Pam dryly. *On first glance, it probably looked like I was the bad guy in this scenario.*

None of the uniforms bore any identifying unit or rank patches, though, which would have been instantly noted in daylight. Plus, each of the dead men wore the standard Coalition issue targeting goggles. How were such averagely humanoid people labeled so positively as troopers? She felt relief they were. Despite the incident with Mott and Shamos, she still wanted to believe Nyorfians, naturalized or native, wouldn't do such things.

~Maybe they're not really humanoid at all. Maybe they used the same sort of technology to change themselves Mott and Shamos did.~

Not now, Pam. But good gods and deities, I hope not.

Omni now in hand, the patrol leader was making notations with a deft speed Rett instantly envied.

Her eyes went back to the bodies in the infantry uniforms. "How are you sure they're Coalition?" asked Rett. "Or—truly humanoid?"

The lieutenant moved past her to crouch near the body closest to Rett. "For the first part—look. Every humanoid Coalition trooper has a number. It's marked on them externally in at least three places. One of which is here." He showed Rett the left palm of one of the snipers, then dropped it. "As to the second, they don't feel it necessary to mark their allied races. However, I can't answer if that applies to people they might have changed like those two agents turned out a month or so ago." He nodded toward Jaq. "Your tech advisor has markings, too. It's not been more than a year or so since that started, but the updates went out to all units in the field. You didn't know?"

"About the marking? No. Our update must have been misdirected." *Thanks to Mott and Shamos,* she added grimly to herself and Pam.

"All right, Sergeant, there are no curfews or restricted areas in Branch, as you were probably told when you checked in, but since weapons were fired I'm going to need to know what you were doing out this way, this late."

Rett nodded and gave him the details, her eyes again drawn by the dexterity of his hands. Wrapping up her summary, she blew a soft breath out her nose. "I still have no idea where exactly 'here' is, Lieutenant."

He nodded and looked up from the notations he was making to his Omni. "Northwest section of town, just about on the edge. You're almost five miles in a direct line from the Old Mill, so deities know how far you actually walked. This used to be a nice residential area, lots of kids. Now just a lot of empty houses and small offices." He shook his head. "I'm really sorry this happened, Sergeant, but thank deities you and the Zetinorian are all right and no one else was around to get hurt. They thought this was their lucky night, huh? Of course they moved on it, with that reward and all. What's it up to? Fifteen million?"

"I don't keep track," muttered Rett.

The patrol leader flipped down his comunit pickup. "Prill, call in for a unit to come out to pick up these bodies and I want this area blanketed—quietly! Also double checks on everyone who's come in the past tenday, records and physical. Have the patrol units verify anyone walking about until further notice."

"Right, lieutenant," responded a voice on the audio.

"I hope this sort of thing hasn't happened in town before."

"We've caught a few here and there. We've found out it's usually to knock off someone or another the Leader thinks is a threat. But since you and F-troop got Circle back…"

"Excuse me for interrupting," Rett said, "But I need to set the record straight. Among others—including the residents of the city of Circle—the 5th and 52nd Divisions were also involved. F-troop and I were not alone."

All the MPs in the room sent her a glance of some sort that indicated this was not how they heard it. She managed to keep the sigh inward and mentally added an item to her list of things to do while in town.

~You don't want to kill the civilian media, Rett,~ thought Pam. ~Not if you want them to back down and leave you alone. Just hurt them a little.~

"Anyway, since Circle is back in Nyorfian control—" the lieutenant looked to Rett for approval and she sent him a tight smile, "we haven't had any trouble. Until now. I'm wondering how they're getting information."

Then Rett knew. "Mott and Shamos. No one's caught them yet and we're still clearing out the mess they made in the 52nd. Colonel Evard's been changing security protocols since he's arrived there, but who knows how much access they still have? Any low level logon to 52nd channels would have been enough to know I would be in town."

The lieutenant's eyebrows rose. "You may have something." Yet another series of notations went into his Omni. "Might explain how these guys sneaked past us, too."

A groan from Jaq's direction brought Rett to his side instantly. "Please don't try to move him."

The MP still near Jaq looked up at Rett warily.

Rett offered an apologetic half smile and knelt alongside her. "I know you had the best of intentions this time, but he caught a stun pulse right between the eyes. Moving him at this point will create the excellent possibility he'll start puking his guts out."

The MP, an older woman, nodded. "Is there anything we can do?"

"Just wait it out for now." Rett sized up Jaq's condition. He was waking up quickly, which amazed her. How much time had elapsed?

Ten, fifteen minutes at most? The unreality of the entire afternoon and evening had totally distorted Rett's own sense of time as well as place. She'd lost the count, that perpetual ticking off of seconds in her head while in combat mode, and didn't even having the excuse of unconsciousness to account for it.

A wave of sadness buffeted her for a moment; one of the first people she'd automatically turn to in a similar situation would have been Kraym.

Just thinking of him triggered her next thought and despite a fresh wash of soreness to her throat, she smiled a little, glancing at the concerned face of the MP alongside her. *I just happen to be in the company of some more of the most detail oriented people in the Free Army.*

"Can any of you tell me how much time has elapsed since you came through that door over there?"

"Seven minutes." Three voices spoke as one and Rett nearly laughed aloud.

"Less than I thought. Good deities, Zetinorians are tough."

Jaq's returning awareness was becoming more visibly evident: from the pale, greenish cast to his face; the sheen of sweat on his skin, and his rapid, shallow breathing. His nose started to bleed. A rapidly swelling and darkening burn-bruise was quickly blossoming across his sweating forehead.

His blue eyes opened, staring and bloodshot, and through the intense, nauseated pain evident on his face, Rett could see he was scared. Sure, anyone'd be scared to feel as if his brain was melting and leaking through his ears and to hear everything as if through whines and static and to be blinded. Not to mention being uncertain of possessing a face.

The nausea was the easy part.

She took his hand and squeezed it, speaking carefully so he would understand. "Just take it easy, Jaq. It's okay. It's Rett. I know you can't see or hear too well at the moment. And believe me, I *know* how sick you feel. Stun beam in the head does that. Caught a few in my time. Try to turn your head to the side a little, your nose is bleeding. It's only temporary. Breathe slow, through your mouth, and relax."

"Is he okay? Do you want a medtech?"

"Thanks, no, Lieutenant, he'll be okay. Lucky for him that SMG was on a stun level. Medtech can't do anything for him, just put him to bed. A good night's sleep is all he needs. I'll take care of him." She looked up. "Sorry about the window," she added.

"Windows can be replaced," said the lieutenant. "The Mayor won't care her office was wrecked as long as it was troopers who were killed instead of Nyorfians." He grinned a bit tightly.

"This is the mayor's office?" Rett looked around at the mess she'd created. "Great."

"Home office. Mostly during the winter. But summers are quiet, and quieter yet for a couple years, ever since the enemy penetrated as far as the Zen's Glacier River district."

She suppressed a shiver. The reminder was much too close to that recollection she had out on the street earlier. She and Pam worked together to bury the memories deeper down. "That didn't last long," she said.

"That's right, you and F-troop pushed them right back to the other side of the river. With the 52nd, of course," he was quick to amend before she pointed out, again, that she and F-troop weren't alone in their efforts.

"Anyway, even the people who live here year round have taken their kids to live out of town just in case. So she's living above her central office, not far from the Old Mill, matter of fact."

She didn't ask him to clarify "in case". There was always a chance the enemy could, and would, use a lot more force and start leveling the landscape instead of attempting to take it with resources and people intact. At least intact enough to be of use to them.

The thought that the mountains of the Branch Range harbored those families in safely was a comfort. There were places in those mountains, especially closer to the Skyraker Range, which the most determined instrument survey from an aircraft or ship in orbit would never penetrate.

"I should get him taken care of and come back here to—"

"Not at all," the lieutenant said firmly. "Don't worry about it. We'll take care of everything."

Acknowledging the sudden note of firmness in his tone, she turned her attention back to Jaq. If she waited any longer to move him, his symptoms would just get worse. "Do you need either of us to hang around for anything else?"

"No, you can go. I'll have you taken to your hostel in a patrol rover. I'd rather not have you an open target until we're certain there are no other infiltrators around."

In the process of maneuvering the Zetinorian, very carefully, to the door and into a small patrol rover, Rett somehow managed to get the lieutenant to take her credit authorization code to cover the cost of replacing the mayor's window. She felt sure he indulged her for the express purpose of expediting her relocation to a more secure area.

Once they were settled, the MP assigned to escort them slid behind the controls. He turned to glance at her as the vehicle moved off.

"Is that usually how SMG stun affects someone? I've never seen anyone who'd been zapped in the head before. We're told to avoid headshots, even with our own stunners."

She glanced at Jaq. She had some concern he wouldn't make it back to the hostel without vomiting all over the rover, but he seemed to have a good grip on himself. So far.

"I suppose there's good reason for it. First of all, it's risky, some have died. If you don't, well, waking up is a hundred times worse than any hangover or migraine headache you could ever imagine. He'll be blind for a few hours and he'll have a headache well into tomorrow morning. Just don't make any sudden turns," cautioned Rett, "or we'll both regret having anything to eat earlier when he starts puking!"

Soon, the MP was helping her get Jaq to the hostel entrance. Rett told him she could handle it from there, since her room was on the ground floor. "Thanks for the ride."

"Okay, Sergeant Rett. I'm going to be on station here until new day if you need anything. Sorry about what happened. We should have—" He stopped and looked down for a moment.

"Don't worry at it," she said dryly, with a sigh. "We can't account for everything. As for me, I'm used to it. Getting shot at comes with the job."

1.4.8 HOSTEL, BRANCH
BRANCH PROVINCE, NYORFIAS
0535.07.37 (LOCAL RECKONING)

JAQ PYM DIDN'T KNOW WHERE he was at first. He woke to sunlight and groaned, covering his eyes, for the brightness seared into his aching head. He'd never been at the receiving end of a stun beam. Now he knew how it felt. Wasn't fun…

"How do you feel?"

Thunder crashed, deafening him. A major earthquake rocked his body. Fortunately, it lasted only a second. He hated the F-troop leader with his entire being as her voice detonated on him from somewhere close by.

"Stop!" he pleaded. Was he the source of that hoarse, high-pitched squeak? He uncovered one eye, then both, finding the brightness considerably diminished. He tried to focus his vision on her. His eyes were crusted and felt like stones. He gradually made out a figure perched on the right side of his bed.

"Good morning, Jaq," she said calmly. "Sleep well?"

"I don't think I slept at all. Unconsciousness doesn't count. Go away." His hands went to his head. "Ow. *Ow.* Lemme alone." This as she grasped his forearms and hauled him into a sitting position. Something cool and damp swabbed over his eyes. "Stop!" He did not pass out, die, or throw up, although Jaq swore that for several seconds he did all three.

"Sleeping more at this point will just make it worse. Trust me. I've been in your place more than once." Her voice was firm yet held a smile. "You're not getting any more coddling from me. You'll be much better after a wash and some breakfast. I brought you some tea."

Jaq groaned again at the mention of breakfast. He had to admit he felt better sitting up and soon realized there were pillows at his back, supporting him. A second later a cup of very hot tea was in his cold hands.

333

He eyed the woman sitting on the bed watching him. Rett patted his knee through the blanket and stood up. "Drink that. Made it myself. Guaranteed to cure hangovers."

"I had nothing to drink last night," he protested. "I don't think I did. Did I?"

"You caught SMG with your head, Jaq. We call the aftereffects you're experiencing a hangover, because that is how it feels."

"What's in this?"

"Either you drink it or I'll pour it down your throat for you." Her expression and tone left no doubt she would.

He sipped the beverage and made a face at the bitterness. Then the hot liquid sent fire down his throat into his belly and the sharp, clean aroma of blue pine shot up his nostrils to his brain. He felt as if someone drilled an icicle between his eyes and poured molten lava into his stomach simultaneously. The icy sensation went straight out through his ears while the heat sank straight to his toes, then both did an about face, toward a collision in his middle.

"Once more," she said.

Jaq tried to protest, but the hand that covered his and guided the mug upward again was too strong to resist.

In a reflex movement, he swallowed again. Tears streamed from his eyes and he gasped for breath.

* * * * *

"Another for good luck," said Rett. This time the Zetinorian was able to protest, if Rett cared to call the pathetic and feeble motion to push her hand aside a protest.

~You're heartless,~ commented Pam admiringly as she, through Rett, watched Jaq's reaction to the tea. ~I've never seen anyone change colors so quickly. Such an attractive shade of purple~.

Rett's lips twitched, but she refrained from laughing as Jaq's bloodshot, now streaming eyes again focused on her. He coughed. She handed him a wipe. He snatched it, blew his nose loudly, and swiped at his eyes. Ripe curses burst from his lips, some in GTC Standard, some in a language or languages Rett didn't know.

~I've been thinking, Rett, that maybe that subconscious memory association was part of the reason you felt…uncomfortable around Jaq prior to last night.~ Pam tendered this idea as they waited for Jaq to realize he felt much better. ~Part of you recognized him, his voice, his aura, I don't know since you hadn't really seen him, with your eyes at least, before. It's crazy, I guess.~

No, thought Rett. *It makes sense. But I'm not exactly ready to go the complete opposite way, you know. Not yet.*

Pam gave her a mental grin. ~I know that. It would be nicer to be friends first before——~

Don't say it, Pam, she warned, glad Jaq was occupied. Pam's mischievous thoughts brought heat to her face. Yes, it had been nice to curl up next to someone so solid and warm; to wake up next to him and watch him while he slept. It was comforting to have someone else there while she cried again for Kraym, for Gerrale, for the others. Even if he had been unconscious. It was nice not to be physically alone. *Now I just have to try it when he isn't injured,* she thought before Pam did. *But I need time before it goes any farther than that.*

Pam didn't push. ~Man, I wish I knew what he was saying. Must have some real select phrases in there.~

Rett's attention returned fully to the cursing Zetinorian. "Yes, and whatever you've said, every word is probably true. But you're still madly in love with me, aren't you?" she asked so sweetly Jaq's blistering soliloquy stalled.

"What?" He blinked and looked her up and down. "You're clean."

Rett looked down at herself. "You have a problem with that?"

"You're in uniform. I thought you were off duty."

"I've errands. Been quite busy already this morning. I see you're feeling much better." She picked up his kitbag and a towel. "When I guarantee something works, I mean it." She tossed his gear into his lap.

"What time is it? Where am I, anyway?"

"It's well after midday and you're in my room at the hostel. You'll be back to one hundred percent after a wash. Go get cleaned up. I'm starving."

Jaq rubbed a hand over his face. "Rett, last night, you didn't run from those guys!"

"I usually don't try to run when I'm cornered," she answered.

"You killed them."

Maybe he's not as tough as I thought. "Are you okay, Jaq? More tea?"

"Yes. No. Well, yes." He grabbed the half-empty mug and gulped back another swallow, only making a small grimace this time. "It's just that it happened so fast. One minute you were Rett, someone grieving and gentle. The next minute you were—"

"Sergeant Killer? Now you know why they gave me that name, huh? I guess I really am two people now," she added with a short, dry laugh. "What did you want me to do?" She threw out her arms. "Say 'Hi! Welcome to Branch! Why yes, I am Sergeant Killer. You found me. And guess what: I'm on vacation from fighting. So don't worry, I'll stand right here. Go ahead and shoot!'? Damn it, Jaq! Those guys were trying to kill us! They intended to do whatever it took."

She dropped her arms and stared at her hands for a moment. "Whatever you may have heard, I don't like killing. I didn't have many options last night. And had things gone farther than that office, who knows how many other casualties there might have been?"

"I've never seen anyone change character so fast," insisted Jaq.

She laughed again without humor. "Stick around. You'll get used to it. It's called survival."

Jaq had lifted the covering and rolled as if to stand up, but froze his motion, staring down the length of his body.

"Now what's wrong? Something missing? Do you need my help to get to the—"

Jaq's feet hit the floor with a thump and he—and the bed covering with his kitbag and the towel somewhere in the folds—disappeared into the lavatory/bathing alcove so fast Rett was left staring after him.

Any ideas? she asked Pam in bewilderment.

~He's shy? Inexperienced? Never been alone with someone he's madly in love with? Butt-naked in her bed, no less?~

"No way," Rett said aloud with a half whistle of disbelief.

~Shit,~ thought Pam in deep disgust, ~you asked for ideas. Admit it, you like him.~

Rett yelped and grabbed her own ribs as mental fingers triggered a tickling sensation. *STOP! I mean it.* She felt Pam back down so quickly she thought her visitor was completely gone. *Pam?*

~I don't know how I did that.~ Pam's mental tone was low and apologetic.

Just don't do it any more. Rett slowed the pulse that had jumped in a reaction of pure fear and sat a moment longer. It was one thing when physical hands tickled her in fun, another thing when it came from inside as something over which she hadn't full control. *I'm all right,* she thought in response to Pam's concern. *Don't do it any more. At least not without some sort of warning. Let's forget it.*

She took a breath and stood up. *And, okay, I like him.* Rett stripped the bottom covering off the bed and remade it swiftly, dumping the bedding into the laundry chute. The hostel provided many amenities, but one kept up one's own room during a stay.

We really have to practice some stuff, you and I. I can see that now. Rett straightened her personal gear, arranging it in her kitbag so that if she were called out, she would already be packed.

~Like that door or barrier thing I do? You're going to want to do that from your side.~

Yes. I've been avoiding it, like I've been avoiding a lot of things. But if we're going to stay merged like this, we should both be able to take responsibility for…keeping stuff in my head that doesn't belong outside of it. Rett raked a hand through her hair. *I hope nothing's wrong with you. I mean, the first merge was a single night of sleep for you, but it was practically an entire day here. And the interval in between for me was a matter of hours, but for you it was a few weeks. You've been merged with me since then for more than two Standard months! How do we know you're even going to have a body to go back to?*

~I'm not going to worry about it,~ said Pam firmly. ~I guess I'll have to find out just how long I was asleep when I wake up. You said ego-merges have happened before, so there must be a reason.~

I wish I knew what that was. Rett scratched at a small nick in her knife sheath.

337

~Well, until we find out, we'll just have to do the best we can. Starting with both of us practicing at setting limits up here. Now that you're using your imagination a bit more again, it shouldn't be much of a problem. I'll remind you later,~ said Pam.

This as Jaq re-entered the main section of the room, completely dressed, raking his fingers through his wet, tousled mane of impossible hair. He dropped his kitbag on a counter and rooted around in it with an intense look of concentration. His hand withdrew with a comb and his eyes, clear now, glanced sideways, toward her.

"Did you say I was in your room? I just realized what a problem I must've been to you last night—"

"No problem. I have to look out for my people."

Jaq studied his comb intently. "Where'd you sleep?"

"Where else? This is my vacation and damned if I'm sleeping on the floor or ground when I don't have to. Why? I mean, we all bunk together back at 52nd HQ and if you have, or have had, a problem with that, I expect to be told. If Zetinorians have some sort of cultural thing against it, then I apologize. I have to admit I know nothing about the social habits of people other than my own."

"No, nothing like that." Jaq mumbled, then blushed, his already ruddy skin darkening with more color that rose to the roots of his hair. His embarrassment surprised Rett.

Shit, Pam, you nailed it or came awfully close. Aloud, she replied: "We didn't have sex or anything, Jaq. You were unconscious, passed out cold as soon as I hauled you through the door over there. You're not all that easy to carry around, you know. Even for me. I was tired." She sighed and shook her head. "I hope you don't think I would have taken advantage of—"

"I don't. I'm sorry." The Zetinorian opened his mouth to say something else, but closed it just as quickly, turning aside to attack his hair. "Did someone drop off my stuff?" he asked.

"I picked up your gear this morning at the MP checkstation. You must have been anxious to find me—I was told you just threw your kit in a corner and went out before they even finished telling you they'd give you a ride." Rett's voice dropped just a bit. She was dressed for business since her first stop of the morning had been to inform Kraym's relatives of his passing with a personal call on vocom. She'd also sought out Kraym's MP friend, first going to his superior. When she explained what she needed to discuss with N'wessar, his commander allowed her to take the MP off his duty for a time.

Last night with Jaq's support had helped, but the shared sympathy with someone who also knew and loved Kraym reached an even deeper level. It didn't make his death easier, but it helped cut the pain. She promised N'wessar she would be available if he needed to talk and he expressed the same. Both of them wanted to share happier memories about Kraym. They'd have time later. She'd be around town for three more tendays.

"I guess you had to call Kraym's family," Jaq said quietly and in such a manner Rett glanced at him, her eyebrows raised in surprise.

"Are Zetinorians telepathic, Jaq? Or empaths?"

"No, not in any strong sense. However, we're wide open to reading nuance. Part of it's this." He indicated his hair.

"Really?"

"Specifically the centerline."

"Your hair really has feeling?"

"It's complicated." He grimaced. "Can we say, for now, that it's an extension of the Zetinorian nerve system?"

"For now," agreed Rett.

"Getting back to this morning, when you said you went out—I could pretty much guess what errands you ran. Those others besides the ingredient gathering for the tea you tried to poison me with." He regarded her intently. "Are you all right?"

"I will be...in time. I'm better than I was." She glanced out the window for a moment. "Thanks for asking. And thanks for being there, too."

"I just wish it was different." Smoothing his combed locks, which were still damp, but already springing into wild abandon, he reached for his cap. She moved closer and intercepted his hand.

"Don't wear that anymore. You've more gear to pick up. I finally tracked that down and it's waiting for you at the Base. I brought one piece of it with me. You're Special Forces now, have to show it or we'll have more mix-ups like last night." She tossed something at him and he automatically closed his hand around it.

"Like what last night?"

"You came here in a hurry, you're dressed generically, and you're... well, definitely alien. There's nothing that instantly marks you as belonging. We weren't too worried about it up at 52nd HQ. There, it was a matter of waiting for the stuff to get sent up. Here, it's going to matter. I don't want to have to threaten to beat up any more MPs because they can't tell you're one of us, so put that on and let's go."

He examined the object in his hand. It was a black headband like hers, except his had a wide, pale amethyst stripe that stood out just a little more from the darkness of the rest of the material.

"That color marks you as an advisor," she explained as Jaq fingered the stripe.

"I can't wear this," he said in a low voice. "I didn't earn it like you and the others did."

"If anyone went through their own version of Special Forces training and testing, it's you." She moved to stand in front of him and took the headband. "You will have this on at all times in public, is that understood, Tech Advisor Jaq Pym?"

She settled it on his head, going carefully around the SMG bruise, arranging his wild, multicolored hair to her liking. Despite its damp-ness, it was all ends and angles, his pale gold crest rampant.

"There. It looks good." She blocked his hand as he reached up to touch it. "Is it hurting you?"

He shook his head, using small motions since her hands were still in his hair. *It really is sensitive,* she thought in fascination, *and not just that lighter part.* Suddenly Rett itched to experiment, but she was all too aware of other errands that still awaited her.

"Good, then leave it there. You'll get used to it. Now let's go. I have a lot to do."

"What do you have to do?"

Her fingers still mussed with the feathering strands of hair that dried as she watched. "Just this morning I received our transfer orders to Epnoce, so, first I have some business to take care of at

MilitaryCentral. The rest of the platoon will be joining us here in two tendays. We also have to pick up your pcom, gear, and uniform, then sort out your billet at the base, where you're going to be stationed with the rest of the 2023rd. That shouldn't take more than an hour or so."

"Great."

"Try not so sound so excited," she said dryly. "You're the one who asked for it. And it's not like you won't have free time. After that, I've arranged to have a little discussion with a few of the local newspeople."

At this, he looked surprised. "You did?"

"I need to set the record straight. I'm not the only one fighting the war, you know, but sometimes they make it sound like that. Those correspondents in Circle took the details all out of proportion. Maybe putting the attention on me is a good thing in some ways...since if it takes Coalition attention off other things it helps our effort. But not for that. Not for that." She had to look away for a moment as her throat tightened.

"Rett." Jaq sounded strangled.

She realized she had clenched her fingers in his hair and quickly loosed them. "I'm sorry." She cleared her throat. "That appointment should only take ten, fifteen minutes tops."

"And then what?"

Her hands left his hair. "I don't know. But we'll have the rest of the day to figure it out."

14.9 HOSTEL, BRANCH,
BRANCH PROVINCE, NYORFIAS
0535.08.02 (LOCAL RECKONING)

~Jaq's coming this morning. At this rate he's not going to recognize you if you come out of here looking all pruny.~ An explanatory image accompanied Pam's thought.

I am not going to look like a ripe blackhip. Rett stretched each of her limbs and flexed, wishing there was some way she could bottle up this bone-deep sensation of complete physical well-being and save it for a time she would really need it again. Her body hadn't felt this good in years.

"Jets off," she said aloud. The turbulence from the therapeutic currents she had been enjoying slowly calmed. Taking a few deep breaths, then a normal one, Rett held it and slid down until she was completely submerged.

~What about that report that someone thinks Mott and Shamos got offworld? You clamped down on that so tight I couldn't follow your thoughts on it. And there was something that they found how long they've been on Nyor——~

A snarl started curling Rett's lip. She fought it back, relaxing muscles that had tensed.

~Bad thought. Sorry.~

No. Getting herself under control, Rett reassured Pam it was an okay topic. *They're not sure. They didn't find those two dead technicians until well after the shuttle would have landed on Epnoce, and technicians have a way of disappearing into the background. Damn it. And the background checks showed they were both on Nyorfias for thirty years. Accepted as naturalized citizens, respected members of the community, and militia.* Rett shook her head a little.

~Think they had anything to do with that attack on you a few nights ago?~

Not really, Rett replied. *I think they had too much else to worry about: surviving, getting offworld. I think they gave the Coalition officers and agents yet remaining on Nyorfias and other commanders the means, but they didn't do anything directly.*

There were still many small pockets of Coalition troopers being smoked out in various locations on Nyorfias. Even in the areas designated, more or less, safe. And there were plenty of places for a determined and skilled group of humanoids to hide in the Branch Range, if not the town of Branch itself.

And I think there's going to be a lot less incidents like that, for a lot of people. Things are looking up now, Rett commented, following Pam's surface thoughts. *Now we're back in control of Nyorfias, land, sea, and air. We can go on to Epnoce.*

~Yeah. And the guys in the white hats are here to back you up.~
White hats?

~The good guys. The Space Rangers or whatever you call them.~

The GTC Rangers are only one element of the Galactic Trade Commission's military, Rett reminded. The long-awaited arrival of Nyorfias's powerful allies had only cemented the reclamation of Nyorfias. Now Rett hoped they would go on together to drive the Yixolryn Coalition from their system for good.

~Which is why you are now underwater getting all pruny since with all this help now, you've earned a break from your usual job of single-handedly saving the universe.~

Rett awarded Pam a mental smack with the back of an imaginary hand. *What's up with you? Deities. Most of the time I can't even save myself, much less the universe.*

~So I'm missing the point of this and why you've suddenly decided to start doing it.~

Bathing? Rett chuckled, keeping it in her thoughts.

~You know what I mean! Putting yourself under two and a half feet of water and staying there until I panic!~

I practice this a lot. And we're going to Epnoce soon. Gravity's higher there. I was trying to use the imagination you've been trying to get me to use and imagine what it would feel like being in a heavier gravity all the time.

-If you wanted to get a grip on conditions on Epnoce,- bitched Pam, -you should have used ice water. Can you stick your nose out at least?-

I've been under less than three minutes. You forget that we pass thoughts between each other a zillion times faster than it takes to talk aloud. Is that what's set the stingfly loose in your pants? Why didn't you mention you have a fear of being underwater? Good thing for us both I'm not in Seacorps.

Before Pam could respond, Rett cut off their communication and went on alert, her body tensing for movement without changing its current position. The increased dismay to her ego-merge companion was instant and obvious, but Rett tuned out Pam's aura. Pushing her awareness outward. Rett tagged and identified the energy from the person who'd just cracked open the door to the cozy hostel room she occupied.

It's Jaq.

-Who else would it be walking in, except one of the hostel staff, who wouldn't show up without calling first? Jaq has your code, after all,- thought Pam.

Deities, Pam, the entire town of Branch is considered a secure area in a safe zone, but a handful of nights ago we were getting shot at by Coalition troopers who managed to get past all that.

Rett sat up, swiping water from her face as it broke into clear air. *Damn it, but the time got away from me this morning.* "I'm here," she said, right before Jaq tentatively called her name.

"Oh. Sorry. I'll wait for you in the common area."

"Don't be a bubblehead. Drop your gear and have a seat. I'm nearly done." She eyed her steaming tank of water regretfully. This routine of soaking out nine years worth of sore muscles by spending a few hours a day up to her neck in the bathing tank had become a quick habit in the time she'd already spent getting caught up with herself. She didn't mourn the recent news that shortened her leave by less than half its original length—the forty days were now only twenty. Not at all. She didn't feel she should have left in the first place, not until the enemy was well gone from the Nyorfian system.

But she also understood the necessity of giving herself a break, physically and mentally. Especially now that she had been away for a time. She was anxious to get back to her platoon, but she knew that when she did, she would be better for it.

~It's too bad he couldn't spend all his time here, instead of a couple hours a day.~ Pam's mental tone was teasing. ~Maybe you'd have done a little more than talk and cuddle by now.~

I'm not sure I'm ready for more than that, and you know he has work to do. Until the rest of F-troop joined them for the upcoming transfer to Epnoce, Jaq spent two shifts a day at the temporary headquarters of the 2023rd. He was also required to billet there. Since the day after he'd first arrived in town Rett had only seen him in the company of one or several other Special Forces people, usually for a meal. But today was a free day for him.

~Maybe the last free day he'll have while you're still on vacation. If you don't get a move-on, it'll be time for him to go back. Let's see, if I had to make a choice between staying in the Jacuzzi or getting out to spend time with a nice guy who really likes me, thinks I'm gorgeous, and wants nothing better than to spend time with me doing whatever I wanted…what would I do? Oh, the decision!~

Annoyed enough to be contrary, Rett leaned in favor of her tank. But as much more interesting she found Jaq's company, her reluctance to leave the luxury of the bath wasn't faked.

"We'll be training to go to Epnoce soon enough, and training again before they let us loose once we get there. It's going to take me a tenday or two to get used to going without unlimited hot water and the time to spend in it," she mumbled as she toggled the drain control with her left foot. "But might as well start now." She stood up and reached for a towel.

~Maybe you can get him to join you in here later. He'll be staying here like he did those other two nights, won't he? Maybe this time——~

Pam, shut up already. Rett supposed she might have suggested Jaq get his own room after that first night, but after more than ten years of military life, she was used to sharing space with any amount of bunkmates. To have only have one—and for such a short time—still seemed as blessedly private as being alone on a remote mountaintop.

~Not to mention you like having him around. You've been having some intense more-than-just-buddy thoughts about him lately. Why do you keep denying yourself? Life's too short.~

Rett swallowed her growl. *Pam, I'm going to do you a favor.* Very carefully she kept her plans in the private part of her mind. She and Pam had been practicing a lot of that lately, so it was time to put the practice to a test.

~Oh, Rett, really?~ Pam's mood changed instantly. ~Are we finally going to a library so I can look up stuff about previous ego-merges and your history and maybe see some maps? Can you get Jaq to talk some more about what he remembers of Zetinor Prime and more about those other worlds he mentioned? Like Kyarta and Uli-Toth and the rest?~

Much better than that. Rett smiled. She prepared herself as best as she could without alerting her ego-merge companion, planning to the hair just how much control of her body to let Pam have for three seconds. *I'm going to give you a nice preview of Epnoce.*

A flick of her wrist opened the manual control for an overhead jet. Water exploded over her head in an icy deluge. As prepared as Rett was for it, Pam's reaction nearly exploded from her throat as a shriek of utmost shock. Only by the barest threads of control did Rett modulate it to a gasp.

"Did that help you cool off?" She palmed off the jet and shook water from her head, the cold droplets flying with the same intensity as the incoherent curses from Pam's mental presence. Smirking, Rett grabbed a towel and attacked her hair with it, as much to warm up her head as to dry off the thick growth.

"What was that, Rett?" inquired Jaq from the outer room.

"Why don't you tell me what you've been doing at the base while I finish up in here?"

Pam had been so thoroughly deceived that she pulled back to her corner to sulk over it. On the other hand, she was thrilled that Rett had kept that from her and that both of them were learning to cope with their unusual situation. And that, despite her recent losses, Rett's battle-weary spirit was lifting, a new energy growing in her that wasn't there before.

346

Her outward tiff was just for show, and didn't last long. She, like Rett, was much too interested in what Jaq had to say about the battle currently being fought on Epnoce and in space. And the feverish mobilization effort underway to move large numbers of personnel there at the first window of opportunity, even though they weren't fully prepared for the heavier gravity.

Gravity. It would be a primary obstacle in the early stages of the new campaign. Many of those being transferred, including at least half of the 2023rd, would have to acclimatize on site. As soon as a safe avenue was opened between Nyorfias and Epnoce, people and equipment would have to be moved, ready or not.

"GTC's sent another troopship and a carrier, enough marines to supplement the troops we already have on Epnoce for a while. That is— if the task force gets the spaceport there on the main continent and the AirSpacefighters secure airspace enough for us to send troopshuttles."

Rett listened as she rubbed on the quick absorbing ointment Med made for her. She had been using it faithfully twice a day since her leave started and was more than gratified at the results. Her scarred skin wasn't nearly as tight and itchy as it usually was, and the extra energy she had as a result of not having to reroute that usual irritation helped to keep her mood elevated. Surprising how such small things made a big difference.

"Huh?" Frowning, she paused in her task and sniffed at her hands. Usually she didn't notice a scent from the stuff. But she'd just opened one of the fresh containers Med had made her take. It wasn't labeled any differently, but according to her nose, Med had altered the ingredients a bit. It didn't smell bad, quite the contrary. It was fresh and clean, slightly spicy.

Oh, this is great. Now people are going to smell me coming.

~Well, you've smelled a lot worse.~

So I have, but that's different. There's usually a good reason for that. Rett shrugged, there wasn't anything she could do about it except hope it wasn't as noticeable to others as it was to her.

~I think Med jazzed it up because Jaq's around now,~ Pam dared to add.

Shut up, Pam.

~Oh, come on, it's very light. I seriously doubt anyone more than an arm's length away is going to take notice. I like it.~

Unaware of Rett's internal conversation, Jaq's mellow voice continued from the outer room. "Oh, Major Yidnar said for you to keep an eye to your message queue. He's going to pull you in for a meeting about some internal redeployment he has planned. He wanted me to make sure you know that he'll try not to make it the same day F-troop gets in, but can't promise anything."

"Wonder what's up with that." Rett swiped her palms together and used a wipe to take off the excess ointment. "Any clues—oh, shit."

It was Pam's turn to smirk.

"Anything wrong?"

"Uhm—no. Keep talking."

~Told you that you shouldn't have taken so long. Now you've got to go out there starkers.~

348

It's not a big deal. Rett had never been uncomfortable about wearing only her skin, and had she been, Special Forces would've trained that right out of her. But Jaq seemed uncomfortable with it. Odd, since he'd adapted without turning one wild hair on his head to sharing space with the entire platoon back at 52nd HQ.

~Then why don't you just go out there? He's seen you naked before. You've seen him naked before. After those Coalition assassins popped him in the head with that stun, you hauled his big handsome carcass in here, stripped him right down, and cleaned him up, clinical as a doctor. Shit, you've even slept in the same bed with him for two nights in a row. If it's no big deal and he's just another one of the platoon, what's the problem?~

You know exactly what the problem is. You were there! You saw how embarrassed he was. Do you go out of your way to do things you know makes your friends uncomfortable? Wait—don't answer that, because you've been doing a fine job on me this morning.

~One day you'll thank me for it.~

Rett growled aloud this time. "Do you know what the problem is? You are!" She grabbed up her towel again and wrapped it tightly around her. It would be enough for whatever Zetinorian hangup Jaq might have with nudity. Her thigh-length sleeping shirt left almost as much exposed and that didn't bother him. If his issue wasn't limited to her, she wondered how he dealt with it all those years he'd spent with the Coalition's military, in which a single private moment was something a regular trooper hardly experienced.

She couldn't help feeling tiffed about Pam's teasing. She knew her friend had her best interests at heart, but everything she said this morning stung. And why? Pam was hitting too close to the target when she talked about Jaq. All right, she had to admit, Pam nailed it dead center.

And that bothered her.

Now that she didn't have the excuse of being on duty to divert her thoughts, she was letting herself think about Jaq in ways she hadn't wanted to think about anyone in years. Worse than that, she was starting to think about him in ways she hadn't thought about anyone else before, ever. It scared the shit out of her. Especially when she knew what the Zetinorian felt for her. Deities, it *was* a curse, this propensity for a Zetinorian to fall deeply, permanently in love with someone, even when that someone else didn't return their feelings. Or couldn't. Or simply wasn't sure what to feel.

~You can just ask him to hand your kitbag to you.~

No. I can't let any issues he has interfere in what I have to do, now or when I'm on duty. Besides, I'm covered up, and if that's not enough for him, he's just going to have to get over it.

Rett strode around the corner of the bathing alcove and toward the countertop where her kitbag lay. "Sorry Jaq, but I left my—"

Jaq had been half-sitting on the window ledge, idly swinging one leg and enjoying the view of the mountains while he went on with his report of the activities underway at the base. At her entrance, he glanced over and nearly went backward but for the grip each of his big hands took on the vertical framework around the window. The Zetinorian's startled breath and arrested gaze had her stop short, the arm reaching for her kitbag freezing in mid-motion. In the next eyeb-link Rett put her back flat to the closest wall and whipped around to face the way she'd come, ready to take on the monstrous alien creature that had to be charging out of the bathing alcove after her.

Of course there was nothing. Could he have possibly sensed Pam? Panic rose strong for a moment. Maybe—

~He would have sensed me a long time ago,~ Pam put in softly, as mystified as Rett.

Maybe we both have figured him all wrong, Rett thought then. She was reminded of what she had felt at first after being merged with Pam. The last thing she wanted, or needed, to be burdened with was someone who was going to be a distraction to the job she had yet to complete.

"Shit, Jaq." She tried to put some lightness in her tone, failed. "Stop staring at me."

He didn't reply, just looked at her—at least the parts of her from the neck down and back up again. He had the strangest look on his face.

Now she felt coldness grow in her belly. A choking sensation constricted her throat even as her next thought surfaced. "Do you have something to tell me? Did I get a message? Someone else from F-troop—?" *Deities not that. Please not that. I already lost too many of them.*

At last, he moved, responded to her. He shook his head, his long, wild, red-brown locks turning into flame as the central white-gold crest caught and reflected the morning sunbeams that came through the window. "No."

"And here I thought I was making *him* uncomfortable," she muttered under her breath. "Then what? Will you tell me what you're looking at?" she demanded, her voice sharper this time.

Her muscles tensed as he came to his feet and shortened the gap between them. Angling her face to keep eye contact with him, she signaled for him to keep his distance with a gesture.

"A miracle," he whispered.

She sucked in a soft breath; her verbal warning dying before it reached her lips. Startled, puzzled, she watched his incredible blue eyes darken with pain and shock as they swept again over the length of her.

Rett glanced down at her body, making sure the towel she'd wrapped around herself in deference to Jaq's apparent shyness hadn't disappeared. *So what's wrong now?* She appealed to Pam, who wasn't in the least teasing any more and every bit as confused.

~Why don't you ask him?~

I figured he'd just come out and tell me, returned Rett to her mental companion. *I mean, come on, you think he would have said something by now, especially with all of us quartered together back at the 52nd.*

And then she knew what he meant, what he stared at, what he must be wondering about for the parts he couldn't see. Although she didn't move a single fingerlength, she felt herself shrinking into herself and her towel. Despite the balm she'd rubbed into her skin, every scar on her body burned, itched, or ached for one endless space of time. Especially those of which she most wanted to forget the sources.

Almost as if he wasn't in control of his own movements, Jaq reached toward her. The backs of his fingers touched the upper part of her left arm. She gritted her teeth and jerked aside as if his touch burned her.

"Don't. I—" *But why should I try to keep any of this from him? He's the one who professes he loves me. He should have a good close look at* 351 *exactly what he hopes to get.*

~Rett,~ cautioned Pam, ~I think you're overreacting a bit.~

Damn it, so what? If anything is going to happen again for me on an intimate level, with anyone, I'm going to have to do this sooner or later.

She lifted her head in defiance and hardened her gaze. Deliberately, savagely, she threw her towel aside. "All right, take a good close look then. I don't know what your problem is with them, but look and get over it. Do you want a tour?"

She spoke harshly, the ugly memories and nightmares surfacing and pressing up so hard and fast she couldn't keep them from spilling out. They clouded her reason with the dusky red haze of old blood, and more words came out with matching dark, bitter venom.

"I can point out a few good ones. Like this…Iheolon's fourth or fifth senior ranking officer, Avok, left her name there with her fingernails, and a few other memos elsewhere. The right leg—that's the best of the lot, after they finished dislocating joints, they started detaching everything else with the full intention of putting it back together—without the bones. Just for laughs. Iheolon was fairly tiffed they had to stop with that because I was losing too much blood and what was the point of that experiment if I was dead? Oh—and this part over here you were looking at before? They peeled that open a layer at a time to put a few—"

"Stop." Jaq sounded strangled.

Some of the crimson haze faded from her sight. Gulping in a breath, she blinked and faltered when she realized there were tears filling his eyes, leaking slowly down his face.

"You forget," he said softly, "that I saw you and many of these wounds long before they were scars. I knew the people who made them and exactly how they did it."

Stepping back, she grabbed the towel from the floor, a hard trembling starting up from her heels. "I didn't forget. Damn it." She shivered, feeling as cold now as she did when she turned the cold water on her head. The balmy warmth of the summer air that filled the room might have been the arctic blasts that scoured and sculpted the polar icefields.

"Why didn't you have your doctors minimize them?"

As if that would make me forget them? Rett's teeth clenched on her thought before it turned into spoken words. Jaq wouldn't imply that. Others might, but not him. She swallowed and tightened up her wavering control. "First of all, our medical people have enough on their hands dealing with more essential procedures. Those that would have impaired my ability to perform have been reduced. Those that extended deep below the surface as well. But the rest were left alone, and I wanted it that way. Minimizing or removing those would have done nothing but give the Coalition room for more the next few times around. That's why they sort of stuck to beating me up and raping me after that. Not much fun to mark up someone already scarred. Takes away a lot of the psychological impact. Not that they had me long enough to get started on more since then, anyway." Her breaths came short and fast, as if she'd been running hard, and her hands made fists so tight her short nails dug through the material of her towel and into her palms.

Pam scrambled to restore some cool balance to the storm surge of emotion in her host. She knew it wasn't the memory of the physical ordeals that threatened the Nyorfian's reason.

~Easy there, Rett. Easy.~ So she was merely sticking band-aids on the dangerous leaks that had oozed the choking darkness into Rett's mind, but it was the best she could do on her own at the moment. ~Breathe. Let this much go. Don't go back any farther.~

Part of Rett was astonished she should so naturally seek the cool light of safety, the comforting deep blue-green and warm earthy brown of Pam's "corner", as a defense against her own mind. What if Pam hadn't been merged with her and this happened? There was a time Rett had thought she had everything locked up so tight and safe nothing would shake it loose.

But her entire life had turned upside down since then. Not that the war hadn't changed it entirely long before her ego-merge. She sent gratitude to her friend and let out a long, slow breath before daring to speak again.

"I'm sorry. I didn't mean to slam into you like that. You were every bit as much a victim of them." She shook out her towel and started wrapping her cold body in it. "I came out to get my stuff. I'll just take it and get dressed, and we can go."

Jaq intervened. His warm hands closed lightly over her arms, in no way even making an attempt to prevent any avoidance or retaliation on her part. For that reason alone she remained perfectly still although her muscles again knotted with wary tension.

"I'm not in a hurry." He was calm now, only a faint streak of drying moisture across one ruddy cheek. His thumb skated along the edge of a particularly deep ridge that ran from her left elbow to her shoulder. "And I didn't mean to startle you with my reaction, either."

"I would have thought you've had opportunity enough to see me from top to bottom already since you've been with F-troop."

"I was trying not to look at those times. I've been making you uncomfortable enough, watching you. I can't seem to help it."

She wasn't about to admit to doing a fair amount of watching him—in a most unmilitary sense—on her own part, at least when she was sure no one was watching her watching him. "So what's so miraculous about me, Jaq? "

"The miracle is that you survived. And that your doctors were able to put you back together. *Look* at you—have you even taken a good look at yourself? I mean, after the last time I saw you. Did you ever *see* the condition you were in after Iheolon got through with you?"

Tight-lipped, Rett nodded. She'd seen images, all right, if only to know exactly what others had seen when they had come upon the mess the Coalition had left for them to find. She tried to tell herself, even now, that she'd seen worse. But those others worse off had also been dead.

Echoing her thoughts, Jaq went on. "I can't even begin to think how much worse you would have appeared later." His mouth closed around whatever else he was trying to say. He looked very much the same way he did waking up from his stun hangover a few days ago.

~Good grief.~ Pam dug in mental fingers and gave Rett a hard shake. ~I can understand the other feelings you have. But not what's coming up now. I won't let you feel guilty over this. You're not responsible for what anyone saw or felt!~

I—

~The bottom line is, that if you hadn't caused that diversion that got you caught back then, there would be no F-troop, an entire community of dead civilians, and far less of the 52nd Division than there is today.~ Pam still didn't know many details about any of the events in Rett's past. But she had enough insight and imagination to make rough sketches to cover what little she did know.

"You're a miracle, Rett," Jaq was saying. "You have complete functionality, mobility, you're every bit as strong and able as you were before. That's not only good medical treatment—that's a miracle. Looking at you normally—I mean, as most people see you daily, in uniform, in motion, it's impossible to imagine that there are any scars beneath the uniform. Even if one knows they should be there. That's what startled me. Every time I look at you, I'm amazed, but seeing what your uniform was hiding completely took me off balance. I expected them to be so much worse. I'm sure there are still complications you've learned to deal with but as I told you that first night, the Major told me that for a while they'd thought you—"

"I can't believe you asked him about something that happened years ago."

"I told you. I had to know."

She was shivering in earnest now, body contracted with cold instead of combat readiness. "It's over. I should have never let it out."

She was dealing with it, complications and all. Her work—the job of fighting the enemy—kept her focused and fit. Her platoon, her friends, the Battalion kept her sane. And until now that had been all she needed.

"It never would have come out, if not for me. I'm sorry." Again his fingers lightly traced her arm. "But since I'm here now, and will always remind you of it on some level, it's time to start healing other parts of you. And me too."

"Jaq—"

"You're part of another miracle, you know. The day I saw your image and fell in love with you I could only dream that I would ever meet the one to which my life and heart wanted to bind themselves. Just as I could only dream about my chance to escape the Coalition and fight them back for what they took from me."

"You didn't dream that part. You've helped so many people, thousands, directly and indirectly, even before you escaped."

Maybe *escape* wasn't the right word. Rett supposed the Coalition would call it defection. But one didn't defect from an organization that had never claimed one's loyalty in the first place. Jaq Pym and others like him were Yixolryn slaves—just as the Yixolryns hoped to make of the Nyorfians.

"I still never thought I would actually be living my dream, that I would be allowed this chance. To be with you when I was finally able to use what I know against them. Those atrocities I saw done to your people—to you—weren't part of my dream. And I need to have some closure with that. So do you."

Held fast by his compelling eyes, she didn't move away, but her shivers grew. Pam's mental support strengthened and she backed into it gratefully.

"It's the only way we can start to let go of the hold they have on that part of our lives."

355

~Easy, easy, easy.~ Pam's repetitive thought absorbed Rett's growing fears, keeping them from going out of control by the reinforcement of soothing, supportive calm.

"I think we should just spend the day here."

"I'm not ready for—"

"I promised you I wouldn't push, and I won't." This time he interrupted, although his manner was far gentler than her own had been minutes before. "*Kelani*, using your scars as armor against the Coalition is one thing. But are you keeping them between us—or between you or anyone else?"

It was a good question. One she couldn't answer.

"These scars aren't obstacles to me, unless you let them be. Nor do I think them repulsive, or that they make you any less desirable to me. Do you think that if they were, I'd be still standing here, looking at you right now?"

"I don't know what to think." Her voice was low, almost catching in her throat.

His fingers moved lightly against her bare arms, leaving lines of soothing warmth. "There's not much that can make a difference in how I feel about you—in how I have felt about you for years. I love you."

"That's *really* bothering me." Rett swallowed. "I've started to care for you in more than a friendly way, but I can't say that comes close to what you feel. I know what you wish for…and I can't promise you. Even if I was sure of how I felt, I couldn't do it. I told you that before."

"I'll take what we have right here, right now. Even if it's only to finish smoothing in your ointment in the spots you've missed." A large reddish finger softly indicated a spot just over her right shoulder. "We can go out and do something else after that."

How many times since Thirdday last had she thought about how secure she felt in his heavy, strong arms? And what it might be like to wake up next to him after something more than a night of simply sleeping alongside him? *Pam, you were right.*

Pam had the good grace not to think a single comment. Nor did she convey anything except that she was ready to back up and support Rett with every breath they took.

"You either trust me or you don't," Jaq said in a whisper.

Rett had to clear her throat and swallow again. "I trust you. It's me I don't trust." She closed her eyes. "Do you remember how I almost lost it that night, when I started to remember where and when I'd heard your voice for the first time? I almost lost control of myself then."

"But you didn't."

"That's not the point. The point is, if I lose control, start feeling trapped or panicked, give in to the flight or flight response that most of us revert to in such situations—you'll be dead before I've even realized I've killed you."

"It's not my intention to make you have such a reaction. I'll take my chances."

"I don't want you in physical or emotional discomfort if I up and change my mind."

Jaq smiled. It was a smile that started to replace her cold, twisting trepidation with tendrils of the same lazy warmth she'd felt while soaking in her tank a short while before. "Then you've yet to complete the research your people have been doing on Zetinorians. Males in particular." He moved his face a little closer to hers, making her breath catch. "It's said that our partners have to be well on their way to getting satisfied before we even start getting…uncomfortable."

"It's said?"

"I have to complete some of my own research on that subject. I was only fifteen when I was taken from my home."

"Jaq, you haven't—?"

"Not…consensually."

No wonder. Rett had heard that life could be brutal for the average Coalition trooper. And the Zetinorians being out of favor already with their Yixolryn masters…She didn't know what to say.

"I'm willing to trust you." He dropped the contact from her arms and took a step back, extending his open hands toward her. "If that's your choice."

Rett's gaze went from his face to his waiting hands and back again. The invitation was apparent.

~You either trust yourself or you don't,~ whispered Pam, and withdrew to her corner.

Rett took a step forward and closed her hands over his.

1.4.10 HOSTEL, BRANCH, NYORFIAS
0535.08.05 (LOCAL RECKONING)

"Sergeant Ariam, F-troop, 2023RD—she'll be staying with me." Rett barely managed to update the hostel clerk on duty before Ariam hauled her out of range. Her sister had a firm grip on Rett's left arm with one hand, her kitbag with the other.

"Easy there, Ari—I don't need a dislocated shoulder. Deities!" She lengthened her stride to ease the pressure on her arm. This was not the time to disengage her sister's grip; she understood the reason well enough. Ariam was hurting, hurting badly, and needed to vent on a level only Rett could provide her. Rett had felt a deep brotherly love for Kraym, had regarded him as a close personal friend. But Ariam had loved him with the depth of heart and soul only lovers and lifemates knew, and Kraym had returned her regard in full. All the same, the prospect of having her return to duty postponed because of an injury wasn't something Rett wanted to consider.

Ariam stopped only when they arrived in front of Rett's door, and only long enough for Rett to bid it open. There were no tangible clues to Ariam's feelings or behavior, not even a trace of color from her aura. Ariam the person was locked up tight inside Ariam the soldier.

It's time to let go now, Ari, thought Rett as she ushered Ariam inside and kicked the door closed. She pulled off her headband and tossed it to the counter. Likewise Ariam dropped her headband and threw her kitbag aside. Then they were sisters again, without any military rank between them, duties to perform, or public appearances to maintain. Ariam collapsed weeping in Rett's ready embrace, her grief as raw as a wound newly open.

Rett gathered the younger woman in her arms as if Ariam was a child and carried her to the big, comfortable chair near the window. She arranged them both, enclosing Ariam with arms, body, legs; absorbing the wild helplessness of Ariam's emotions in the same manner as her shirt became saturated with the tears.

* * * * *

Pam felt at once left out and drawn into the curious handshake effect that Rett and Ariam's bond as siblings induced. Stunned and wondering, she felt the conscious minds of two unique individuals merge into one. Soon it was impossible to tell where Ariam ended and Rett began. Any distinction between them was blurred as effectively as the camouflage of their combat uniforms faded them into the landscape.

Equal now in their communion both sisters wept, for Kraym, for Gerrale, for Jubos and Talivri and the rest. For their mother and brother. For others with names they knew and names they would never know. For what horrors they had seen and endured, and for what they had yet to see and endure.

And Pam cried with them even as she held them both, glad for the opportunity, relieved that the bond between them did more than release deep emotions otherwise tightly controlled.

Rett kissed the golden hair she had made wet with her tears, smoothing loose ends of it away from Ariam's hot face. Ariam lay limply in the cradle of her body, too emotionally spent for the moment to do anything but breathe and stare with red-rimmed, half-lidded eyes at a slice of bright sky outside the window. A breeze, warm and smelling of distant rain, stole in to bless them, as light as the caress of a mother to a sleeping baby.

"Will it ever stop hurting?"

Rett pressed her cheek against Ariam's forehead and closed her eyes. "No, Ariam," she whispered. The same question, and the same answer, had been exchanged between girls aged eleven and not quite sixteen. "It'll hurt as long as we love them. But it will get easier to take in time."

Ariam adjusted her head against Rett's shoulder. "Med said that Kraym was well beyond feeling anything when he let go."

359

Rett reached for a wipe from the dispenser on the counter, just managing to snag one at the fullest extent of her reach. Wiping Ariam's face gently, she said, "Then we must believe Med, who's always told us the facts. And be glad of that much."

Ariam nodded, but shivered all the same.

"I'm sorry I wasn't there."

"It wouldn't have changed what happened."

Rett let out a breath and used the back of her right hand on her own face. "Did Kraym ever tell you about his friend N'wessar?"

"Kraym and Newi. The terrors of Bolle's Marsh." Ariam smiled a little. "Yes. I couldn't believe the stories, or that he wasn't given the responsibilities of a citizen until he was thirteen. Even though I knew he was telling me the truth."

"Well, Newi's an MP here in town. I told him all about you. Come to think of it, I don't know too many people I haven't told all about you."

"Kraym had mentioned Newi had been assigned here. He saw him last time he had a long leave." Ariam wriggled around a bit more, getting comfortable.

"He's charming. The news was hard for him to take, but he loves talking about the old days. It seems to help him." Rett chuckled. "Helps me too."

"It helps to remember the good and fun things."

"Well, then you'd like talking with him, Ari—he'll tell you stories that will curl you hair."

"Hope I get time to meet him. We won't have too much off it. Am I squishing you?"

"Oh," Rett said dryly, "horribly."

"Good. Because I just got comfortable and I'm not inclined to move at the moment. Pam's all right? I felt her before—so close that I was sure if I opened my eyes she would be physically right next to you."

"Yes. She's here."

"It was nice to feel three minds in the link again."

"You felt her thoughts? That deeply?"

"Impressions, emotions, yes. She was right there, Rett, just like with you. It was almost like when we were kids, and Tova and I would pull you in, remember?"

"Yes."

"She's very supportive."

Rett tightened her arms around her sister and sent a mental smile to Pam. "You know, she's almost as big a pain in my ass as you are."

"We might not understand the reasons ego-merges happen, but yours couldn't have been better, in my opinion. I'm glad you have her."

"I'm glad I have you both."

"And Jaq?" Ariam tilted her head back a little. The contact between them was still far too close for Rett to even bother trying to block her talented sister. The smile that grew on Ariam's face eased the remaining heaviness that sorrow had left there. "Are you going to give me any details, or do I have to ask Pam for them?"

Don't even think about it, Rett warned Pam as she felt her mental companion give a small, playful push as if testing just how much control Rett had right now.

~Then you better talk. You know how miserable little sisters can make your life when big sisters keep secrets.~

"I don't know, Ariam," she said aloud. "It's my guess F-troop has some sort of scheme going on over this and you're right in the middle of it."

"So what else is news? Tell me anyway. That way, if I win this pool, I'll share it with you."

"*This* pool?"

"You know there's more than one," stated her sister, matter-of-fact.

"Good gods and deities." She lifted her gaze ceilingward and shook her head. "All right. Jaq," she said, in a tone of confidential awe that brought a gleam to Ariam's gray eyes, "is incredible. When he came to tell me about Kraym, I was upset and tiffed off at him. Just off and left him standing there. But he came looking for me."

Ariam's eyes widened. "No one can say our Jaq's not brave."

"Mmm."

"But you *left* him? Alone?"

361

"Well, not really. I went up to the rooftops and just followed him from there. That way if any MPs showed up, I'd be right there before he could get in trouble for being on the street unescorted. And before I could get in trouble for letting him. Pam convinced me that I wasn't being fair; reminded me he was one of F-troop now and I would never treat one of my people that way."

"Good for Pam."

"So I went down and talked to him. He was very sweet and understanding. And supportive."

"And?"

"It was such a beautiful night, a quiet street in a part of town mostly deserted since they were winter homes, or homes belonging to families who went to the mountains for safety. No one but us. I was upset, and he just held me. So after a while, we were standing there wrapped up in each other's arms."

Ariam shivered, this time in anticipation. "Did he kiss you senseless again, like he did in the rover?"

Rett neatly avoided a direct answer. Instead she borrowed a very convincing, languid little sigh from an obliging Pam. "And then things got really hot."

Which they did, since those Coalition assassins who'd infiltrated the edge of town opened fire on them.

"I think my pulse rate went up about three hundred percent in a matter of seconds."

Mostly because she was rapidly relocating herself and Jaq to avoid getting hit by the SMG fire coming out of the night.

"Deities, Ari, what happened next was simply amazing. I never knew it was possible…"

Ariam was solidly hooked. "Possible for—"

Rett closed her eyes. She let out another slow exhale, her voice going low and dreamy. "I never, ever in my life dreamed that anyone could catch SMG stun right between the eyes and wake up in less than ten minutes."

Suddenly she found herself landing on the floor with a thump.

"When I get done with you," snarled Ariam, "I'm going to yank Pam right out of you and start in on her, since I know damn well you couldn't have pulled that over without help."

"Yeah—you and what army?"

Ariam leaned over with a sweet, dangerous smile. "You forget—I know your weakness." She flexed her fingers in a manner that replaced Rett's amusement with alarm. Before she could get out of range, Ariam's knees landed in her stomach, pinning her to the floor. Her sister's steely, slender fingers drove the remaining breath from Rett's lungs in a wheeze of protest and helpless laughter.

1.4.11 A PLACE OUTSIDE OF TIME

"You might have taken the first level, neophyte," sneered Pheasyce's opponent. "But the second is yet to come. And the rules change. All the opening advantages will be mine this time."

Pheasyce was well aware of that.

"And I will take great pleasure in watching how it affects you just as much as I will enjoy the slow destruction of your key Player."

"None of us know how our Players will react, Xonomer."

"Yours will have no defense." As if to prove this point, Xonomer started to reach toward the two Nyorfians.

"The second level has not yet started, Xonomer. Touch any of my Players now and you risk forfeit."

"Do not presume to tell me the Rules, neophyte."

The dark mass of energy spun closer to Pheasyce, so close and taking on such enormous proportions that she started feeling her life force smother.

"I have already proven myself to my own Order. Time, and time again. I have defeated Guardians of Light as well as Guardians of Balance. I have sent neophytes back into the matrix of the universe with as little effort as your key Player could blow a speck of dust off her hand. It is you who should forfeit. Spare your people further suffering. Forfeit now, and I will be merciful."

Pheasyce moved back, gathering her essence tightly. "Merciful? As you were to the Zetinorians? To the Uli-Toth?"

"Very well. If you insist on seeing this doomed match to its conclusion, I will make sure you have much to watch. I am sure it will be most entertaining." The dark entity came slightly closer. "For me."

And then it was gone.

The glimpse of just how powerful Xonomer was left Pheasyce shaken. The agent of Dark was ancient, experienced, and had never lost a match—the only reason Xonomer yet existed on this plane. And here she was, just starting.

Xonomer was right. The next level could very well be the end. Pheasyce could only hope the strategy she had chosen was the right one.

END OF BOOK ONE

THE ADVENTURE CONTINUES IN

GRAVITY

JOURNEY TO NYORFIAS, BOOK 2

PLEASE TURN THE PAGE FOR A SAMPLE

AN EXCERPT FROM JTN2 GRAVITY

UNDETERMINED AREA, COMPLEX 63, EPNOCE
0535.13.24 (LOCAL RECKONING)

RETT SWIPED HER FOREARM ACROSS her chin, smearing her face with blood. "Fang Med, I need an ETA."

The medtech's reply was lost in a blaze of static from energy weapons.

Jessek stiffened and ground his teeth together as she used her knee to apply pressure over the blood-soaked bandages at the top of his thigh. She'd applied them in haste, with no thought other than to keep his leg attached long enough to move him into a safer area. Well, they weren't going to get much safer than this, and now that they had the time, she had to think about him bleeding to death.

I have to do better than this. She put her weapon aside and rummaged in her utility belt for more medical supplies, laying them out in easy reach.

"Stay with me, Jess. I'm letting up. Deep breath."

The partial release of pressure on his groin pushed Jessek beyond all temptation of movement. What smidgen of color remained in his cheeks washed out with the clammy sweat that slicked his skin. The young sharpshooter's nostrils flared with each breath with his struggle to keep his pain in control; to regulate his breathing and heart rate as he had been taught.

Stripping the old dressings away with careful speed, Rett poured the antiseptic coagulating powder liberally into the wound before pushing the mess of torn and crushed tissue together as best she could. She opted against the adhesive. Strong as it was, the adhesive wasn't meant for something as massive and deep as this, unless she started applying it from the inside out. Instead, she reached for the specially pretreated bandages they carried as part of their personal medical kits.

To her eyes, his leg was all but severed; the heavy thighbone crushed and fragmented. Deities knew what had kept the big femoral artery from rupturing. As far as she could see, that artery and the long muscle on the inside of the thigh were all that kept the limb attached.

In her former life as a logger, crushing accidents happened occasionally, no matter how careful they were. She recalled with graphic clarity the first time she'd seen the victim of a similar accident. That one had died as they performed emergency treatment—much the same as Rett now was performing for Jessek.

Rett bit the inside of her cheek. Jessek wasn't the only casualty, but the other two with her didn't make it. She'd left them back there, one of her newest personnel and one of R-troop's longer term people, who'd come along to relay information back to Sergeant Tris.

~It's awful they died, Rett, but right now, what matters is that it didn't happen to Jess. If he was going to die of shock, he'd be dead already, especially considering it took you a couple minutes to get him out from under that door. Immediately after which you dragged him a hundred or so lengths and around a corner or two before ever slapping on the tourniquet, much less the first bandage.~

That's just it, I should have—

~What, stopped and given first aid right then? You're both still lucky to be breathing! I don't think that a mosquito could have made it through the SMG at the time, and the way the shots were bouncing everywhere. Now, focus!~

Rett winced. Pam was right. But who knew what she added to Jessek's trauma by that rough handling—

~Hel-LO! That's not the point! Jess knew how bad it was before you ever got him out. If he was worried about permanent damage, he wouldn't be here with you now.~

A sharp twinge twisted in the muscle of her left upper arm. Ow! Damn, how did Pam do that? *All right. You're right.*

Jessek was determined to live, no matter what. He would have asked her for mercy otherwise. Rett sent gratitude for Pam's heading her back on track.

She compressed her lips in the same manner her bandaging compressed Jessek's mangled flesh. Of course there was a chance to save the leg, but only with the timely arrival of a medtech and a quick dispatch of Jessek to a hospital facility.

And we were just about set to pull back. Come ooonnnn, Tris, com me! she growled inwardly.

Then she realized her thoughts showed on her face, and Jessek was watching her.

"Back with me then, Jess?"

"Ass is smoking," he informed her in a raspy grunt. "Come'ere." He lifted his right hand.

She swung her hips a bit closer to his reach, since her hands were occupied. Strange how she only noticed the spot of heat after Jessek flicked away whatever it was that had been slowly charring its way deeper through her uniform and into her flesh.

"Check for anything else, Jess, would you? I'm a bit busy here."

His contact was firm, although as his fingers felt along her length for any hotspots, a steady tremor betrayed the weakness and pain. "That was it." Jessek let his hand fall to his chest. "Guess I bled on you enough to put out anything else. Shit. It's bad, isn't it? How's it look?" He tried to lift his upper body enough to see.

"Lie still. It's bad enough. A few fingerlengths higher and to the right, you'd have to learn a new way to piss."

Jessek's answer was a short laugh that sounded more like a groan.

"Easy." Making sure the bandage lay snug and smooth, she finished it off at the top of Jessek's thigh, watching as it puffed up and tightened to keep its own pressure on the wound. She slid a finger beneath to check—good, not too tight, just enough. She hoped. "Easy. Don't move any more. Just breathe."

He had a good grip on himself now; it would just take a minute or so more to coordinate everything and lock it down…if he stayed conscious for that long.

"Stay with me." Rett smoothed the furrowed lines in his forehead with her filthy hand.

"Minute," he murmured. "Just a minute."

"One minute," she said. "You're on the chrono."

If he can't lock it down, I'll have to get him to go into deepsleep. It was a last resort, and while it had its advantages, it had just as many drawbacks. If it came to that, she'd have to guide him down, and do it while he was still coherent. For someone not in total control of the process, there was the risk of the sleeper going so deep he or she would die instead of merely slowing metabolism.

Rett sat back on her heels, easing some of the pressure on tired muscles that had once again forgotten what it felt like not to feel pain of some kind. Then, using the plotters on her VARs, her senses— natural and trained—and factoring in the terse communications over her pcom, she updated herself to within several fingerlengths as to the current location of her people and what each of them were doing.

Two days earlier, the infiltration of Complex 63 had started right on plan, but all sorts of minor complications had cropped up. Since they left plenty of room for alternate plans and quick changes, the overall progress was still on the chrono. Although Easy Force's units were still fighting on this level, Rett was ready to receive the order to start replacing her people with the advance infantry units.

As second in command and Combat Team Leader for Easy Force, she'd been directing the replacement of teams from the four other platoons besides F-troop that made up the special assault group. Since then, however, F- and B-troops had encountered a stiffer opposition, requiring Rett's direct attention and participation. So she'd turned over the matter of redeployment to R-troop's Sergeant Tris, who acted as Rett's backup.

F- and B-troops were engaged, yes, but nothing they couldn't hand off to the infantry now. And by her estimation, Tris should have finished routing the new teams in place for her so they could start the transition. Rett took a breath, ready to com him herself.

As if cued by her thought, Tris's voice sounded in her ear. "Fang Lead, we're all go for—"

Sergeant Trebor interrupted on the priority frequency. "Fang Lead, there's a group of kids between us and the rest of the complex. Just spotted them moving into a side corridor. If they keep going that way, they'll be heading into a live sector."

You just had to tempt more bad luck, didn't you? Thanks a flaming lot, Pam, groused Rett.

~I didn't do anything!~ Pam protested.

You were thinking we were almost finished up here.

~Well, sure…but so were you. Don't blame me. It wasn't like I was bored enough to yank kids out of my ass and throw them into the live fire zone.~

The static from Trebor's end was answer enough why he hadn't sent anyone after the kids himself. His group was hot.

"You saw what, Fang Two?" The Easy Force commander, Lieutenant Evetez, jumped in on the conversation. "Kids in…Sector 17?"

To hear a report of a civilian in that location was something unexpected. Sector 17 housed the main power units, generators, and machinery that ran the basic environmental controls for the west side of the complex. Even under normal circumstances, it was a low-maintenance area, always monitored and routinely inspected, yet never assigned permanent staff. As such, the sector was far from any areas normally frequented by the civilian inhabitants. Occasionally a maintenance worker, but they'd stay away if the area was hot.

Unstaffed or unpopulated as those areas might be, Coalition troops were aggressive in safeguarding them. Not all of the various humanoid and alien races filling the ranks were able to adapt to sharp changes in heat, cold, or air quality, so a drastic, sudden change in environment might cause unexpected and intense problems for them.

"Fang Two has never made a sighting report in error, Easy Lead," Rett said, her tone very dry. For once she wished he had.

"Damn." This from Tris, and he sounded tiffed. "No time to wonder how and why. Better have someone from your group get them, Fang, you're closest. Can you spare a team? What about Razor Fourteen and one of yours?"

Rett kept the pained sigh in her thoughts. "Razor Fourteen and Fang Thirty-two didn't make it. But we're on it, Razor Lead." Already she was checking the gear she carried.

"Good," said Tris after an extra second of hesitation. "We've already started deploying infantry into this level, so we'll keep them there since they're needed, and advise extra confirmation before they shoot at anything."

"We can't finish our pullback now in any case, until we make sure no civilians are going to get caught in the line of fire," Evetez said.

Rett signed off her direct links with Tris and Evetez and spoke to her second in command. "Fang Two, I need details."

371

"I saw three bodies, but caught only enough to identify two. Boy, red-brown hair, about a length and a quarter in height. A teenager, girl or boy, hard to tell. Thin, length and a half, can't miss her, her hair is as silver-white as Razor Lead's." He followed with coordinates of the place they were spotted; the direction the children were headed.

Trebor must have only seen them for half an eyeblink not to have more detail to report than that. She was glad he'd had that much time. She briefly consulted her Omni, calling for the map of their level to match the picture she'd formed in her head with Trebor's coordinates.

"That means if I cut through the service corridor at 45 West B345 I should intercept."

"Yes. But you'll have to move fast. Must go, things have just heated a bit more here. Luck, Fang Lead."

Rett glanced down at Jessek. His eyes were closed, but he was listening, to her and whatever was coming over his pcom on the general bandwidths. She touched gentle fingers to his throat, noting his pulse was steadier now. "Good, that's it, sport. Lock it down. Com connect Fang Med—how long?"

This time Med's answer was clear. "Two minutes. I heard. I guess there's no protesting your going this time." He sounded resigned. "I have help with me. So go ahead, be careful. Did you give him anything?"

"No. He has a grip, and I thought it was best he stay alert until you or someone else had matters in hand."

Med spoke Jessek's com number to include the wounded man in the conversation. "Once Fang Leader gets you situated, don't move. You move and I'm going to kick your ass. Dead or not."

"Yeah, Med," mumbled Jessek, rolling his eyes.

Rett tousled Jessek's straight hair as she signed off with Med and opened a direct link to Trebor. After getting the accessway location where his sighting had occurred, she gave him a quick update and switched back to Tris. "I'm on it. Fang Two has the team until I'm back." Rett cut her com with a voice command and looked down again.

Jessek was alert and in solid control. He pushed something damp into her hand—a wipe. "Better use this, Sarge. You don't want to scare those kids off, and your face is all over blood. At least get it out of your eyes."

"Suppose you're right." She scrubbed the treated material over her face and hoped she exposed some skin instead of smearing the mess even more. It would take a lot more than one wipe for a thorough clean, but there wasn't time for that.

~You're going to be more visible out there too, with blood mucking up your uniform,~ said Pam.

Rett acknowledged the reminder, grateful for it.

"You'd better get going," Jessek said. He lifted his head and shoulders, his forearms and fisted hands pressing hard to the floor.

Guessing his intention, Rett quickly intervened. "Damn it, Jess. I said don't move, so did Med."

"Med said after I was situated, and I want to sit up," said Jessek with a determined frown.

"Then I'll help you," Rett said. "I've time enough for that." She settled him in a sitting position, his back braced against the wall. "Better?"

"Little easier to shoot this way than flat on my back." The senior corporal's skin was as pale as the snow outside the complex, his dark brown hair and eyebrows making the contrast even sharper. Tense lines tightened and aged his face, but his lake-blue eyes were bright, perhaps too much so. He bared his teeth at her in a grin of sorts. "Good to go," he told her as she handed him his weapon.

She nodded, made sure anything else he would need was in easy reach. So many words rose into her throat, but she swallowed them, unable to find the right ones.

Instead, it was Jessek who spoke. "Sarge, I—"

She completed Jessek's sentence for him. "—am going to hold this section of corridor until relieved. And you're going to damn well watch my smoking hot ass until you can't see it any more."

The apologetic expression that had started creeping into Jessek's too-bright eyes transformed into purpose, and as he nodded, Rett tightened her utility belt a notch.

"Depending on where those kids are by the time I catch up, either I'll be back with them or we'll sit in a safe spot until the shooting stops." She slapped the outside of her right boot to make sure her locator was active. "I'll check in when I can."

"Jammers," reminded Jessek.

"On," Rett said after taking a moment to feel the subtle vibration from her wrist bracers, which indicated the targeting jammers were active. "Don't disappoint me, Jess."

He gave her a smile. "Never, Sarge. Get those kids safe."

Keeping to the shadows, Rett raced through the narrow accessway to where she hoped she'd intercept the group of youngsters Trebor reported. Sounds of battle echoed into the access from the main corridors and open spaces in the local area. She kept every sense she had wide open, and found time to wonder just why in three moons, and how, these kids had become separated from their parents at a time the citizens of the complex were told to hold tight.

The Yixolryn Coalition troops had learned to contain complex inhabitants in their residential areas at the first sign of trouble. They'd found out the hard way that the majority of Nyorfians on Epnoce, for so long a time sulky and compliant under Coalition occupation, made an instant transition to fierce guerrilla fighters once Free Army forces backed them up.

Except for here, Rett thought. *We haven't had any contact with civilians here at all.*

While the greater part of her was on alert as she moved, a small inner part of her fretted over Jessek. The responsibility to protect civilians at all costs came first, but it didn't mean she had to like leaving one of her own alone in such a condition, and in such an unsecured area.

The Coalition troops pinned inside, especially those guarding the complex commander and any escape route they had, would hang tough no matter what. The enemy needed this place. Complex 63, devoted to agriculture and food production, was an important, renewable source of food and the only one the enemy had access to. Food—prepared food—was something the surface troops of the Yixolryn Coalition were hurting for. They slaughtered large numbers of animals on Epnoce, like they had on Nyorfias, but much went to waste, since many of them hadn't the slightest clue how to prepare or eat something that wasn't packaged or ready-made.

The lack of culinary skill was a good thing for the families that lived here. Since the Coalition desperately needed bodies to make the food they couldn't make for themselves, the people of Complex 63 received a better level of treatment than civilians elsewhere.

~Not to mention the kids would be the first ones threatened if the adults failed to produce said food,~ Pam put in. ~That could be why you didn't get any civilian help on this job like the others.~

Rett had to wonder if Pam wasn't absolutely right.

Jaq had told some unbelievable tales of troopers going hungry amidst some of the lushest supplies of naturally growing food plants on Nyorfias. Rett wondered what sort of impact that dependence made on this agricultural community. Would the average Coalition trooper starve if nobody existed to prepare what was harvested here?

Maybe the GTC reinforcements produced the most visible results in the Nyorfians' twelve-year struggle for freedom. But the matter of food and fuel, especially food, and the Coalition's complete dependency on technology to get both, was rapidly becoming the Nyorfians' greatest asset.

~Wise Earth generals, even in ancient times, said that an army marches on its stomach~, Pam thought. ~I guess they had a point.~

And for once, Rett had to instantly agree.

As more distance and time opened up behind her, temptation to pcom Med about Jessek was strong. She told herself there wasn't a damned thing she could have done. At the same time she was sure two extra seconds and her own body length would have made the difference between the young sharpshooter's coming along with her on this retrieval, or his sitting back there wondering if he was going home with one leg or two. That was, if he didn't bleed to death first. The pressure properties of the bandages she used only lasted so long.

She emerged into a slightly wider corridor, once more focused on her mission. If she'd timed it right, she should—

Yes. There. She caught sight of a small figure with red-brown hair. If there were others, they must be ahead; already around the corner this one was fast approaching. In that same moment, the child's face turned toward her. Trebor had nailed the gender correctly—a boy. She saw his mouth open in an expression of astonishment. With a yip, the boy broke into a run and turned the corner.

Rett launched herself after him, wishing she had been closer before allowing herself to get spotted, but then again, she wasn't expecting Nyorfian kids to run *away* from her.

The russet head peered around the corner. Rett gestured, a sign that any school-age child would recognize and respond to from an adult, especially during an emergency.

Stop. Wait for me.

But the child quickly pulled back.

Anywhere between seven to ten years old from her guess. But why the avoidance? Surely the kids knew the difference between the Nyorfian and Coalition troops. *Must be he's seeing something else I'm not scoping yet.*

Before she focused her awareness ahead, a niggle of warning from a different direction had her flattening to a wall. A stray SMG shot from

375

a side corridor on her left zinged past, well spent by the sound of it, but still hot enough to cause serious burns. The bolt hit the opposite wall, the glossy smooth surface bouncing it up toward the ceiling, where it ricocheted at least five times from wall to wall before vanishing with nothing more than the scent of ozone and a wisp of smoke.

When a startled yelp reached her ears from the direction the boy had gone, concern overshadowed her caution. She took the same corner a second later...

GRAVITY
Journey to Nyorfias, Book 2
Available at your favorite bookseller

ABOUT....

TERRY ROY

TERRY (T.M.) ROY'S PRIMARY CAREER is as a book designer, writer, editor, and graphic artist. By any other time she's a fiction writer, artist, illustrator, and anything else life demands she must be.

In 2003, Roy's novel, *Discovery*, was a finalist in the 2003 EPIC Awards for Best Science Fiction Romance. She prefers to write adventure stories in sci-fi settings, some of which have been over twenty years in the making.

She was lost in a wormhole for a while and stranded in North Dakota for eight years, but found her way back through the event horizon into the Pacific Northwest. A random tesseract then transported her back to the Upper Midwest where she now resides in the Minneapolis-St. Paul metro area with an opinionated Quaker parrot named Apple and a Senegal parrot, Sir Hugo the Naked.

When she's not writing, formatting, or drawing, she is campaigning to save the honeybee, gardening, "putting up" food, and when she can afford it, flying small airplanes.

She likes hearing from her readers. Feel free to drop an email to tmroy@zapstone.com or visit her Facebook pages:

Author page: http://www.facebook.com/pages/
TM-Roy-Terran-Moffat/297327413694111
Blog: https://teryvisions.wordpress.com/

ACKNOWLEDGEMENTS

MY ENDURING THANKS TO CATHY Wiley, for editing, insights, long Skype sessions, business partnership, and sushi by mail. And to all those who've encouraged, discouraged, inspired, been around, were gone, listened, ignored...I thank all of you, too. Really. It's helped shape me and helped shape my stories. My past and recent editors: Sara, Karli, Mary N., Cathy, Debra, and Linda. Most of all to my family, my brother Tim; my sisters Cathy (a different Cathy), Nancy, Sharon, Maria, and Laura. Parts of all of you are thick in this story. Especially Sharon, who perhaps gave many qualities to Rett.

www.ingramcontent.com/pod-product-compliance
Lightning Source LLC
Chambersburg PA
CBHW020513260626
47156CB00006B/1993